DETECTIVE SCHOOL 101

A Detective School Mystery

J.R. Ripley

Beachfront Entertainment

Published in the USA by Beachfront Entertainment.

First edition 2020
Trade Paperback: ISBN 9781892339447
Ebook: ASIN B08BWL6B45

Please contact us at beachfrontentertainment@outlook.com with any issues or comments regarding our books. We appreciate the feedback, and we love reading and hate errors as much as you do.

Cover design by: http://www.stunningbookcovers.com

DETECTIVE SCHOOL 101

1

There has to be more to life than this, Jane Bright was thinking as she stared dully at the dry brown grass circles in Mrs. Terwilliger's otherwise immaculate backyard lawn.

Mrs. Terwilliger smelled of geraniums. That smell came out of a perfume bottle. The yard smelled sweet and flowery too. The light breeze sweeping east to west over a nearby circular patch of pink and white stargazer lilies carried that natural scent to her nostrils.

"It's the trolls, I'm telling you." Mrs. Terwilliger tugged at a head of wavy, red hair—the kind that came out of a bottle too— that showed signs of its natural gray. "I don't know what to do about them." Her white gardening gloves had seen cleaner days.

"Yes, Mrs. Terwilliger. Trolls." Jane toed the dry grass with the tip of her shoe. It didn't take a genius, a master detective or even a master gardener—none of which she was—to figure out this mystery.

Mrs. Terwilliger nodded firmly. Her floppy white-straw hat flapped like a lazy seagull around her head. "There's more of them than ever. I'm sure new ones are moving into the neighborhood."

"Yes, ma'am." Jane hurriedly placed her notebook over her mouth to hide a looming yawn. This was not what she had gone to journalism school for. Then again, who went to journalism school anymore? Newspapers were dying. Real journalism was all but dead.

"It's all the new construction. It is driving the trolls east." Mrs. Terwilliger grabbed a skinny rake with sturdy green plastic tines and attacked a brown patch of lawn.

"East?"

"Out of the Everglades. Where they belong."

Jane pulled her brows together. Wasn't the Everglades where alligators, herons and panthers belonged?

Then again, if she was a troll and alligators and panthers were roaming loose in her neighborhood, she'd be looking to relocate to a nicer one like the Terwilligers' roomy estate, too.

"South Florida is done. They ought to stop building." Scratch scratch scratch. Bits of grass flew as Mrs. Terwilliger vigorously attacked the blemish. "That's what they ought to do."

Jane had seen it a thousand times before. The root of Mrs. Terwilliger's problem was a fungus called rhizoctonia. Not trolls. Better known as brown patch lawn disease, the grass-destroying fungus thrived under hot, humid conditions.

Welcome to Florida.

As for trolls, Jane wasn't so sure where they thrived. But she was positive they did not come out after midnight and pee in Mrs. Terwilliger's garden as she had suggested on Jane's arrival.

Then again, the woman in question was the wife of the Broward County Times biggest advertiser. And, as Lou Edelstein, the paper's publisher and editor, liked to remind her each and every time she complained about her assignment, Jane's main, priority number one, job was to keep the advertisers happy.

Funny, the University of Miami's Department of Journalism & Media Management hadn't taught her that. It must have slipped through the cracks in the curriculum.

The Terwilligers had a fancy house in Hidden Acres, a posh neighborhood in Plantation, Florida. The community sat near Sawgrass Mills, the area's, and possibly the country's, largest outlet mall.

Due to the many and regular trips Jane had been making from the Fort Lauderdale office of the Broward County Times to the Terwilligers' home, she could practically have made the drive blindfolded.

Benjamin Terwilliger owned a chain of laundromats called CLEAN BEE spread across Broward County and dipping across the line into Miami-Dade County. The roofs of their trucks sported yellow- and black-striped bumblebees.

Mrs. Bethany Terwilliger didn't give a hoot about dirty laundry. What she wanted was a spotless garden.

"Here's what I think you should do." Jane was supposed to be writing up stories and taking accompanying photos for the newspaper's Gardening and Southern Living section. Instead, she was doling out advice on how to eradicate troll pee stains from this woman's backyard. "Be sure to water early, not in the evening. What sort of fertilizer are you using on the lawn?"

"I'll have to ask the gardener." Mrs. Terwilliger frowned. "I hope he understands me. My Spanish is poor and his English is atrocious."

"I understand. Tell—" Jane paused. "What's your gardener's name?"

"His name?" Mrs. Terwilliger's mouth fell open. A

bee threatened to explore her esophagus but she shut it again as it approached her pink, wet tongue.

"Never mind. It's not important. Tell your gardener he might want to try applying a fungicide."

A thin line of sweat formed along Mrs. Terwilliger's forehead at the hairline. She wiped it away with the side of her glove. "You think that will keep the trolls away, Jane?"

"Yes," Jane lied. "Trolls don't like fungicide. It's a well-known fact."

Mrs. Terwilliger beamed. "That is a relief."

"I'll write this story up when I get back to my desk," Jane promised. She had already taken several close-up shots of the brown patches in the expansive backyard.

"How soon will you publish?"

"The article should appear in the paper in about two weeks' time." And Lou Edelstein, her editor, would be charging Mr. Terwilliger for a full-page, full-color ad for CLEAN BEE on the opposite page. Like he always did.

Mr. Terwilliger, Jane decided some time ago, was a saint.

Jane was already mentally composing her story. She would write an article giving her readers insight into brown patch lawn disease. Not trolls.

Bethany Terwilliger, Jane had learned, never read the articles, she simply liked seeing her name in print and bragging to all her friends about it. Jane always put Mrs. Terwilliger's name in the first paragraph.

Still, Jane thought, adjusting the car window visor as she headed east into the sun, there had to be something better out there.

2

"Don't get me wrong." Jane was back at her desk. Lou Edelstein hovered over her shoulder, decaf coffee in hand. Both his wife and his doctor had pressured him into giving up caffeine. Owning the paper gave him jitters enough, according to his wife, Pepper, who was forever urging him to sell up and retire to, of all places, New Jersey.

Of course, that's where the Edelstein children and grandchildren lived. So it sort of made sense, but Jane wouldn't move to New Jersey for anything or anybody. Not that there was anything wrong with New Jersey.

If you liked snow, which she did not. And congestion, which was even worse in parts of NJ than it was in South Florida.

"Mrs. Terwilliger is sweet but nuts." Jane nudged her PC's mouse with her fingers, bringing her computer out of its sleep. "Like a Mister Goodbar."

"You just write it up and make Bethany look good."

"I always do, Lou."

Lou was a small man, made smaller by the passing of time. His hair had thinned, the skin around his eyes drooped. His flesh was pale. Lou and his wife avoided the sun like it was a cosmic plague. Jane never understood why they had moved to Florida. When she'd asked, Lou's answer had been "Because that's what everybody was doing."

Lou had made a small fortune in the newspaper business, as he liked to say, by starting with a large one—that one inherited from his father who had been a successful clothier with a factory in NYC's garment district.

Lou pressed his fingers into her shoulder. "Make sure you include Mrs. Terwilliger's photo. Ad revenue is down month-to-date."

"Yes, Lou." She removed Lou's fingers from her person. "Can't you give me something bigger to work on?"

"You mean like the annual Fairchild Gardens spread?" Lou slurped his decaf and adjusted the window shade. This time of day the sunlight was harsh and glaring.

The Fairchild Tropical Botanic Garden was twenty minutes south in Coral Gables. It was big—and lush and wonderful—but it was not what Jane had in mind. "I mean big as in that story about the vice mayor taking bribes from that healthcare company exec in Oakland Park."

Lou waved his fat hand in the air. "Eduardo has got that covered."

"Eduardo couldn't properly line a bird cage with the Sunday funnies." Not that she had anything against the swarthy but slick reporter, but Eduardo Sanchez was far more interested in chasing the ladies than he was in chasing down a news story.

Lou tapped some papers on her desk. "You stick to the stories I assign you."

"Yes, Lou," sighed Jane.

3

James dragged himself outside.

It was midday. The downtown streets were busy this time of day, littered with the gainfully employed.

Staring balefully up at the glittering high rises with a frown on his face, he couldn't get the pug-faced club owner out of his mind. The man had been condescending and cold. "Yes," he said. "You can perform in the Banana Reef Bar & Grill."

"No," he added, "I won't pay you a single red cent. You can work for tips," Mr. Pug-Face had said. "Like everybody else does. So long as you play plenty of Jimmy Buffett tunes." Mr. Margaritaville was popular with the locals.

Singing about cheeseburgers was not James' idea of paradise.

After declining the less than generous offer, James had dejectedly hauled himself off the rust-pitted chrome barstool with its torn green vinyl top that stuck to his pants like gluey flypaper and declined the offer.

Waitresses earned more in tips than musicians. He knew that from experience. Playing for three solid hours for a handful of pocket change wasn't going to pay his mounting bills.

Mr. Pug-Face should have named his joint Stale Beer & Body Odor rather than the Banana Reef. That's what it had smelled like, James reflected, not ripe tropical fruit.

Mostly armpit sweat.

The downtown Fort Lauderdale bar had been his last hope. What few live music venues there were wanted mostly younger faces. The hotels wanted monkey-suited piano players who'd mindlessly cover *Piano Man* night after night for the out-of-town mojito sippers.

The city-sized cruise ships plying the shark-infested offshore waters wanted slick Vegas-style performers with big phony smiles. Shipboard sharks, men and women alike, were looking for somebody to share their beds or change a light bulb for them.

No, thanks. That wasn't his scene. Plus, he got seasick easily.

But what to do?

The money was practically all gone. Needing to free up some cash, he'd been living on the proceeds from the sale of his Ocean Palm condo. When that money ran out, he was reduced to renter status. With his kid brother as his landlord, to boot.

He needed something and something quick.

It was another sweltering summer afternoon. This being Florida, there was nothing extraordinary about that.

In fact, James was pretty sure the bright, muggy conditions were responsible for creating all the crazy in Florida—the same way the dark and dusty corners in kitchen cabinets seemed to create cockroaches out of nothingness.

The heavily traveled and stickered black guitar case dangling by the leather-wrapped handle gripped in the fingers of his left hand felt like a hunk of sculpted lead. It was as if rather than hauling around his prized Martin guitar, he was hauling a freshly landed 200-pound Marlin billfish. He shifted the case to his other side.

Maybe a 250-pound Florida Marlins third baseman.

"Hi!" A very sexy blonde with a coppery tan and blue eyes that could suck your soul up through a straw without once blinking was holding up a sign. "Act now," she said with hope and cheer.

James paused. The guitar case banged against his knee. "Excuse me?" He squinted into the sun, unable to find his sunglasses. Had he left them back at the bar? If so, they could stay there. His dignity wouldn't let him step back inside the Banana Reef.

The blonde glanced at her sign then at James. "Act now." She struggled to hold on to her optimism.

The stiff red cardboard sign was about 18 inches long and 12 inches tall. The front side read: *Act Now*.

The back side read: *Bruno Caliostro's School of Detection*.

"The first class is free," explained the blonde. By way of comparison to the sign she held, the curvy young woman was about 5 foot 4 inches tall and as perfectly proportioned as any woman in his dreams had ever been.

Unlike her sign, there was no writing on her skin at all. None that was visible, anyway. In the current tattoo renaissance, there was no telling what lay beneath her clothes. It didn't hurt to imagine.

"I'm Cindi. With an *i*."

"I'm baffled." James held up his guitar. "With a guitar case."

She appeared nonplussed rather than amused. Pity, it had been a clever line too. He was going to have to use it again. On somebody with a sense of humor.

The woman gave no sign of moving out of his path. James went around her, carefully dodging two men in dark power suits as he did so.

"I love the guitar!" she called after him.

James slowly turned around. Her dress was cobalt blue and wasn't hiding a thing. Her heels were red and lifted her two or three inches off the ground. "I love it too. That was my mistake."

He set the butt of his guitar case on the sidewalk and rested his elbow on the top end. "What are you selling?"

She ran her finger along the words on the sign as if reading from a cue card. "Bruno Caliostro's School of Detection. Mr. Bruno says to tell everyone that the first class is free."

Despite the heat and humidity, she sounded as perky as she looked.

"School of Detection? What is that exactly? Something to do with ESP? Magic classes?"

"I'm not sure. I think the guy who hired me is a PI."

"A private investigator?"

She blinked and warmed him with her smile. "I think that's right. My job is just to hold up the sign."

"No *just* about it. You are doing a great job."

"Do you really think so?"

"I really do. Good luck."

"Wait!" She gripped his shoulder. "Aren't you going to check it out?"

"Well..." Meaning not likely.

"Please?"

"A PI school?"

"Yes. Hardly anybody has shown any interest. You are like the first person to even stop this afternoon. Mr. Bruno says he might fire me if he doesn't see some response to the advertising." She batted her long eyelashes. "I really need this job."

"What do I have to do?"

She bent to a pill-shaped yellow purse nestled against the red brick wall of the real estate office occupying the entire ground floor, showing a length of leg in the process. She extracted a pack of gray and white business cards held together with a green rubber band.

She plucked one from the deck and handed it to James. "All you have to do is show up." She pressed her brows together. "I guess."

"Yeah, we guess." James scratched his temple with the edge of the business card. "There's no address. Not even a phone number."

"Turn it over."

He flipped the card over. More words. He read: *It's up to you to find us. Find us if you can.*

James looked up and down the busy sidewalk. "Is this for real? Is this some kind of gag?"

"No," she said breathily. "At least, I don't think so." Cindi's forehead wrinkled ever so slightly. "Mr. Caliostro told me it's like a test."

"No hidden cameras?" James thought he saw some funny movement in the office building across the street. Were those guys in that cubicle watching them? Were he and Cindi with an i being filmed? Were those guys in the office window getting close-ups of his puzzled reactions so they could replay the scene for the whole world later on YouTube?

Not if he had anything to say about it.

"No. Scout's honor." She placed a hand over her heart. Finely-manicured fingers drew him closer into her sphere. He smelled something flowery and alluring coming from the region of her neck.

"I'll tell you a secret," she stage-whispered while motioning with her sign to a narrow concrete stairs that cut into the side of the building. "It's up those steps."

James took a look. Sure enough, he discovered a sign painted on the wall in bold blue lettering:

Bruno Caliostro's School of Detection.

Bruno Caliostro, PI to the Stars, Director.

"When's the next class?"

Cindi visibly brightened. "There's a new session starting tonight. Seven o'clock."

That was fast. Faster than he liked to think, let alone act, on any thoughts—good, bad or indifferent.

"If you go, please give Mr. Bruno the card I gave you. Tell him I sent you. He promised me a twenty-dollar bonus for every new student I bring in."

"I tell you what, I'll think about it." James slipped the card into his breast pocket. "Will you be there?"

"Me? No. I'm a model. And an actress. That is, I want to be an actress."

James promised again to think about it as Cindi with an i went bouncing off in search of fresh pedestrians to lasso.

James' thoughts lingered more on Cindi with an i than they did Bruno Caliostro's School of Detection. If she had promised to be there, he might have given the class a second thought.

As it was, he'd left college after two years of law school, hadn't looked back and didn't see school of any kind in his future.

As he had tried to explain to his much-disappointed parents, and his brother, and his brother's wife, school was not his thing. Their beagle, Pete, was the only member of the family who seemed to understand. Dogs were good that way.

If James had a dog, which he did not, both he and the canine would agree to skip dog obedience class.

The guitar at James' side was a 1966 Martin D-28, a gift from his mom and dad on graduating college. It had been nice of them not to demand it back the day he dropped out of law school.

Nineteen sixty-six, that was the year of *Yellow Submarine*, *Good Vibrations* and *These Boots are Made for Walking*.

"And that's just what I'll do." James entertained the bemused passers-by with a poor impression of Nancy Sinatra as he followed the sidewalk to the little street where he'd tucked his car not quite legally in front of a fire hydrant. He wasn't worried. In his experience, the city rarely towed vehicles from the downtown streets.

Besides, he was lucky that way. A small ray of sunshine in an otherwise cloudy life.

4

It was a short drive from downtown Ft. Lauderdale to Pompano Beach. James' current home was one half of a small duplex with a concrete tile roof and stucco walls. In its latest incarnation, it held a sloppy baby blue paint job done some time ago. He had helped his brother paint it in exchange for knocking a few bucks off the rent for three months. Rust stains, caused by the iron in the water, climbed the walls and green mold rushed down to meet it from the eaves.

The window shutters, more decorative than functional, glowed brilliant yellow. If a hurricane hit and, this being the Florida coast, it would, the shutters would make great blades, slicing the air at 80 mph and removing the heads from anybody foolish enough to be outdoors running around in the middle of a hurricane.

Again, this being Florida, there would always be a fool or two running around in the middle of a hurricane for no good reason at all—mostly to brag that they had done it and survived.

James pulled his little Nissan into the sandy yard and killed the engine. A shiny, late-model black BMW convertible sat up close to the front door. He knew the car and its owner well.

James listened for several minutes to the tick-tick-tick of his car's motor cooling and his heart beating before reluctantly moving along.

Sure enough, Roger was waiting in the living room. At least he had come alone.

"Hey, bro." James' brother waved from the sofa. There was a cold beer in his hand and his heels were attached to the coffee table.

James said hello and went straight to the fridge. Settling his guitar case on the kitchen table, he extracted a cold can of dark beer. He drank it quickly standing behind the green sofa. His eyes flicked to the baseball game on the TV. It was the bottom of the seventh inning and the Marlins were losing.

Beer foamed out of the can and dribbled down the back of the sofa. No sweat. The only thing good about the sofa was that he could, and had, spilled just about everything including pea soup on it and no one was any the wiser.

If all furniture was food- and drink-colored, the world would be a better place.

The brothers bore a strong family resemblance. The same noses and cheekbones, brown eyes and thick brown hair. But that was where things diverged.

Roger liked to point out that he stood an inch taller than James' own six-one. His brother was also four years younger, fitter, more successful and, if James was totally honest with himself, quite possibly smarter.

A commercial for senior diapers interrupted their brotherly quality time. Roger swung his head around. "It's the end of the month. You got the rent?" His feet fell from the coffee table. "I mean, I am sorry to ask but Sheryl insisted."

James fell into the matching chair. "Sorry. Not yet."

The duplex's best feature was the weedy canal out back. Its worst feature was that his brother and sister-in-law owned the place. Then again, he'd been more or less squatting for months, so who was he to complain?

Roger shook his head. "Sheryl isn't going to be happy."

"Is Sheryl ever happy?" James rose, grabbed two more beers and tossed one to his brother.

"No comment. I've got to hit the road."

"Give my love to Sheryl."

"Very funny." Roger set the beer on the table. "Fine. I'll bail you out. Again." Brushing potato chip crumbs from his trousers to the purple area rug the last tenant had left behind, he stuffed the can of beer in his pocket. For later.

"My CPA thinks I'm crazy to keep paying *your* rent on *my* property through *my* business account." Roger scooped his car keys from the little table next to the front door. "Sheryl, on the other hand, will divorce me if she finds out."

"Are you kidding?" James followed him onto the porch. "Sheryl is my number one cheerleader."

Roger snorted as he settled himself down in black leather luxury behind the wheel of the BMW. "Dream on, James. Dream on."

Roger's wife of seven years, Sheryl, had had it in for James from the beginning. She considered James the black sheep of the family, made worse because he was the big brother. She was constantly berating him. Being the older of the Stewart boys, she felt it was incumbent upon James to set a good example for Roger.

"Mom likes me," James said. "Just ask her." Their parents were retired and had moved to an expat community in Belize. If Roger wanted confirmation, it would take a long distance call. The folks were on a no-computer kick. That meant no Skype.

"Likes me better," came Roger's usual comeback. "What am I going to tell Sheryl about the rent?"

"Tell her I'm working on it," James shouted as his brother maneuvered the BMW around his Nissan.

Roger braked. "You want me to lie? Again?"

"No. This is legit. I'm working on something new." He fished the business card from his shirt and waved it in the air.

Roger's head loomed over the windshield. "What's that?"

"A new business opportunity," James said. "I'll tell you about it later."

"I can't wait," Roger said unconvincingly before roaring off.

5

James showered and threw on a fresh pair of jeans and a blue chambray shirt. Stomach rumbling to remind him that he hadn't eaten since before noon, James snatched an overripe Valencia orange from the lowest branch of the neglected tree in the front yard to eat in the car on his way downtown.

He parked in a gravel and dirt lot beside some railroad tracks. The Edsel Building served as home to various businesses besides the detective school. Many of these, judging by the placard dangling on a chain nailed to the brick on the front of the three-story building, appeared to be nefarious or insubstantial at best.

James scratched his head. What was Monkey Shoes, Inc.? And how did an enterprise that boasted it still rented both beta and VHS tapes keep its doors open?

Climbing the narrow stairs to the single red door standing ajar, he went inside.

A mismatch of battered folding chairs, old office swivel chairs and long, chipped tables filled the room. To his right, hunkered a cheap cherry veneer desk littered with papers, books and a PC that looked remarkably newer than anything else in the room. Mounted side-by-side to the wall behind the desk, a whiteboard and a similar-sized blackboard loomed.

A cloth navy blue *Bruno Caliostro's School of Detection* banner hung from one side of the low ceiling to the other.

The boxy room air conditioning unit hanging precariously out the single window emitted an electronic hum. It was either broken or somebody's idea of ideal room temperature was 85 degrees Fahrenheit.

"Are you here for the class?" Inside the door to his right, a pretty woman about his age sat behind a small desk. She held a clipboard in her hand.

"Yeah. I guess so."

"You guess so?" She arched a dark judgmental brow. "Or you are so?"

What a piece of work.

James had half a mind to turn around and go home. But he had come this far. It couldn't hurt to spend an hour here. And Cindi with an i would earn her twenty-dollar bonus. He wondered how many of the others in the classroom were here at her behest. Cindi could be cleaning up.

"Yes. Here for the class. Cindi sent me. She said to give you this." He handed her the business card Cindi had given him.

She gave the card a funny look.

"This is the School of Detection, isn't it?" James asked. It looked more the sort of place where miscreant high schoolers hung out for after-school detention. He'd been there, done that.

"Thank you." She tossed the business card into her gaping purse. "Sign in, please." Her voice was all frost and ice.

Pity the attitude. She was attractive, with bright green eyes, thick chocolatey brown hair and pale skin.

"Then find an empty seat."

"No problem." There were far more seats than people.

James scribbled his name across the sign-in sheet and took a seat between two others, an overweight man in a cheap blue suit and a young kid with pimples and a sunburnt nose.

At the sound of wheezing and the thud of approaching steps, all heads, but for the receptionist's, turned to the open door.

After a quiet moment, broken only by a bout of uncontrollable coughing, a top-heavy man with broad, sloping shoulders and narrow hips, fell into the stuffy room. He wore a buttery yellow button-down shirt with significant sweat stains under the arms and pleated tan trousers. The dull brown penny loafers swaddling his wide feet were missing their pennies.

"We ready?" he asked the young lady at the front desk.

She handed him the clipboard. "This is it."

With a final rasping cough in a vain attempt to dislodge whatever it was that had stuck in his throat, the man turned to the eight of them in attendance. His lips moved silently as he took a head count. Satisfied, he clapped his hands loudly. "Let's get started, shall we?"

James noticed that this was the embodiment of the man in the gold-framed picture fixed to the wall between the blackboard and whiteboard. He had a triangular face, more hair than most men his age—which James was pegging at near sixty—and a squat, fleshy nose.

Did private investigators get punched in the face a lot? If so, he was adding that factoid to the list of reasons he should drop out. And soon.

James didn't like getting punched. And he liked his nose the way it was.

Bruno Caliostro's ruddy cheeks sported the same humungous mutton chop sideburns that Elvis Presley had flaunted in the seventies.

"I'm Bruno Caliostro, PI to the stars!" He hitched a hand under his belt. "Tonight, I am going to—" The detective frowned as a hand flew up in the audience.

"Can you tell us some of the celebrities you've worked for?" inquired the redheaded kid to James' left.

The man loomed over the table. "Who are you?"

"Arthur Montgomery, sir," squeaked the kid in the red-and-white gingham shirt and blue jeans.

Arthur Montgomery looked like he belonged in a remedial high school English class, not a detective school for grownups.

"Do you know Miami Sound Machine, Artie?"

"It's Art. Or Arthur," the young man corrected. "No, I am not familiar with Miami Sound Machine, sir."

Mr. Caliostro snarled unhappily and scratched the top of his head. "Gloria Estefan, Artie?"

The young man struggled to conjure up an answer and failed.

A strong voice came from the table behind us. "Gloria Estefan. I love her music."

James swung back for a look. A Hispanic woman with short-cropped hair and dark eyes with long, curly lashes glared back. She was shy of James' age and primly held a pen in one hand. A brand new notebook sat on the table in front of her.

James had brought nothing to class. Not even an apple for teacher.

"Precisely." Bruno smiled to show his pleasure. "I worked for Ms. Estefan on a very confidential case."

The woman to James' right leaned into him. She had taken the seat at the front row table with James, between him and the big guy in the shiny blue pinstriped suit. "I heard he found her poodle for her."

James turned and stared. This speaker was a large woman with a double chin, wearing a flowery muumuu. Colorful beads circled her neck and both wrists.

"Lost the poor thing shopping at the Neiman Marcus in Coral Gables," she added thickly.

The large man in the shiny suit snorted. James kept his mouth shut because Bruno Caliostro was looking murderously at all three of them.

"Please hold your questions until the break." Mr. Caliostro snatched a wooden pool cue that had stood in the army-green metal trashcan beside the desk. He proceeded to wave it about, utilizing it as a pointer as he pontificated.

James learned that about Bruno Caliostro quickly. He didn't talk. He pontificated.

The next hour and a half passed in a funky haze. Most of the class seemed to drift in and out of consciousness as Bruno Caliostro offered them an introduction into the world of the private investigator. James snuck looks every few minutes at his smartphone. Time was passing at a glacial pace.

Bruno Caliostro dimmed the lights and showed slides on an ancient black projector. The cone of light highlighted every mote of dust. He followed this display with a short film on the history of private detection beginning with the Pinkertons.

Boring.

The only thing worth looking at was the receptionist in the tan skirt and white blouse seated at the desk near the entrance. She paid Caliostro no attention, too busy looking at who knew what on her smartphone throughout his presentation. No doubt she'd heard it a million times before.

Finally, mercifully, the introductory class was over.

James yawned as he waited in line for what was to be his exit interview. And exit was all he was itching to do.

Mr. Caliostro wanted five minutes at his desk with each potential student before they left. James impatiently waited his turn. The way he saw it, Cindi with an i owed him big time.

Finally, Arthur Montgomery, carrying a new spiral-bound book in his hand and a dazed look on his face, stumbled out the door and into the night. "See you next class."

James smiled. "Not a chance," he said under his breath.

Caliostro waved him over. "Have a seat, Mister—?"

"James Stewart."

Caliostro's brows went up. James couldn't blame him.

"Like the actor that had that invisible rabbit for a best friend? What did he call it?" Caliostro leaned back in his swivel chair and swiveled. "Herman?"

"Harvey. Same as the name of the movie. Yes, that James Stewart. What can I say? My folks have a sense of humor. But to be clear, I do not see invisible rabbits. At least, not regularly. Even if I did, I'm not sure how useful he'd prove to be on stakeouts."

Funny, there had been Major League ballplayer for a handful of years with the name James Stewart. He'd played with a number of clubs, including the Chicago Cubs and the White Sox. Nobody ever mistook him for that guy.

"Interesting." Bruno Caliostro yanked open the upper right-hand drawer of his desk, twisted the white lid off a bottle of lime-green pills and popped one. "So, James, why are you interested in becoming a private investigator?"

"To be honest," James squirmed. "I'm not quite sure. I have been looking for a new direction in life."

Or maybe life was demanding a new direction of him. Either way, what he'd said was not a lie.

Bruno Caliostro ran James through the same list of preliminary questions that he'd asked the other potential students, including whether he was a US citizen or legal resident, had a criminal record, was of good moral character, had a history of illegal drug use, alcoholism or mental illness.

James answered all to his satisfaction—as for honestly, that was debatable.

"What else have you done?"

"You mean jobs?"

"Yeah." Bruno Caliostro scooted closer and planted his elbows on the desk. "Anything related to investigatory work?"

"Does searching for the lost chord count?" An obscure Moody Blues reference.

Bruno Caliostro frowned. "Do you like adventure?"

"Maybe. Sort of." Frankly, he wasn't sure.

"Huh." Bruno Caliostro tapped the sharp end of his pencil against the desk, leaving an array of tiny gray dots in the wood surface that looked remarkably like a pixillated raccoon clinging to a pogo stick. "What about puzzles?"

"Puzzles?" James repeated, puzzled by the question.

"Yeah, do you like solving them?"

"I like doing the USA Today crossword. Does that count?"

"No, no. I'm talking about real puzzles, involving real people. Mystery, intrigue—"

"Who's cheating on who?"

"Yeah." Bruno shrugged. "There is that."

"Why am I not surprised?"

"Hey, it pays the bills. Besides, tailing some of those cheating spouses can be a real hoot."

"I'll bet."

Bruno Caliostro retrieved his bottle of pills and popped a second one.

"Should you be taking so many of those?" scolded the receptionist. She handed him a glass of water to wash it down then retreated to her desk without waiting for a reply.

"Thanks, honey." Mr. Caliostro ran his moist tongue over his lips. "Any other special skills, James? How are you with computers?"

"I can hold my own."

"Do any photography?"

"No, not really."

"And you say you're a college graduate?"

"Yes, sir. I did have two years of law school, in addition."

Bruno Caliostro brightened. "That's something. That's a real bonus. Some of these folks, the only previous experience they have is watching TV cop shows."

"Do you reject them?"

"You mean turn them down?" Bruno Caliostro sounded aghast. "James, I don't turn any wannabe student down. It wouldn't be ethical."

Or profitable, thought James, cynically.

"Ready to sign up?"

"How much is the tuition?" James hesitated to tell him the truth that he'd only come as a favor to a woman he didn't even know.

Bruno Caliostro, in his earlier overview to the class on the PI business in Florida, had explained that applicants for a Class C Private Investigator's License in Florida must have two years of experience. The majority of applicants opt to apply for licensure as a Class CC Private Investigator Intern first.

"You remember what I said before? Prior to applying for the intern license, you gotta complete at least forty hours of professional training pertaining to private investigation and Chapter 493 of the Florida Statutes? Offered by an accredited school?"

"Yes." Barely.

"Forty hours. That's the law. But forty hours isn't good enough, James." Bruno Caliostro shook his head as if it were a very sad thing indeed.

"It isn't?"

"Nope. The PI game is competitive. Very, very competitive. But," he said, meaningfully twisting the solid gold watch around his wrist, "it can also be very, very lucrative. I'd be doing you and all my students a disservice if I didn't offer them the absolute best education possible."

Bruno Caliostro paused a moment to let that fact

sink in. "So I don't insist on forty hours? No, siree. What do I do?"

James waited for the answer.

"Do I double it? No, sir." Bruno banged his fist on the desk. His PC monitor went plummeting over the edge of the desk. James snatched it before it smashed his toes into pudding.

"Thanks," Bruno said. He set the monitor to one side, looping the cord around his index finger and holding tight. "No, James. I quintuple it."

"Quintuple it. Right."

"That's six hundred and fifty hours of professional investigatory training."

James suppressed a frown. He was no accountant but he was pretty sure the numbers did not add up.

"For one very, very low price."

"Which is?" They had finally circled back to James' original question.

Mr. Caliostro named the price of a small import coupe with all the options. Plus the extended warranty.

James blinked.

"Shall I sign you up?" Not missing the slight hesitation on James' part, he added, "I've got a monthly payment plan. Super low interest."

"Define super low interest." James squirmed. The noose was tightening around his financial neck.

"That's difficult to say. It's pegged to the prime rate but I don't charge a cent more than the bank charges me. Plus, there is no application fee and, as a student of Bruno Caliostro's School of Detection, you won't have to fill out any papers. You qualify."

James had a feeling that anybody, dead or alive, would qualify.

Figuring he could always call and cancel the contract tomorrow, James said, "Okay, I'm game." Cindi with an i would get her twenty-dollar commission and he'd get on with finding a real job. Which meant probably having to sell cars on his brother's lot like Roger had been bugging him to do.

Oh joy.

"Excellent." Caliostro pointed to the signature line on the first page. "Sign here."

James signed then quickly flipped through the pages of the contract, skimming a phrase here and there. There was no point reading the school's contract. The font size was far too small for any human to make out—not to mention the precious time it would have taken him to read the thing cover to cover.

At Bruno Caliostro's instruction, James quickly initialled the bottom of each page and put his signature once more and the day's date on the last.

"One copy is for you," explained Bruno Caliostro, sliding it across the desk. "The other is for our records."

"Thanks." He eyed the contract. "Out of curiosity, how much is this going to cost me on a monthly basis?"

"Next to nothing, James." Bruno Caliostro scooped up his copy of the contract and shoved it in a drawer atop a pile of others.

"How next?" Not that it mattered. James had had a hard time staying awake through the intro. He'd never survive a second class.

"We can talk about that at the next class." Mr. Caliostro answered slickly. He grabbed two spiral-bound books identical to those he'd handed the others and laid them on the desk between them. The sheet of paper stuck in the plastic sleeve on the front of the top one read *Bruno Caliostro's School of Detection: Volume 1, Class Handbook.*

The book was a solid two inches thick.

Volume 2 proclaimed itself to be an exercise book.

James frowned at the materials. That equalled four inches of sheer hell.

Bruno Caliostro slid the books towards James. "I don't expect you to memorize anything. Yet." He chuckled. "But read chapter one for Thursday. And do the first set of exercises. That's pages one through three in Volume 2."

"Thursday?" James pushed his copy of the contract inside the school binder.

"That's our next class." Bruno Caliostro smiled. "You are now an official private investigator in training."

"Do I get a school jersey and a class ring?"

"You have an interesting sense of humor, James." Bruno Caliostro tented his fingers and studied him. "I'm not sure that will be of benefit to you as a private detective. This is a serious business. Our clients depend on us for our skills, discretion and gravitas."

"Gravitas. Of course, sorry." James seriously wanted to get out of there.

"And if you wanna be a detective, you're gonna need a haircut."

James' hands went automatically to his skull. "I am?"

"Getting a little bushy around the ears there. A good operative must be innocuous, unremarkable and blend in with his surroundings."

"Right." This from a man with sideburns the size and shape of Delaware.

6

James had been the last student remaining to be interviewed. The receptionist offered a stiff good night, a whiff of Chanel, then locked the door behind him.

The sky was a spatter of black and white. The street was deserted. James shambled back to the gravel lot around the corner of the Edsel Building. He figured he would stop at a drive-thru joint and enjoy what was left of his night with a burger and a beer out on his back deck overlooking the narrow canal.

Maybe play a little guitar if the iceberg next door didn't get on his case. Iceberg was the pet name James and Roger had for the woman renting the other half of the duplex. If she ever cracked a smile, he was pretty sure her face would shatter as quickly and completely as a mirror hit with a hardened-steel hammer.

The parking lot was quiet. A steel chain with finger-thick links blocked the entrance. Steel eyebolts driven into sturdy wooden posts securely held each end of the dangling chain.

"What the—"

There was no sign of his car.

He cursed, stomped in a circle, and cursed some more.

He angrily tugged at the chain to no avail.

A deliveryman just wrapping up his shift stopped

his truck at the curb.

"What's the problem?" asked the driver, leaning toward the open passenger side window. He had close-cropped hair and smelled of fresh-baked bread.

"They towed my car." James pointed to the metal warning sign at the entrance to the lot, the one he had ignored and which read *Towing Enforced*, followed by the usual scare tactic, pseudo-legalese mumbo-jumbo. The name *Smiley's Towing Service* and a phone number followed.

"That's a drag," said the driver.

"Tell me about it." James folded his spiral-bound books under his arm. It was going to be an expensive night. Surely, they didn't tow cars after business hours. "I'm hoping it's a mistake."

With the driver watching, James punched in the telephone number of the towing service on his smartphone. It went straight to voicemail. "No answer." He thrust his phone in his pocket. "What kind of sadist names their towing service Smiley's?"

"Smiley's? That's that yard up the tracks at the corner of Dixie and Carter." The driver gestured for James to get in. "I'm off duty. Come on, I'll drop you off."

"Thanks."

A mile up the railroad tracks, the driver deposited James outside a one-story building with white vinyl siding and a black shingled roof. The small parking lot in front sat deserted. An eight-foot chain link fence created an impassable barricade to the larger lot that circled behind the building and faded into the distance.

For anybody even thinking about climbing up and over that tall fence, the nasty ribbon of razor-sharp wire running along the top of the fence was bound to make them think twice.

A big yellow and red smiley face hung over the front door, rotating slowly round and round—its fatuous smile mocking him.

James saw no trace of his car. The door to Smiley's stood to the right with windows to the left. James stepped inside. He found a heavyset man wheezing behind a desk, a cigarette in one hand and a cellphone in the other.

"Hold on!" the man barked into his phone. "You want something?" he demanded of James.

"You towed my car." The cramped and cluttered interior was icy cold. The air conditioner hummed in a desperate attempt to maintain the arctic temperature. James was surprised not to see icicles hanging off the overworked unit and from the man's nostrils.

"Call you back." The man at the desk slammed the cellphone down on a thick blue ledger and climbed out of his chair. He wasn't tall, but he was big. His face was wide and his nose was flat. Like Kansas. Crow-black hair spilled over his ears.

"What kind of car you got?" He blew out a puff of warm smoke and coughed on the fumes.

James described his Nissan.

"Ain't seen it. Could be out on a truck yet."

"Can you find out?"

"I'm closing for the day. In fact, it's past closing time. How about you come back in the morning, buddy?" The man marched to the front door and threw it open. "We'll fix you up then. Bring your checkbook. Three percent surcharge for credit."

"Listen," James said, "I need my car. Your operator shouldn't have towed it. I was parked over at the Edsel

Building *after hours*."

"The Edsel Building? Down by the tracks?"

"That's right."

"There ain't no after hours at that lot." He pulled out a pack of cigarettes and lit one up with a cheap plastic lighter. With his back against the door, he asked "Didn't you read the sign? You gotta have a sticker to park there. Twenty-four seven."

A tow truck rumbled into the parking lot.

"That your car?" asked the man.

James poked his head outside. "No. That's a Buick." A maroon Buick hung off the back of the tow truck like the catch of the day. This guy ran a tow company and he didn't even know one make from another?

"So it is." The man stepped out and said something to the driver. When he turned around, James was standing inches away.

"I am not leaving here without my car."

The man flicked his cigarette. "Yes, you are."

"No, I'm not. You had no right to tow me."

"You hear that, Adam?" he said to the burly tow truck driver.

"No. Tell me again, boss." His mustachioed companion, Adam, smirked. The tan shirt struggling to contain him had the Smiley's logo stitched to the pocket. The shirt was loosely tucked into greasy brown trousers. He held a stainless steel travel mug in his meaty hand like a modern day club.

"This man tells me I got no right to tow his car." He chuckled. "Mister, I own this place and I got a business license on the wall inside that tells me I've got every right."

He thumped his finger against James' chest. "Now,

you'd best get off my property before I call the authorities and have *you* towed away!"

The owner and the tow truck driver stood shoulder to shoulder.

"You haven't heard the last from me," warned James. He didn't normally let things get under his skin, but this guy was too much.

James marched off before he did something stupid.

7

Tucking his detective school books under his arm —tempted to hurl them as far as he could but knowing that, with his luck, a cop would be passing and he'd get ticketed for littering—he followed the railroad tracks back the way he had come.

Hopefully, Bruno Caliostro and his assistant would still be upstairs at the School of Detection. Maybe he could bum a ride back to his place with one of them.

He should have thought of that earlier instead of wasting his time at Smiley's.

A couple of upper floor lights glowed in the Edsel Building. A blue van sat parked on the street outside. James remembered seeing it earlier. He worked his way towards the building.

Beep! Beep!

James turned to see who was honking. The driver of a shiny black Jeep Wrangler minus roof and doors had pulled off the road near him.

"Hey, Guitar Guy!"

James found a smile. Not that it was easy with a hole where his car used to be. "Cindi with an i." He approached the Jeep. "What brings you here?"

"I was passing by. Curious to see if anybody I handed a card out to showed up." She wore the same clingy blue dress James had first met her in. "What about you? Did you go to the School of Detection?" A shiny red leather shoe pressed down on the brake pedal.

"I did."

"Thanks!" Cindi appeared genuinely pleased. She drew her brows together. "Need a ride?"

"I do. My car has been towed."

"Wow. Bummer."

"Yeah." James kicked the sidewalk. "Some jerk named Smiley."

"Did you say Smiley?" Cindi grinned from ear to ear.

"Yes. What's so funny?"

"You are not going to believe this."

"Try me."

"Smiley is my brother-in-law."

"You're kidding."

"I told you you wouldn't believe me."

"Smiley is your brother-in-law? Black hair? Black mood?"

"Yep. I am so sorry." She looked stricken. "I feel to blame."

"Not your fault. I should have parked on the street." James resigned himself to the situation. "Besides, I might have to apologize to you."

"How do you mean?"

"Smiley and I didn't exactly hit it off. I may have had a harsh word or two for him." He explained his earlier confrontation.

Cindi laughed. "His name isn't really Smiley. It's Kevin. He may look all rough and tumble on the outside but he's not so terrible. Must've been having a bad day."

She dug her phone from the red purse on the passenger seat. "Maybe I can help. Let me call him on his private number." She pressed the phone to her ear a moment. "No answer. I know. How about if I buy you a drink? Maybe dinner?"

"Thanks, but I really should get back."

"We can try Kevin again a little later. Maybe your car will show up by then. Worst-case scenario, I drive you home tonight. I'm sure your car will be fine until tomorrow. What's the worst that could happen?"

James hesitated. He didn't like it when nothing went as planned. Then again, things rarely did.

She leaned across the Jeep. "Come on, hop in. Dinner's on me. It's the least I can do to pay you back for showing up for that kooky class. And my being responsible for you getting your car towed."

James climbed aboard. "I'll settle for a lift home. I don't want you blowing your twenty-dollar bonus on me."

"By the way, what's your name?" Cindi revved the engine and cut in front of a motorcyclist who then weaved past and shot them the bird. Cindi merely smiled, raised her hand above the windshield and waved to the rider.

James regretted the Jeep's lack of doors. And crash helmets.

"James. With an s," he couldn't resist adding.

"Cute." She tapped a fingernail against her teeth, driving one handed. "I have an idea. We can go to my apartment."

"Your apartment?"

Cindi's golden hair flew like a wild beast on the breeze. "Sure. I'll fix us up dinner." She took her eyes off the road just long enough to ask, "You are hungry, aren't you?"

"Starving." The last thing he remembered eating was that orange.

"Good. I'm no master chef but I'll fix you right up." Cindi suddenly swung the Jeep hard to the left.

James dug his hands into the sides of the seat to keep from planting his face in the asphalt flying towards him at light speed.

"Trust me," she said.

James nodded. But the last time he had trusted someone he had been a twenty-seven-year-old law student at Arizona State University. His fiancé, Lindsay, was a year younger. She was in the film school. They shared a small one-bedroom apartment a few blocks from the Tempe campus. One day she announced she had to go to LA to work on a film project with a couple of her fellow students.

As it turned out, there had been only one other student, John Holder. She never came back to Arizona, at least not while he was there. She asked one of her girlfriends to remove the rest of her things from their shared apartment. The girlfriend did a good job. After she closed the door behind her, no trace of Lindsay remained.

Not long after that, James had decided law school wasn't for him. Ditto, Arizona.

Lindsay's name popped up from time to time in film credits: Lindsay Hicks, Director of Photography—whatever that meant. Either she had never married or had refused to change her last name.

Before he knew it, Cindi was parking in the big lot of a tall white stucco building with a peach-colored portico over the entrance. The stuffy elevator stopped on the tenth floor. James ran his fingers through his hair checking for bats and moths he might have picked up on the drive as she led him along the exterior walkway leading to her apartment halfway down.

"Nice place," James said, taking in the view of the Intracoastal Waterway. The ICW ran from Florida to points north. How many points north he didn't have a clue. At least as far as Washington, DC.

James slid open the door to the terrace and stepped outside. The night sky was clear and starry. The lights of a jet coming in for a landing at Fort Lauderdale International Airport blinked in the distance.

Various yachts shimmered below on the black water. Florida was a great place to be if you were rich. High rises sprouted up along the Intracoastal. Somewhere beyond them was the ocean. The corner of a golf course sprinkled with sprawling estates was visible further south.

Cindi appeared at his side with a cold can.

"Thanks."

"Have a beer while I see what I've got to eat."

James followed her inside. "Can I help?"

"Nope. I've got this. You relax." Cindi kicked off her heels at the door and moved to the galley kitchen at the front of the small apartment.

Minimal furnishings, all neat and stylish, occupied the main living area. A small futon sofa stood against the wall, surrounded on each side by armless accent chairs. Fashion and movie magazines covered the glass table in front of the sofa.

A stereo and TV occupied the opposite wall. There was a short hallway with a bathroom at the end and doors on each side, which James pictured leading to bedrooms.

Would he discover the truth behind at least one of them later?

He studied the highly-stylized photos on the wall. Some were black and white, others sepia tone and full-color. He recognized Cindi in most of them.

"The others are friends," Cindi said, catching him looking.

"You look great on camera." One black and white headshot in a slender black frame was particularly sexy.

"Thanks. That's my standard headshot. You can have one, if you want. I've got a drawer full of them."

"I might take you up on that." Her name, Cindi Keach, and the name of the photographer and a modeling and acting agency located down in Miami Beach ran along the bottom edge of the picture.

"Very impressive," James remarked, studying the photo-filled wall. A gold-framed magazine cover featured Cindi standing in front of a splashing coquina fountain outside a palatial Palm Beach home, showing off a multicolored sequined gown. James had seen the South Florida design magazine around town.

"I've had a few jobs. I'd like to do more acting though. There's more money in it. At least, so I hear."

"Is there much opportunity here?" James drifted to the kitchen. "Wouldn't you be better off in LA or New York?"

"Maybe. But I'm a Florida girl. What about you?" She dropped a skillet on the burner and smeared a stick of butter across it. "Where are you from? Grilled cheese, okay?"

"Sure. I'm a Florida boy. Born and raised."

"Cool. It's sort of my go-to comfort food." She tossed Swiss cheese between thick slices of sourdough bread and dropped them on the hot skillet.

James finished his beer. "Do you think you could try your brother-in-law again?" The Nissan wasn't much but it was his sole source of transportation. The sooner he got it back, the better he'd feel.

Plus, he was hoping that if they could sort things out now, Cindi's brother-in-law would see fit not to charge him to get his car out of impound.

"What's your hurry?" Cindi glanced at her wrist-watch. "Don't you like my company?" She batted her eyelashes at him.

"No hurry," James amended quickly. On second thought, a towed car might have been the best thing to happen to him in a very long time.

"After we eat then. Promise. There's wine in the fridge."

Cindi pointed with her spatula. "Nothing fancy. I hope you don't mind. I'm on a budget."

"Don't worry. Me, too." James opened the fridge and pulled out a box of sangria.

"Glasses are up there." She pointed this time to the cupboard nearest the refrigerator.

James filled their glasses. Cindi plated the grilled cheese. She tossed some baby carrots on both plates, adding a pile of potato chips to his.

"I have to watch my diet." She led him out to the long narrow balcony holding a single chaise lounge, a small round table and two chairs. "I have a photo shoot tomorrow."

"Cindi!" a voice called from inside.

James lurched, spilling red wine in his lap as a woman in tight indigo jeans and a black scoop-neck top burst through the front door. She swayed forward and gripped the corner of the wall.

"Cindi?"

"Out here!"

James wiped at his trousers with a paper towel. "I think that woman knows you," James stage-whispered.

Cindi sighed and licked her fingers. "That's my sister, Alyssa. I hope she hasn't been drinking again."

"I'd say it's too late to hope for that." James watched as the woman stumbled towards the patio. She was about Cindi's size and shape but with jet-black hair. "You want me to leave?"

Cindi scooted back her chair and slid past James. "No, please stay. I'll see what she wants." She pecked James on the cheek. "Don't go anywhere."

James looked out over the railing. The only place he could go was straight down. Ten stories down. Given the option of facing the drunken sibling of a woman he barely knew or a three second freefall to his death, he chose to do as Cindi requested. He could think of better places for his final resting spot than being splashed across the parking lot of a South Florida high-rise.

Unable to turn away, James sipped his sangria and nibbled the corners of his sandwich, awkwardly watching the two women huddled in the kitchen. He couldn't make out what was being said between them.

Finally, Alyssa hung an arm over Cindi's shoulder and allowed herself to be led down the hall.

Several minutes later, Cindi reappeared. She dropped her sister's sandals at the side of the front door and went to the kitchen. Carrying the box of wine, she returned to the table and sat.

"Sorry about that, James."

"Everything okay?"

"Alyssa has been drinking again." Cindi worried her fingers. "I'm afraid she has a bit of a problem."

"Sorry to hear that."

"It's not your problem." She glanced inside. "It can be mine sometimes though. I put her in the guestroom to sleep it off for a few hours."

"She doesn't live here?"

"No. She's married."

"Oh, right." James polished off the last of his chips. A pile of cold baby carrots remained on his plate. "To Smiley."

"Yeah." Cindi ate half a carrot and washed it down. "He's really a good guy. Don't let the tow unduly influence you. Besides, he rarely tows anybody himself anymore, unless too many drivers are out sick. He's mostly in that office of his. He's got lots of employees. I bet it was one of them."

"I understand. I met one of them. Adam."

"Kevin will be disappointed to see that Alyssa's been drinking again." Concern colored her eyes. "I think it might be best if she stays here tonight."

"Won't Kevin worry?"

"I'll give him a call. Tell him we're having a girls' night." Cindi beamed. "I need to telephone him anyway, for you." She dialed and left a message explaining on her brother-in-law's voicemail.

Cindi reached across the table, revealing a hint of tanned cleavage, and touched his wrist. "Would you mind doing me a favor?"

"What's that?"

"I need to run to the store and pick up some aspirin, maybe some antacid or some sort of hangover cure for Alyssa when she wakes up. Would you mind terribly keeping an eye on her while I'm gone?"

"No, I guess not."

"Great. We'll deal with your car when I return. Don't worry about Alyssa. I'm sure she'll be no trouble. She's probably dead asleep already."

Cindi stood and reached into a pocket. "I took her keys from her. I don't want her hurting herself." Cindi handed them to James for safekeeping.

"Or anybody else," added James, accepting the keys.

"Right. Turn on the TV if you get bored. Help yourself to anything. I'll be back in a jiff."

"Does that anything include you?"

"Guess you'll just have to wait and see." She pecked him on the nose, grabbed her purse, slipped on her shoes and disappeared.

8

Sometime later, James heard a key turn in the lock and fought his way back to consciousness.

"I'm back." Cindi tossed her keys on the kitchen counter. "How did everything go?" She dropped a plastic grocery bag on the counter.

"Quiet." James shut off the television. One of the oldies cable channels was running *Vertigo*. He'd had little interest in the classic detective movie. In fact, he'd had enough of detectives, period. One class with Bruno Caliostro had seen to that.

While Cindi was out, he had given his detective school handbook a desultory look and wondered what he had gotten himself into. There had to be something better he could do with his life than shadow suspected adulterers and insurance cheats. Maybe he would ask his mom and dad what the job opportunities were like in Belize.

James joined her as she pulled out a small bottle of aspirin, some antacid and a jug of tomato juice, setting them on the counter.

"Alyssa didn't give you any trouble, I hope."

"Not a bit." He dropped Alyssa's keys beside Cindi's.

"Cool. Sorry it took so long. I stopped for gas." Cindi slid out of her shoes, braced one hand against the counter and rubbed her foot. "It's been a long day."

"Yeah." James glanced at the digital clock on the oven. It was merely nine thirty but he had to agree, it had been a hell of a long day. "I really should be going."

"Are you sure? What about your car? I haven't heard from Kevin yet. Let me try him again."

"I'm sure. Don't worry about the car. I've decided to put it out of my mind until tomorrow. Thanks for supper."

"Can I give you a ride?"

"I'll call a Lyft. You don't want to leave your sister alone."

"That's true." Cindi turned a worried eye on the hall. "You sure she didn't give you any trouble?"

"I heard her moan once or twice. Otherwise, nothing." He had been dreading Alyssa would emerge feeling sick and he would be forced to help her to the toilet. He'd lived through enough dorm mates vomiting into toilet bowls to last him a lifetime.

"Good."

James pulled open the door and stepped outside.

"Wait, James!" She pranced over to the credenza and back. "Here's my card." She slid a silver business card with black lettering and a photo of herself on the left into his palm. "Call me?" Her lips brushed his.

"Definitely." James handed her a card from his wallet. They were cheap, black and white and advertised that he was available to play private parties, weddings and bar mitzvahs.

He drew the line at birthday parties for five-year olds. The only thing that made the kiddies happy was him singing the SpongeBob SquarePants theme song. They couldn't get enough of that.

He could.

As for Cindi, she had to be ten years younger than him but, if she didn't mind and wanted to see him again, who was he to complain?

He couldn't remember the last time he'd had a steady relationship. Was it his fault, like his sister-in-law claimed?

James skipped the Lyft. It was a balmy night and the walk would do him good. Spending time with Cindi with an i left him with energy to burn, unlike money of which he had little to burn.

Lyfts cost money.

The longer James walked, the more his thoughts turned to his towed vehicle. He jingled the keys in his pocket with satisfaction. Brother-in-law or not, Smiley wasn't going to get the best of him.

It was a fifteen-minute walk to Smiley's Towing Service. A dark blue Mercedes-Benz with tinted windows sat parked near the entrance. It had been there earlier as well. He placed a hand on the hood. Cold.

A row of tow trucks faced the street. Titans waiting to do battle the following day.

James saw no sign of his car. The windows of the office were dark. Pressing his face to the glass door, he noticed a faint light coming from farther down the hall.

James fiddled with his keyring. If he could just find his car and drive it away, he could save himself maybe several hundred dollars in tow fees. It may not have been quite ethical but then neither was towing his car in the first place as far as he was concerned.

He moved quietly to the right side of the building. At this hour, every step sounded like a slap. He stuck to the shadows, not wanting to be seen from passing cars.

Somebody had failed to pull the gate shut all the

way, leaving a noticeable gap between the gate and the fence. The tall chain link gate rested on wheels and rolled easily.

The sad, dark silhouettes of dozens of captive automobiles, trucks and vans filled the expansive lot. Some were victims of parking violations, others represented the mangled remains of car crashes.

Smiley's did a brisk business.

By the dim light of his cellphone's flashlight, James started up the first row of vehicles in search of his Cube. The ticking of insects and throaty chatter of frogs filled the night.

Thankfully, there were no vicious guard dogs on duty. The mosquitoes, on the other hand, were out for blood. He was constantly swatting at them as they buzzed his face, neck and ears.

Two flat-roofed extensions hung off the rear of the main building. The sign over the smaller of the two indicated this was the shop. The larger wing on the other side was unmarked. A couple of overspilling dumpsters and a four-post car lift separated the two structures. A tin shed stood in the middle of the back lot. It appeared unoccupied.

Brilliant LED fixtures mounted on the eaves washed the larger annex with harsh white light. James edged closer. If Cindi's brother-in-law was around, he'd maybe have to rethink taking possession of his car. The guy struck him as the shotgun carrying, shoot first, ask questions later type.

Window blinds tilted downwards prevented him from peering inside. James crept to the door. Or what was left of it. The glass had been shattered. Ice-cold air spilled out-of-doors. Had Smiley's been burgled?

Was it being burgled now?

The door opened into a dead-end hallway with a single doorway to the right. Light spilled from within, cutting a wedge into the linoleum tiles.

Burglars could be armed. And dangerous. He needed a weapon. And that medium-gauge nylon guitar pick in his pocket wasn't going to cut it.

He remembered seeing a tire iron lying next to one of the dumpsters. He ran back for it and returned to the broken door. Bits of glass crunched underfoot as he tried the door handle. An electric hum came from the interior.

"Hello? Anybody here?"

Gripping the tire iron like a club, he stepped into the narrow hallway. An alarm pad mounted to the wall on his right blinked green and made no sound. "Hello, Kevin? Are you here?"

No reply.

"Don't be alarmed. I'm a friend of Cindi's."

The walls refused to speak.

James tiptoed up the hall to the doorway, keeping close to the wall. Prepared to turn and run if somebody came at him. Taking a deep breath, hearing nothing but an unidentifiable, steady hum, he turned the corner.

James didn't know what surprised him more, seeing a room filled with an elaborate tabletop HO train layout or the body of Smiley himself slumped over the railroad tracks with a shiny little train engine pushing futilely against his flaccid cheek.

9

That little engine could keep huffing and puffing and pushing all it wanted. It wasn't going anywhere.

Neither was Kevin. Kevin, aka Smiley, looked balefully at James through a solitary half-opened eyelid. Okay, so that was James' imagination.

It was not his imagination that Cindi with an i's brother-in-law was dead with a d.

James' pulse quickened. Despite the polar temperature in the train room, sweat oozed from every pore. He dropped the tire iron and ran.

The green glow of the alarm box beckoned like a beacon in a thunderstorm. He stopped and punched the button for the police. The alarm box pulsed an angry red. Electronic alarm horns spread around the property sprang to life as if all hell had broken loose.

As far as James was concerned, it had.

He stumbled out the door, slip-sliding through the hundreds of shards of broken glass. Huffing and puffing, he ran out the gate and into the parking lot.

He stopped dead in his tracks.

A police car, light bar aglow and siren shrieking shrilly, fixed a pair of brilliant LED headlights on him.

A navy blue-uniformed officer jumped out the passenger side door and drew his weapon. "Police! Hands on your head!"

James threw his arms in the air. Nobody was going to have to ask him twice.

"I said on your *head*."

"Oh, right." James shifted his feet as he planted his hands atop his skull.

The woman who'd barked at him approached, lowering the muzzle of her weapon ever so slightly. "What's your name?"

The officer's partner joined her, talking on his clipped-on radio as he came. Both looked grim. James couldn't blame them.

"James Stewart."

"Very funny, wise guy." The woman frowned, took a step back and raised her weapon once again.

"No, it's true! That's my name!" His parents' whimsy was about to get him arrested or shot. Maybe both.

Keeping his hands firmly atop his head, lest she get the idea he was up to some sort of funny business and shoot him, he motioned with his chin. "My driver's license is in my back pocket. In my wallet. But listen, there's a—"

Her olive-skinned partner, who fit the description of gym rat, thumped a short black baton across his palm. "Show us. Slowly."

James nodded, keeping a wary eye on the woman who seemed to be waiting for an excuse to shoot him dead between the eyes. Slowly lowering his right hand, he extracted his wallet. "I'm the one who set off the alarm."

"Hand it to Officer Deen."

James handed his thick wallet to the officer.

"I'm Lieutenant Byrd." She flashed her own ID.

"You work here, Mr. Stewart?"

"No." Out of the corner of his eye, James watched nervously as two more police cars appeared, blocking the entrance to the parking lot. This annoyed the driver of the EMS vehicle that roared up behind them. Words were exchanged and the two police cars separated long enough and wide enough for the EMS vehicle to squeeze through.

"But you set off the alarm?" The lieutenant had replaced her weapon in its holster but her wide stance showed she was ready for James to make any sudden moves. He had no doubt she could wrestle him to the ground.

Probably single-handed.

"Yes."

Three more police officers had joined them. The four of them formed a loose circle around James. Each face presented a stern, concerned, no-nonsense look as if they had each been cast from the same grim mold. James pictured a bent-back sadistic sculptor carving the mirthless clay molds in a low-lit windowless basement atelier somewhere under the streets of Paris.

"Why? There's no fire. I don't see any disturbance. What is the nature of your emergency?"

While this was going on, Officer Deen held the mic to his lips as he read James' license information to whoever was at the other end.

"There's a dead man," James explained.

"A dead man? Who?"

"Smiley. I mean, Kevin. I'm not sure of his last name." Had Cindi told him?

The officers exchanged a look. Radios crackled. The EMS crew stood beside their vehicle, waiting to spring into action or for word that they weren't needed here. The fire department had joined the party. The crew appeared bored. James figured it must have been the lack of flames. Nothing duller than a building that was not on fire.

Having knitted his hands together atop his head once again after giving over his wallet, James asked, "Can I put my arms down now?"

She nodded in the affirmative. "Show us this body."

Officer Deen stayed behind, returning to his vehicle with James' license.

James led the officers through the open gate. "He's this way."

James came to a stop outside the annex housing the toy train setup. The alarms were wailing and gave no sign of quitting anytime soon.

"Did you smash this door?" she demanded.

"No." James shivered. "It was like this when I got here."

"Can somebody call the alarm company and turn the damn thing off?" Lt. Byrd barked. If she wasn't in charge, she should have been.

One of the men pulled out his cell phone and made a call while the others followed James inside.

The HO-scale maroon-and-yellow Rock Island locomotive hadn't managed to move Cindi's brother-in-law off the tracks but it had managed to make a dent in his face. The wheels spinning wildly against the track created a stomach-turning metallic burning odor.

"One of you shut this train off. But be careful of fingerprints," Lt. Byrd cautioned. "We have a crime scene here."

She had aimed those words at James.

"He was like that when I found him." James scrambled to defend himself. Even though he knew he had done nothing wrong. Well, nothing serious.

"I've got it, Lieutenant." One of her fellow officers went to the train controls on the far side of the table, slipped on a nitrile glove and killed the power.

"Have you been here long?" James was asked.

"No. I arrived a few minutes before setting off the alarm. I was in class before that, then visiting with a friend."

"Class? Are you a teacher, Mr. Stewart?"

"No, I'm in detective school."

"Detective school? You're a police officer?" Her shoulders relaxed.

"No. Not that kind of detective. Private investigator school." James heard snickers behind his back.

"A PI?" Lt. Byrd was trying not to smile. And failing miserably.

"Bruno Caliostro's School of Detection."

Titters turned to snorts.

James twisted his head around. The other officers were openly grinning. He turned back to the lieutenant. "What's so funny?"

"Nothing." The lieutenant warned her team with her eyes. "I'm still not clear. You didn't break the window but you did set off the alarm?"

"Yes, but not by breaking the glass. I punched the emergency button."

"Right." The lieutenant rubbed her chin in thought.

Silence but for the collective breathing of all but one body in the room—not his fault, he was dead—filled the large room.

James suddenly realized somebody had finally managed to turn off the alarm. It was about time. His eardrums were going to be bleeding for days to come.

"What was it? Heart attack? Stroke?" asked the officer blocking the entrance.

Lt. Byrd was standing directly behind the body. "His skull's been caved in." She was looking at James again. "You know anything about that?"

James gulped. "No."

She slipped on a pair of examination gloves. "Wait for us outside. Go with him," she instructed the officer at the door.

The officer led James out to the parking lot and deposited him in the back seat of Officer Deen's vehicle. The EMS crew hustled inside the building.

10

After forcing James to sit in the stuffy back of the car for over an hour, feeling like a criminal, Officer Deen delivered him to the Ocean Palm Police Station.

The officer led him to a small, windowless room with periwinkle blue walls, a pair of white plastic chairs, and a white plastic table floating in the center of the room.

"What, no TV and donuts?" quipped James as Officer Deen told him to have a seat and wait. "Budget cuts?"

"The lieutenant will be with you shortly," answered Officer Deen, refusing to rise to the bait. "You want coffee?"

"How about simply telling me what I'm doing here?"

Officer Deen folded his arms under his biceps to show James just how big his guns were. "Is that a no on the coffee?"

James nodded.

"Suit yourself." Officer Deen shut the door to the tiny room on his way out.

Another hour went by. Despite his best efforts, James had fallen asleep, his feet propped on the table, his back against the wall. Sitting all alone in a sensory-deprived cube in the bowels of a police station was possibly even more boring than listening to Bruno

Caliostro pontificate on the convoluted Florida statutes regarding the rights and obligations of a state-licensed private investigator.

He was wakened by the sight and sound of Lt. Byrd throwing the door open and rapping her knuckles on the table. "Wake up."

"I'm awake." James leaned his chair forward and scrubbed his hands across his face. "Can I go home now?"

She pulled out the second chair and sat. "I have a few questions for you first, Mr. Stewart." The lieutenant crossed her legs and gave him a stern look.

Lt. Byrd's above-the-shoulder brown hair was straight, parted on the left across a high forehead. Her light complexion made those brown penetrating eyes of hers all the more unsettling as she brazenly studied him.

"Such as?"

"Such as what were you doing at Smiley's?"

"I wanted to talk to him about my car." A yawn interrupted James' explanation. "It was mistakenly towed earlier tonight."

"Smiley's was closed. It was after hours."

"Yeah. I realized that. But I saw a car out front and noticed some lights on."

"So you thought you'd smash a window and have a look around?"

James felt a surge of anger. "Should I be calling a lawyer now?"

"You tell me. Should you?"

They glared at one another for a mini-eternity.

James caved first. "Look, Lieutenant. My car was towed, like I said. I was hoping to talk to Kevin."

"You knew the victim?"

"No. I mean, I had a brief conversation with him earlier tonight. I knew his name. That's all."

"What time was this?" She whipped out a narrow leather-bound notebook and starting scratching at it with a silver pen.

"I don't know. Around eight, eight thirty, maybe?"

"Tell me about it."

James did so. He explained that he was hoping to get his car out of the tow yard but it hadn't shown up yet so there was nothing to be done.

"Then what did you do?"

"I left."

"Where were you between the time you left Smiley's and ten thirty?"

"I was with Kevin's sister-in-law for most of that time."

"You just told me you didn't know the victim, Mr. Stewart. Would you care to amend that statement?"

James chewed on his lower lip. The lieutenant listened skeptically as he explained how he had met her on the street that day when she was hustling students for Caliostro's detective school. "I ran into her again tonight. She offered to give me a lift."

"And?"

"And we hung out for a while. Then I left."

"You say her name is Cindi Keach?"

"That's right." He watched as Lt. Byrd underlined the name on her notepad. "And she's Kevin Rain's sister-in-law?"

"Yes."

"Yet you never met Kevin until tonight."

"No. Like, I said, I didn't even know his last name

until you said it. I only met Cindi today." James fidgeted uncomfortably. He had to admit that it all appeared a bit unbelievable even to him. The next time a beautiful woman stopped him on the street, he'd keep walking.

Yeah, right.

"So what happened to Rain anyway? My guess is he surprised a burglar." James reminded her of the smashed glass in the door.

"Maybe." Lt. Byrd leaned back. "Do you have an address for Ms. Keach?"

"I have her phone number and the number of her agency."

"Agency?"

"She's a model-actress."

"I see." The lieutenant studied the card James handed her. It was the one Cindi had given him.

"She lives in the High Tide Apartments on Fourth. She'll confirm that I was with her all evening."

"I'll do that." She stabbed the table with her pen. From the marks on the table, she wasn't the first to do so. "Is the address on your driver's license up-to-date?"

"Yes."

"Where are you employed?"

"I'm sort of between gigs at the moment."

"Gigs?"

"I'm a musician."

"When you aren't in PI school," she said with a grin.

James flushed. "Something like that." He climbed angrily to his feet. "Can I go now?"

"In a minute." She looked over her shoulder. "Wait here."

She exited the room, returning a minute later

with a man in denim shorts and a floppy Charlie Daniels Band T-shirt looming behind her. A blue bandana wrapped tightly around his forehead.

The man looked vaguely familiar.

"Is this the man?" Lt. Byrd asked the man peering over her shoulder.

"Yeah," the man grunted. "That's him. He took a swing at Kevin but hit me instead when I stepped in the middle of them."

The man lifted his shirt revealing a hairy potbelly and a bruise the size of a softball in the middle of his chest. "I was trying to protect Kevin. Wish I had stuck around. Kevin would still be alive now."

"Thanks. That will be all, Mr. Mitchell."

James suddenly realized where he had seen the man before. "Hey, you're that driver." He snapped his fingers. "Adam, right?" The tow truck operator who'd arrived at Smiley's as he was leaving. "I never hit you. I never hit anybody!"

"Take it easy, Mr. Stewart." Lt. Byrd put her hand on his shoulder. "Relax. You'll get your turn."

"I hope you give him the chair," the man hissed. "Because if you don't kill him, I will. Poor Kevin."

"Yes, that will be all." Lt. Byrd gestured to an officer who took Adam Mitchell's arm and started to lead him away.

Mr. Mitchell mumbled something incomprehensible and disappeared.

Lt. Byrd folded her arms as she looked at James. "Mr. Mitchell claims he witnessed you having a heated argument with Kevin Rain earlier this evening. Is that true?"

"I told you, Lieutenant. I went to talk to him about

getting my car back."

"Did you argue?"

James tugged at his collar. "We discussed the whereabouts of my car. I wouldn't call it arguing exactly."

"Mr. Mitchell says you threatened his boss. Is that true?"

"You mean Smiley, er, Kevin?" She nodded yes. He answered, "No, it is not true." James jumped to his feet. "It is definitely not true. I didn't threaten him and I definitely did not take a swing at him."

"Sit down, Mr. Stewart," ordered Lt. Byrd, pointing to the chair that he had knocked over in his excitement.

James picked up the chair and fell into it. He was definitely going to need a lawyer. Then again, if he insisted on one, the police would only think he was guilty. And he hadn't done anything.

Except find a dead body. What was the crime in that?

"Do you want to tell me about the tire iron?"

"What tire iron?" he asked warily.

"The one we found outside the smashed window."

"Oh, that." James relaxed. "No big deal. It's not mine. It was there at Smiley's. I found it lying out back. Near one of the dumpsters. When I arrived and saw the broken glass, I thought somebody might be inside. I picked it up figuring I could use it as a weapon."

Lt. Byrd smiled but that smile held no friendliness. Rather, it was of the cat that swallowed the canary variety. And it scared him. It scared him a lot.

"And did you?" Lt. Byrd asked quietly. Her words sizzled in the air like a snapped live wire.

"Did I what?" James felt the blood thumping

against his eardrums.

"Did you use the tire iron as a weapon?"

11

"Thanks for getting me out of there." James squinted up at the sun. Not a cloud in the sky.

So why did it feel like such a stormy day?

"Don't thank me." Roger pointed to his BMW. "Thank Sheryl."

James cringed. Sheryl glared at him from the front passenger seat. With the dark sunglasses hiding her gray eyes and white silk scarf wrapped around her head, she looked like a young Audrey Hepburn. A young and angry Audrey Hepburn.

James marched awkwardly to the car. "Good morning, Sheryl," he said with as much bonhomie as he could muster, climbing into the backseat.

Roger shrugged at James and got behind the wheel.

"What were you thinking, James?" Sheryl shot her head around and at him.

"What do you mean?" James struggled to find a seatbelt.

"Did you kill that man?"

"Sheryl!" Roger exclaimed. Momentarily losing control of the BMW, he swerved quickly to avoid a mail carrier.

"No, Sheryl. I did not kill that man." James finally found and fastened his seatbelt. "For the record, I've never murdered anybody."

"The police are pretty sure you did," Sheryl said. "In fact, if it was up to Lt. Byrd you would be behind bars now. Your fingerprints are all over that tire iron, dumbass."

James leaned toward the front. "I said thank you." How had he been so stupid as to leave his fingerprints all over the murder weapon?

Then again, when he had picked it up, he'd had no idea there had been a murder, let alone that he would be accused of being the killer.

How had his life gotten so screwed up?

Roger dumped him off outside the duplex. James' eyelids felt like they had ten-pound lead weights attached to them. Dragging him inexorably towards the ground.

"We can't keep bailing you out, James," Sheryl said as he extracted himself from the car, taking his spiral-bound detective school books with him. The police had given them back after deciding that they weren't evidence of anything criminal. "Stupid, maybe," Officer Deen had quipped. "But not criminal."

"You didn't have to bail me out this time. Technically."

"This isn't funny, James. A man has been murdered and you were found at the scene of the crime. As if that weren't enough, you were seen arguing with him earlier."

"Believe me. I am taking this very seriously."

"Come on, guys. Do we have to fight?" Roger cut in.

"I don't think you are, James." As usual, she ignored Roger's plea. "The police have serious questions about your character."

"What's that supposed to mean? What's wrong with my character?"

"It means you are middle-aged, unemployed, broke and shiftless."

"That's not true."

"I think a couple years in prison could be good for you. You can maybe learn a vocation." As Ocean Palm's city attorney, Sheryl had helped move quite a few miscreants along to the Florida State Prison as well as other fine Florida correctional institutions.

"I've got a new vocation."

"What? That detective thing?" She snorted. "I heard all about that from Lt. Byrd. Give me a break. You can't find your car keys. You can't even find yourself. You've said so yourself. How are you going to find somebody's lost cat?"

"How hard can it be to find a cat?"

Sheryl ignored the question. "I mean it, James. When are you going to get a real job? You don't see Roger running around penniless and practically homeless. Chasing after..."

She stopped and shook her head. "After I don't know what."

"Yeah," James muttered, as Roger's BMW kicked up dust and backed into the street. "I don't see him smile too often either."

"Stay out of trouble," Roger called.

James waved desultorily and went to see if there was anything in the mailbox. The twin black metal boxes attached to a post in the ground carved to resemble a manatee leaned to the right. He gave it a kick to let off some steam.

The wooden gray manatee crumbled to the

ground on his left side.

"Great." He bent to pick up the mail that had spilled out of the boxes.

"Not only is that vandalism, I'm pretty sure it constitutes cruelty to animals," called a firm feminine voice.

James' hand tightened around a wad of bills. He stood and turned. "Did you just make a joke?" It was his neighbor, Iceberg. What was her name? She had told him once. Maybe twice.

He bent and picked up her mail, reading the name of the addressee: Roberta Higgins. He handed hers over.

"Thanks. Somebody was looking for you." She riffled through her pile of mail, which included two gardening magazines. Iceberg was tall with auburn hair and cornflower blue eyes. He placed her in the ballpark of forty.

She favored a pageboy haircut. A yellow and black jogging outfit clung to her skin, making her look like a skinny queen bee. James wondered if that had been the intent.

"Who?"

"Some girl, your daughter maybe. She said her name was Candy something."

"Cindi?"

"Yeah, that's it." She arranged the stack of mail neatly in the palm of her hand.

"What did she say? What did she want?" How had Cindi found him? His address wasn't on his business card.

"I couldn't begin to imagine," came Roberta Higgins' frosty reply. She turned on her heel and headed to her side of the property saying, "I suggest you fix the mailbox before I report it to the landlord."

"Go ahead." James grinned smugly. "That's my brother."

"I know that. I'm talking about Sheryl."

Damn, she'd won the round.

"Screw you," he said under his breath, but not under enough for her bat-like ears.

"In your dreams."

James scowled. He had made that too easy for her.

She stopped on her front porch, looking down at him. "I could report you to the postal authorities. Mailboxes are federal property. Violators can be fined up to two hundred fifty thousand dollars, or imprisoned for up to three years, Mr. Stewart."

"Any suggestion how I might do that?"

"Go to prison? Just keep doing what you do."

"Very funny. Fix the mailbox."

Her answer was to close her door firmly behind herself as she retreated indoors.

James nudged the manatee's tail with his foot. "The joke's on her, buddy. I'll probably be going to prison for murdering Smiley before they can send me away for kicking you to the dirt."

Over his shoulder, he saw Roberta Higgins watching him from her front window. The woman never let up.

"She probably will call the police, too." James let loose a string of curses as he scoured the yard. Noticing some garden landscape rocks up near his porch, he carried an armload of them to the street. He propped up the mailbox post with the stones. It was wobbly but he figured it would hold until he could get around to finding a better solution.

At least Iceberg had finally moved away from her window.

James let himself into his apartment and locked the door behind. It had been a long night. All he wanted was sleep. And to wake up and discover the last twenty-four hours had been a bad dream.

He padded to the master bedroom. The windows faced the narrow canal, which itself was lined on both sides mostly with typical seventies-era South Florida housing. Several of the quaint single-story houses and duplexes had been torn down over the years to be replaced with larger, more opulent single-family homes.

As James pulled at the dark curtains, he spotted a blonde woman sitting in one of his weather-beaten teak lounge chairs, staring up at the sun through a pair of green-tinted shades.

"What the hell?" He rapped a knuckle against the window.

The woman turned and slid her feet to the deck. She wore a buttery-yellow shirt with tan slacks and open-toed leather sandals.

"Who are you? What are you doing here?" he shouted through the glass.

The blonde raised a hand over her eyes as she came towards the window. "Mr. Stewart? I'm Jane Bright."

She hastily pulled a bent business card from the pocket of her slacks. She waved it in his direction. "Broward County Times. I'd like to interview you about the murder, Mr. Stewart."

"No."

"How about a quote?"

"Here's a quote: Go away." James yanked the curtains shut.

Throwing himself down atop his sagging mattress—another cast-off from the previous tenant, he squeezed his eyes shut and kicked off his shoes.

A moment later, she was banging her keys against the sliding glass door leading to the deck. "Damn reporter." James planted a king-sized pillow over his face. If it didn't drown out the noise, maybe it would smother him to death.

He was good either way.

"How does it feel to be a murder suspect?" Jane Bright shouted.

James cursed and leaped out of bed. He pressed his nose to the slider. "What the hell is wrong with you?"

She held a small black and silver digital recorder in her hand. She had borrowed it from Eduardo—when he wasn't looking. "Come on, Mr. Stewart. How about a statement?"

James cursed her six ways to sundown.

"Is that a confession?"

James unbolted the sliding door and threw it open. He grabbed her by the shoulders and dragged her inside before the neighbors heard her.

"Hey, careful!" Jane complained. Nonetheless, she allowed herself to be led indoors. She made herself at home in a puke green armchair stuck in the corner where the kitchen peninsula jutted from the wall.

James yanked open cabinets and drawers in search of coffee. He found a rubber-banded, half-full bag behind a jar of green mayonnaise in the refrigerator and prepared a pot of coffee. Why not? His chance for sleep was shot.

Then again, Kevin Rain's days had ended permanently.

"How did you know the victim?" Jane Bright leaned forward, elbows pressed into her knees. "Are you cool with me recording this interview?"

James handed her a cup of coffee and plucked the recorder from her hand. "No."

"Hey! That's company property!"

"You can have it back when you leave." James fiddled with the controls, making sure the thing was off. "Which I hope will be soon." He set it on the peninsula counter and flopped himself down on the sofa. He shoved a pillow behind his back and drank his coffee black.

The reporter took a sip from the chipped Disney's Snow White and the Seven Dwarfs mug he had given her and spat.

"Not very ladylike, are we?" James said.

"This tastes terrible." Jane spat again.

"Sorry," James said. "Next time, try Dunkin' Donuts."

Jane set the mug on the matted blue carpet. "I only drink organic, shade grown coffee." She sniffed. "Bird friendly."

"And I only buy Newark's finest, grown along the sunlit banks of the Lower Passaic River." James gulped a mouthful of coffee and grinned with satisfaction. Okay, so it tasted like crap. He'd die drinking it before he'd tell her that.

The reporter gaped at him a moment then cleared her throat officiously. "Kevin Rain, owner of Smiley's Towing Service was found dead in his office last night."

Jane slipped a small spiral notepad from a brown suede purse and clicked her pen to life. "According to the medical examiner's office, Mr. Rain died due to a blow to the back of his head. What can you tell me about that?"

"That it must've hurt?" James lifted his cup to his lips and sipped slowly.

"Very funny. I'm serious." She tapped her pen annoying. "Well?"

"Look, I can't tell you anything about it, Ms…?"

"Bright. Jane Bright." Her teal blue eyes swept side to side as she reviewed her notes. "The police have listed you as a person of interest, Mr. Stewart." She glanced up at him. "Is that your real name?"

"Would I make a name like that up?"

"Listen, I'm merely trying to get a story here—"

"And I'm trying to get some sleep."

"It's morning."

"And I've been up all night," James snapped. "So unless you'd like another cup of coffee or to continue this conversation from my bed, Jane, I'm going to have to ask you to leave."

He stood and unzipped his trousers, letting them drop to his ankles.

Jane Bright yelped. Hastily snatching her recorder from the counter and thrusting it in her purse, she marched to the front door and threw it open. "Jerk!"

The door slammed behind her.

12

James tried phoning Cindi but his calls went straight to voicemail. His texts all went unanswered. She was probably pretty shook up. He wanted to offer his condolences. He also wanted to ask her who might have wanted to put her brother-in-law permanently out of commission.

This was going to call for the personal touch.

Being without wheels, James was forced to call Roger and beg a loaner. Roger had grumbled but come through for him, arriving at the duplex an hour later with a car off the lot.

However, this beast in front of him wasn't what James had been expecting.

"A Ferrari? Seriously?" The red over tan car was long and angular with a wedge-shaped nose. It looked like a Ferrari, then again, it did not. It was like somebody's 1970s idea of the future.

A future that had, thankfully, never come to pass.

It was the last thing he expected to see when he stepped outside his duplex.

"A '74 Dino 308 GT4, to be exact," Roger proudly replied.

"Yeah," James scratched the top of his head, "but a Ferrari? You trust me with this thing?" He turned to his brother.

"Don't get excited. It's not like it is a million-dollar McLaren. In fact, it is the cheapest vehicle I have on the lot at the moment. And I didn't even want it. I took it in trade from Mike Mirage. He's one of my best customers. I couldn't say no to him."

"I won't say no either." James squeezed his guitar and amp into the Dino's sleek, yet cramped, rear seats. "Don't worry, I'll take good care of it."

"You'd better. By the way, Sheryl promised to pull some strings to get your car out of the impound lot."

James had learned that his Nissan was indeed at Smiley's and had been all night. The driver had dumped it towards the back of the impound lot and James hadn't spotted it. The police had found and gone over the vehicle and declared it clean.

Now all he had to do was get it released from the lot. With Smiley's owner in the morgue, that could get complicated.

"Where are you going with the gear? Got a gig?"

"Something like that." James turned the key in the ignition. The car rumbled to life. Iceberg poked her head out from her front door. Roger hopped in on the passenger side for a ride back to his car lot.

The Ferrari bucked like the prancing horse on its hood.

"You should have called me the minute you'd gotten hauled to the station," Roger said as they drove.

"I was hoping it wouldn't be a big deal."

"You didn't think finding a dead body was going to be a big deal?"

James left the question unanswered. Answering would only make him look stupid.

"Man." Roger whistled out the open window.

"Sheryl hit the roof when she heard."

"I'll bet. Still, it can't be that big of a deal, only one reporter had followed up." James told his brother about the not-so-delightful Jane Bright. "And she works for one of the tiny rags, the Broward County Times."

"Didn't you hear? That's because there was a bigger news story breaking. A trawler filled with cocaine beached last night in Fort Lauderdale. There was a gunfight between the cops and the cartel. Fortunately for you, your little adventure didn't make the front page. The world doesn't care about a small businessman bludgeoned to death when there's a big shootout on the beach. Especially when it involved drugs."

"Yeah, lucky me."

"Besides, nobody cares much what goes on in Ocean Palm. We're a sleepy little burb in comparison. All the big stories are in Miami, Ft. Lauderdale and Palm Beach."

"And I'd be happy to keep it that way. If only this particular story didn't involve me."

After dropping off his brother at the dealership and topping off the red beast's thirsty belly, James drove to Cindi's apartment. He didn't see her Jeep but it was a big parking lot. Hoping for the best, he knocked on her door anyway.

No answer.

So much for expecting the best.

He drove to city hall and wandered down the warren of halls holding small offices. The building had once been a public school and didn't function all that well as a bureaucratic center—it was more a bureaucratic labyrinth/nightmare.

Then again, maybe the mayor and city council had

instructed the architect and interior designer to complicate the insides as much as possible. All the better to confuse the tax-paying public and baffle anybody flagrant enough to stop in, unannounced and unescorted, hoping to speak to one of the myriad minor officials hiding behind their closed doors, hoping to collect their government paychecks undisturbed.

He opened one of those closed doors without bothering to knock first. Sheryl sat ramrod straight at her desk, dressed in her usual navy-blue power suit. "Go away, James."

"How do you do that?" he asked. She hadn't looked up and his toe had barely crossed the threshold.

"Instinct." She flipped papers from one side of her desk to the other. "Survival instinct." Finally, she deigned to look at him. "What do you want?"

"I want to know if the police have pulled in any suspects on the Rain case yet."

"Besides you?"

James fell into a creaky guest chair. "The lieutenant seems convinced it was murder."

"She's also convinced it was you who did the murdering. I can't say I blame her. As for murder, I've yet to see a case where somebody committed suicide by bashing themselves in the back of the head with a tire iron."

"It wasn't me."

"I hope not."

"For my sake or yours? I imagine it might sully the family name if your husband's brother gets convicted of bludgeoning a tow truck operator to death."

Sheryl smiled. "Don't worry. We're getting used to you sullying the family name."

"Ha-ha." He pressed his fingers into his knees and

pressed his luck. "So can I get my car back?"

"It might take a day or two. In the meantime, stay out of the way."

"What's that supposed to mean?"

"James, you're family and I love you, so don't take this the wrong way. Don't stick your nose into this. Stay home. And stay out of trouble until this case is solved."

"What if it's not solved, Sheryl? Did you think about that? Everybody is going to think I killed Kevin Rain. They'll probably be considering that the only reason I got away with it is because you covered up for me."

Sheryl laughed. James had to admit the comment was laughable. Sheryl wouldn't cover up a parking violation committed by her own mother.

Sheryl's assistant, unused to such happy noises coming from her boss's office, stuck her head through the connecting door. "Everything all right, Ms. Stewart?"

Sheryl assured her everything was fine and the assistant returned to her desk with a puzzled look on her face.

James stood. The visit had been a waste of time. He should have known better.

"Let the professionals handle this, James. Trust me, we know what we're doing."

"I might not be as useless as you think, Sheryl."

That put a smile on her face. "Prove it."

He fixed his eyes on his sister-in-law. "I might just do that." How he would love to show her up. He was getting tired, very tired, of being considered a loser. "Goodbye, Sheryl."

James turned quickly and smashed into a solid

blue wall.

The blue wall retreated a step. "Mr. Stewart. Perfect timing."

"Lieutenant Byrd."

"Follow me."

Despite the fact that she couldn't have had any more sleep than he'd had—which was zero—she appeared sharp, fresh and alert. Murder brought out the best in her.

"Hi, Sheryl." Lt. Byrd set her brushed aluminum briefcase on the corner of Sheryl's desk and snapped open the lid. She pulled out a pair of sunglasses wrapped inside a plastic evidence bag. "Recognize these, Stewart?" She held the bag by the corner.

Sheryl bit her lower lip and remained mum.

"Those are mine." James turned them over in his hand. The funky orange-rimmed sunglasses were unmistakable. One of the bands he had gigged with about a year ago at a club in West Palm Beach had had them made up as a freebie for their audiences. Their name *Orange Blues* was imprinted on the left-sided temple. "Where did you get them?"

Sheryl pushed out of her chair and leaned over the desk.

"You admit they are yours?" The lieutenant snatched them back and raised a brow in Sheryl's direction.

"I just said so, didn't I?"

"These sunglasses were found in the knee hole under Kevin Rain's desk. Inside the office of Smiley's Towing Service."

"I don't understand," James said.

"Neither do I," said Lt. Byrd. "But I would like to.

What happened? Did you drop them when you were searching his office for your car keys or maybe some loose change?"

James spluttered but nothing comprehensible came out.

Lt. Byrd went in for the kill. "After you murdered him?"

"That's ridiculous." James leaned against the doorframe. "I could be wrong. Those might not even be mine. The band must have given out hundreds of pairs of those."

"Maybe," conceded the lieutenant. "But this pair has your fingerprints on it."

"They do?" James' chest tightened. "Believe me, I have no idea how those got in Rain's office."

Sheryl stepped from behind her desk and lifted the baggy for a closer look. "You probably dropped them when you stopped by his office earlier when you were looking for your car. It's interesting, Robyn," she said to the lieutenant. "But circumstantial."

"Yeah." James wiped his wet forehead. It wasn't like Sheryl to throw him a lifeline but he took it. "That must be it. That's what happened."

The truth was he had forgotten the sunglasses at the Banana Reef the other day. But what was the point of saying so to Lt. Byrd? She'd never believe him. And how could he prove it?

No, he couldn't blame her.

She wanted to know how they had then ended up in a dead man's office. And James didn't have a clue.

Lt. Byrd carefully placed the sunglasses inside her briefcase and snapped it shut. "It's your call, Sheryl. I wanted to make you aware of it. And keep you apprised of the investigation."

Sheryl tapped a pencil against her lip. "I appreciate it, Robyn. And I am also sure that James will do everything in his power to cooperate with you in your investigation. Won't you, James?"

"Absolutely. In fact," James said, rolling back on his heels, "since I'm friends with Kevin Rain's sister-in-law, I was thinking I might get a lead on his killer from her."

"Excuse me?" Lt. Byrd squared her shoulders.

"You know, see if she has any idea who might have wanted her brother-in-law dead."

"Don't you dare," said Sheryl, locking her arms over her chest and shaking her head.

"Any interference from you and I'll lock you up for obstruction," threatened Lt. Byrd. She looked at Sheryl for confirmation.

Sheryl nodded. "Go home, James. Better yet, go job hunting. Leave hunting killers to the police."

"The lieutenant thinks she's already found her killer."

Lt. Byrd's eyes danced with amusement. "No offense, Sheryl, but your brother-in-law does make an ideal candidate for this one."

"I know," Sheryl grumbled, reaching for her ringing desk phone.

James departed as Sheryl picked up and began speaking in clipped, hushed tones. The lieutenant followed him out, swinging her briefcase at her side like it was the sword of justice. They walked shoulder to shoulder down the narrow hallway.

"You know, if it wasn't for Ms. Keach alibiing you, I'd have locked you up."

"Nice talking to you, too." James threw open the

door and went quickly to his car.

He had never been happier escaping from a woman.

The ticket stuck under the wiper blade for having an expired parking meter was a bonus he didn't need.

13

James still hadn't heard from Cindi. He tried her phone, her apartment and the number of her agency more times than he cared to count.

No luck.

Was she avoiding him?

She probably thought he was some psycho stalker at this point—in addition to being the killer of her beloved brother-in-law. A second date, if that first night counted as a date, which in his book it did, could now be out of the question.

James parked, very carefully and very legally, in a slot near the Edsel Building that cost him a flat five dollars for afterhours parking. He hoped he might catch sight of the lovely Cindi with an i on the street trying to hustle up some new customers.

Again, no luck.

James drove a hand through his hair as he climbed the steps to the School of Detection.

The woman at the door seemed surprised to see him. "Mr. Stewart. You came."

"Why wouldn't I? I signed up, didn't I?" James waved his class workbook at her. His contract was tucked into the sleeve inside the back cover.

James had been intending to cancel. The contract had given him twenty-four hours to do so. Who knew that in the space of that twenty-four hours he would find a dead man and find himself accused of the murder?

"What is this, third grade?" James muttered, scribbling his required signature on the attendance sheet. Learning a few detective skills might just help him out of the jam he was in.

He grabbed a seat in the second row next to the Hispanic-looking woman and Arthur Montgomery knowing he could catch a little breeze shooting up the stairwell that way. For some reason known only to the wearer, aka Arthur, the kid had chosen to be seen in public decked out in pleated khakis, a print shirt—green turtles on a pink background—and a shiny black bow-tie.

Several minutes later, with the small class chatting quietly amongst themselves, there came the sound of an emphysemic hippopotamus—lost on its way to the nearest watering hole—forcing its way up the steep stairway.

Sure enough, Bruno Caliostro, self-proclaimed PI to the stars, appeared. Clutching both sides of the door-frame in his meaty fingers, he pulled himself inside the stifling room. Sweat stained the arms and neck of his raspberry polo shirt. "Welcome back, everyone, to Bruno Caliostro's School of Detection."

Bruno Caliostro glanced quickly at the sign-in sheet and rubbed his hands against the sides of his legs. He moved to the front of the room. "I trust you have all read chapter one and done the first set of exercises?"

Heads bobbed.

Bruno's heavy-lidded eyes fell on James. "Mr. Stewart." He glanced at his assistant at the door. His jaw twisted side to side. "I wasn't sure if we would be seeing you. You have had a rather eventful time since you attended our introductory class."

James squirmed in his chair. He'd been hoping that neither his classmates nor the detective had heard the news of his little misadventure. "It was nothing."

James looked at the others. He stretched a grin. "One of those wrong place, wrong time deals. That's all."

James cleared his throat and opened his book to chapter one and started scanning the words on the page. How was it that he was the only one in class not to have read the first assignment?

Bruno's loafers slapped the gray-flecked linoleum as he paced up and down in front of the class. He stopped to address the group. "We have an interesting situation, class. My assistant, Ms. Lorenzo, is still running routine background checks on each and every one of you. You can't be too careful in this business."

Several faces appeared concerned, others amused. The fat guy with his chin resting on his chest appeared asleep.

Bruno Caliostro rubbed his chin thoughtfully. "If you get a police record, Mr. Stewart, you're done for in the detective biz. You can't be a PI with a criminal record."

James nodded his understanding.

"Did you really kill a guy?" whispered Arthur.

"Shut up, Artie," hissed James.

"You try anything with me," warned the Latin woman on his opposite side, "my boyfriend will cut you. I will cut you." She demonstrated, running a fine-pointed fingernail along her dark neck.

"The police came to see me, Mr. Stewart." Bruno

Caliostro's hands did a little dance. James half-expected he was about to see a magic trick of some sort. "I had to cooperate, of course."

"Of course," James agreed. "I explained to them that I had been in class earlier. I guess they wanted to check my alibi."

Bruno rested his bulk on the edge of his desk. "And do you have an alibi for the murder?"

"Yes, I do." James slammed his book shut. "Look, I came here to take a class, not get interrogated." He levelled his eyes on his classmates. "Or get accused of murder."

"Relax. Relax, James." Bruno motioned for James to sit back down. James hadn't even realized he had been standing. "Enough. Let's get started."

James sighed. The hot-tempered Latin woman noisily scooted her chair out of arms' reach.

When the two hours were up, James had never felt more relieved. Gathering up his things, he raced down the steps.

Bruno Caliostro's assistant was hanging around at the bottom of the staircase. She tilted her long, fine neck and took a slow drink from a bottle of mineral water. Her black skirt fell to just above the knee. Her short-sleeved white shirt was unbuttoned just enough to make him look.

James stopped next to her. "What do you think?"

"Excuse me?"

"I guess I'm not exactly on my way to being the teacher's pet."

She narrowed her eyes at him and rolled a pink tongue over her full mauve lips. "He does not like pets. Never has."

"Right. Did you hear him? He practically accused me of murder. In front of the whole class, too. Bruno Caliostro, PI to the stars. What a laugh."

"Just between you and me, I'll bet I'll make a better detective in a week than Bruno does in a lifetime. In fact, I hear he's barely competent to find missing pets."

"Is that so, Mr. Stewart?"

"Yep. In fact—" James turned at the sound of approaching footsteps. It was Bruno. With him were two of his students, Claudia Suarez—she was turning out to be a real suck up—and Artie Montgomery.

Bruno's assistant gently pushed James aside. "Ready to go, Dad?" She slung her arm through Bruno's.

"Bruno is your—" James felt his blood turn hot. He stumbled numbly to the curb.

Bruno and his daughter followed.

Bruno whistled through the gap in his teeth. "This your car, Stewart?"

The classic red Ferrari sat alone under the glow of a yellow streetlamp. Moths and mosquitos circled the light overhead.

James thrust the key in the driver's side door lock. "What do you think?"

"You drive this," Bruno said, "I think you're gonna stick out like a sore thumb, Stewart." Tick-tock noises tumbled out of Bruno Caliostro's mouth. "If a PI needs to run a tail, and being a PI you are bound to, you need yourself a vehicle that blends in with the background. Know what I mean?"

He pointed to a dusty blue van on the opposite side of the street. "Like mine."

"I'll keep that in mind, Mr. Caliostro." James fired up the engine and flinched. Even though he had come to expect it, the dissonant rumble rattled his teeth and scared him every time.

"You think you might want to sell it?" Bruno Caliostro ran his hand lovingly down the hood of the sports car.

"Sorry, it doesn't belong to me. If you're interested, talk to my brother, Roger. He owns Stewart Classic Motors on Federal Highway. Give him a call. Tell him I sent you." If Bruno bought, maybe his brother would give him a commission.

"Good night, Mr. Stewart." Sophie Lorenzo smiled coyly. "It's been a pleasure chatting with you."

"Same here," replied James, although he didn't think the woman knew what pleasure was.

As he spun away from the curb, he couldn't help worrying that she was going to rat him out to her father.

14

Mid-morning the following day, James tossed on a clean T-shirt and a pair of jeans that had seen better days. Better nights, too, for that matter. He didn't have a washer or dryer in the duplex and he found laundromats depressing. He stretched his clothes, like he stretched his money, as long as possible.

James had come to the conclusion that if he wanted his privacy back and for the world to forget about him, rather than stay under the radar, as Sheryl had admonished him, he was going to have to find some answers—even if that meant sticking a target on his back.

Oh, yeah, and find Kevin Rain's killer.

The first thing he had to do in that regard, at least one of the first, was to find Cindi. Hopefully, she had some answers. As Kevin's former sister-in-law, she might know a thing or two that would help his case.

And, if he couldn't find a single model/actress, what hope did he have of finding a killer? Yep, finding her was key.

Cindi might look like a ditzy blonde but she struck him as having some smarts about her.

Maybe some of those smarts would rub off on him.

The question was: where was Cindi? With her brother-in-law dead, she could be anywhere since it had crossed his mind that Kevin could have been originally from out of state, like so many Floridians. Cindi and her sister might be busy making funeral arrangements in some far off city.

If that was the case, he was out of luck until she got back. He wasn't in the mood to sit around and wait.

After peeking out his front window, checking to see if the coast was clear of nosy reporters, James slipped outdoors.

Unfortunately, Iceberg, aka Roberta Higgins, was squatting on her knees in a flowerbed outside her door.

"Decapitating flowers now?" James quipped as he stepped off the shared front porch. "Have you graduated from pulling the legs off spiders?

"It's called dead heading." Roberta Higgins snipped another gardenia with a small pair of pruning shears. She tossed the shriveled flower in a tiny pink plastic pail on the grass.

"Have fun with that." James headed for the Ferrari.

She climbed to her feet and dusted off her hands. "Nice car."

"Thanks."

"For a drug dealer."

James pressed the gas pedal to the floor and delighted in watching the amused expression on her face turn to fright and then disgust as the vibration and noise rattled her bones.

15

James chuckled all the way to Smiley's Towing Service where he sat idling at the curb on the opposite side of the street so he could keep an eye on things.

Smiley's was open for business. The death of its owner had been nothing more than a speedbump. One tow truck was pulling out. Another was pulling in with a fresh catch dangling off its back.

Despite Lt. Byrd and Sheryl both telling him to stay out of the investigation—or maybe because of it—James was determined to find out who had killed Kevin Rain. James didn't particularly care why he had been murdered, he just wanted the guilty party caught and himself exonerated.

Lost in his own thoughts, James didn't see the big man coming for him. One minute James was leaning against the inside of the driver's side door pondering his next move, the next minute his next move was made for him and he was tumbling face first to the pavement.

James' palms scraped across the asphalt. A heavy-booted foot, moving in a blur, kicked him in the stomach. He rolled over, throwing up his hands in self-defense.

"What the hell are you doing here?"

James scrambled to the front of the car, putting some space and some metal between himself and the berserker confronting him. "What the hell is your problem?"

"You are my problem!" bellowed Adam Mitchell, the tow truck operator who had ID'd him as having argued with Kevin Rain the night of the murder. A beefy, much-muscled arm jabbed out at James.

James flinched.

"Why aren't you locked up?" Adam snarled.

"Me? You're the one who ought to be locked up." James' ribs throbbed. His palms were raw and bleeding. "Animal."

A dark-haired young woman came running across the street. "What on earth is going on out here?" Her wide eyes swept from James to Adam. "What's wrong with you, Adam? Haven't we been through enough?"

Adam's eyes narrowed and he snorted like a cartoon bull. "This is the guy that offed Kevin."

The woman gasped. Her hands went to her cheeks.

"That's not true. I only found him. That's all. He was already dead." James pointed. "This guy, this employee of yours, I take it, attacked me for no reason. I was sitting in my car minding my own business."

That wasn't quite true but it was close enough for these two clowns. "With a temper like that, how do I know you didn't kill your boss, Mitchell?"

Adam Mitchell lunged for him. James fled to the opposite side of the car. It was a little embarrassing being chased around a car by a gorilla, but less embarrassing than being beaten to a puddle of marrow, soft organ tissue and blood in front of a pretty woman.

The dark-haired woman clutched Adam Mitchell's arm, cursing as she tried to hold him back. "Damn it, Adam, stop!"

He suddenly stilled and hung his head. James remained vigilant.

She tilted her head at James. "You're James Stewart, aren't you?"

"That's right." James clutched the passenger side door handle in the event that Adam got loose and came after him again. The plan was to get inside the Ferrari, lock the doors and drive away. Fast. If he ran over an extremity or two that belonged to Adam Mitchell in the process, so much the better.

It may not have been the bravest option but it was very likely the safest. The survival instinct was one of James' best instincts, if he did say so himself.

"Wait," James said. "I know you. You're Cindi's sister, Alyssa. I didn't recognize you at first." What could he say? That she looked different, better sober than she had when he had first laid his eyes on her in her wasted condition the other night?

"Yes." Alyssa pushed a lock of dark hair behind her ear. "Sorry, I don't really remember you all that well." She smiled her apology.

"I'm not surprised."

"Cindi can't stop talking about you. She says what a nice guy you are."

"I'm sorry about your husband."

Alyssa groaned and her face fell. "Maybe if I hadn't been out drinking and had stayed home…Kevin would still be alive."

Alyssa's chest heaved. Her hand loosened from Adam's elbow. The oaf was a lost man, not knowing what to do.

"You can go, Adam," she said softly.

"Yeah," James couldn't resist tossing in a trademark smirk. "You can go, Adam." He flicked his fingers as if to say *scat*.

Adam swore a goodbye and thudded back across the street. He climbed behind the wheel of his tow truck and rumbled off.

"Why don't you come inside, Mr. Stewart?"

"Call me James."

She did.

Her jeans bore the name of a Miami designer. Despite the heat, she had pushed the sleeves of her modest black blouse down to her wrists.

Alyssa was everything that Cindi was and then some. Young, fit and beautiful—and that was without visible makeup. Raven haired rather than blonde like her sister. Whose was natural and whose came from a bottle, he didn't know. James had never been good at distinguishing. Maybe he just didn't care.

She led him into the office where the temperature was much more temperate than it had been on his first visit to Smiley's.

They were alone. She took a seat and offered a chair to James. The lines on her face betrayed both weariness and sadness. And probably a lot of stress. Her husband had been brutally murdered only a couple of nights earlier. For all she knew, she was staring at his killer.

Looking across the cluttered desk at Alyssa, he wondered if she was sleeping and how she was coping. By the red canals visible in the whites of her eyes—coupled with what he'd seen of her the other night—there were probably drugs and alcohol involved in the process.

He didn't blame her.

Alyssa scrubbed her hands up and down her face as if trying to move things around to a more comfortable position. "Coffee?" She raised a coffee-stained Styrofoam cup in his direction.

"Thanks."

She poured him a cup from a small setup atop a metal gray lateral filing cabinet. "Sugar or sweetener?" Her hand hovered over packs of each.

James said sugar and she tossed two packs his way. She handed him his coffee.

Sighing as she leaned back in her chair, Kevin's chair, she said, "So you found my husband, huh?"

"Yes." James ripped open the sugars one after the other and dropped the contents in the cup. There was nothing to stir with, so he sloshed the liquid around a bit. Some landed on his trousers. Alyssa didn't seem to notice.

He sipped. The coffee was bitter despite the sugar. "There was nothing I could do. Like I said, he was already dead when I discovered him."

She nodded silently, folding her hands over a stack of invoices in front of her on the desk.

"Your husband loved his trains."

That evoked a smile. "Kevin was obsessed with them. He used to have a really big setup at home. After the divorce—"

"Divorce?"

"Not me and Kevin. Kevin and Felicity, his first wife. Felicity got the house. And the kids." Alyssa's mouth puckered each time she said Felicity. It was as if the word was bitter lemon-flavored.

"Were you and Kevin married long?"

"About four years. Kevin got the trains as part of

their settlement. And no place to keep them. We live in a condo. So he built an addition here at his office."

"It's quite a setup."

"Yeah." Alyssa finished her coffee and tossed the Styrofoam cup in the trash. "I don't know what I'm going to do with them." She pushed her hands through her silky tresses. "Do you like trains?"

"I wouldn't have any place to keep them. Do you two have any kids? Maybe they'd like them."

"Kevin's children are grown. I don't think you'd catch either one of them playing with trains. Kevin said they always thought his hobby was kind of dumb."

"Sorry. Maybe you can sell them?"

"Yeah, that's an idea." Alyssa sniffed. "There's so damn much to do. A funeral to arrange, a business to run."

"It must be tough with Kevin gone."

"Tell me about it. He ran the whole shebang." Alyssa shoved the papers around. Several fluttered to the floor. "I don't know a thing about any of this."

She screamed as the phone jingled to life on the wall behind her. "Excuse me." She yanked the red telephone receiver off the wall and shouted into it. "You need to call back later!"

The panelling nailed to the wall behind her rattled as Alyssa slammed the phone back into its cradle. "Sorry about that," she said sheepishly. "The answering service is supposed to be handling all the incoming calls."

"No problem."

"Was there something special that you wanted, James?"

"Now that you mention it, I would like to get my car back." He explained how Smiley's had mistakenly towed his Nissan the night of the murder.

"Right. Cindi asked me about that too." Alyssa scooted her tongue over her lips. "I'd like to help you. I'm waiting for the paperwork to come back from the PD." She smiled to show her commiseration. "Evidence and all that crap. Know what I mean?"

"I'm afraid I do." James stood. "Thanks for the coffee." He dropped his half-empty cup in the trash. "How's Cindi holding up? I've been trying to reach her."

Alyssa pulled herself up from her seat. "She's an angel. I don't know what I'd do without her. She's staying with me at the condo."

"I guess that explains why I haven't heard from her."

Alyssa laid a friendly hand on James' arm. "Believe me, she'd love to hear from you. It's just she's been busy helping me with funeral arrangements, talking to the police, running interference with Felicity and the kids. All around giving me a shoulder to cry on," she said wistfully. "Wait."

Alyssa ran back to her desk and scribbled something on a pad. She tore of the sheet and handed it to James.

It was a Smiley's Towing Service pad. On it, Alyssa had jotted down an address. "That's our condo. Go say hi."

"I'll do that." James stuffed the small square of paper in his pocket.

Alyssa followed James to the door and let out a sad sigh, leaning her back against the doorframe as he passed out-of-doors. "Maybe I'll take Adam up on his offer, after all."

James stopped. "What offer is that?" If it was from

that gorilla, it couldn't possibly be any good.

"He says he's got some money set aside. He wants me to make him partner." Alyssa pulled a crumpled pack of cigarettes from her pocket and lit up. "Nasty habit."

She studied the burning tip of the cigarette. "I just started again, after, you know..." Her voice trailed off. There was no reason to continue.

"You were saying something about Adam being made partner."

"Right. I told him no way. I mean, Kevin isn't even in the ground yet and the guy is pushing me to cut him in on the business." She sucked on the end of her cigarette and blew out a cumulonimbus cloud of death. "Still...Adam says Kevin kept promising to make him partner."

"And did he?"

"Did Kevin promise Adam? Not that he ever told me." Her eyes sparkled. "You've met Adam. You've seen him in action. Can you imagine that ape running a business?"

"I can see that ape tearing a business apart with his bare hands. But running it? No, I'm with you." James squeezed her free hand. "Hang in there, Alyssa. You'll figure things out."

She tossed her cigarette. James watched it somersault down the steps to the parking lot. "You think so?"

"I'm sure of it."

"Felicity and the kids are trying to squeeze me out. A former employee filed a lawsuit. That's a joke." She pushed her hands through her hair. "Then there's Ronnie."

"Who's Ronnie?"

"Ronnie Tench. Owns Tow The Line. Fairly new in

town but Kevin's biggest competitor. Wants to buy me out. Lock, stock and tow truck."

James gave her words some thought. A dead husband, an empty room full of toy trains and a surly tow truck driver or two. "You want my advice?"

"Sure."

"Take the money and run."

"I wish I could do that," Alyssa said dreamily.

"But?"

"The problem is that Kevin wasn't the world's greatest businessman. He was up to his eyeballs in debt." Her face soured. "Debt that is now mine."

"That's tough." Debt was something he knew too well.

"Lucky me." Alyssa frowned. "If I sell, I'll be lucky to break even." She grabbed another cigarette from the pack. "Then what do I do?"

James had no idea.

16

The scrawny seventy-something security guard chilling inside the gatehouse waved lazily to James as he rolled up to the barrier gate arm protecting Tarpon Bend Isles from the rest of the world. A small TV tucked next to the leather-skinned, gray-headed uniformed man's padded stool was airing a senior tour golf match.

"I'm here to see the Rains."

The guard took James' word for it, handing him a flimsy paper ticket with a number on it. He told him to stick it on his windshield. The guard pressed a button to raise the white gate arm then returned to the tournament before James could thank him or even roll up his car window.

Tarpon Bend Isles was one of a thousand condominium complexes that had overtaken the South Florida landscape like kudzu. It was located in the Tarpon River neighborhood of Fort Lauderdale, south of the New River. The New River is a tidal estuary connecting the Florida Everglades with the Atlantic Ocean, albeit in a circuitous route due to the myriad man-made canals that had been carved out in between.

The Rains lived on the third floor of a seven-story building with a view of a mirror-image block across a narrow walkway lined with foxtail palms.

James knocked on the Rains' door.

"Come in! It's open!"

Cindi sat on a barstool at the kitchen counter. She was talking on the telephone. She raised a finger in James' direction and mouthed that she would only be a minute.

James took a quick swing around the condo's main living area. There wasn't a lot of furniture but the pieces were decent, if bland. A flat screen TV, as wide as James was tall, filled the wall across from the taupe sectional. A furry zebra skin rug held a glass coffee table.

Several HO-scale train engines and an assortment of tiny cars and cabooses sat on shelves behind the sofa. The framed posters on the walls all featured trains and train stations.

Cindi dropped her phone, leapt from her stool and threw her arms around James' neck. "I'm so happy to see you!"

James let her hang there, enjoying the feel of her body pressed against him. "Are you?"

"Uh-huh." She unwound herself and beckoned him to join her on the sectional. She wore snug black leggings and a man's white dress shirt. She was barefoot.

"I want you to know that I had nothing to do with Kevin's death," James began, feeling like he had to defend himself.

"I know that." Cindi patted his cheek. "Poor baby. I heard the police have been giving you a hard time."

"I guess they're just doing their job. Speaking of which, thanks for confirming my alibi."

"My pleasure. I feel responsible for getting you into this mess. If I hadn't begged you to sign up for Mr. Caliostro's detective school, you wouldn't be in this jam in the first place."

"True." James scooted closer. "But then I wouldn't have met you and I wouldn't be here now. What do you say we get some lunch? I know a great place at the beach."

"Sorry. Kevin's kids are coming by with their attorney. I'm expecting them any time."

"What for?"

"They want to poke around." She scrunched up her nose in disgust. "They think there might be some personal effects here that belong to them."

"Tell them to get lost. They don't have any right." He still remembered a thing or two from law school.

"I can't do that. Besides, Alyssa told Felicity, that's Kevin's ex, that it was all right. My sister doesn't want to make more trouble than necessary."

"I get that. Things are hard enough."

"Yeah," Cindi answered softly. "Personally, I wouldn't give his ex-wife the time of day, let alone those two jerks."

"Kevin's kids?"

She nodded. "Kourtney and Dale. They never did like Kevin. In fact, Kevin told Alyssa that Kourtney once pulled a gun on him and threatened to blow his brains out. Can you believe it?"

"Did you or your sister tell the police that?"

"No. Why?"

"I'm not saying his kids are guilty but if what you say is true, it seems to me one or the other of them is capable of murder."

"Murder their own father?" Cindi clutched her chest. "That's sick. Can I get you a drink?"

"No, thanks. You know, I had a run-in with Adam

Mitchell at Smiley's today. He's got a temper."

"So I've heard. He's always been nice to me."

That was no surprise. When you looked like Cindi, men fawned, not feuded. "Your sister said Kevin promised to make him a partner."

Cindi shrugged. "I don't know much about that. Kevin was the boss. He liked to talk trains more than he liked to talk shop. Alyssa didn't have much to do with the business either. Felicity wouldn't have tolerated it."

"The ex? What's she got to do with it?"

"Felicity got twenty percent of the business in the divorce settlement." Cindi massaged her thighs. "Boy, was Kevin mad about that. She had absolutely nothing to do with starting the business or running it."

"What happens to Smiley's now that Kevin's dead?"

"Business as usual, I suppose. Alyssa is doing the best she can." She rose and crossed to the refrigerator. "Under the circumstances. Are you sure I can't get you something?"

James declined and she poured herself a glass of unsweetened iced tea, squirting lemon from a plastic bottle into the glass and stirring it with a pink plastic straw.

There was a heavy-handed knock on the door.

Cindi stiffened. "That must be them."

James climbed to his feet. "I'll leave you to it." He didn't want to get in the middle of a family squabble. He had enough of those with his own family. Why add somebody else's?

Cindi opened the door and a woman swept in on a cloud of Chanel as if she owned the place. She had light blonde hair, a deep tan and venomous blue eyes.

A younger man and woman with angry, pinched faces flanked her.

The younger woman, this would be Kourtney, clutched her mother's arm. The boy, Dale, planted his hands on his hips and glared at James. "Who's this? Your lawyer?"

James stuck out his hand. "James Stewart, attorney. You must be Dale Rain." He glanced behind the incomers. "Where is your counsel?"

"Parking his car," the ex-Mrs. Rain answered icily. "You didn't tell me Alyssa was bringing her attorney into this."

Cindi shook her head. "James is joking. He's a friend of mine." She grabbed his wrist and led him to the door. "He was just leaving."

"Wait a minute." Kourtney stepped in his path. "You're the man the police think had something to do with Daddy's murder."

Dale pushed past his sister, his face purple. "Is that true?"

"No," James said. "Wrong James Stewart. You're thinking of the actor. I never had the pleasure of meeting your father." That much was true. Meeting Kevin Rain had been no pleasure.

Kourtney Rain pinched her brows together. "What do you mean the—"

"Never mind all that," snapped Felicity Rain, chopping the air with her hand. "Ronnie Tench called me again, Cindi. Tell that sister of yours that it is urgent she phone Tench back."

Cindi rolled her eyes. "Whatever."

A man in a gray suit with jet-black hair whipped off a pair of expensive mirrored sunglasses as he pushed through the open door. He wiped his brow with a silk handkerchief. "Sorry. I couldn't find a spot. I had to park in a handicapped space. Can we get on with this?" he urged Felicity.

"I'll walk James down," offered Cindi.

"That's not necessary," James replied.

"Yes," Cindi replied, pulling him by the hand, "it is." After a few steps, she said, "I can't stand those people."

"They aren't the friendliest bunch, are they?"

"No."

"How can you be sure you can trust them alone in your sister's condo?" James asked as they took the stairs to the ground floor.

"Don't worry. I can handle them."

"Was that the same Ronnie you sister was telling me about? Ronnie Tench?"

"Yeah. Owns Tow The Line, they are, or were, Kevin's biggest competitor."

"And they want to buy Smiley's?"

"They did. I don't know what will happen or if Smiley's will matter to them now that Kevin's dead."

James stopped in the center of the parking lot. The heat bouncing off the blacktop was twice as hot as that streaming from the sun millions of miles overhead. How was that possible?

"I take it Kevin did not want to be bought out?"

"No. Kevin hated Ronnie and swore he'd go broke before he'd ever let Tow The Line get its hands on Smiley's. He started the business himself, one used tow truck and twenty-hour days. He put every cent he had into that business. He put his whole life into it."

And now his death. "I get that. Smiley's was

Kevin's baby." Maybe Cindi was right, maybe Kevin hadn't been such a bad guy after all.

"Ronnie Tench and Kevin have been feuding for a year or more. Ever since Ronnie set up business in Broward County. They've been doing everything they can to put each other out of business."

"And now Kevin is out of the way. Permanently."

"Do you think it had something to do with the business?"

"I don't know what to think," admitted James. "It's just one more funny little thing that makes me wonder."

"Makes you wonder what?"

"Who really killed Kevin and why."

"It must have been a burglar. A mistake. An accident. Kevin was a good guy."

"So you've said," James commented as he moved toward his car. "Not to speak ill of the dead but he seems to have had his fair share of enemies."

"I suppose." Cindi sounded uncertain.

James extracted his car keys from a pocket as they walked to his car. "How about dinner later?'

Cindi pouted. "Sorry. I sort of promised my sister I would hold her hand for a few days. Know what I mean?"

He did. James yanked open the door of the Dino. "I'll call you in a couple of days."

"Wow, a Ferrari *and* detective school." She did a slow circle around the bright red car. "You'll be like Magnum PI."

"You know that show?" She probably hadn't even been born when the program originally aired.

"I've seen the reruns." Cindi yanked open the passenger side door. "Can we go for a drive?" She batted her eyes at James over the top of the sleek automobile.

"What about Felicity and company?"

"Screw them. There's nothing in the apartment worth their stealing."

James jumped behind the wheel. Cindi might just be on to something...

All he needed was the Hawaiian shirt and a tan. He could be Thomas Magnum. And once he got his license, he'd be a PI, too.

Life could be worse.

17

James and Cindi cruised Fort Lauderdale beach along A1A, taking in the sun, the sand and the sights. James felt like a rock star. How could he not? He was driving a red Ferrari with a red-hot young blonde in the passenger seat beside him.

In your face, Tom Selleck.

"It must have been something finding Kevin like that," Cindi said, long blonde hair flying in the breeze shooting through the open window.

"It's not something I'm soon to forget, I'll tell you that."

"And you didn't notice anything odd? I mean, you didn't know anything was wrong until you found him?"

"No. That is, except for the broken glass in the door."

"That's what makes me think he must have surprised a burglar."

"Me, too. The only problem is that the alarm hadn't gone off."

Cindi gave that some thought. "Kevin sometimes locked up without turning on the alarm. Especially if he was inside. I mean, why bother?"

"I guess so." Though he could have answered to keep from getting murdered. "Still, you'd think he would have heard the intruder breaking the glass. The trains weren't that loud."

A kid on a bicycle shouted "Nice wheels!" James waved to him. "The police grilled me incessantly. There's a Lt. Byrd who is convinced I'm guilty. All because Smiley's towed my car and I wanted it back."

"That's ridiculous. Plenty of people get their cars towed every day."

"Yeah. Tell them that."

"But you have an alibi."

"I know. Thank goodness for that. Not that the fact that I was in your apartment seems to impress them with my innocence."

"Lt. Byrd interviewed me too." Cindi rubbed her legs and James couldn't help watching. "I don't like her."

James forced his eyes forward. "That makes two of us."

"The police really don't have any other suspects but you?"

"If they do, they aren't telling me. That's why I'd like to learn more about Kevin's enemies, like this Ronnie Tench, Adam Mitchell and Kevin's ex-wife and kids. I need to prove that there were plenty of other people who might have wanted Kevin dead. No offense," he added hastily.

"None taken. I'd be just as anxious if I was in your position." Cindi fiddled with the radio dial until landing on a Top 40 station.

"I hope your sister doesn't think for a second that I had anything to do with her husband's death."

"Don't be silly."

"That's good."

"I can tell you this much, Alyssa is hoping that Kevin's ex did it. If not her, one of the kids."

"Do they have alibis?"

"I have no idea."

James was going to have to look into that too. The problem was he had no idea how. He made a note to himself to check his school books. Maybe there were some pointers in there on how to go about proving one's innocence and finding a real killer.

"If you can think of anything else or anyone else who might have had a hand in Kevin's death," James begged, downshifting into third as they approached a traffic light, "let me know, will you?"

His eyes drifted for the umpteenth time to her legs. With the heat, she had pulled off her leggings and balled them up. The shirttails barely covered her thighs.

Cindi held up her hand. "I promise."

18

After dropping Cindi back off at her sister's place, half an hour and half a tank of gas later—the Ferrari burned fuel at an alarming rate—James pulled into a gas station to top off the beast.

Once he had refueled, he parked in front of the convenience store and pulled up Tow The Line's address on his smartphone. The enterprise was located a little further north in the City of Oakland Park.

James went inside the store, grabbed a rubbery cheese sandwich from the cold cabinet and a soda from the fountain dispenser. Like the Ferrari, he had been running on empty.

As he stepped outside, he noticed a woman in a green Volkswagen Beetle parked at the edge of the service station. She glanced at him then looked guiltily away.

"Damn." It was that reporter woman who'd stalked him to his duplex. Setting his food on the roof of the Ferrari, James moved towards her.

The Beetle sprang to life and took off down the street.

"Oh no, you don't!" James jumped behind the wheel of the Ferrari and went in pursuit.

After playing cat and mouse, Dino vs Bug, for a couple of blocks, he caught up with her in the parking lot of a seafood restaurant at the end of a dead-end street. He swung the wheel, blocking her in, and leapt from his car.

James rapped his knuckles against her driver's side window. "Why are you following me?"

Jane Bright clutched her steering wheel, avoiding eye contact, looking straight ahead. James cursed and pushed his face against the windshield. "I said, why are you following me?"

The reporter reluctantly rolled down her window. "I am not following you, Mr. Stewart. *You* are following me." She picked up her cell phone and stuck it in his face. "Maybe I'll call the police and report you."

"You do that." James folded his arms over his chest and waited, tapping his foot.

She dialled 9 then 1, then cursed, tossing the phone down on the empty seat beside her. "I don't know why you are being so difficult."

"Me? Difficult? I'm just trying to live my life. You're the one invading my home—"

"*Please*. I was sitting on your patio. You yanked me inside."

"Tailing me like somebody out of a John le Carré novel."

"Frankly, I'm surprised you even know who John le Carré is." She flecked imaginary lint from her skirt.

"Very funny."

"I'm merely trying to get a story. That's my job."

"At least you have a job."

"I won't much longer if I don't break this story."

"Poor you. If the police don't find who really murdered Kevin Rain, I could spend my life in prison." James stabbed his thumb into his chest. "The police think I did it."

"Didn't you? You are acting very guilty," Jane Bright pointed out. "Running around with the widow's sister, drag racing in what is probably a stolen Ferrari."

James spat. "Excuse me? You try finding a dead man and then being accused of his murder and see how you react!"

"If I was smart," she said frostily, "and I am, I would cooperate with someone who might be able to help me figure out who the real killer is. If I wasn't the real killer myself."

She finally turned off her motor. "I wouldn't be running around like a crazy person. You know," she plucked a tube of lip gloss from her purse and ran it in a circle around her lips, "if the police had seen the crazy way you were driving that midlife crisis car of yours, they'd probably have arrested you for reckless endangerment."

She stared James down. "How do you think that would make you look on top of everything else?"

James gritted his teeth and clenched his hands.

"Like a criminal," she said pithily. "Is that what you want, Mr. Stewart?"

James gulped in some air and forced it back out again. His head was about to explode. "What I want is some grub. But I seem to have left mine smeared all over the parking lot at the gas station back there."

"Not my fault."

James bit his tongue. It was completely her fault but he refrained from saying so. He glanced at the sign above the restaurant: Seminole Seafood. He straightened his smile. "Buy you some lunch?"

The reporter returned his smile. "Sure. Move your

car so I can park properly. Some of us like to obey the law."

"Very funny." James went back to the Ferrari, which was blocking several spaces and eased into a slot on the perimeter. Jane Bright smiled, started her engine, and blasted off down the street, waving her hand out the window as she flew by.

For one mad, anger-driven moment, James considered chasing after her. In the end, he shook his head and let her go.

"Good riddance," he mumbled, kicking at the road.

19

In contrast to Smiley's, Tow The Line was being run out of a sleek steel and tinted glass building with a strip of grass at the street and palm trees flanking the doors. Somebody had spent some big bucks on this place.

James pulled into a spot near the front. Two shiny late-model red tow trucks with all the bells and whistles sat side-by-side on the far side of the parking lot. An attendant was wiping one of them down with a white cloth.

What James didn't see was an impound lot to hold the vehicles they collected each day. With shops and businesses crowding all around them, he couldn't imagine where they hid the confiscated vehicles. Not underground, that was for certain.

Underground in Florida meant underwater.

Inside, a glossy, black-granite counter spread across the plum-colored back wall. A clean, well-appointed waiting lounge stood to the left of the entrance with two big-screen televisions, a sectional and several nice leather chairs, a magazine rack and a snack and beverage center. Several customers sat in the lounge, their brains wrapped up in mindless TV programming.

An etiolated young man in a short-sleeve white button down shirt and skinny black tie tucked into his black trousers approached him. "Can I help you?"

"Is Ronnie here?"

"Do you have an appointment?" He was half a head shorter than James with emotionless grey eyes and razor-sharp dark brown hair. Red stitching above his shirt pocket spelled out Tow The Line.

"No, we're old buddies."

"I see. What is your name?"

"James Stewart." James gave Skinny Tie a friendly smile.

The name didn't seem to ring any bells for the young man, not as a suspected murderer or a dead film star. Apparently the kid didn't read the newspapers and was too young to remember the Oscar-nominated actor.

"Ronnie and I go way back. I'm in town for a few days. I thought I would surprise him." He closed the deal with a conspiratorial wink.

Skinny Tie smiled back. With a deft move that James hadn't seen coming, he twisted James' arm behind his back and pushed him to the door. "Let's go." He somehow managed to open the door with his free hand and shove James out with the other.

"What the—" James stumbled against a parking curb. "Wait until Ronnie hears about this!"

Skinny Tie folded his unexpectedly strong arms across his chest. "Don't worry, Mr. Stewart, I will be certain to let *Ms.* Tench know you dropped by."

Ms. Tench?

Damn.

20

Outside the duplex, buckets of rain fell. Thunder rattled the roof and jagged bursts of lightning slashed through the black sky as if the gods of Mount Olympus were hurling down angry fire bolts upon the mere humans below.

James, stretched out on his sofa, skimmed the pages of volume one of the School of Detection's class handbooks. "There has to be something in here about finding a killer," he muttered.

The door shook and he ignored it as the work of the thunder. When it shook a second time, he realized somebody was knocking. "If you're a reporter, let me warn you, I've got a baseball bat!" he hollered, leaving the threat open-ended.

"Open the damn door!"

"Oh, it's you." James plodded to the door and peered into the peephole. Yep, it was his brother. He unlocked the door. "Why didn't you just let yourself in?"

As family and landlord, Roger had two reasons to have the key to James' duplex.

"Because I don't have my keys with me. Here." Roger thrust a wad of wet mail at his brother. "I found these in your mailbox. And I found the mailbox face down in the mud. What's with that?" He brushed his wet sleeves.

"I think Iceberg backed into it with her car. You ought to have a word with her about that."

"Right." Roger frowned skeptically and moved to the living room. "What are you doing?" He dripped over the open book on the coffee table.

"Drowning." James complained, tossing the fresh pile of unpaid bills onto the chair.

Roger looked at James' shoes. "Your feet aren't even damp."

"Very funny." James frowned. "You know what I mean. I'm talking about those."

James pointed to the latest pile of debts his brother had carried inside. He pushed his hands through his hair. "I'm tired of being looked at everywhere I go like I'm a murderer, too. I can't do this anymore." He fell onto the chair oblivious to the soggy mail under his butt.

"What?" Roger's baritone chuckle came out like the purr of a diesel truck as he helped himself to a soda from the fridge. "Finally thinking of giving up the entertainment business?"

"Lately, it has been anything but entertaining." James waved his arms around. "Look at me. I need a job."

James grabbed a handful of soggy bills from under him and waved them in the air. "I'm a thirty-six-year-old law school dropout and washed up musician. May as well add failed butcher, baker and candlestick maker." He sighed. "I don't know what I'm gonna do."

Roger claimed the sofa, pressing his elbows into his knees. "What are you going to do? I'll tell you what you're going to do. Come work at the lot."

"Oh, no. Not a chance. No offense. I'm going to give this detective school a shot. A real shot." Anything was better than having to face working for his kid brother. "Besides, I'd make a lousy salesman."

"Are you out of your freaking mind?"

"No. I'm out of freaking money."

"If you're so broke, how are you going to pay for this detective class?" Roger's already naturally unnaturally large eyes grew two sizes as he noticed the extremely visible gap in the corner where James' Martin guitar used to reside. "Tell me you didn't."

"Okay, I didn't."

"The hell you didn't!" Roger jumped to his feet. "You hocked the Martin?"

"And the Vox. Yeah." Saying it out loud gave James the chills.

"No? The vintage amp, too?"

"I've still got the Guild to doodle around on."

"You have lost your mind."

"I merely hocked them. I haven't lost them." James paused. "Yet." All he had to do was find a way to make a few bucks and he could get them back. "The pawnshop is giving me ninety days." At thirty percent interest.

"And you expect to become a detective and earn enough to get your gear out of hock in that time?"

"I refuse to answer on the grounds that it may incriminate me."

"Make you look stupid, you mean. James, James. Bro." Roger approached and squeezed his brother's shoulder. "Listen to yourself. You are going to give up playing music to play cops and robbers?"

"Something like that."

"It's a mistake. I'm telling you, you are making a big mistake." Roger paced.

"In case you haven't noticed, my whole life has

been a mistake. I'm taking a do over."

"I think you're having an early midlife crisis, a pre-midlife, midlife crisis."

"You think? Maybe I'm destined to die young and this is my mid-midlife crisis."

Roger paced faster. "What about going back to law school?"

"I can barely afford PI school. Law schools are hellishly expensive. Besides, it's not the career for me."

"And being a detective is?"

"It might be."

Roger swirled his soda. "This isn't doing it for me. I'm getting a beer. You want one?"

"No, thanks. I've got class. Teacher frowns if we show up drunk."

Roger grabbed a warm six-pack from the kitchen cupboard. "I'll take these for the road."

"Fine. Deduct it from my rent." James followed his brother out the door. The rain had stopped. Roger did his best to avoid the mud comprising eighty percent of his front yard. He stopped next to his BMW and looked at his muddy shoes. "Crap. What a mess."

"Tell the landlord to put in a proper driveway."

"Maybe if the landlord had tenants who actually paid their rent, he might do that." Roger kicked his shoes gingerly against the bottom of the car door and laid a newspaper on the floor mat. "How's the Ferrari treating you?"

James glanced at the glistening car. "Like it thinks I'm its sugar daddy."

"When are you going to let me fix you up with a real car?"

"Cubie is a real car." James had bought the dark

gray eight-year old Nissan Cube secondhand from a local florist. It served him well.

"No." Roger rolled his eyes. "Cubie is not a real car." James had insisted on giving the misshapen vehicle a name. In Roger's opinion, it was unworthy of one. "Definitely not. I can pick you up a sporty little Fiat at the wholesale auction. It won't cost you much."

"Cubie is sporty." James ran his hand along the door of his brother's Beemer. "I even added a racing stripe. Remember?"

"That's a scratch. Somebody keyed Cubie while you were picking up groceries."

"One man's scratch is another man's racing stripe. Besides, it holds all my gear."

"You hocked all your gear, remember?"

James winced. Parting with the guitar and 1960s-era Vox amp had been not-so-sweet sorrow.

Roger squeezed into his German wonder and hummed off.

21

Bruno Caliostro was in a foul mood. His jaw was set as he paced stiffly at the front of the room. His daughter, Sophie Lorenzo, shook out a wet black umbrella and dropped it noisily into the trashcan beside her desk. She glared at James as she took her seat.

Had he done something wrong?

Once everyone had settled into their seats, Bruno Caliostro cleared his throat and picked up his pool cue. He aimed the long stick at James like his head was the cue ball and he was getting ready to break. "The police, one Lt. Byrd, came to see me again, Mr. Stewart. Do you know what she said?"

James flushed. "I can't imagine."

"She said a pair of sunglasses belonging to you was found under the victim's desk."

"Yeah, his desk. Not his body." James forced himself to sit straighter. It didn't pay to show signs of weakness, not around the likes of Bruno Caliostro, let alone his classmates. "Besides, why would she come tell you that?"

Bruno's grin made James uneasy. "Because she strongly suspects you of murdering Kevin Rain."

"I have a solid alibi. I dropped my sunglasses at Smiley's earlier—when I went to talk to him about my car." Maybe if he repeated the line enough times it would become the truth.

"Talk or have a heated argument and physical altercation with?" came a voice from behind.

James whipped his head around to see who had made the nasty insinuation. All he saw were zipped lips and stony faces.

What a bunch of weasels.

Bruno shook his head. "If only those sunglasses were the only problem. We could dismiss the sunglasses, don't you agree, class?"

No one deigned to say so out loud.

James scratched them all off his Christmas list.

"I admit that they are circumstantial evidence." Bruno scratched under his armpit with the pool cue. "Behavior, class. A good detective must closely examine a suspect's behavior. You will learn a lot by observing the object of your investigation carefully."

"What's that supposed to mean?" James was painfully aware of the entire class mutely watching them, hostile eyes transfixed on the exchange between pupil and teacher.

Why hadn't Bruno waited until after class to have this conversation?

"A reporter came to my office this afternoon. A very persistent reporter." He turned to his daughter. "Isn't that right, Sophie?"

Sophie nodded once and flashed a pair of scornful eyes at James before turning away.

"Shouldn't we get started?" James opened his handbook and turned to chapter one.

"Unfortunately, class has been cancelled," announced Bruno Caliostro.

Murmurs and cries of dismay and confusion came

from the small group.

"Why?" demanded Claudia Suarez, leaping from her seat directly behind James.

"Mr. Stewart, I am afraid I cannot continue to have you as a student at this time."

"Why not?" demanded James.

"Because having you as a student, with all of your negative notoriety, does not reflect well on the Bruno Caliostro School of Detection. My name is on this school. I have my reputation to think about."

"But I'm innocent." Caliostro couldn't be serious. "Innocent until proven guilty, right?"

"In my experience, Mr. Stewart, in the public's eye, the opposite is often true. Joe Public assumes a person is guilty until proven innocent."

"This is ridiculous."

"If or when you are exonerated in the murder of Kevin Rain, then you can resume classes. In fact, we'd be delighted to have you back. Wouldn't we class?"

You could have heard a pin drop until Arthur Montgomery finally said, "Yeah, man."

"But I paid. I have a contract with the school."

"If you will read your contract carefully," cut in Sophie, "you'll note that there is a subparagraph clearly stating that all students must conduct themselves in a professional manner so as to not besmirch the school's or my father's reputation."

James cussed and gathered together his books. "I want my money back."

"I'm afraid that's not possible." Bruno Caliostro looked saddened to say so but James knew better.

"No refunds," snapped Sophie.

"So," said Bruno Caliostro, "Mr. Stewart, we must

say goodbye. And class," he hung his head, "I must say goodbye to you all as well."

"What?" gasped Arthur Montgomery. "Why us? We didn't do nothin' wrong."

"We require a minimum of eight persons for our class." Bruno leaned his butt on his desk. "Until we can find another student, classes are suspended."

He didn't really but, like he'd told his daughter, he wasn't climbing those hellish steps for seven lousy students. It wasn't worth the effort or the money. "Canceling class will motivate the others to ferret out a new student," he had quipped, explaining his reasoning to Sophie.

"Idiot!" Claudia savagely kicked the back of James' chair. "Look what you've done, *imbécil*! I need this class!"

"Hey!" James swung around. A meaty hand fell on his shoulder.

"It ain't worth it, Stewart." The man in the shiny blue pinstriped suit shook his finger at James.

James jumped to his feet and shoved his chair into the table behind him. "This isn't over. You can't take my money and then kick me out."

"I gotta think about my reputation," Bruno Cagliostro said. "You clear yourself, you come back to class."

"Not in a million years." James stomped out.

22

James needed a drink and he knew just where to get it. The Banana Reef Bar and Grill. This was where his latest streak of bad luck had started. If nothing else, maybe he could drown those troubles in a pint of brew.

And look for answers. The trail had to start somewhere and this was as good a place as any.

The Banana Reef was packed and most of the crowd had to be under thirty. Loud music banged out of a pair of PA speakers set up in the corners near a trio of pockmarked dartboards.

A solitary singer-guitar player with silvery ropes of hair stroked an amped acoustic guitar. He was belting out Neil Young's *Comes A Time* with a high-pitched, nasally whine.

He wasn't any good but James had to give him credit for putting his soul into it—especially considering that there was a good chance none of these Millennials even knew who Neil Young was.

James shoved his fingers in his ears as he jostled his way through them. If the music was loud, the people struggling to carry on conversations were even louder. He wondered how they could stand it.

Pushing his way between a couple of women in casual business attire at the bar, James ordered a draft beer. "Is the manager in?" he hollered to the bartender.

"Duke?" The bartender swung his head around. His face was bright red, like a boiled lobster. "He's here someplace. What's up?"

James threw some money on the bar and sipped. "I left my sunglasses here the other day."

"Hold on." The red-faced bartender helped out a customer at the other end of the bar. He returned a minute later, crouched and pulled up a battered cardboard box. "Help yourself." He dropped the box heavily on the bar.

James looked inside. A couple of keyrings, a scarf, a pair of high heels, lots of lip gloss tubes, a strip of packaged condoms and two smartphones. He gave the box a shake but nothing else appeared. Nothing that he was willing to touch anyway.

"You don't understand," he said. "I lost them a couple of days ago. Somebody already picked them up."

"Then what are you busting my balls for?" The shaven-headed man grabbed the box and threw it under the counter.

"I was wondering who picked them up."

The bartender looked at James as if he had just met the dumbest man on the planet. Maybe he had. "How about whatever effing friend returned them to you, buddy?"

"It wasn't a friend. The police found them."

"The police?" The bartender eyed James with newfound suspicion. "What's going on, buddy? Who are you exactly?"

"My name's James. I was in here auditioning for Duke the other afternoon. I left my sunglasses behind." He slapped the bar. "Here."

"So?" The bartender ran a cloth around the insides

of a beer mug.

"So someone picked them up. Then the police found them at Smiley's Towing. I'm trying to find out who that someone was."

"Smiley's Towing?" The bartender looked thoughtful as he poured a draft from the spigot and handed it to a waitress in a short black skirt and spangly halter top. "Isn't that where that dude got murdered?"

"Yeah, something like that."

"You a cop?"

"No. I told you, I was auditioning for a gig here."

"Look, I have no clue. In case you haven't noticed, a lot of people are in and out of the club." The bartender indicated the crowd.

"Where's Duke? He was here. He might know."

The bartender scowled and searched the crowd once again. "Over there. Talking to Wayne."

"Thanks." Although for what, James didn't know. He slammed back the rest of his beer. He'd paid for it. No point letting it go to waste.

Duke, manager of the Banana Reef, sent Wayne away as James approached. "Can I help you? You look familiar. I know you?"

"I was here the other day. I play guitar."

"Oh, yeah. You wanted to get paid." He jerked his head toward the stage where the tall, dreadlocked guitar slinger was doing his best now to sound excited about cheeseburgers in paradise. "You hear that? Rick knows what the customers want and is happy to give it to them."

"Good for Rick." If anybody was listening, they were doing a good job pretending they weren't. "I wanted to ask, you remember when I was here auditioning? I left a pair of sunglasses on the bar."

"Look in the lost and friggin' found box." Duke started to move off.

James stepped in front of him. "They aren't there. The police have them."

"Then go talk to them." Duke stroked a thick black beard that looked like it had been glued to his face. "I've got a business to run."

"Do you recall who picked them up?"

"Listen, kid." Duke had about fifteen years and forty pounds over James. He looked oddly out of place in a bar catering to the hip South Florida youth in his rumpled blue chinos, paisley shirt and espadrilles.

"I don't even remember seeing your lousy sunglasses, let alone who mighta picked 'em up. Could've been another customer, you know?" He pushed James aside. "You like 'em so much, go buy yourself another pair."

Duke disappeared into the throng of drinkers near the bar and soon landed at his pal Wayne's side once more. James was about to do a disappearing act himself when he spotted a pair of familiar faces, Kourtney and Dale Rain, seated at a high-top table in the corner with a third person.

The three of them looked lost and out of place in the Banana Reef.

Kourtney was a younger version of her mother, long aristocratic nose, high forehead, a haughty look that seemed to come natural to both Rain mother and daughter. Kourtney's auburn hair was threaded with blonde and done up in a chignon. She wore a simple blue dress that left everything to the imagination.

Dale visibly bristled when he spotted James working his way towards them.

"I gotta run," gasped their companion, a man in his midthirties, with sloped shoulders and a paunch surrounded by a wide black brace of some sort. His light brown hair was thinning fast. "We'll talk later."

He grabbed at an aluminum crutch leaning against the wall. Sliding himself carefully off his tall stool, he planted the crutch under his armpit and hobbled slowly out the door.

"Was it something I said?" quipped James, helping himself to the vacated seat.

"What do you want Stewart?" Dale's hands tightened around a glass of something blue. He rattled the ice.

"He's following us, Dale. Call the police," Kourtney urged. "Tell them that the man who murdered our father is hounding us."

"Hey, I'm only here asking about my sunglasses." James laid his hands on the table.

"Sunglasses?" Dale asked.

"I don't suppose either of you know how they ended up in your father's office?"

Kourtney's laugh came out like shards of sharp broken glass, hard-edged and nasty. "What are you waiting for, Dale? Call."

"Hold on a second." Dale drummed his fingernails on the table. "Hold on a second. Maybe Mr. Stewart can help us."

"I doubt it," said Kourtney with a look that would have withered a lesser man.

James doubted it too. Still he asked, "How can I help you?"

"Cindi says you're a detective. If you didn't murder

Dad, find out who did."

Kourtney slowly smiled. "That's a good idea. I like it." She took a sip of her own unnaturally blue concoction.

"Cindi may have exaggerated," James began. "You see, I'm not—"

"We'll pay you two hundred dollars a day," offered Dale.

"Plus expenses." Kourtney batted her eyes. "Isn't that customary?"

James scratched his neck to buy some time. He knew nothing about being a detective. On the other hand, he knew plenty about being broke. "I don't know. I'm busy with a lot of other cases at the moment."

"Look at it this way, Mr. Stewart," Dale pressed. "Not only will you be helping to find the man who murdered our father but you will be clearing your own name at the same time. And getting paid to do it."

"You do make a good point."

"My brother is very smart." Kourtney unlatched her patent leather purse. She opened an alligator skin wallet and extracted some bills. "Here's four hundred dollars to get you started." She placed a mix of fifties and twenties on the table.

A signal passed between brother and sister. "Do we have a deal?" Dale asked.

"I'll have to shuffle a few clients around," James lied. "But sure. You've hired yourself a detective."

"Great. What are you drinking?" James answered and Dale told the waitress to come back with a beer. She did.

James enjoyed the free drink while his mind raced to come up with step one in his pursuit of Kevin Rain's killer, refueled and reinvigorated by the infusion of money on the table.

This was going to be tough. On one hand, he wanted the killer found fast and himself exonerated. On the other hand, dragging the "case" on for a few weeks would do wonders for his solvency issues.

"Do you have a business card?" Kourtney interrupted his thoughts. "How do we reach you, Mr. Stewart?"

"I'm all out at the moment." He patted his pockets. "I've got new ones on order."

"Here, use one of mine." Dale extracted a slim leather card holder from his jacket. "Write your number on the back of one of these." He handed James two thick, glossy business cards.

James read the card. Dale Rain was president of DK Mortgage Brokers with an address up the street. James wrote his mobile number on the reverse side.

"Keep the other card for yourself," said Dale. "In case you need to reach me."

James pocketed the card. "Do either of you have any idea where to start? Who might have wanted to see your father dead?"

Besides the two of them and their mother, he could have added. But then they might have wanted their four hundred bucks back.

"Our mother," James was very surprised to hear them say together.

23

Back at the duplex, James discovered the manatee mailbox standing upright once again. How had that happened? Had the Save the Manatees group rescued him?

Inside, he found his brother chilling on the sofa, beer in hand, Marlins vs Braves game on TV. "This is beginning to become a habit."

"You're home early." Roger glanced up from the screen.

"And you aren't home at all." James' brother liked to escape from Sheryl now and then. Lacking a man cave at his condo, he often appropriated James' living room as his man cave away from home.

"Scoot over." James dropped a six-pack on the coffee table and reached into a bag of cheese puffs.

The first of a string of commercials came on and Roger said, "What happened? You drop out of detective school already?"

"No. Kicked out."

"Kicked out?" Roger's feet fell from the table. "What the hell did you do?"

"I didn't do anything." James explained about how his being under a cloud of suspicion in the murder of Kevin Rain had led Bruno Caliostro to expel him. "So now I am *persona non grata*."

"Man, I can't believe he kicked you out."

"Yeah." James stuffed a handful of cheese puffs in his mouth and chewed. He'd opened the bag a month ago. They were stale and tasted like salty, cheddar-flavored chalk. "At least temporarily. Caliostro says if I can prove my innocence, I can go back."

"Screw him. Come work for me."

"Thanks but no thanks. I found something to tide me over."

Though the game had resumed, James held Roger's interest. "What's that?" Roger asked.

James explained how he had gone to the Banana Reef looking for answers on how his sunglasses had ended up at the murder scene and found Dale and Kourtney Rain instead. "They offered to pay me to find out who murdered dear old dad."

"Don't tell me you buy their act?" Roger said. "They sound like a pair of phonies."

"You've never even met them."

"No, but from what you tell me—"

James cut him off. "Besides, it doesn't matter if they are lying to me, their money is real enough." James patted the pocket holding all that lovely greenery. He pulled out the bills and waved them under his brother's nose.

"Did you stop to think that maybe those two could be setting you up?" Roger snatched the money before James knew what was happening and thrust it deep in his own pants pocket. "Thanks, I'll put this towards your arrears. Keep Sheryl happy."

"Hey!" James protested but knew that it was futile. The money was gone. "Speaking of Sheryl, has she said anything?"

"If you're asking if she's spilled the beans about an ongoing police investigation, the answer is no. You know better than that."

"True." Roger's wife took her job a little too seriously.

Roger cursed as the Braves scored on a walk with bases loaded. "Change the damn pitcher already!" He threw a pillow at the television. "You believe this?"

"You really think Dale and Kourtney Rain might be setting me up?"

"Why else would they be paying you to find their father's killer? You're no detective."

"They don't know that."

"If you're smart—which I on occasion question—you won't mention you are investigating to Sheryl. The shit's gonna hit the fan if she hears you are not only sticking your nose in a murder inquiry but passing yourself off as a PI."

"Yeah." James wracked his brain. "If Dale and Kourtney are setting me up, I don't see how. Or for what possible reason."

"Neither do I," Roger admitted. "But that doesn't make it any less conceivable."

"Did you ever stop to think that maybe Dale and Kourtney honestly do want to find out who murdered their father? And," James continued, seeing that his brother was about to cut him off with a response, "that they think that I can help them?"

Roger snorted.

"That's insulting."

"Come on, man. You can't find your way out of the mall."

"One time," James snapped angrily. "One time.

One time and you won't let me forget. And that was the Aventura Mall. Anybody could get lost in there. It's a jungle. It's downright labyrinthine."

"Yeah, labyrinthine. Yet little old ladies with glaucoma burdened down with purses the size of bowling ball bags and overstuffed Bloomingdale's shopping bags manage to get in and out on a daily basis without any problem."

"Shut up." The doorbell rang cutting off any further comeback. Which was probably a good thing, because telling his brother to shut up was the best he could come up with.

"You expecting somebody?" Roger asked.

"No. Maybe it's Sheryl coming to drag you home."

"Not funny." Roger frowned at his watch. "I should be getting back though. Besides, I can't stand to watch this anymore." He punched the power button on the remote, bringing an end to his anguish.

Grabbing his jacket, Roger followed James to the door as the bell rang for the third time. James looked through the peep hole. "Crap."

Roger shouldered him aside. "Who is it?" What he saw was a pretty, young blonde with pale blue eyes and a pert little nose. She held a bottle of red wine with a blue label in one hand and a white paper bag in the other. A purse hung over her shoulder on a black leather strap. "Nice. Who is she?"

"She's a nosy reporter. The one I was telling you about," whispered James, his back against the door.

Roger raised his brow. "Aren't you going to invite her in?"

"No."

There was a loud rap on the door. James stiffened.

"I can hear you in there!" boasted Jane Bright.

"You big chicken." Roger laughed and threw open the door. "Hi, come on in. I was just leaving." Cutting off James' protests, he added, "Have a good time, you two."

24

James smouldered as Roger honked and the lights of the BMW swung past the reporter's VW at the curb and disappeared down the street.

"What do you want?"

"I brought lunch." She held up the bag and the bottle of wine.

"It's a little late in the day for that, isn't it, Ms. Bright?"

"Jane." She offered her hand but James wasn't taking the bait. "Come on, James. I can call you James, can't I?"

She cracked a smile. "I feel bad about the way I treated you before. Plus, I owe you a meal. You said so yourself. Let me make it up to you."

While James was making up his mind whether to let her in or slam the door in her face, Jane Bright slid past him. James followed her to his living room.

She set the bag and wine on the coffee table. Whatever was inside the sack smelled delicious. "I see you've eaten. Beer and cheese doodles. An American classic."

She flopped down on the sofa with James glaring at her. "I brought lobster rolls and a nice merlot. I hope you like lobster." She sloughed off her purse.

Jane dug into the paper sack and unwrapped two thick lobster roll sandwiches. "What are you waiting for? They aren't laced with arsenic. Join me."

James sat tentatively on the edge of the armchair near the sofa, as if waiting for a bomb to explode. She slid a lobster roll towards him then grabbed the wine bottle. "Do you have a cork screw?"

James carried the bottle to the kitchen, opened it and filled two glasses generously.

"What do you think?" The reporter asked several minutes later.

"About what?"

"The lobster." She pointed at his half-eaten sandwich. "Do you like it?"

"Yeah, it's fine. Great." Actually, it really was delicious. He'd never had a lobster roll before but would definitely be adding them to his menu. If he could afford them.

A couple hundred years ago, people considered the crustaceans cheap and hardly worth eating. Now, people considered boiled red lobster on the plate a sign of luxury dining.

Of course, from the lobster's point of view, life had been better two hundred years ago.

Jane nodded. "I get them at Deen's up on Federal Highway. Do you know the place?"

"I've been by it. Never went inside," he said, still not willing to give more than necessary. James swirled his glass and took a gulp. The wine was on the sweet side. "You want something, Ms. Bright. What is it?"

"Jane," she reminded him, showing a mouthful of brilliant white teeth.

She wasn't bad looking when she smiled. There was a certain girlish charm about her. But then, snakes could be charming, too, just before they sank their fangs in you.

James waited as she polished off the last bite of her roll and licked her fingers clean.

Like a cat, he thought.

"I want to help you."

James tilted his head at her. She had taken him by surprise. "I thought you were convinced I was a cold-blooded murderer?"

"No," Jane said slowly. "I said you sometimes behave like one." She waved a scolding finger at him. "There is a difference."

"You said you wanted to help me." James leaned forward, pressing his elbows into his thighs. "Why?"

"Because I want a story. Like I said before."

"If you're looking for a confession from me to run in that little paper of yours, you can forget it."

"Are you even listening to me?" Jane surged toward him and thwacked him in the side of the head with her finger.

"Ouch! Dammit!" He rubbed his skull.

"I'm sorry but you really are a lousy listener."

"And you're certifiable!" James jumped to his feet. "I think you should leave."

Jane rolled her eyes. "Don't be so dramatic. I think *you* should sit down."

James seethed, as she waggled her finger at him the way his high school English teacher, Mrs. Maupin, used to.

James fell into the chair with a sigh of defeat.

He hated that finger.

Mrs. Maupin had wielded that same power—the power to crush him. His former teacher had crushed his soul under her boot of authority more times than he cared to remember. There was that English class where they had been told to write a short story in the style of Jonathan Swift, as if the satiric author was alive today. James had thought he'd done a pretty good job of it.

James got his story back with a big fat F on the top. An F minus, actually, as if to pour salt in the wound. Mrs. Maupin had added a written message next to the failing grade stating in no uncertain terms that if Jonathan Swift were alive today he most definitely would not write as James had done.

James tried arguing, even pleading. All attempts were met with a fortress-of-steel visage and a waving forefinger. He had lost that battle. He would probably lose this one too...so why fight it at all?

Better to hear Jane Bright out. The sooner he allowed the reporter to have her say, the sooner she would leave.

"That's better," Jane said, smiling. "You finished with that?"

"Huh?" James looked at the remains of his lobster roll. "No." He grabbed it and chewed dully while she wadded up her wrapper and dropped it in the bag.

She rose, stretched her arms overhead with the rumpled bag in her right hand. "Trash?"

"What?" James swallowed and reached for his glass.

She jiggled the bag.

"Under the sink."

Jane cast him a scolding look. "Not good. You'll attract cockroaches that way." She pulled open the cabinet under the sink and dropped the bag in the plastic trashcan. Without so much as a how-do-you-do, she moved his green trashcan to the narrow space between the refrigerator and the wall. "That's better. Any dessert?"

"There's a lemon pound cake in the fridge." James was getting used to her bossy behavior and shorthand speech. It probably went with the news reporter territory.

"Awesome." Jane pulled open two upper drawers before stumbling on the silverware. "What a mess," she remarked. "You ought to keep your silverware closer to the dishes."

She plucked out a butter knife, rinsed it, then used it to cut two generous slices of cake.

He thought it especially generous considering she had helped herself to a cake that did not belong to her.

The pound cake was part of his mother's bimonthly care package. One week she'd send him a homemade dessert, a couple weeks later it would be something healthier, like blueberry muffins or a loaf of whole wheat bread.

Jane carried two small plates to the coffee table and handed him the larger of the two slices. "This is terrific," she said, inhaling her first mouthful.

"Mom has a lot of time on her hands." Not that he was complaining.

"Your mother made this?" Jane said, wide-eyed. She stabbed the cake once again with vigor. "I'm definitely going to need this recipe."

"I'll let Mom know." In about a million years.

"Do you know what I do for a living, James?"

James drew his brows together, plate nestled between his pressed knees. "You're a reporter."

"I work the gardening section mostly." She sucked the crumbs off her fork then licked her empty plate before setting it carefully on the coffee table. "Do you know what that means?"

James spoke with his mouth full of lemon, "That you write about gardening?"

She nodded. "Flowers, shrubs, palm trees. Did you know there are over twenty-five hundred species of palm trees? I mean, I'm not saying they are all in South Florida, but still, that's a lot of palm trees, right?"

James struggled to keep up.

She eyed his dessert and he ate faster. "I also cover related things like mulch, potting soil. And don't get me started on the pollinators."

"Pollinators?" What the hell was this woman going on about and what did it have to do with her showing up on his doorstep? Was she some lonely, loony looking for somebody to talk to?

"Birds, bees."

"You should talk to my neighbor, she's really into gardening." Like right now. Peas in a pod, those two.

"I mean, don't get me wrong, I've got nothing against plants. But it's not a career. You know?"

"I suppose," he said cautiously. "So where is this going?"

Jane's smile filled her face like he'd just told her she had won the Florida lottery. "We work together, James. I have my resources, you have yours. I mean, as the prime suspect and brother-in-law of the city attorney, you can find out things I can't."

Her finger waggled between the two of them. "We solve this murder."

25

One bite.

That was all it would take. One bite and that finger would wag no more.

"And you get off the gardening page."

"That's the idea."

James nodded slowly, wheels turning. "Forget it."

"What?"

"I said forget it." James stuck out his chin. "No deal. I don't need your help to solve this murder. I can solve it myself." He ignored her piglike snort of derision. "Not only can I, I'm being paid to do so."

"Paid?" Her brow ridged up. "Who would want to pay you to solve a murder that you're suspected of having committed?"

"I have an alibi. I did not murder Kevin Rain. I'm simply, unfortunately, the man who found him," James replied angrily. "And I wish I hadn't."

James drained the dregs of the wine into his glass. He stood. "It's late, Ms. Bright." He motioned towards the door.

She ignored him, crossing her legs and jiggling her foot. "I guess you didn't hear then, did you?"

"Hear what?" James heard himself asking although he was already dreading the answer. She looked far too smug.

"Your alibi doesn't hold up," Jane said victoriously.

"What do you mean it doesn't hold up?" James was getting a sinking feeling.

"It means that the police, in running a routine check on Cindi Keach's movements on the night of the murder, found some discrepancies."

James sat on the arm of the chair. "Discrepancies? What sort of discrepancies? And why would the police be checking on Cindi? She's not a suspect. And how does that affect my alibi?"

"Everybody is a suspect until proven otherwise," Jane replied. "In tracing Cindi Keach's movements, the police have learned that she left her apartment for quite some time."

James shook his head. "Cindi didn't murder her brother-in-law. That's crazy."

"No. I'm not suggesting she did. In fact, from what I've learned from my sources, her movements prove just the opposite."

"Get to the point, would you?"

Jane reached into her purse and extracted her notebook.

While James gnawed at his lower lip, she skimmed her notes. "Cindi Keach is known to have been out of the apartment for approximately one hour. There are credit card transactions and CCTV video recordings of her having stopped for gas, purchased groceries and waited in line at a pharmacy for a prescription."

The reporter looked up at James as if waiting for a response.

He gave her one. "So? All you've done, all the police have done, is prove her innocent. That pharmacy you mentioned is miles in the opposite direction from

Smiley's. There's no way she would have had time to murder her brother-in-law and do all that other stuff and get back when she did."

"Yes." She slid her notebook back inside her purse. "Would you mind? Could I take a slice of that cake home with me?"

"Get to the point!"

"Wow. Temper, temper." She pressed out a wrinkle in her fitted skirt. "The point is that this tells the police that while you stated that you were in Cindi's apartment during the time of Kevin Rain's murder, you could have left, killed him in a violent argument and then returned. All before Cindi returned."

James felt a sudden chill and sank back into the armchair.

Jane fetched him a glass of cold water. "Do we have a deal, James?"

26

"Shh." James put a finger to his lips and rose slowly. "Did you hear that?"

"Hear what?" Jane gave him a funny look.

"I heard something. At least I thought I did." He tilted his head and listened intently.

The reporter followed suit. "I don't hear anything," she said after a moment. "I think you're avoiding the question. Do we have a deal, James?" She crossed her legs and faced him.

He waved for her to be quiet. "There it goes again. I hear voices."

"They're probably in your head," Jane quipped. "Or maybe it's your neighbor and her TV or radio or something."

The reporter sighed as James tiptoed to the sliding glass door. As he drew back the drapes to take a look, he heard a scraping sound followed by running footsteps.

"Hey!" James yanked open the slider and ran out the door. He crashed into a deck chair and cursed. A light came on in Roberta Higgins' place next door.

James ran barefoot around his side of the duplex. He heard the sound of a car starting up further down the street. It sped off in the opposite direction.

James hobbled over the rough stones back to his place, cursing with every step.

Jane was standing on the deck with her arms folded. "Find anybody?"

"No," James snarled.

"What's going on over there? Mr. Stewart, is that you?" Roberta Higgins was glaring at him from her kitchen window. The layout of her unit was the mirror image of his.

"Yes, Ms. Higgins, just chasing away a burglar." After a breath, he added with uncloaked sarcasm, "Or a murderer. Probably saved your life. You're welcome."

The sharp bright beam of a high-powered flashlight shot from the Iceberg's kitchen window, illuminating his face. He held up his hands protectively.

The beam of light played over Jane, who waved to Roberta. "Hello."

The window rolled up. "I would appreciate it if you and your girlfriend would keep it down over there, Mr. Stewart. Some of us are trying to sleep."

"Sorry," cooed Jane.

James jabbed his finger at the reporter. "This woman is not my—"

The window slammed down.

Following Jane back inside the unit, James wiped his dirty feet on the scrap of carpet that served as a door mat. The bottoms of his feet were bleeding. "Great. Just great."

Jane tossed him a roll of paper towels that he kept next to the kitchen sink. "You never did tell me who was paying you to investigate Kevin Rain's murder. By the way, is that even legal? I mean, for you to investigate. You don't have a PI license. I'm surprised the state even gave you a driver's license."

"Ha-friggin'-ha." James ripped off a wad of paper

towels and dabbed at his lacerated feet. "It's none of your business who's paying me. And I don't need a license to try to find out who killed Kevin Rain."

Unable to stem the flow of blood, he swaddled his feet in paper towels.

Jane giggled.

"What's so funny?"

"Not a thing." She made a face of disgust, picking up the bloodstained paper towels he'd dropped and depositing them in the trash can. "So who's paying you?"

"I told you." James took a chair at the small wooden dinette table in the corner.

"No. You told me it's none of my business."

"Exactly." James touched a finger to his nose. "Now go home." He aimed said finger at the door.

She folded her arms under her chest. "I'm not leaving here until you tell me who's paying you. Go ahead. Pull down your pants, if you want to," she said, only she knew she was bluffing. "It's nothing I haven't seen before. And better."

James bit his lip. "Fine. Dale and Kourtney Rain, that's who. There, are you happy? If so and, even if not, please leave," he ended sternly.

"Dale and Kourtney Rain, eh?" Jane paced the small dining room space. "Kevin's kids. Sick but, yeah, that could work."

"What could work?"

"I'll bet Dale and Kourtney offed their dad and are setting you up for the fall." She was grinning.

"I don't see anything funny about that."

"No?" Jane shrugged a shoulder. "I don't know. It's sorta funny when you think about it."

"There is nothing funny about it at all. There's

nothing funny about this entire situation." James climbed to his feet, sliding on the fresh paper towels he'd applied.

Jane was staring at his feet. Okay, so his paper towel bandaged feet did look funny. That was beside the point.

"This isn't a game. We're talking about murder. Not mulch or pollinators or palm trees!"

"I can see you're tired." Jane helped herself to another wedge of his lemon pound cake.

James watched in stunned silence as the reporter peeled a clean paper towel off the roll and carefully wrapped the cake inside. She placed the wrapped slice gently in her purse. "Get some sleep."

At the front door, she added, "We'll talk in the morning."

The minute she left, James grabbed the green trashcan with both hands and threw it under the kitchen sink where it belonged. The trash can bounced off the drainpipe, tipping sideways and dumping garbage all over the inside of the cupboard. What didn't land inside spilled out onto the kitchen floor.

James gaped at the mess. This was all Jane's fault. "The hell with it. I'm going to bed."

27

Felicity Rain lived in a pale yellow, two-story Mediterranean-style home in an upscale country club community in Boca Raton, a pricey city approximately thirty miles north of Fort Lauderdale. James had gotten the address from her obliging kids, Kourtney and Dale.

The community boasted a heated Olympic-sized pool, sixteen clay tennis courts, complete with a six-figure yearly income tennis pro, eight pickle ball courts, and a putting green.

What it also boasted was that it had absolutely no swing sets, no sandboxes and no slides. Not even a basketball court. This was no place for kiddies. Never would be. And proudly so.

The developer had built Boca Banyans Estates for the fifty-five and older crowd. This was something of a catch-22 for potential residents who, while wanting to live unencumbered by the youth who only reminded them of their own extended and ever-advancing years, were forced to show legal identification proving they met the age requirement before association approval for permission to reside at Boca Banyans Estates.

And nobody in Boca Raton over fifty-five wanted to admit to their true age.

James had been tailing Felicity Rain since around 8 a.m. when she left her house in the company of a two-tone Mercedes-Benz driving woman with two-toned hair. The luxury sedan was blue and silver. So was her hair.

They drove to a bagel shop squeezed between a skincare center and a Rolex store in a red-tiled shopping center on Military Trail in the heart of Boca Raton.

The two had been lingering for half an hour already over coffee and bagels. During this time, Felicity had managed the merest bite of what looked like a whole-wheat bagel. The woman with the two-tone hair had no trouble gobbling hers up completely, cream cheese and all.

Seated in his car, James watched from the parking lot. The Ferrari might have looked out of place most anywhere else but here in Look-at-me-I'm-rich Boca Raton, the normally rare red sports car was just a car. Nothing special at all.

With his eyes glued to the two women in the bagel shop window, Jane Bright took him by surprise as she threw open his passenger door and plopped down on the seat beside him.

"What are you doing here?" James hissed.

"What are you up to, James?" Jane deftly ignored the question and tilted up the sun visor to see better. "Who are you watching? Somebody inside the bagel shop? Is it those two ladies? The ones in the window? They look harmless."

James bit his lip. "Yes." He reluctantly took his eyes off his prey and planted them on his antagonist. "Why are you here, Bright?"

"Jane." She shrugged. "I was following you. That's my car, right back there. See?" She swiveled her neck and pointed out the tiny back window. "Some detective.

You never even spotted me."

James turned away so she couldn't see him blush with embarrassment. "I saw you," he lied. "I chose to ignore you."

"Right. Anyway, I was bored so I thought I'd come sit with you."

"Again, why are you here? And I don't mean in my car. I mean here here, in this parking lot."

"I was on my way to your house this morning when, lucky for me, I spotted this gaudy red homage to testosterone pulling out or I might have missed you." Jane squinted out the window.

She smelled of lilac blossoms.

"Shame on you." Jane wagged her finger. James resisted the urge to snap at it with his canines.

"Shame on me for what?"

"For planning to leave before I got to your house."

"I didn't know you were coming to my house." His fingers tightened around the steering wheel. "If I had, I would have left earlier."

"What's that supposed to mean? We had plans to talk."

"No we didn't. We had no plans at all. Talk or otherwise."

"I'm pretty sure we did, James." She tilted her head at him. "You're not a very good listener, are you?"

Peering through the windshield, paying little attention to the babbling reporter beside him, James observed Felicity and her companion rise from their table and collect the purses strapped to the backs of their chairs. "No, we didn't."

"What about our deal?"

"Deal?" James watched as the women waved to a

valet for their vehicle. At the same time, his brain struggled to figure out what this garden section reporter who wasn't supposed to be there was talking about. Then he remembered, she wanted them to work together.

"I don't need your help." He started the Dino, the noise of which woke late-dozing retirees nestled in their garden villas two blocks away. "They're leaving. Get out."

"Not a chance." The reporter clipped her seat belt. She had dressed casually for the occasion in stretch denim jeans, low-heeled black shoes and a light cotton shirt that hung loosely at the waist, deemphasizing her figure.

"What do you mean not a chance? You need to go."

The valet opened the door for the driver of the Mercedes, who handed him a five. Felicity patted her coif and waited patiently for him to do the same for her on the passenger side. Apparently opening her own door was too plebian a task, or maybe the motion threw off her tennis stroke.

"I am going." Jane rolled up her window. "With you."

28

James swore, at both Jane and the woman driving a silver Range Rover the size of a Calistoga wagon that she was struggling to inch out of the slot behind him. Until she moved, he was stuck.

The Ranger Rover was fitted with twenty-one inch wheels and four-wheel drive, all the better to get over those pesky speedbumps in front of public elementary schools, which were surely intended only for lowly Toyota and Honda drivers—the bumps and the public schools.

The Mercedes was already at the traffic light at the corner and making the turn as the Range Rover cleared his path. James sped up and followed at a careful distance.

Some minutes later, the woman at the wheel of the Mercedes dropped Felicity off at the edge of her paver-clad driveway. The woman then headed swiftly away, ignoring the curses and gestures of an elderly fellow in the crosswalk propped up by an aluminum-framed, two-wheeled walker. He'd been trying to cross the street and been forced to swerve to avoid being plowed down by the Mercedes that seemed to have no intention of stopping or even slowing.

James and Jane watched from two doors down.

"Aren't you going to follow her?"

"The woman in the car? Nope."

"Who is she?"

"The driver? I have no idea."

"Get her license number?"

"No."

"Why not?"

Damn. Because he'd forgotten. Hadn't even thought about it. "Because she's not the person I'm interested in. This one is. That lady walking up to the house is Felicity Rain."

"Ex-wife of the dead man?" Jane arched her brow. "That's interesting. So what do we do next?"

James lifted his foot from the brake. "I go interview her. You wait in the car." James pulled into the drive and climbed out of the Ferrari. Never an easy task even at his relatively modest size. The sports car was small and low to the ground.

Jane jumped out and joined him as he started up the path to the front doors, two eight-foot tall, carved mahogany statements of wealth and status.

"I said wait in the car."

"Do you really think Felicity Rain is going to talk to you?"

"I guess we'll find out."

Clutching her purse, Jane said, "Let me handle this. I'm a reporter. I'm used to interviewing people."

"Yeah, little old ladies about their rosebushes. I'm trying to find out about a murder, not what to do about aphids."

"That's sexist. And stupid." The reporter matched him step for step. "Everybody knows a little soapy water will get rid of an aphid infestation."

"Yeah, what was I thinking? Everybody knows

that." James rolled his eyes.

Jane grabbed his arm. "Maybe I can get her to tell us why Kourtney and Dale might have wanted to murder their father."

James pulled her back behind a large traveler palm in the well-tended front flowerbed. "I told you last night, Kourtney and Dale hired me to find his killer."

"And you think it's her? The ex?"

"*They* think it's her."

Jane whistled softly. "Interesting. Interesting twist." She shot past him and rang the doorbell before he could stop her.

James fumed.

"Felicity Rain?" The reporter smiled. James had never seen a phonier looking face in his life. "I'm Jane Bright. I'm with the Broward County Times." She offered Ms. Rains her business card.

"Yes?" Felicity Rain looked quickly at the card, holding it in her fingertips like it was poison ivy. "What do you want?" She gazed suspiciously down at the two of them.

Kevin's ex-wife was dressed in a light pink tennis outfit, matching skirt and blouse with a diamond necklace circling her long, tan neck. Her designer white sneakers didn't look like they had ever touched a clay court, let alone done any running after tennis balls.

"We were hoping to have a word with you about Kevin Rain," James interjected.

Felicity blinked at James. "Aren't you the attorney friend of that tramp Alyssa's?"

"No. I'm the one who discovered your husband's body."

"My ex-husband," corrected Ms. Rain with a steely

tone.

"Do you have any idea who might have wanted Kevin dead, Ms. Rain?" asked Jane.

A small dog yapped somewhere inside, its voice echoing across the polished travertine floor. Felicity Rain stepped outside, shutting the door behind her. "Few people wanted my ex-husband alive, Ms. Bright. Like Alyssa. He was her golden ticket, wasn't he? As for who wanted him dead, take your pick. Everyone from employees and ex-associates and his competitors, to every loser—his word, not mine—whose car he had towed."

James shifted uneasily. He was one of those losers. And he'd been found at the scene of the murder with his prints all over the murder weapon.

That made him Super Loser.

Felicity ran her fingers through her hair. Everything about her screamed high-maintenance, from the two hundred-dollar haircut to the one hundred-dollar pedicure. Being married to her must have cost Kevin Rain a bundle. The divorce might've actually saved him some money.

"I know all about you, Mr. Stewart." Tiny diamond studs accented delicate ear lobes. "The police suggested once again that you might be involved. I don't believe it for a second."

"Thank you," James replied. "I'm glad somebody thinks so."

"Of course." Glued-on eyelashes fluttered. "I mean, look at you. A man your age and you can barely hold down a job."

"That's not—"

"Ah-hem." Jane cleared her throat, ballpoint pen

poised over her notebook. The two of them bickering wasn't going to get this investigation anywhere. "Who's your number one suspect, Ms. Rain?"

Felicity cocked her head ever so slightly. "This is going to sound terribly catty of me..."

"Yes?" Jane smiled encouragingly.

"If you must know," sighed Felicity, "Kourtney and Dale weren't exactly lining up to give Kevin presents on Father's Day."

"You think his own kids murdered him?" Jane asked, wide-eyed. This family was creepy.

"I would not put it past them."

"What about Adam Mitchell?" James asked. "I heard he wanted your ex to make him a partner."

Felicity smiled delicately, not wanting to cause any fracturing or wrinkling of her painstakingly surgically enhanced and expensively maintained features. "Adam Mitchell does have a temper. He and Kevin fought any number of times."

"You mean they argued? About the business?" Jane inquired.

"I mean they came to blows physically," Felicity said rather cooly.

"But what exactly did they fight about?" James asked. "And why didn't Kevin fire him?"

Felicity smiled. "You'd have to ask Kevin that, wouldn't you?" She looked pointedly at a diamond-studded gold watch on her left wrist. "I'm sorry but my trainer is here."

Sure enough, a sleek black Mercedes-Benz Sprinter with Famous Fitness written on the side pulled up to the curb. An athletic woman in gray-striped leggings, cross-training sneakers and a halter top hopped out.

"Thank you for your time," Jane said.

James wasn't ready to go. Kourtney and Dale had accused their mother of murdering their father and vice versa. There had to be reasons. You couldn't blame everything wrong with these people on a shallow gene pool. "Where were you the night your ex was murdered?"

"Home taking a bath." Felicity stepped off the porch and greeted her trainer.

"Can you prove that?" James pressed.

The trainer carried a Famous Fitness nylon duffel bag in her right hand. Felicity told her she would meet her inside and the blonde-haired fitness fiend disappeared through the front door.

Felicity's countenance darkened once her trainer was gone. "Be careful who you accuse of what. Both of you."

"We're only trying to find your ex's killer," protested James. "Please, Ms. Rain. If there is anything you can think of that would help shed some light on the murder, I would really appreciate it. I'm still the main suspect."

Felicity Rain tapped her manicured fingernail against a capped front tooth. "Have you spoken to Phil Adler yet?"

"Who's Phil Adler?" Jane asked.

"The ten million dollar man."

The lithe blonde instructor stuck her head out the door and clapped her hands. A small curly-haired white dog with black eyes peered anxiously between her ankles. "Time's ticking, Felicity."

"Please call first next time," Felicity said, starting for the house. "That's the problem with not living in a gated community," they heard her complain to her trainer before slamming the door behind them. "You can't keep out the riff-raff."

29

"Weird," sighed James as he and Jane took the walk of shame back to the Ferrari.

"What's weird?"

"When I saw Felicity, Kourtney and Dale at Alyssa's condo, I got the impression they were united. Mostly in their contempt for Alyssa."

"So? Alyssa is the new, younger version of Felicity. Can you blame them?"

"No, but then why are they throwing each other under the murder bus now?"

"Good question." Tall clouds hung in the air, diffusing the sun. One of South Florida's near ubiquitous landscaping crews tumbled from an open-backed truck on the opposite side of the street. They began unloading mowers, blowers and clippers with well-practiced ease.

"What's next?" Jane slid into the passenger's seat as James cranked the engine to life in frustration.

They had learned nothing. How did private detectives do it, James wondered? He couldn't force Felicity Rain to talk to him and tell him everything he wanted to know. If he flat out accused her of murdering her ex, she could file a defamation suit against him or some such thing.

He couldn't risk that.

"Kourtney and Dale gave me another lead." James slowly weaved his way out of the neighbor and turned onto Yamato Road, one of Boca Raton main east-west arteries.

"What is it?"

"You'll see."

A couple minutes later, he turned into the palm-lined drive of a tangerine-colored, twelve-story office building with a two-tiered, green-roofed parking garage jutting out on the left side. The tower's glass sides glittered bronze in the sunlight.

"This is it." James pulled up to the main entrance. "Hop out. I'll find a spot and meet you inside."

"Sure." Jane extracted herself from the Ferrari and stretched her arms overhead. "Who are we looking for?"

"I'll tell you inside." James smiled for the first time that day as he sped out the drive, tires squealing as he hit Yamato and floored it.

He could practically hear Jane Bright's angry curses buzzing in his ears. She ran helplessly after him then stopped in the middle of the road, slamming her purse down on the pavement as she realized the futility of her actions.

A mile away and safely out of the pestering reporter's reach, James drove into a small shopping center anchored by a Dunkin' Donuts and killed the engine. Pulling up the Internet on his smartphone, he searched for Phil Adler.

For once, the gods—at least the gods of detection—were on his side. There were only a handful of P Adlers in the entire state. Better yet, only a couple of Adlers, and a solitary Phillip Adler, in the immediate vicinity. This one lived in the Town of Davie.

James mapped the address. The town was southwest of Ft. Lauderdale. Historically, Davie had been the region's cowboy country. It still was to some extent. Years ago, James had attended a concert at the Bergeron Rodeo Grounds: A Cowboy Christmas Carol. Not his finest memory, but his then high school girlfriend, a Texas transplant, had been thrilled.

James couldn't find a telephone number for Adler but that didn't matter. He wouldn't have used it anyway. Better to pay a surprise visit in person, discover who this Phil Adler was and what part he might or might not have played in the murder of Kevin Rain.

James detoured into a gas station to refill the ever-thirsty beast, then followed the voice directions coming from his phone.

Like much of South Florida, Davie had sprung to life due to the overzealous draining of the Everglades swamps by land hungry developers. That zeal had created the Frankensteinian patchwork of neighborhoods and canals that defined the region.

If the predictions were right, much of South Florida would be underwater once again, only this time it would be drowned up to its penthouses in seawater rather than freshwater.

Following a narrowing and little-traveled road that turned from blacktop to hard-packed dirt, past grazing horses and scrawny cows that the cattle egrets were using as mobile perches, James landed at a small cul-de-sac with a solitary and forlorn ranch house at the end.

A faded red pickup truck with rust-pitted wheel covers sat inside the carport. A motorcycle protruded from under a torn and dusty rain cover. Several overspilling garbage cans lined the back. It was late afternoon, yet all the curtains in the house were pulled tight—gashes of neon green clashing with the muddy brown stucco someone had amateurishly smeared across the walls.

A long, silver propane tank rested on cement blocks surrounded by tall weeds in the middle of the front yard. Phil Adler apparently did not have to worry about any homeowners' association rules and regulations out here like they did in Boca.

The first thing James noticed of significance was the shiny Tow The Line truck parked in the rutted dirt driveway out front. The second thing of significance was the eight-foot tall wood picket fence circling the backyard.

James took a last refreshing moment to enjoy the cool AC then shut off the Ferrari's engine. The front door of the house opened. This action was followed by the thick steel-barred screen door swinging outward.

The third thing of significance were the devil dogs—two muscular and bloodthirsty Rottweilers that came snapping their razor sharp teeth as they made a beeline for him the moment he opened his car door and set foot on the ground.

The lead dog grabbed his foot and chomped down. James screamed and kicked, leaping sideways into the car. The dog bounced off the door, falling on his back, legs kicking. The second dog leapt over its mate and lunged at him.

James slammed the door shut as the dog slammed into the driver's side window, spitting and snarling. The other Rottweiler jumped onto the hood.

"Damn." That was gonna leave some nasty scratch

marks. Roger wasn't going to like that. James planted himself in the driver's seat and flipped the ignition. He punched the gas pedal. The rear wheels spun madly then grabbed dirt. The Ferrari lurched forward. One Rottweiler bounced over the hood, the other bit into the front tire.

He slammed the Ferrari into reverse, spun the car around and sped off. The demon dogs gave chase and didn't give up until he'd gone a quarter mile down the road and the beasts were nothing more than nasty specks in his rearview mirror.

30

Glancing in his rearview mirror to be certain the devil dogs hadn't picked up his trail, James didn't stop until he reached a discount supermarket nearer to civilization and farther from rampaging Rottweilers.

The top of his right leather shoe was punctured and the laces torn. He tugged off his shoe to examine his foot and was relieved to see he wasn't bleeding too badly.

Sticking his shoe back on his foot, he ran inside the supermarket for some bandages and something to eat. Tossing the bags in on the passenger side, he couldn't help noticing that, in addition to the deep scratches crisscrossing the roof, long, wide scratches ran up and down the front fender and there were teeth marks in the front tire, which itself wasn't flat but was clearly losing air. He was going to have to do something about that.

Damn dogs. Adler ought to clip his Rottweilers' nails once in a while. Not to mention, one of the brutes had clamped his fangs into the side view mirror like it was a piece of raw meat for the taking.

There wasn't much left of it now.

Roger was going to notice that too.

James' smartphone rang. He grabbed it off the dash. "James here."

"Mr. Stewart, it's me, Dale."

"Hello, Dale. What can I do for you?"

"I'd like an update. Have you made any progress on the case?"

James glared at the hot phone. "I only started today."

Dale Rain sounded unimpressed by the fact. "You spoke to Mother. What do you think?"

"I think she looks quite fit for a woman her age."

"Do you think she murdered Dad?"

James sighed and sunk into his car seat. "She didn't tell me so in so many words, no." He tugged at the sweaty collar of his shirt. "I only have your word and your sister's for it."

"Mother is a clever woman."

"You never did say why exactly your mother would want your father dead, Dale. The divorce was some time ago, wasn't it?"

"Let's just say the wound has not healed. Besides, Mother was unhappy that he refused to sell Smiley's."

"To Tow The Line?"

"That's right."

James did some thinking. "Who's Phil Adler?"

There was a long silence during which James pictured his just-bought frozen dinners reaching the melting point. He started the Ferrari and cranked the AC down to sixty degrees.

"Are you there, Dale?"

"Phil Adler filed a lawsuit against Smiley's."

Felicity Rain's ten-million-dollar man. "A ten-million-dollar lawsuit."

"That's right."

"Why?"

"Mr. Adler claims he was injured on the job."

"I'm sensing a but, Dale."

"But our father was positive that Mr. Adler is faking his injuries. He was just unable to prove it. And believe me, he tried. Dad even hired a private detective."

That got James' attention. "He did? Who?"

"A PI by the name of Caliostro."

"*Bruno* Caliostro?"

That really got James' attention. His pontificating, gasbag teacher, Bruno Caliostro – PI to the Stars, had a direct relationship to the deceased. A relationship he had failed to mention although there had been plenty of opportunities.

"What happens to the lawsuit now that your father is dead?"

"As far as I know, it continues. The lawsuit names Smiley's Towing Service, in addition to Dad personally."

"What about your mom?"

"Are you asking if she's named in the lawsuit?" James said he was and her son continued. "Yes, as part owner of the business, she is one of the defendants."

James figured since he had nothing to lose and he had the kid on the phone, he'd ask, "Do you happen to know a woman who drives a blue two-tone Mercedes S-Class, Dale?"

Dale snorted.

James frowned. He'd had that coming. This was South Florida, Mercedes of all shapes and sizes were ubiquitous and practically indigenous—like blood diamonds and Gucci handbags.

"What is Adler's relationship with Tow The Line?"

"There is no relationship, so far as I know, Mr. Stewart. Why?"

Why, indeed.

Why was a Tow The Line truck parked outside the ranch house belonging to a disgruntled former Smiley's employee?

"Before his injury, what did Phil Adler do at Smiley's?"

"He was a driver and occasional mechanic, like eighty percent of the employees. Is it important?"

"Let me do a little digging," James replied vaguely. "And get back to you on that." He ended the call before Dale Rain could press him further.

Dale would want to know what James' plan of action was going to be next. That was a tough question to answer.

Because James was stymied and had no idea.

But he couldn't do anything if he didn't have wheels.

He ran back inside the grocery, found a can of miracle flat-fixer in the household goods aisle. Following the microscopic directions on the back of the can, he screwed the nozzle to the valve stem and pulled the trigger. Yellow-white foam shot out the nozzle. Some managed to make it inside the tire, the rest landed on his feet.

At least it might fill the Rottweiler holes in his shoe leather.

31

James planted a soggy microwave dinner of Lite & Licious rigatoni with vodka sauce on the grungy glass plate in the countertop microwave. One of these days, he'd wash that plate. At least, that was what he had been telling himself every day for the last three years.

James nuked it for the prescribed three minutes, let it cool for another minute while he opened a beer, and carried everything out to the deck. Standing, he balanced the box and the can on the guardrail. White lightning danced in the distance. He popped the plastic food covering with his fork and took a bite. The noodles were a little tough and a little cold.

And the sauce could have used more vodka.

He thought about the murder.

This detective stuff was hard—harder than it looked on TV. Almost impossible really. He had spent the day chasing one dead end after another. All he had to show for it was a pocketful of gas receipts for a sports car that had seen better days.

Felicity Rain had been vague and confrontational. Phil Adler had sicced his devil dogs on him.

What was the point?

How was he ever going to figure out who killed Kevin Rain?

"Boo!"

James flinched, knocking his microwave tray over the side of the railing, through the cattails and into the canal with a dull splash. The beer can followed with a bigger splash.

He spun around to see Jane Bright stomping up the deck stairs, grinning.

"What are you doing here?" James clamped his hands on the rail, looking sadly at his sinking dinner. It would be tomorrow morning's duck food. "Look what you made me do."

"Sorry," Jane said mechanically and without a trace of sympathy. She veered straight for the sliding door, pushed it open and stepped inside.

James hurried after her. "You still haven't told me what you're doing here."

Her head was stuck in the refrigerator. "You got any more of that lemon pound cake left?"

"No." James stared at her backside.

"Wrong. Here it is," she said glibly, her hands pushing foodstuffs around on the middle shelf. She pulled out the remains of his foil-wrapped cake and set it on the counter.

The reporter cut herself a generous slice—again, especially generous considering it wasn't her cake—and placed the rest back in the fridge. She hadn't even bothered to ask James if he wanted a piece of his own cake.

James fumed as she slowly chewed, then licked her lips with relish.

"Thanks for stranding me, by the way," Jane said, breaking another chunk free with her fork—his fork. "I really appreciate that."

James snatched a fresh can of beer from the refrigerator and carried it to the sofa. His stomach grumbled over its missed meal. "Being left behind at a state-of-the-art office building in the middle of Boca Raton is hardly the same as being abandoned on a deserted island in the South Pacific."

"Without my car? In the heat?" Jane puffed out her cheeks. "You try it sometime."

"I did, if you'll recall," James replied. "The night my car was towed. That's what started this whole mess. Reminds me, I need to pick it up tomorrow."

Roger could have the Ferrari. And none too soon. The cost of running it was too high. The only question was whether his brother was going to make him pay for the damages the Rottweilers had inflicted. If so, Phil Adler was the person who ought to pay.

"I had to walk for miles." Jane slipped off a shoe, cast a reproving look at him while rubbing her foot, then joined him on the sofa.

"Walking is good for you. It's healthy. In fact," James reached into the bag of cheese puffs that had been sitting out on the coffee table since the other day, "how about walking to your car right now?"

"Very funny." She picked up a single cheese puff, sniffed it suspiciously. She scrunched up her pert little nose and dropped it back on the table. "I found out who she is."

"Who who is?"

"The woman that Felicity Rain was having coffee and bagels with this morning before you unceremoniously ditched me. Speaking of coffee, you want some?" She practically flew off the sofa and headed for the kitchen.

"I've got beer."

"Coffee's healthier."

"Says who?" James muttered.

Jane scrubbed out the coffee pot before filling it from the tap. "You really ought to use filtered water, you know." She got the pot going.

"So, who is she?" James was leaning over the kitchen counter now. The reporter was acting like she owned the place.

"Who?" She batted her eyelashes at him.

"Don't be coy. You know who. The woman with the two-toned hair that Felicity Rain met with this morning."

"You owe me an apology."

"For what?" exclaimed James.

"Now who's being coy? Where are the clean cups?" She looked skeptically at a couple of mugs filled with dirty water and floating food debris sitting in the kitchen sink.

"Cabinet to your left."

Jane opened the cabinet and pulled out two glasses. "Jelly jars? Really? At your age?"

She returned the glasses to the shelf. She proceeded to give the mugs in the sink a thorough wash. By now, the coffee was ready. She poured two cups and handed him one. "Well?"

James took a cautious sip, keeping his eyes on the reporter. The coffee was hot, almost as hot as his temper. "I'm sorry for ditching you back there. I shouldn't have," he forced himself to say.

"No, you shouldn't."

"It was a lousy thing to do," he found himself saying.

"Yes, it was." Jane smiled. "Don't you feel better

now?" She sashayed—there was no other word to describe it—to the sofa, mug in hand. "Come. Join me." She patted the cushion beside her as if calling her pet collie.

James flung himself down as far from her as possible, balancing his mug on his knee. "The woman?"

Tiny, nearly invisible wrinkles appeared at the corners of Jane's eyes. "Ronnie Tench."

"Ronnie Tench? Owner of Tow The Line?"

"The very same."

"I thought Ronnie Tench was a man." James drank thoughtfully. The coffee was delicious and he hadn't even added sugar like he would normally.

"It's because I washed the pot and cleaned the filter," Jane said as if reading his mind.

"Tell me about Ronnie Tench. How did you find out about her?"

"I have my sources." There was no way she was going to tell him she looked up the Tow The Line webpage and found Ronnie Tench's picture plastered there. "Veronica Tench, one tough cookie. Built the business practically single-handed."

Jane set down her coffee and reached for her purse. "Opened her first Tow The Line territory in the Jacksonville area." Jane read from her notebook. "She's been working her way down Florida ever since. Gobbling up the competition or putting them out of business in the process."

James whistled. "Married?"

"Me?"

He frowned. "Ronnie Tench."

"That's an interesting question." Jane tapped her finger against the page of her notebook. "Her husband disappeared off the coast of Bimini about a decade ago.

Leaving Veronica a very wealthy widow. He was a developer and insured to the hilt."

"Drowned?"

"Either that or she fed him to the sharks."

James sipped thoughtfully. "I'd like to meet her. I went by her office but got rebuffed by some smarmy kid in a skinny tie."

Jane was smiling brightly—like her name.

"What?"

"Play your cards right, James, and I'll let you join me."

"At what?" James stomped to the kitchen for more coffee to which he added a shot of amaretto. "You want some?" The caffeine was going to make him jittery. The amaretto would stave off the effect.

Jane declined. "I have an appointment with Ms. Tench tomorrow morning at ten."

"How did you manage that?"

"I'm a reporter, James. I have a way of opening doors."

"Yeah, and entering them uninvited."

"That's not a very nice thing to say. Do you want to come with me or not?"

"Yes," James hated to admit. "I do. What time?"

"Ten a.m. Sharp." She'd been stretching the truth with James but had plenty of confidence in herself. All she needed was a little time to come up with a plan for getting in to see Tench.

"Fine. That gives me time to pick up my car at Smiley's first. I'll meet you at Tow The Line."

"Great. Now that we have that settled, tell me what you learned today."

James hung over the counter with his mug in

hand. "I learned that Adler is suing Smiley's for ten million bucks and that he does not like uninvited guests."

"Hmm. That is interesting." She riffled through the pages of her notebook. "I googled Mr. Adler. He claims to have been injured on the job. He filed for disability, which Kevin Rain contested."

"Yeah and guess who Kevin Rain hired to find some dirt on Adler?"

"Who?"

"Bruno Caliostro."

Jane arched her brow. "The plot, as they say, thickens."

"Thickens or sickens. Either way, I'd sure like to know what's going on." He was finding it hard to breathe. Like somebody, Lt. Byrd most likely, was tightening a noose around his neck at that very minute.

His too-young-to-be-strung-up-for-a-murder-he-didn't-commit neck.

32

The following morning, James arrived at Smiley's at nine thirty. Plenty of time to pick up his Nissan and meet Jane at Tow The Line. A couple of cars and a solitary tow truck sat in the front lot and the smiling face over the door rotated as if nothing bad had ever happened there.

James opened the door expecting a blast of cold air but it was remarkably warm inside. If anything good was going to come from the death of Kevin Rain, it was that Smiley's monthly electric bill would decrease.

James loosened the top button of his cotton shirt. He had opted for a pair of rarely worn brown slacks, an Oxford shirt and tan loafers. If he was going to play detective, he figured he ought to look the part. Maybe it would make the subjects he needed to interview take him more seriously than if he showed up in blue jeans and a T-shirt.

All he needed was a checkered sport coat and he could be Jim Rockford.

"I'm here to pick up my car."

Adam Mitchell was making himself at home behind Kevin Rain's desk. A smug smirk sat on his face. "Are you now?" He folded his python-like arms across his thick chest and swiveled lazily side to side. The phone on the wall rang incessantly.

"Is Alyssa around?" James looked about. No one else was in the office but he heard sounds coming from down the hall.

"She's taking a couple of days off." Adam Mitchell pushed his elbows against the desk. James swore he heard it creak. "The murder and all."

"Right. About my car. It's a gray Nissan Cube." James cocked his head as Mitchell displayed a couple rows of unhygienic yellow teeth. "Something funny?"

"It's a cube, all right."

"What's that supposed to mean?"

Adam Mitchell shuffled through the papers in a plastic letter tray teetering on the far right corner of the desk. Finding one he liked, he slammed it against the desktop and turned it for James to read.

James' face fell and his blood quickened as he scanned the document. "You had my car taken to a junk yard?"

"Not me." Adam Mitchell laced his fat fingers behind his thick head. "I'm not in charge here."

"You're saying Alyssa did this?" He couldn't believe it. "Here I am trying to help her find out who killed her husband and she has my car hauled off to a junk yard?"

The tow truck driver sighed like he didn't mean it. "Could've been anybody. All I know is that the order came in to send it off due to delinquent payment of fees owed."

James' eyes burned red. "I was going to pick my car up today. Take care of the charges." He waved his checkbook in the air. "Not that there should have been any charges. My car never should have been towed in the first place!"

"Don't yell at me, Stewart. I only work here."

"If you had anything to do with this—" James balled up his hands.

"Is that a threat?"

"Yes, is that a threat, Mr. Stewart?"

James spun on his heels. "Lt. Byrd!" He took a step back. "I'm surprised to see you here."

"Why? I've got a murder to solve. What about you? Do you really think you should be here?" she said icily. "Not planning on providing me with a second corpse are you?"

James colored. "No, I only wanted to pick up my car. Mitchell says it's been relegated to the scrap heap."

"Is that so?" She was looking at Adam Mitchell.

"Yes, ma'am." The tow truck operator showed her the paperwork. "All I know is that it was taken on a hauler this morning. Standard procedure. All official like."

Now Lt. Byrd was looking at James. "Everything looks in order. It seems to me you should have paid your bill promptly."

"I didn't think—that is, how was I to know..." He squeezed his eyes shut. "I want to file charges, lieutenant."

"What sort of charges?" Lt. Byrd tipped her hat off her forehead.

"Criminal charges. Mitchell here has had my car hauled off to some scrap yard."

"I told you. It wasn't me."

"Yeah, right."

"Besides, I only work here. You want to file a criminal complaint, file it against Alyssa. She owns this joint. You want to press charges against the new widow, Stewart?"

"No." He did not. Besides, what would Cindi think of him if he did?

"Sounds like a civil matter to me," cut in Lt. Byrd. "Talk to a lawyer, Mr. Stewart. I'm really thinking you're gonna need one."

"What I need is my car."

The tow truck driver's grin widened. "If you hurry, Stewart, you might just make it in time to prevent it going to the crusher."

"You son of a—"

Adam Mitchell tipped back his head and laughed. James lunged out the door with the staccato beat of Adam Mitchell's glee ringing in his ears.

Lt. Byrd's wiry fingers dug into James' shoulder as he reached for the door of the Ferrari. "Got a minute?"

"What do you think?" James took a step back, forcing her to let go. "You heard him, lieutenant. My car is about to be squashed like a bug."

"What are you worried about your car for?" Lt. Byrd looked pointedly up and down the length of the rare Ferrari. "You've got a car. In fact, it seems to me you're moving up in the world."

"This car's not mine. It belongs to my brother. You know, the guy that's married to Sheryl Stewart, the city attorney." James knew better than to antagonize the officer but he couldn't help himself.

"Ms. Stewart can't save you if you're guilty." She fanned her face with her cap.

"I'm not guilty so it doesn't matter. Besides, I can save myself." He fell against the hot car. Sweat dribbled down his forehead.

"Don't get involved, Stewart."

"I am involved, whether I like it or not." He pushed

off from the car before he ended up with second-degree burns from the hot steel. "Why are you here?"

"Following up leads. Re-interviewing witnesses." She slapped her hat against her palm. "All standard operating procedure. Take you, for instance."

"What about me?"

"Your alibi doesn't hold up."

"I didn't do anything. I don't need an alibi."

"You were alone in Cindi Keach's apartment," Lt. Byrd went on, ignoring James' feeble retort. "You admit you had the keys to Alyssa Rain's car. You had plenty of time to drive to Smiley's Towing Service, bop the victim on the back of the head while he played with his toy choo-choos, and return to the apartment before Cindi returned."

James tugged at his shirt collar.

"That's motive—you argued with him over impounding your car. Means—the tire iron found at the scene with your fingerprints on it. And now," she said, pulling back finger number three, "opportunity. And let's not forget the sunglasses."

"Yes," snapped James, "let's not forget the sunglasses. Can't forget the sunglasses."

She ignored his sarcasm. "You took Alyssa Rain's car while she was sleeping off a bender and murdered her husband. Wait." Her eyes flashed like tiny novas. "You aren't having an affair with the widow, are you?"

"What? That's crazy! Have you lost your mind? I never met Alyssa Rain until the night her husband was murdered. And I tell you what, I wish I'd never met her, her husband or anybody else related to this case!"

"Can you prove you never met Alyssa Rain before?"

"How can I prove a negative? Besides, I'm dating

her sister. Sort of. Do you really think they'd be okay with that?"

"Okay, okay. Alyssa Rain corroborates that. She only has a vague memory of meeting you the night of the murder."

"She was incapacitated."

"She was drunk. Cindi, on the other hand, was sober when she lied to us."

"She never lied."

"She told me she was with you the night of the murder."

"So she went out shopping for a few things and forgot to mention it. No big deal."

"It is when it provides you with an alibi."

"A lot of people wanted Kevin Rain dead, Lieutenant." At least, that was the impression practically everybody involved in his life was giving him. "Have you talked to Felicity Rain?"

"Yes, as a matter of fact, I have. Why?"

"Come on, we both know that spouses are often murdering one another."

"Except in this case, Felicity Rain is the ex-spouse with little to gain from Kevin Rain's death."

"Maybe."

"You know something I don't?" She gave him a searching look.

James shifted uneasily. "No." He debated telling her about Kourtney and Dale's suspicions concerning their mother and decided against it. What Jane had said could be true. The pair could have been misdirecting him when they were themselves the guilty parties.

The last thing he wanted was to look like an idiot in front of Lt. Byrd. She already had a dreadfully low opinion of him. Besides, he could use another day or two on Kourtney and Dale's payroll.

Lt. Byrd tilted her head, waiting him out.

"Fine. I happened to see Felicity Rain meeting with Veronica Tench. She's the owner of Smiley's biggest competitor, Tow The Line."

"So?"

"Maybe the two of them conspired to murder Kevin Rain."

"In an attempt to take over the business."

"Something like that." James stuck his chin out, pulling his car key from his pocket. Kourtney and Dale had intimated that their mother wanted to sell Smiley's to Tow The Line and reap a big payday. But was it true?

"And you just happened to see them together."

"I was getting a bagel. There they were."

"What a coincidence."

"Yes, it was, wasn't it?"

"Any other coincidences I should know about?"

James did some thinking. It couldn't hurt to tell her about Phil Adler. The more suspects, the merrier. "An ex-employee by the name of Phil Adler is suing Smiley's for ten million dollars."

Lt. Byrd twitched. "Adler, you say?" She pulled a notepad from her belt and began writing quickly.

"That's right. He was injured on the job. Claimed workers compensation or something. I'm not quite sure." James pulled open the car door, forcing Lt. Byrd to move aside. "I'm still looking into it."

Lt. Byrd grabbed the end of his shirt sleeve. "Don't look into anything, Mr. Stewart. That's what the police are for."

He climbed into the Ferrari and twisted the key in

the ignition, getting some satisfaction in watching her jump a foot in the air in response to the brash noise that blasted from the engine compartment. Maybe there was something wrong with the muffler or the tailpipe. Maybe he would mention it to Roger.

Maybe he would just continue to enjoy watching people's startled reactions.

James slammed the door and rolled down his window. "It's nice to know the police are good for something."

James made an angry three-point turn, hit the road and glanced nervously in the rearview mirror, realizing he probably shouldn't have come off so strong. The smoldering look Lt. Byrd was giving him was definitely of the *can kill* variety.

33

Jane glared at her watch but the face she saw belonged to James Stewart. Where the heck was he?

Here she was, wasting time sitting in her VW, watching the sun bake the wilting palm trees. He had been supposed to meet her here at Tow The Line over an hour ago. "Men."

Jane had had enough. She threw open her car door and slammed it behind her. "You can't count on them to do anything right."

The reporter tugged at the hem of her pale green skirt. She had half a mind not to share what she learned interviewing Ms. Tench with James. If he was going to continue to be difficult, he could darn well take care of himself.

Marching to the entrance, she studied her reflection in the shiny windows. Hair in place, blouse tucked in. Check.

A pale-faced young man with short dark hair and calculating eyes handed a cup of coffee to a woman seated in the lounge with an open magazine balanced on her lap. "Good morning, miss. How can I help you?"

Jane handed the man a business card. "Jane Bright, Broward County Times."

The man adjusted his skinny black tie. His equally pale arms protruded at odd angles from his short-sleeve white shirt. "How can I be of service?"

"I'm here to interview Veronica Tench." Having failed to come up with a reasonable ploy, she had opted for the take-them-by-surprise approach.

"Oh? May I ask what this is in regard to?"

"Of course." What was with this guy? Why was he being so obstructionistic? It wasn't like she was trying to get in to see the governor. Were all men out to get her goat today? "I wanted to interview Ms. Tench about her plants."

"My plants?"

Jane looked over the man's shoulder. At the top of a broad concrete staircase bordered by a sleek aluminum railing, a woman stood. Veronica Tench. She recognized her from her photo and the bagel shop the other day. "Hello, Ms. Tench?"

"That's correct." Ronnie Tench was dressed elegantly in silvery-gray silk slacks and matching jacket with a white blouse underneath. She moved slowly down the stairs, tapping an ink pen rhythmically against the railing as she did so.

"What's this about my plants?" With a nod of the head, she shooed her assistant away.

"I'm Jane Bright. I'm a reporter for the Broward County Times. Perhaps you've heard of it?" She suddenly realized she may have to tread carefully here. Was she one of the paper's advertisers? She cursed herself for not checking first. Because, if so and Jane made her mad, Lou would be furious with her.

Ronnie Tench said nothing as she took the business card Jane offered her and scanned her eyes over it before setting it down on a nearby credenza.

"I wanted to speak with you about your office

plants."

"Honey." She patted Jane's shoulder solicitously. "I've already got a service for that. I'm quite happy with them. Sorry."

"No, that's not what I meant." Jane dug in her heels as Ronnie pushed her toward the door.

"What did you mean?"

"I write a gardening column. I thought our readers would be interested in reading about your collection."

Ronnie eyed her with not unreasonable suspicion. "My collection? Honey, all we've got around here is a bunch of potted plants." She waved her arm in circle. "And we rent these on a monthly basis."

"I see." Jane thought quickly. "What about at your home? Our readers are always interested in what local business owners' personal gardens are like." Did that sound as inane to Ronnie Tench as it had to her? Jane hoped not.

Ronnie frowned. She picked at her teeth with Jane's business card. "They are?" she asked dubiously.

"Sure they are. It means lots of free publicity. Why, some months ago," please don't check, she prayed, "we did an article on another company similar to yours. Smiley's Towing Service. Perhaps you've heard of them?"

Ronnie waved to her skinny-tied assistant. He hastened to her side. "You did, did you?"

"Y-yes," Jane replied nervously.

"I suppose you've heard that the owner of Smiley's is now dead?"

"Yes, I did hear something about that."

The guy beside her was smiling.

"And do you know *why* he is dead?" Ronnie Tench

asked in a voice hard as nails.

"No." Jane gulped. The last visitor had left and the three of them were alone in the austere office.

"Because he didn't know how the world works."

"I'm afraid I don't understand."

"Exactly. You have to understand how the world works. Otherwise you might end up dead. Or worse."

"What could be worse than dead?" Jane made the mistake of asking. Jane's heart thumped against her chest as Ronnie eyed her in terrifying silence.

Finally, Ronnie Tench said, "Honey, you do not want to know."

With another brisk nod of the head from his boss, Tench's assistant escorted Jane outside. Leaning in, he whispered in her ear, "Get lost and stay lost."

Jane didn't bother to respond.

Skinny Tie stood, arms folded, watching her carefully, until she disappeared down the road.

Had she just been threatened?

It was a scary and chilling, yet at the same time thrilling, sensation. Maybe she was on to something. She smiled. *In your face, James Stewart.*

34

Southern Autocyclers, the establishment listed on the paperwork Adam Mitchell had shoved in James' face, was way out at the west end of Broward County. Roger had offered to run him out there in the BMW and picked him up at the duplex that morning.

When Roger noticed that the Ferrari was nowhere in sight, James told him he had dropped it off at a car wash/detail service to get it cleaned up for him.

The truth was he'd hidden it under a tarp in the carport of a buddy of his up the street. Until he could figure out what to do about it, he didn't dare let Roger see it.

Due to road construction, it was nearly noon when James and Roger pulled into the crowded Southern Autocyclers lot.

Stepping into the cluttered trailer office, a sweating bear of a man with a thick black beard and bulging brown eyes greeted them. "Buying or selling?"

"Hello. I'm James Stewart. I was told that my car was brought here this morning. From Smiley's Towing Service. A silver-gray Nissan Cube."

"Looks like a big, ugly toaster on wheels," quipped Roger.

"Not helping," James said.

"You got a VIN or plate number?" The man's hands

hovered over a grimy beige keyboard and his eyes locked onto a computer screen planted on the chest-high countertop.

"Maybe. You see it never should have been towed and then it was brought here. I really need it back."

"So gimme something to go on, buddy."

"Right." James fished around in his wallet. "Here it is." He read off the license plate number and VIN.

The man repeated what James had said and keyed the numbers into his computer. His forehead twitched. The big boxy fan on the table behind him hummed noisily, rustling his thinning hair. "What's the matter? You leave something valuable in it?" His fingers paused over the keyboard and he grunted.

"The whole car is valuable."

"Uh-huh," he replied disinterestedly.

Roger chuckled.

"Well?"

The man's eyes flicked up. "Too late. You wanna look at the remains?"

James gulped. "Remains?"

"Yep. She's stacked up in quadrant C12." He turned and pointed towards the rear of the trailer. "If you go back out front and turn left through the gates, then follow the—"

"Never mind." James turned on his heels. He had already seen one dead body too many. He didn't need to see his dead Cube.

"Sorry, bro." Roger cupped his hand over James' shoulder. "You can keep the Dino as long as you like."

"Thanks." James slumped into the passenger seat. It was going to be a very long day. "Don't tell Sheryl. I don't need her getting all over me for getting free use of one of your vehicles."

"Bank on it," replied Roger. "She'd kill us both, if she knew. She thinks I'm enabling you."

"Seriously?" James' eyes flew from the road to his brother. "To do what?"

Roger shrugged off any answer. "Sheryl means well. She wants to help you."

"I'd hate to see what she's like when she's trying to hurt me."

"Let's hope you never do," Roger said, tapping the brakes as they hit a patch of slow-moving traffic. "Let's hope you never do."

After his brother dropped him back off at the duplex, James retrieved the Dino and ran to a drive-thru for a sandwich and a soda. Waiting in the pickup line, he dialled Dale Rain's number. They arranged to meet at his office downtown and James arrived some forty minutes later.

"Business must be good." James rubbed the supple leather chair.

"It is." Dale Rain sat across from him behind a desk as big as a battleship. "If you're in the market for a property and need a mortgage, I can get you an excellent rate."

James smiled. "Not with my credit rating, you can't."

Dale played with an 18k gold fountain pen. He had a great view of the city skyline from his corner office. Outside his door, a comely secretary sat at her desk, keeping the riff-raff at bay and serving beverages to their well-heeled clientele. "What can I do for you, Mr. Stewart? I'm expecting a client any minute."

"It's like this. The first time I met your mother, at

Alyssa's apartment, if you remember?" Dale nodded and James continued. "I got the impression that she wasn't fond of Ronnie Tench."

"And?"

"I saw your mother and Ronnie Tench having a meeting in Boca."

If Dale was surprised, he wasn't going to let it show. "In commerce, Mr. Stewart, you don't have to like someone to do business with them."

"Is that your company motto?" When Dale didn't laugh at his joke, James plunged ahead. "Why would Ronnie Tench want to buy a business that Alyssa Rain says is up to its eyeballs in debt? That sounds like a pretty dumb move from where I sit. And Ronnie Tench, from what I've learned, is not dumb. Not by a long shot."

"I really wouldn't know. You're the detective. That's why I'm paying you, remember?" Dale glanced past James as his secretary stuck her head.

"Your clients have arrived, Mr. Rain."

"Ply them with espresso and biscotti, would you? I'll be finished shortly."

His secretary nodded and left.

"Will there be anything else, Mr. Stewart? I'd think your time could be spent better elsewhere. And, like I said, I am paying you for that time. Rather handsomely, too, I might add."

James was liking this guy less by the minute. Despite the money he was getting from him. He took a moment to settle his anger. "Does it surprise you that your mother and Ms. Tench had a meeting?"

"Nothing my mother does surprises me. As for Tench, have you spoken to her yet?"

"Not yet. But I plan to." Because of his car troubles,

he had missed his appointment with her and Jane Bright.

Now the reporter wasn't answering her phone. Not that he was going to tell Dale Rain any of that. How would that make him look as a PI?

James ran his hands up and down his thighs. "You know, if your mother is implicated in any of this, she could go to prison."

Dale Rain smiled for the first time since James had stepped across his threshold. It wasn't much of a smile but his lips were curving ever so slightly upward. "My mother can take care of herself."

"I'll bet. Her and Ronnie Tench."

Dale rattled his pen against the desktop. "You think they may have conspired together to murder my father?"

James shrugged. "It's possible, isn't it? By the way, I also learned through my sources that Ronnie Tench is a widow. It seems her husband disappeared at sea, leaving her very wealthy."

"Lucky her."

James cocked his head. That wasn't the reply he had been expecting but it was doozy.

"Is there anything else?" Dale Rain stood, his black tie dangled over his desk like a snake searching for a rat to swallow. He reminded James of an undertaker in his somber black suit with fine gray pinstriping.

James took the hint and climbed to his feet. Nobody had even offered him so much as a glass of cold water, let alone biscotti and espresso. "I'm looking into Phil Adler too. There might be something there."

"Oh?"

"Did you ever meet him?"

"Never. Like I said, I never had much to do with Dad's business."

"Yet you know the name."

"I must have heard it mentioned."

"Right. I went by Adler's place out in Davie."

"Did you talk to him?"

"The timing wasn't right." Once again, he'd only look like the blundering incompetent that he was if he mentioned to his paying client that he had been run off by a duo of hungry Rottweilers that'd tried to make a meal of his car. "He had company."

"Do you know who?"

"There was a tow truck parked in front of his house."

"One of Smiley's?" Dale asked as he swept around the side of his desk and headed to the door of his office.

"Nope. Tow The Line."

"Tow The—"

James was pleased to see that something that he had said had finally gotten under Dale's skin. Shaken him up.

"He's all yours, folks," James said to the nervous young couple holding hands on the sofa, about to sign their lives away on an overpriced house in the burbs, no doubt.

"Sorry to keep you waiting." Dale Rain's cool, smug mask had shattered. He now looked fazed and confused.

Like Humpty-Dumpty must have looked in free-fall.

James wondered exactly what he'd said that had cracked Dale's cool façade.

35

James carefully angled the Ferrari out of the parking garage and shoved his ticket in the pay station slot. His cellphone jangled. He let it ring as he dug out his wallet and grabbed a credit card.

As James paid for his parking—there would be no more daring the gods of street parking from him for a long time to come—the phone went silent but for a beep signalling that he had a new message.

Once outside, James sidled up to the curb to check his phone. It was Roger. Without bothering to hear the message, he dialled his brother. "What's up?"

"Where are you? I've got a buyer interested in the Dino."

"I'm on Las Olas but—"

"Great, see you in ten. Don't worry, I'll scrounge you up something else." Roger cut the connection.

Knowing he would have to face the music and the consequences for the damaged Dino sooner or later, James drove to Stewart Classic Motors.

Roger was showing a slim gentleman in loose brown slacks and a white shirt a preowned Porsche 911S convertible. With them was a young woman with very long and very straight straw-colored hair. She was half the gentleman's age. This being South Florida, that didn't narrow things down much. She could be either his daughter, his nanny or his new bride.

James parked the Ferrari up near the entrance. Two young men, SCM employees, were busily detailing a white on red BMW M3 under the canopy attached to the building.

Roger left his customer and hurried over to his brother. "Perfect." He cocked his head. "That's them over there. Sid Hornsby. He's bought a dozen cars from me over the years."

"Who's the girl?"

Roger smiled. "Mrs. Hornsby. Katrina."

"Lucky guy."

"Yeah, Sid says fourth time is the charm."

"Fourth? I'm surprised he has any money left for cars."

"His pockets run deep." Roger began moving around the Ferrari. "And he likes exotics. This Dino is about as exotic as it gets."

Roger tapped his watch. "Where exactly have you been driving? This thing is filthy." Roger poked his head in the open window. "Beer cans, hair, sand, fast food wrappers. I can't show Sid a car looking like this. There's crap everywhere," he complained with a loud sigh.

"You didn't give me much notice."

"Maybe I can get him and the wife to have a drink down the street while I get the Dino detailed."

"What the hell?" Roger had reached the opposite side of the car. "What happened?" He looked across the roof of the car at his brother. "What did you do to the Dino?"

Roger stepped back, eyes filled with horror as he took in the jagged scratch marks and gnawed remains of the sideview mirror.

"It wasn't me," James stuttered. "There were these dogs—"

"Dogs?" Roger looked aghast. "You let dogs in the car? I told you you could borrow the car James but I didn't tell you you could use it to haul dogs around town. And the hood!" He clutched his head between his hands.

"That's not what happened."

Roger pulled James aside. "So what did happen?" The brothers were aware of Mr. and Mrs. Hornsby eyeing them from the shade thrown by the canvas awning over the office entrance.

"A couple of Rottweilers started chasing me. It's a good thing I got away when I did. I mean, they could have done more damage. Maybe even eaten the whole car. As it was, they only ate the one tire and I was able to fix that...sort of. You're lucky."

"Lucky, right." Roger swore. "Scratches up and down the door panels, the fender. And look at this mirror!" He gripped the sideview mirror. "It looks like one of them took a bite out of it."

The mirror split in two. He cradled the pieces, a look of horror on his face. "Dogs don't just do this sort of thing. You must have provoked them. You provoked them, didn't you?"

Sid Hornsby and his wife strode over, holding hands like a pair of young newlyweds. Katrina sported a wedding ring with a diamond the size of a tennis ball. She was young and she was pretty.

And she knew it.

Katrina cast a *you-can-look-but-you-can't touch* glance at James and shook her perfect head. "Is this the car, Sid, sweetie?" She sounded disappointed.

Who could blame her?

Sid Hornsby had an eye for cars like he had an eye for brides. "I'm surprised in you, Roger. The way you described the Dino, I was expecting something in much superior condition." He tilted his thick eyeglasses down his nose as he studied the marred red surface of the Ferrari.

"Me, too," Roger said tightly. "I'm sure once the guys detail it—"

"It's hot and baby is thirsty." Sid patted his young bride's cheek. "You call me if you get anything special in."

"I'm sure those marks will buff right out," promised Roger. Of course, nothing could be further from the truth.

Sid merely waved and slid behind the wheel of a huge silver Mercedes AMG sedan with Katrina at his side.

"Sorry about that." James watched the Mercedes bounce out of the lot. "I didn't mean to cost you a sale."

"Sure." Roger thrust his hands in the pockets of his navy blazer. He heard a tear and saw the fingers of his right hand poking out the bottom of the torn pocket.

Roger swore and marched to the office. James followed. Roger hung his blazer on the brass stand in the corner behind his desk, threw himself into his chair, and began scanning his email and text messages.

A car dealer's life was a hectic one.

James skipped the guest chairs and fell onto the short black leather sofa against the wall after helping himself to a plastic cup of water from the cooler in the corner. "This is probably the worst possible time to bring it up...but you did say I could keep the Dino a little longer."

"You're right." Roger paused and carefully set his phone atop his mid-century modern desk. "This is the worst possible time."

James squirmed.

"Then again," relented Roger. "I don't suppose you could do it any more harm."

"Right. And I swear I'll reimburse you for the damages."

"If you do any more damage, do me a favor and total the damn thing." Roger pressed the heels of his hands against his eyes. "I'd rather have the insurance money at that point. It's probably lost half its book value already."

"Sorry." James dragged his teeth over his lower lip. "It really wasn't my fault. Those dogs—"

"Let's drop it," Roger said wearily. "Though, it is kinda funny. I can just picture it." He suddenly burst out laughing then stopped just as suddenly. "Sheryl can never know."

"Trust me, my lips are sealed."

Roger leaned over the desk. "You got pictures, didn't you?" He thrust out his hand. "Give me your phone. I want to see them."

Roger waved his hand impatiently. "Did you video those Rottweilers chewing on the Ferrari? Oh, man. We could post this on YouTube. This could go viral. Hey, it might even be good for business. We can run the Stewart Classic Motors banner under the video and—"

"I don't have any pictures, Roger."

"You don't?"

"No pictures. No video." Thankfully.

Roger fell back in his chair. "Too bad."

"Would you please stop grinning?"

Roger poured himself a mugful of iced tea from the thermos bottle that Sheryl prepared for him every day. She insisted that green tea was good for him and that he drink two cups per day whether he liked it or not.

"Sorry," Roger said finally. "This is really not your day."

"I'm glad you're finally coming to realize that. This being a PI thing is hard."

"Yeah." Roger planted his elbows on the desk, laced his fingers and rested his chin on his thumbs. "But I'll bet it's nothing compared to being charged with murder."

James was afraid to ask what Roger was talking about but knew he had no choice. "Are you trying to tell me something?"

Roger's chair squeaked as he leaned back. "I'm not supposed to say anything...but Sheryl's under a lot of pressure to charge you for the murder of Kevin Rain. She's taking a lot of heat."

"I'm sure she can handle it."

"Maybe. The mayor herself is pressing her on this. She says it's making the city look bad having a murderer running around loose."

"I suppose."

"Mayor Toms thinks the city would look much better and the voters would sleep better too knowing that there was a suspect in custody."

"Makes sense." James refilled his cup and sipped.

"I'm glad you understand." Roger propped his tasseled Italian leather loafers on his desk. "Sheryl is going to announce your arrest tomorrow."

36

"What?" James leapt off the sofa, throwing water in every direction.

"Hey, watch it!" Roger pulled out a paper towel and dabbed puddles of water off his papers.

"Can't you stop her? Talk her out of it?"

"Yeah. There is one way," Roger said with hesitation. He grabbed a handful of wet papers and shook them out. "You got water all over these contracts."

"What way?"

"I'll tell you." Roger smoothed out the typed contracts on his desk. "But you're not going to like it."

"Spill it, already. I'll do anything."

"Sheryl wants you to get a job." Roger leaned on the corner of his desk.

"I've got a job. I'm going to detective school."

"You got thrown out, remember?"

"Temporarily. And I've already got a paying client."

"You'll be tossed out of school permanently if you're arrested for murder. Plus, I doubt Kourtney and Dale Rain will be paying you for your services if you're the one charged with killing their dad. Kids can be funny about things like that."

Roger was clearly enjoying himself. "Besides, Sheryl wants you to get a real job."

"A real job? Where am I going to get a real job at

this point?" His resumé, lousy to begin with, had been made worse by this whole murder thing. What could he list as his last position of note: Finder of dead body?

"James, I'm glad you asked." Roger draped an arm over James' neck and dragged him behind the desk. He slid open a two-drawer oak cabinet.

James watched warily as Roger pulled out three light blue polo shirts and three khaki-colored pairs of cuffed slacks. Each piece was new, wrapped in clear plastic.

And hideous to behold.

Roger dropped the pile of clothes in James' hands.

"What's all this?" James eyed the geeky clothing.

"I almost forgot." Roger grabbed a covered hanger from the brass rack and unzipped it. "Your new blazer."

James' mouth fell open. The blazer and the clothes were identical to his brother's. "You don't mean—"

Roger flashed a victory smile. "Sheryl wants you to work here." He held out his hand. "Welcome to Stewart Classic Motors, James."

"Oh, no. You can't be serious." James dropped the pile of clothes on Roger's desk. "This is a joke, right? You're putting me on."

Roger pulled out his smartphone and offered it to James. "You want to call Sheryl? Ask her to verify?"

"You think I won't?" James snatched the phone from Roger and speed-dialed his sister-in-law. His brother was lying. Conning him.

"Hello, Sheryl? It's me, James. Roger's been feeding me a bunch of garbage about how you're going to charge me with murder if I don't—" James winced. "Yeah, but —" He tugged at his collar. "Sure, but you see I—"

Roger smirked as Sheryl continued talking and

James' face grew whiter and whiter. For Roger, it was nice, very nice not to be on the receiving end of Sheryl's wrath for once.

After a minute during which his brother's complexion and demeanor had changed from that of a cocksure wannabe PI to that of a day-old corpse, James handed Roger back the smartphone.

Roger said goodbye to his wife then turned to James who was slumped on the sofa, a hangdog expression chiseled on his face. "You start tomorrow."

James managed to lift his head just enough to make eye contact with Roger. "You're enjoying this, aren't you?"

"Of course. Isn't it obvious?"

"About the Ferrari..."

Roger threw up his hand. "You know my motto."

"You don't have a motto."

"I do now." Roger spread his hands like a Broadway marquee. "You scratch it, you—"

"Bought it." James finished the sentence, not wanting to give Roger the satisfaction. He pushed himself off the sofa and plodded to the door.

"Don't forget these." Roger shoved the shirts, slacks and blazer at his brother.

"Thanks." James shouldered his way out. He dumped the clothes on the passenger seat of the Dino and climbed in. "How am I expected to pay you back for the Ferrari?"

"You can make payments." Roger folded his arms. "Sheryl also said to take your rent out of your paychecks. I'll do the same for the Dino."

"Let me get this straight." James' foot played with the gas pedal. "You're going to pay me to work here but deduct the rent on the duplex, plus a monthly payment on the car?"

"You got it. That's the deal. Cheer up. It won't be so bad. In a few years, we'll be square. Plus, she told me to add in the back rent a little each payday."

"How am I going to make any money?" James complained. "It seems to me everything I make goes back to you."

"And it seems to me that you, big brother, are going to have to hustle your butt and sell some cars, if you want to get ahead." Roger leaned against the roof of the Ferrari.

"I don't like it."

Roger and James stared each other down until a housefly landed on James' nose. He blew it away with a puff of hot breath.

"You don't have to take the deal, James. You can always say no. Of course, you will face the wrath of Sheryl. And maybe twenty to life."

James fixed his hand on the gated shift knob and shoved the Dino into gear. "I'm facing it now."

Roger slugged James in the upper arm. "She only wants what's best for you, bro."

"Yeah, you keep saying that." James rubbed his shoulder. "How do you sleep with yourself at night?"

"I don't," Roger said slickly. "I sleep with a beautiful young woman with a killer sex drive. You should try it sometime. It'll do wonders for you. In fact—"

James sped off, coaxing every bit of obnoxious noise out of the mufflers as he could. The fact was, the last thing he needed or wanted were any more facts or words of advice from his kid brother. Especially not about his sex life.

Extra-especially not about his sex life with Robo-Attorney.

37

"Thanks for coming tonight, Cindi." James pulled the cork from the bottle and poured. He had gone all out. Candles flickered on the table. Soft music played on the stereo.

The duplex had never looked so good.

Okay, so maybe Roger's parting shot had rattled him. Maybe he did need a good, steady woman in his life.

Cindi accepted her champagne and sipped. "Mmm. It's nice to get away from...things for a little while."

"How's Alyssa holding up?"

"Not so bad. Under the circumstances."

James nodded. They both knew what those circumstances were. Cindi was set to stun in a scoop-neck red dress and matching heels. She smelled good too. This was going to be James' last night of freedom and he planned to enjoy it to its fullest.

Tomorrow he would add used car salesman to his resumé, on the line right after murder suspect.

"Dig in." He had ordered tandoori chicken from a Punjabi restaurant on Oakland Park Blvd. The bags were in the trash. In the bin *under* the sink where it belonged.

"This is delicious." Cindi poked a bit of tender chicken with her fork and dropped it on her tongue.

"Thanks."

She delicately wiped her chin with a paper napkin. "I've never dated a guy who could cook like this." She set the napkin in her lap. "Who could cook at all, for that matter."

"I try." It wasn't a lie. He did try. He just wasn't any good at it.

"I'm sorry about your car."

James dropped his fork. "You heard?"

"Yeah." Cindi appeared dismayed. "Alyssa told me. I was there when Adam called from the office and told her she might be hearing from you."

"Your sister didn't have anything to do with that, did she?" James asked cautiously.

"Of course, not." Cindi shook her head. "How can you say that? Alyssa hasn't been going into Smiley's much. She got really mad at Adam. He swears it wasn't him though. If you ask me, it was just some sort of paperwork mix-up. Those things happen. Kevin wasn't the best at keeping things organized."

Cindi smiled wanly. "Except for his trains. Alyssa kept telling him he ought to get a secretary but he didn't want to spend the money."

"In an operation that size, I'm surprised he didn't have some sort of clerical help."

"Felicity used to handle all that. Before the divorce. Things went downhill after that."

"Speaking of Felicity, Kourtney and her brother, Dale, have asked me to look into Kevin's murder."

"Really?" Cindi scrunched up her nose. "That's weird."

"What's weird?"

"Those two never liked their father much." Cindi swirled some rice on her plate with her fork. "It wouldn't surprise me if one of them killed him."

"That's a popular opinion."

"Huh?"

"Don't they have alibis?"

"Sure," Cindi said pointedly, "each other."

"That's interesting." Very interesting. "I heard a man named Phil Adler filed a ten-million-dollar lawsuit against Smiley's."

"Alyssa is really worried about that. Lawyers' fees are eating up what little profits there are. She's pretty strapped for cash."

"So why doesn't she sell out to Ronnie Tench?"

"I keep telling her she should. But Alyssa says Kevin wouldn't have wanted her to. She wants to respect his wishes."

"I can understand that. Still, sometimes you have to—"

Cindi put a finger to her lips. "Shh." She leaned across the table and whispered. "Did you hear something?"

James watched the candle flame dance in her blue eyes. With a little luck, the flames of romance would soon follow. "No. Like what?"

"I thought I heard something." She stared out through the sliding glass door. Shadows cloaked the deck. The sluggish waters of the canal reflected the moon's face. Lights were on at the house across the way but, other than that, not so much as a night owl alligator was stirring.

James refilled their glasses. "It must have been the wind. Or maybe my neighbor." Probably spying on him. Needed to get a love life of her own.

He should have shut the drapes, but it was such

a nice night. Few clouds obscured the stars. Maybe they'd take the rest of the champagne outside after dinner. Dessert under the moonlight. He'd bought a cherry cheesecake for the occasion.

"There it goes again!" Cindi reached out and gripped James' hand.

"Huh?"

"Voices. I definitely heard noises."

James slowly set his glass at the edge of the table. He'd heard them now too. That was the second time in days that someone or something had been prowling around in the yard. "Maybe it's a cat."

"You have a cat?" Cindi perked at the thought.

"No. I'm not sure about my neighbor though." He wracked his brain but couldn't remember if he'd ever seen Roberta Higgins with a feline. He wouldn't have been surprised if she did. Probably lived with a whole herd of them.

"Maybe it's a raccoon or a possum." James slid back his chair. "I'll take care of it."

If it was Jane Bright, he was going to toss her butt in the canal. That might put a stop to her nasty habit of creeping up on him.

Cindi rested her hand atop James'. "Don't hurt it. It might bite."

"I won't. I'll just encourage him or her to move along." He pictured Jane sputtering and treading water in the foul canal.

Approaching the sliding glass door, he released the lock and slowly pushed the slider open. He poked his head outside and peered into the gloomy shadows.

Nothing.

James stepped outdoors. Lights were on in his

neighbor's unit, casting a small yellow patch on the weathered decking. "Here, kitty. Psst. Psst. Psst."

Still nothing.

Whatever or whoever it was had gone.

James moved to the end of the deck, placing his hands on the railing. For once, the weather was neither too hot nor too humid. This was definitely the place for a romantic lovers' rendezvous.

As he turned to go back inside and invite Cindi outside, a glint of something shiny caught his attention. He peered over the rail.

A dark hulking shape pressed right up against the bottom of his deck, which had a decorative latticework running around it. The glint had come from something in the person's hand.

He held his breath.

What was going on?

38

"James?" Cindi moved closer to the door. "Everything okay?"

"Yeah, fine. Stay inside," he said softly. He tiptoed to the rusted out barbecue grill at the corner of the deck, another cast-off of an earlier tenant.

Lifting the lid, he retrieved the stainless steel spit inside. The rod was thirty-two inches long, wicked sharp at one end with a handle at the other—a suburbanite saber.

James waved it silently in the air. Whoever was hiding down there was going to have a headache in the morning once he whacked them on the skull.

Moving stealthily back to the edge of the deck, James raised the spit over his shoulder and prepared to strike.

"He's going to hit him!" a man's alarmed voice shouted in the darkness.

"Quiet!" ordered a woman's voice, this coated with a thick Spanish accent.

James spun around. The voices had come from the other side of the deck. "Who's there?"

"Is everything okay?" This voice had come from whoever had been skulking at the back of the deck.

Moving instinctively, James brought the steel spit down on the dark silhouette as it jumped up at him, striking the stranger solidly on the shoulder.

"Ouch. He hit me!" A soft splash followed, like the sound a catfish makes struggling in the shallow water.

"My camera!" The stricken man howled in anguish. "He made me drop my camera!"

"Stop!" A woman's hand grabbed James' spit-wielding arm as he brought his arm back to strike again. Sharp fingernails dug into his flesh.

The patio light flicked on.

"I'm calling the police!" Cindi shouted.

"No!" James recognized the woman clutching his arm. "Suarez? What the hell is going on? What are you doing here?" He allowed his arm to relax and lowered the spit to his side.

In a moment, they were joined by Art Montgomery who was dragging the big guy from class—what was his name? Oliver something?—along with him.

The two men tromped up the deck steps.

Claudia Suarez let go of James and ran to the others. "Are you okay, Ollie?"

"Yeah." The big guy was clutching his shoulder. He sniffed. "He hit me and I dropped my camera."

"Don't worry. We'll get it back." Suarez's eyes glowed yellow as she glared at James. "What did you hit Ollie for?"

"What did I hit him for?" James replied with Cindi pressing up against his side. "I saw somebody lurking off my deck. It could have been a burglar or a murderer."

"Or a peeping tom." Cindi clutched James' forearm. "You'd be surprised how many of those I've had to deal with."

"*Dios mio*." Claudia Suarez let loose a string of foul words. At least, they sounded foul by the intonation and vehemence with which she spat them out.

Being flung in Spanish, James wasn't quite sure what each word meant but he got the gist of it.

"Give me that before you hurt somebody." Claudia Suarez snatched the spit from James' hand and sent it skittering across the deck.

"He was lurking in the dark. Taking pictures of us. If anybody is a peeper—"

"Come on, everybody." Claudia Suarez gave the injured man a shoulder to lean on. "Let's go inside."

"Sure," grumbled James, looking at the moon hovering up in the night sky like another opportunity lost. "Make yourselves at home."

"What about my camera?" moaned Ollie.

"We'll get it," promised Claudia Suarez. "If not, James will buy you another one."

"Oh no, he won't," said James.

"*Sí*," Claudia vowed. "He will."

"Hi." Artie walked up to Cindi. "I'm Arthur Montgomery. You seeing anybody?"

"Artie!" scolded Claudia. "Get the door."

"Sure, Claudia." Artie cowered and shuffled toward the house.

"See if you can find some ice for Ollie's shoulder."

"I will."

James pulled the door closed once they were all inside and shut off the patio light.

Artie had his nose in the freezer. "No ice tray?" His voice echoed in the box.

"Keep looking," James said truculently. "It's in there someplace."

James slumped down beside Cindi on the sofa as Art Montgomery, Claudia Suarez and the big guy, whose name seemed to be Ollie but that didn't seem right to James, made his home their own.

"Sorry," James mouthed to Cindi. Their shoulders touched and then their lips melted together. James felt a thrill but the sensation was short-lived.

Ollie pulled open the fridge. "Hey, cheesecake!" He lifted the lid of the plain white box he had found inside and sniffed. "Gotta be from Zelda's. She makes the best cheesecake."

Ollie twisted the box around in his hands. "There's no name. But I'm right, right? Zelda's?" He eyed James hopefully.

"I thought you made dessert?" Cindi blinked her troubled eyes.

"I did," James said through clenched teeth.

"Yeah, I'm right. Told you," he said to Art Montgomery. "Here's the bag. I found it."

James twisted his neck. Ollie had rummaged around under the kitchen sink and had found the bag from Zelda's in the trash. A summer shower had struck just as James was picking up the cake and the clerk had wrapped the box in a plastic bag.

James blushed.

"Who are all these people?" Cindi's soft breath tickled James' ear.

"Classmates."

"Huh?"

"From the School of Detection."

"Oh, Mr. Caliostro's school. Cool." Her head swivelled from one moving misfit to the next. Art Montgomery was snooping around in James' upper cabinets.

Ollie had set the cheesecake box on the counter and was slavering over it. The big guy's shoes were muddy and his gray pants were wet above the ankles from stepping in the canal.

"Were you guys like planning to have a study group tonight?" Cindi wanted to know.

"No," James replied adamantly. Where was that crazy cubana?

"Maybe I should go." Cindi's fingers inched towards her purse.

"No, please. Stay. I'll get rid of them. I promise."

"If you're sure..."

"I'm sure. Believe me, tonight is all about you and me."

Cindi smiled. "I'd like that."

So would he.

Claudia Suarez burst in from around the corner. "There's nothing in the bedroom."

"What were you doing in my—"

"Don't you have a flashlight in this dump?"

"In the bathroom, under the sink."

"What do you keep it there for?" Claudia planted her hands on her hips and scolded him with a look that sent Latin men as far away as Cuba diving for cover.

She turned, went into the bathroom, returning a minute later with a heavy black flashlight. She thumped it in the palm of her hand, flicked the switch on and off a couple times to make certain it had batteries. "Be right back."

39

Ollie and Artie had pulled out chairs and made themselves comfortable at the kitchen table. The cheesecake box sat between them. Ollie did the slicing.

"Listen, guys," James approached the kitchen table. "Cindi and I were kind of in the middle of something here." He nodded towards his date. "Know what I mean?"

Cindi smiled and waved from the sofa. "Cindi Keach. Pleased to meet you."

"Arthur Montgomery," the skinny kid repeated in case she didn't remember him introducing himself five minutes ago. "But you might as well call me Artie, everybody else does."

"I'm Greg Oliver." The big guy slid a generous helping of cherry cheesecake on Artie's plate. "Call me Ollie."

"Right, Ollie. How's the shoulder?"

Given his size, his fleshy face, deep-set brown eyes and the shock of dark hair that made him look like a walking chia pet, James predicted the man was going to find it difficult conducting undercover PI work.

"Stings." Ollie reproached James, "What did you have to hit me for?"

"I'm sorry, Ollie. I didn't realize that was you down there." Hiding off the end of my deck. On private property. Peeping on me and my date with a camera equipped with a telephoto lens.

"Yeah." Ollie shrugged it off. "You want cake?" He looked at Cindi. "Cheesecake, Cindi?"

"Yes, please."

James' date pranced to the table and joined the others. James blew out the candle—a waste of perfectly good beeswax—and pulled up a chair.

"James tells me you are all in school together," Cindi said. "That is so totally cool."

Artie spoke up. "Ollie is a trained chef. He was executive chef at a resort and caught his wife cheating on him."

"I came off shift early and found the two of them in bed," Ollie said glumly.

"Now he wants to learn detective skills," explained Artie.

"Poor Ollie." Cindi tilted her head and pouted.

"I'm a full-time student. Broward Community, in the criminal justice program," babbled Artie. He liked to talk but, like many talkers, wasn't much of a listener. "I'm gonna be a private detective."

Claudia Suarez, clad in an olive green blouse loose over a pair of light khaki shorts and sturdy hiking boots, returned from her trek outdoors.

"Got it." She held James' flashlight in one hand and a dripping long-lens camera in the other. Wet weeds clung to its sides.

Ollie looked crestfallen as she set the camera gently on the counter. It looked like a drowned small mammal.

Cindi gave him a hug. "Cheer up, Ollie. I'm sure your camera can be fixed up good as new. In fact, I know this guy. He's a real genius photographer. I should know.

I'm a model, you know. And actress.

"I'll give you one of my cards. In case, you know, you hear of anything." She whipped a card from her purse and slapped it in Ollie's hand. "Anyway, he's a whiz with these things."

"Really?" Ollie's watery eyes filled with hope.

"Yep. How about if you leave the camera with me? I'll take it to him in the morning."

"You're sweet. She's sweet, James." She rewarded him with a kiss on the forehead.

"Yeah, sweet." James' night was going downhill fast. That kiss should have been for him. He angrily buried a fork in his cheesecake and shoved a bit in his mouth. "Isn't it about time you tell me what you all were doing prowling around my backyard?"

James aimed the question at Claudia Suarez as she guzzled the rest of his champagne straight from the bottle.

She drained the bottle, plopped it on the coffee table with a bang. "Isn't it obvious?"

"If you're spying on me in the hopes of finding evidence that proves me guilty of murdering Kevin Rain, you are wasting your time. I didn't murder anybody." He squeezed his fingers tightly around his fork. "Yet."

"No offense but men are idiots." Claudia tore a side off the cake box, grabbed what was left of the cheesecake and used the cardboard as a plate. "Any halfwitted woman can pull the wolf over a man's eyes."

"Wool," interjected Artie, raising his finger.

"Yeah, wool over a man's eyes."

"Gee, why would we be offended? Right, Artie?" James was running out of patience. "And what does wool have to do with why the three of you have invaded my home?"

"Be nice, James," Cindi said. "These are your friends."

"These are not my friends." James jumped to his feet and paced. "In fact, I barely know them."

Claudia crossed her arms. "He got us all kicked out of school. Some friend."

Cindi's eyes grew wide. "Why would you do that?"

"I didn't do that. Not exactly."

"Mr. Caliostro says he requires a minimum number of students to hold a class," explained Artie.

"And with James booted out because of the whole murder thing, Bruno has suspended classes until further notice."

"Meaning," continued Artie, picking up for Ollie, "that we get another student or James gets cleared of murdering Kevin Rain."

"Which is why we are here." Claudia tossed the remains of her cake in the sink. "To help you, moron." She stuck out her chin. "Take a seat, Stewart."

James locked eyes with the high-strung cubana and lost.

40

James reclaimed his chair at the kitchen table between Ollie and Artie. Cindi dug his last six-pack of beer from the fridge and handed out the bottles.

Claudia yanked off her small green nylon backpack and set it on the table. Next, she carried a barstool to the table, sat and began rummaging around in her pack.

"Make yourself comfortable, everybody," mumbled James, fondling his unopened beer.

Claudia ignored him. "Here it is." She extracted a medium-sized notebook with a blue cover, one of those cheap ones you can buy anywhere for a buck or so.

Pulling a pair of tortoise-shell reading glasses from a pouch sewn onto the side of her pack, she slipped the glasses over her nose and read. "Kevin Rain, the deceased. Are you listening?" she smacked James in the ear with her notebook.

"Ouch." His hand flew to his ear.

"Pay attention. This is important."

Claudia had caught him looking longingly out the window at the stars, regretting every choice he had ever made in his life. Because it had all led to this moment. This miserable moment.

"Are you crazy? Of course, I'm listening." He jammed the opener onto his bottle cap and pried it off. "Keep talking." He tipped the bottle and chugged.

"Felicity Rain divorced Kevin seven years ago but, from all indications, their marriage was not a happy one prior to that."

James wiped his fingers across his lips—lips that should be kissing Cindi with an i right about now. "How do you know?"

"Save the questions till later," Claudia snapped, waiting to be sure James would comply before continuing. "Felicity Rain and Veronica Tench have been communicating with one another."

"We think they may have wanted to bump off Kevin and take over his business." Artie smiled at Cindi.

Claudia continued. "The two kids, Dale and Kourtney, have had little contact with their father and took their mother's side in the divorce. We also found that an outstanding lawsuit has been filed with Smiley's Towing Service and Kevin Rain named as defendants."

"I know all that," James risked interjecting. He was suddenly weary. Of the murder, of being a suspect, and of all these people cluttering up in his house. Eating his food. Drinking his drinks. "So, thanks for coming but, if you don't mind, Cindi and I would like to be alone now."

He stood.

"Did you know that Bruno Caliostro had once been hired by Kevin Rain?" Claudia asked.

"Yes," James replied. "Dale and Kourtney already explained to me how their father had hired Caliostro to investigate Adler. Kevin was sure that Adler was faking his injuries."

"Wow." Cindi extended her hands and studied her glittery pink fingernails. "Small world."

"Interesting," said Claudia. "But that's not what I was referring to."

"I don't get it." James shoved his hands in his pockets.

"Rain hired Caliostro to tail his wife," Ollie stated.

"He thought she was cheating on him," added Artie. He winked at Cindi.

What was the wink all about? wondered James.

"And guess whose payroll our Mr. Caliostro is on now," Claudia lowered her glasses as she aimed her words at James.

"I have no idea. Whose?"

"Felicity Rain's."

James was amazed—both that there was a connection between Bruno Caliostro and the Rains and, even more so, that these clowns had found out about it. "How did you find all this out?" He grabbed the pad and riffled through their meticulous notes.

"Basic detection," said Ollie.

"We broke into Caliostro's office," boasted Artie.

"Artie. I told you to keep your mouth shut." Claudia slugged him in the shoulder.

Artie whined. "Ouch. That hurt." He rubbed his upper arm. "I didn't know you meant James. He's one of us." He smiled at James, showing off the prominent gap in his two upper front teeth. "Right, James?"

James leaned back in his chair and banged his head against the wall. If only the wall would swallow him up...

"What does it all mean?" wondered Cindi.

Claudia snatched her notebook out of James' hands. "It means there is something very fishy going on. And we are going to get to the bottom of this ball of worms."

Cindi tapped James on the knee. "Ball of worms?"

"I think she means can of worms," he explained.

"Right. If Bruno and Felicity are involved, that proves you are innocent." Cindi smiled. "You should tell the police all this, James."

James fell forward, pressing his palms against his temples. "Tell them what exactly?" He shook his head slowly. "No, it's not that simple."

"You tell anybody we broke into Caliostro's office and I'll cut your tongue out," snarled Claudia. She chopped the air with the side of her hand.

"I worry about you." Violence seemed to be the hotheaded Latina's solution to everything. Could she have murdered Kevin Rain? He didn't dare ask her to her face if she had known him. He would have to do some discreet digging.

"What do we do next?" Ollie wanted to know.

"We need a plan." Artie scratched his nose with the tip of his beer bottle. "That's what the book says."

"Book?" said Cindi.

James kept his eyes glued to the table, afraid to look. When he finally did, all eyes were on him. "Don't look at me, I don't have a clue."

Ollie nudged Claudia. "Show him the book."

"Right, the book." Claudia's hand dug once more into her magic backpack.

"What book?" James demanded.

"Here it is." Claudia withdrew a large hardcover book with a tattered cover and yellowed pages. A bargain two-dollar yellow price sticker was plastered over the barcode on the backside.

She slid the book across the table as if it was the map to the treasure of the Sierra Madre.

James flipped the book over and read the title. "*The*

Beginner's Guide to Detection by Parker McRaney." He looked at them skeptically. "Really?"

"We picked it up in a used bookstore at the Swap Shop."

"I'm not surprised."

The Swap Shop was famous. What had started life as the Thunderbird Drive-In Theater in 1963 was now 88 sprawling acres holding a flea market, an arcade, an amusement park and even a Ferrari museum among other things.

And you could still go to the movies there, if you wanted to, on one of its 14 big outdoor screens.

James riffled through the worn pages of the book, stopping on the glossy photo of a smiling man with perfect teeth and sweptback tinted brown locks on the back cover. He looked vaguely familiar. "It's written by an *actor*. From an old eighties TV show."

"It wasn't just any old TV show," gushed Ollie. "We're talking Rocky Rhodes, PI. It ran for eleven seasons. It's still running, if you count reruns."

"But," James repeated more slowly in case all these lunatics had missed it the first time, "it was a *TV show*. Fiction. Make believe. You know, Hollywood? Lights, camera, action?"

"Yeah." Artie grabbed the book from James. "But Rocky Rhodes knows his stuff."

"What makes you think so? Besides, like I said, this Rocky Rhodes is a *fictional* character."

"Are you kidding?" exclaimed Ollie, who now snatched the book from Artie. "That show was a big hit. I've seen every episode a hundred times. Parker McRaney *was* Rocky Rhodes. He must know what he's talking about."

"I never heard of him," confessed Cindi.

Claudia had. "Rocky Rhodes was huge in Cuba when I was a girl. He drove that fancy American sports car and always dressed so nice."

From the look in her eyes, James couldn't tell if she was mooning over the TV star or longing for the lost days of her youth.

Figuring there was no point arguing with his partners, clearly been bedazzled by Parker McRaney's TV stardom, James asked, "What does the book say we should do?"

41

The insistent knocking at the front door deprived James of an answer.

"I'll see who it is," offered Artie.

James pushed Artie down in his chair. "I'll get it." He couldn't let these people take over his house and his life. Not entirely anyway.

This was one of those times when James wished he had a peephole. He kept asking Roger to install one. Roger kept asking him to pay his rent. It was one of those push-pull situations that he was doomed to lose.

James twisted the knob and let the door fall open. "What are you doing here, Bright?"

Jane Bright stood on his front porch in a mid-length tan coat, jeans and white trainers. Her hair was pulled back severely across her head and knotted in a ponytail.

"I saw the gang was here so I thought I'd stop by too." She muscled her way past him and marched purposefully into the living room as if she owned the place.

"Gang?" James hissed as he followed behind her. "What gang? There is no gang."

"Hi, gang!" Jane Bright waved brightly to the others filling up his tiny living space. "I'm Jane." She unbuttoned her coat and tossed it over the back of the sofa, revealing a tight V-neck blouse the color of a newborn chick.

Claudia leapt to her feet and thrust out her hand. "I am Claudia Suarez." She introduced Artie and Ollie.

"A pleasure." Artie leered.

"And you must by Cindi Keach." The two women shook hands. "How is your sister, Alyssa, managing?"

"To tell the truth," Cindi replied, "she's having a hard time coping."

"I can understand that completely," sympathized Jane. She took James' seat and his beer. "You don't suppose she would be up for an interview do you?"

James looked down at his hands and saw two fists. One by one, he mentally struggled to loosen his fingers.

"What?" Cindi didn't understand.

"She's the reporter I told you about," explained James. "Jane works for the Broward County Times."

"Oh. Right."

"Believe me, I have nothing but sympathy for Alyssa. I'm sure our readers would too."

Cindi looked to James for help but James was busy looking for something on the shelves to calm his stomach.

"It might even help find her husband's killer," Jane put out. "A reader might come forward with some special bit of information."

"I'll ask her." Cindi sounded uncertain.

"That's all I'm asking. Here's my card." Jane offered Cindi a business card from her purse.

Finding nothing better, James settled for a handful of saltines and washed them down with a cupful of warm tap water. "You never did explain how you knew all these people were here."

"Isn't it obvious?" Jane lifted his now empty beer

bottle. "Got any more of these?"

"No." James waved his hand at her. "Continue. You were explaining."

"I saw the truck."

James frowned. "What truck?"

"Are you kidding?" Jane smirked. "Hard to miss a food truck. Ollie's Delights. I saw it parked up the street. That thing is huge. Takes up half the road." She turned to Ollie. "Frankly, I don't know how you manage to handle that in downtown traffic."

"It isn't easy," explained Ollie. "But one gets used to it."

"He's got the best sandwiches in town," boasted Artie. "Man, I could use one right now. All this drinking on an empty stomach is making me hungry."

Ollie climbed to his feet. "I could whip something up for you. The rest of you guys want anything?"

Everybody said yes except James, who said something else. "I want something. I want you all to leave."

"James!" gasped Cindi. "Don't be rude."

"I'm sorry but I never asked any of these people to come to my house." He stomped across the floor. "Nor did I even once ask any of them for help."

"Yeah, because you're too *stupido*," snapped Claudia. "I suppose you'd rather go to prison. Is that what you want?" Her volume climbed with every word. "Let the police lock you inside a cell so you don't have to worry about doing anything, including thinking?" She finished with a snort of derision.

"I'm going to tell you the same thing I told that pain in the butt, Lt. Byrd." James got in her face. "I did not murder anybody. I'm sorry that Kevin Rain is dead but frankly I wish I'd never met him or anyone that knew him!"

There was a stunned silence.

Cindi burst into sobs.

"Oh, Cindi." James reached for her arm. She pulled back. "I didn't mean you."

"Yes," sniffed Cindi. "You did." She scurried out, slamming the door behind her.

James' heart sank.

"Now look what you've done, moron," scolded Claudia.

"What I've done?" James said in disbelief. "She's the one causing all the trouble." He pointed at the reporter.

Jane cocked her head and addressed her words to Claudia. "Just like a man, isn't it, Claudia? Blaming a woman for all his troubles."

"Tell me about it, sister," Claudia extended her arm and they slapped hands.

"Amen, sister," quipped Artie.

James slapped him upside the head. "Whose side are you on?"

"Ouch." Artie lips turned down.

Ollie sniffled.

"What's wrong with you?" James twisted Cindi's vacated chair around and sat, leaning his arms over the top rail.

"Cindi forgot my camera," he said forlornly.

James rolled his eyes. "I'll give it to her tomorrow."

"Are you sure?"

"I promise." It would give him an excuse to see her. And apologize.

Artie popped open The Beginner's Guide to Detection. "It says here that stake outs are good. We should do a stake out."

"What's this?" Jane narrowed her eyes at the spine of the book. "The Beginner's Guide to Detection?"

"By Parker McRaney," Ollie said. "You know, the TV star."

"Sure." Jane angled for a closer look. "I remember him. Randy Rhodes or something."

"Rocky Rhodes, PI," corrected Artie.

"He drove that sexy red and white fifty-seven Chevy with the soupy engine," Claudia added.

"She means souped up." Artie loved correcting people.

"Souped up, soupy. What's the difference?" Claudia asked in confusion.

"The difference is—"

"It doesn't matter what the difference is." James cut Jane off. "Look, these guys found an out-of-print how-to-be-a-detective book at a flea market bookstore. Now they seem to think that if we follow what this Hollywood actor says," he jabbed the book with his finger, "we'll find out who really killed Kevin Rain. Gimme a break.

"The actor probably hadn't even written the book himself. McRaney and his publisher probably paid some hungry ghostwriter a big chunk of change to pen it for him."

"Jealous?" accused Claudia.

Jane smiled. "I think that's a great idea."

James frowned. "Don't be ridiculous."

She lifted her brow. "Have you got a better idea?"

"Yeah," chimed Claudia. "You got a better idea, smurfy-pants?"

Artie tapped James on the shoulder. "She means

smarty-pants."

"I know what she means, Artie."

What James wanted to do was to go running after Cindi. Past experience told him not to. Better to let her cool down some, then approach. He kicked off his shoes and stretched out on the sofa.

"What sort of a stakeout did you have in mind, Artie?" He stared up at the popcorn ceiling. Was there asbestos in it? Was it slowly killing him like everything else in his life?

42

"How about Smiley's?" suggested Artie.

"Too obvious," dismissed Claudia. "Maybe Tow The Line. That Veronica Tench is one hard ass woman. I did some digging. She put the squeeze big time on a man named Larry Dobb up in Palm Beach County. Forced him out of business."

"We should definitely talk to him," Ollie agreed.

"Let's do it first thing in the morning," suggested Artie.

Keeping his eyes fixed to the ceiling in the hopes that it would fall and crush him to death, James said, "We can't all five of us go talking to suspects."

"Dobb isn't a suspect," Jane pointed out.

"You know what I mean," James snapped. "Anybody we talk to is going to clam up if five of us show up to interview them."

"He's right," Jane admitted. "They'll be too intimidated. I could do it. I'm a reporter. I know what I'm doing."

"*I'll* handle Dobb," insisted James.

"But I'm the reporter," complained Jane.

"Yeah, but I'm the guy with his head in the noose."

"Fine," Jane huffed. "Be that way. I'll see if I can get Parker McRaney to talk to me."

"What for?" Ollie wanted to know.

"He wrote this book. Plus, he played a PI forever. He might have some pointers."

"True," agreed Claudia. "We can't ask Bruno Caliostro because he may be mixed up in this."

"And he's the only other real detective we know," added Ollie.

James bit his tongue. They were all nuts.

He propped himself up on his elbows. "Sounds good to me, Jane. Shall I book you a flight?" Los Angeles was a world away. He figured she'd be gone for three days minimum.

"I don't have to go to LA. I happen to know he is retired and living right here in Fort Lauderdale."

James groaned.

"What about the rest of us?" Ollie asked. "What do we do?"

Claudia provided the answer. "There are more than enough suspects to go around. I say we split up and tail them. See what we can find out. We regroup tomorrow night, right here to compare notes."

Great, thought James. Not only was he now part of a gang of misfits, his house was their official clubhouse.

Claudia, Artie and Ollie debated over following Dale, Kourtney and Felicity Rain, Bruno and his daughter, and Adam Mitchell. Claudia wrote furiously in her notebook.

They were getting nowhere.

"Let's get back to the stakeout idea." James threw his feet on the floor. The others gathered around. "Phil Adler has a ten million dollar lawsuit against Smiley's. What else do we know about him?"

"According to my sources, the police interviewed him. He was home at the time of Kevin Rain's murder,"

Jane said.

"Alone?" James asked.

"Yes. He lives alone. But it doesn't matter. Phil Adler is an invalid. That's what the lawsuit is all about. He claims he was injured on the job. Now he's permanently disabled."

"What happened to him?" asked Claudia.

"The boom control on the truck he was operating failed. He injured his back and shoulder. The lawsuit claims that the equipment was poorly maintained. Phil Adler couldn't have murdered Kevin Rain," the reporter said in conclusion.

"I'd still like to talk to him," persisted James. He explained how he'd gone to the house and been rebuffed by the Rottweilers the moment he'd stepped out of the car.

"He keeps that place locked up tight. The curtains are drawn shut and there is an eight-foot tall fence around the property."

"Sounds to me like somebody with something to hide," Claudia said.

"Me, too," agreed James. "Ideas, anybody?"

"I saw this program on TV once—"

James squeezed his eyes shut. Here we go again, he thought.

"The TV presenters were examining this myth on the ways that you could distract trained attack dogs. They got this bitch in heat—"

"What? You watch your mouth!" Claudia waved a fist at Ollie.

"He's talking about a female dog." Jane patted Claudia on the arm and the cubana settled back down.

"Did it work?" Artie asked.

"Yep. Nothing like a little sex to take a dog's mind off his job." Ollie giggled then blushed when he realized there were ladies present.

"That's good to know," James said. "But I have no idea whether those dogs of Adler's are male or female."

"But you saw them," Jane said.

"Sure, for about one nanosecond. And they were running straight at me."

Silence fell over the room.

"All right. It's late. I tell you what." James handed Parker McRaney's book to Artie. "How about if you go home and study this and see what else it recommends. Read it." He roped an arm over Artie's shoulder. "Cover to cover. We can talk about it later."

That would get rid of them.

Claudia gathered up her things. The men followed her faithfully to the front door.

Jane Bright had remained behind. In the short time James had been away, she had cleared and wiped the table. Now she was rinsing the empty beer bottles in the kitchen sink.

"Those are for the recycle bin." James inspected a sudsy bottle. The woman was a neat freak. "You don't have to rinse them."

She grabbed the bottle from his hand, upending it. She gave it a shake and dried the outside with a frayed kitchen towel. "They like it when you rinse them first."

"They who?"

"The recycle people."

"Wouldn't want to upset the recycle people." He noticed she had returned his trash can to the space she preferred— squeezed between the counter and the refrigerator. "Shouldn't you be leaving like the others?

Don't you have a column about flowers or ferns or something to write?"

"Easy peasy. I only do my columns twice a week. Plenty of time."

She placed all the empty bottles plus the carton and anything else that was appropriate neatly in his recycle bin just outside the sliding door. She washed her hands under the tap then wiped them with the same towel she had used on the rest of his stuff. "I thought you might want to go over the case."

"You thought wrong. What I want to do is get some shut eye." He threw his arms overhead and acted out a yawn.

"We could make a list of all our suspects." Jane ignored him and went back to the spotless kitchen table. It hadn't been that clean in all the years he had lived there. Was it really that white? All this time, he thought it was yellow.

"Then make columns for what their motives might be, alibis. That sort of thing." She had her notebook open and was scratching in it with a pencil.

James stared wordlessly at her. Was she that oblivious to his hints? What did he have to do, physically lift her up and toss her out?

She smiled his way. "I'll go first." She wrote a name in small, tight letters. "Bruno Caliostro." She underlined it with a flourish. The pencil hovered above the paper as she waited expectantly for him to continue the process.

"Good night." James turned and headed for his bedroom.

"Fine." Jane scooped up her belongings. "I'll let you know if I get a chance to talk to Parker McRaney."

"You do that." It would be a cold day in Hell before he would take advice from a washed-up old actor. "While we wait to see what Claudia, Ollie and Artie come up with, I'm going to dig into Bruno Caliostro's background a little deeper. After I've had a chance to interview Dobb."

"Do you really think they'll turn up some leads?"

"Could be." Mostly, James was glad to have them all busy and out of his hair. He'd be tried and convicted if he had to rely on those misfits to save his butt.

43

Working at Stewart Classic Motors was every bit as bad as James had feared. The sun beat down on him, the new clothes itched and the brown penny loafers Roger had forced him to buy at the shoe warehouse up the street pinched his toes. Might as well stick his feet in a pair of vises.

Worse yet, the shoes squeaked with every step.

If it didn't stop soon, he was thinking of resorting to motor oil.

It was midafternoon when Roger finally cut James some slack and let him go for the day—just as he was contemplating slitting both wrists with a box cutter, jumping in the ocean and yelling "Come get me!" to any sharks that might be passing through the neighborhood.

James hadn't sold a single car but then neither he nor his brother had expected him to. Still, a little cash in his pocket would have been nice.

While he'd been talking to a prospective buyer earlier, Jane Bright had phoned and left a message on his cellphone telling him she had a surprise.

Lucky him.

He ignored the message and tried calling Cindi from Roger's office. "Hi, Cindi. It's me, James. The jerk, not the actor."

Maybe levity would work. She had been avoiding his calls the way he'd been avoiding the reporter's. "I really didn't mean what I said last night. Sometimes my mouth gets ahead of me."

He paused, hoping she would pick up.

She didn't.

James swore.

"No luck, huh?" Roger asked.

"Nope." James stuck the phone in his pocket. "I'm out of here."

"See you tomorrow." Roger waved.

"Sure, rub it in," quipped James.

"Come on, James. Lighten up. Is selling cars really that bad?"

James held his tongue. To say anything would be to insult his brother's chosen profession.

"Sheryl said to tell you that she's really proud of you."

"I don't suppose she mentioned that the police have any new leads? Maybe a hot new suspect?"

Roger shook his head. "Sorry, no."

James felt silly dressed up like a used car salesman but didn't feel like taking the time to change. Roger had even splashed him with some godawful spice cologne when he arrived at the dealership that morning.

Roger said the customers liked it.

James stank. Now the Ferrari stank. He rolled down the windows as he cruised up I-95. Larry Dobb lived in a rundown apartment complex out near Palm Beach International Airport.

A 737 rumbled overhead as James knocked on the door to his second-floor unit. "Mr. Dobb? Larry Dobb?"

"You got him." The man gripping the doorknob

had sagging flesh and a long face with wideset eyes. He appeared in floppy plaid shorts that nobody should be wearing outside of a Florida golf course and a thread-bare sleeveless T-shirt. Television sounds came from within.

"My name's James Stewart. I'm a private detective investigating the murder of Kevin Rain." He had practiced the line in the car. Firm but not overly aggressive.

He liked the sound of it: James Stewart, Private Detective.

Dobb grunted. "You're the guy accused of clocking him. You telling me you're a PI too?"

James' bravado deflated. Larry Dobb knew who he was. "May I come in? I wanted to talk to you about Mr. Rain and Veronica Tench."

Dobb released the doorknob and shuffled inside, following the track in the worn carpet. James trailed, closing the door behind him.

Larry Dobb's small condo boasted a galley kitchen to the left with a small dining and living area to the right. The living area led out to a patio just about wide enough to turn around in—if you were a pigeon. Dobb was carrying around more than a few extra pounds. James couldn't picture him pirouetting out there or using the balcony for his morning yoga-with-pigeons routine.

"Nice place." James noticed an unmade bed at the end of a short hall.

"You want to bullshit me or you want to talk?" Dobb parked himself on a dumpy plaid sofa. "Make yourself at home. By the way, you stink." He waved his hand in front of his nose.

"I blame it on my brother."

"That's funny, most guys blame it on their fathers."

James liked the man already. He spun a chair away from the dinette set and moved it closer to Dobb. The man's eyes vacillated between the game show on the biggest thing in the room—the TV—and James.

"So talk already, Mr. Stewart. I ain't got all day. Well, I have but, no offense, I don't want to spend it with you. Is that your real name by the way? James Stewart? Or is that your made-up PI name?"

"It's real. Would you mind turning the TV off?"

"Very much," Dobb said, smiling on the edge of his seat as a contestant requested a vowel when everybody could see what he needed was a consonant. "Idiot," Dobb muttered. "Him, not you. So you gonna talk or what?"

"Did you know Kevin Rain personally?"

"Sure, I knew him. Not well, but I knew him. Knew his whole family. The kids were spoiled brats and the wife was a real piece of work. A real green worshipper. And I'm not talking about Mother Earth. I'm talking about this."

Dobb rubbed his thumb against his fingers. James knew what that meant. It meant money. "But Kevin..." Dobb nodded. "He was okay, you know? He was like a big kid. Loved his trains."

Dobb's countenance darkened. "Say, you didn't kill him, did you?"

"No."

"I didn't think so. You don't look the type. Then again, you don't look like a PI either." He ran a tattooed forearm across his forehead. "Hot in here."

It was. Crazy hot. "Now that you mention it—"

"Can't afford the A/C. Too expensive. That's the electric company for you. Always ripping everybody off. And me on a fixed income. I'm retired, you know." He groaned when the contestant on the screen screwed up again.

"I know." James loosened his collar. "Any idea who might have wanted Kevin Rain dead?"

"Like I said, I never saw him much. We were friendly competitors you might say. He pretty much stayed off my turf and I stayed off his."

"And then Veronica Tench came along."

Dobb's face darkened. "Yeah. Twenty-two years I ran a successful business. I worked my butt off and grew my business until I had me more than a dozen truck operators. Then Tench shows up and I'm out of business in less than a year. The woman's like the black plague. That's a thing, right?"

"How could that be? How could she put you out of business?"

"Intimidation, sabotage. She would intimidate my employees and my accounts. My vehicles were tampered with. She cut her prices to the bone. I couldn't match her. That was her tactic. She'd move into a territory, bleed money until her competition sold out to her or was forced out of business by her."

"Did you go to the police?" James felt a trickle of sweat roll down his neck and settle into his sternum.

"And tell them what?" Larry Dobb reached for a pack of Camels on the glass coffee table. He thumped the pack against his palm, shaking a cigarette loose. He lit up and puffed hungrily. "I had no proof about the sabotage or intimidation tactics. She and her thugs were careful like that."

Smoke poured from his nostrils.

"As for her rates, it's a free country. If she wanted to provide a towing service at below cost, the police weren't going to shut her down over it." Larry Dobb chuckled humorlessly, scratching the apex of his near-bald head as he reflected. "You name it, she'd do it."

"Do you think she would stoop to murder?"

A smile turned the tired man's lips upward. "Stoop? I don't think Tench or her goons would have to stoop at all."

"Meaning?"

"Meaning Tench and her goons are already as low as it goes." He pushed his bristly brows together. "What's the opposite of stoop?"

James shrugged. "I don't know."

"Hmm. Be a good question on a game show, wouldn't it?"

Rather than answer the question, James asked another. "Is there anyone else you can think of that might have wanted to harm Kevin Rain?"

Dobb smiled, revealing two uneven rows of cigarette-stained teeth. "I thought you'd never ask."

44

James drove south to Ft. Lauderdale with more questions than answers circling around in his head. Larry Dobb told him that Kourtney and Dale had murdered their father. He'd had no proof, merely a hunch.

James didn't like hunches. Even more, he didn't like the thought that the two kids really could be guilty. If they were charged with murder, all their money would be spent on defense attorneys and he wouldn't see another cent from them.

Sure, it was a mercenary thought. But these were desperate times. He didn't want to end up a used car salesman for the rest of his life.

Worse still, working for his kid brother.

Larry Dobb's remark that Kevin Rain had once joked with him that he was the bane of his children's existence had him curious. Larry Dobb claimed Kevin hadn't explained what he had meant by the odd statement. Dobb said he had not pushed Kevin on it because it was none of his business.

James was going to make it his business, clients or not.

James exited I-95, checked the gas gauge, which was dangerously low but would do, and headed to the Rain residence because Ollie's water-damaged camera was lying on the floor behind his seat wrapped in a plastic grocery bag.

Hoping Cindi had cooled down and was ready to forgive him, he went straight to Alyssa's condo and knocked on the door.

"Hello, James." Alyssa wore a conservative black outfit and no makeup. The smell of tobacco filled the air. "Cindi isn't here."

"Too bad." The bag holding the camera dangled heavily in his hand. "I brought this. It's Greg Oliver's camera. Cindi promised him that she would ask a photographer friend of hers to take a look at it and see what he could do to fix it up."

"Sure." Alyssa took the camera from his hands and set it on a console table near the door.

"It fell in the water."

"So I heard. Come on in." Her eyes were flat and her voice lacked emotion. She seemed to be taking her husband's death hard yet. No surprise.

James followed her to the sitting room. A single lamp in the corner by the sofa provided a soft glow. A rumpled pillow and herringbone-patterned knit throw lay across the sofa.

Alyssa stooped and picked up a paperback romance novel that had been lying on the floor beside the sofa. She set it on the coffee table. Tucking her legs under, she lit a cigarette and took a sip from a tall glass. "Vodka and orange juice. Would you like one?"

"No, thanks. I really can't stay. Tell Cindi I called, would you?"

She nodded and blew out a ring of smoke.

"Are you sure you're going to be okay?"

She turned up her lip, the cigarette smoldering. "Yeah."

"Maybe you should get out. See some friends."

"Don't worry. Sometimes I like to be alone. Tomorrow I'm going into the office. Packing up Kevin's trains."

"Did you find a buyer?"

"I'm donating all of them, plus the tables, to a children's hospital."

"That's a great idea."

Alyssa dragged the throw over her knees.

James said goodbye but stopped himself at the door. "There is one thing."

"What's that?"

"Can you think of any *concrete* reason why Kourtney and Dale would have wanted to harm Kevin? I mean, it's nice to accuse them and everything but..."

Alyssa puffed on her cigarette for a minute. James was beginning to wonder if she would ever reply when she said, "Because Kevin always paid his mortgage on time."

"That's an odd reason to want to murder your father, don't you think?" James' hand rested on the doorknob. Being with Alyssa was uncomfortable. Was she on drugs?

Her smile crossed the distance between the sofa and the door. "We're an odd family, James. You might want to keep that in mind."

45

Jane found Bruno Caliostro's office easily enough, located on the second floor of the Edsel Building in downtown Fort Lauderdale. Bruno rented a private office in the main building. The School of Detection occupied space on the same floor, accessible only via an exterior stairs.

Pulling open the door of the puny and deserted lobby, the foul-smelling odor of mildew and mold assaulted her. Seeing no elevator, she climbed the slick wooden steps.

Caliostro's cramped little office was tucked into a corner of the building. Dirty windows looked out over some railroad tracks and a three-story parking garage.

Waltzing through the gaping door, Jane found Bruno sitting at his desk skimming some paperwork. A computer hummed on the floor next to a battered plastic trash bin. A game of solitaire was in progress on the computer monitor on his desk.

The detective perked up when the young and pretty blonde entered. "Good afternoon."

Bruno brushed hoagie crumbs from his shirt and struggled to his feet. "Have a seat. Tell me how I can be of service."

Jane squeezed her purse in her fingers and looked skeptically around the office. Stacks and stacks of paper covered the cheap furniture and beige linoleum floor. A coffee maker was parked on the floor next to a vacuum cleaner that was itself layered in a year's worth of dust. The vacuum cleaner cord was a tangle of knots.

"Are you Bruno Caliostro?" She saw a ruddy-cheeked man with chipmunk cheeks and overgrown mutton chop sideburns. His nose was sunburnt. His pleated trousers were rumpled and there were sweat-stains under his armpits.

This wasn't quite the action figure she expected a PI to look like. Hadn't he ever read a Raymond Chandler novel?

"That's correct, Ms—"

"Jane Bright."

"Have a seat, Ms. Bright."

"Thank you." Jane sat, resting her purse in her lap. "I'm interested in the School of Detection." If she told him she was a reporter, and a gardening and lifestyle one at that, he would never open up to her.

Bruno's smile widened and the creases in his face deepened. "Wonderful." He rubbed his hands together. "You know, a new semester has recently started up."

His eyes glittered with hope. "Are you interested, Ms. Bright?"

If he signed her up, classes could resume.

Truth be told, he could have continued with a single student if he felt like it. But why bother? Kicking Stewart out and postponing classes was meant to provoke the rest of the students into finding his replacement.

Now he had found that replacement himself. He wouldn't even have to shell out a finder's fee.

"Yes, very much. I've heard so much about your

school. I always wanted to be a detective."

"Take it from me, it is the best profession in the world. Glamour, intrigue, excitement."

Jane looked around the office, which was none of those things. "Sounds wonderful. I'm looking to make a change."

"May I ask what line of work you are in currently?"

"I'm a secretary at a boat storage firm." It was the first thing that sprang to mind.

"Sounds boring, if you don't mind my saying."

"Not at all," Jane replied. "It is."

"Don't worry. You'll get plenty of excitement being a detective, Ms. Bright. Although it is very hard work. Being a private investigator requires a great amount of training. But I'm sure you're up to it. You're smart. I can tell. You have the makings of a successful private detective."

"I hope so," she said with mock sincerity.

He offered her a drink. She declined. Dog hair covered the brown dormitory room-sized refrigerator on the floor. The desiccated remains of a packaged meal and a dirty plastic fork rested atop a cheap microwave oven that screamed to be wiped down or taken out and thrown in the nearest and deepest dumpster. Red smears of nuked ketchup covered the insides, visible through the gaping door.

The only thing that Jane could see coming out of ingesting anything of the liquid or solid variety that this office had to offer was a good case of dysentery.

"I have been following that murder case."

Bruno steepled his fingers. "What murder case is that?"

"The one where that musician killed the man for

towing his car."

"Ah." Bruno nodded. "An interesting case, that."

"Oh?" Jane fluttered her lashes. "I don't suppose you would know anything about the case, would you? The police can be so secretive."

Bruno bared his teeth. "Trust me, the police don't know everything."

Jane leaned forward in her seat. "What do you mean?"

"They follow the rules, stay in the box. Follow the letter of the law."

"And you don't?"

"Don't get me wrong, Ms. Bright, we follow the *spirit* of the law."

"Jane."

"Jane. But a detective can find out things that the police could never hope to uncover. The police would be lost without us."

Bruno's swivel chair gave a gerbil-like squeak of pain as he leaned back and folded his hands over his flabby torso. "Believe me, I could tell you a thing or two."

He leaned forward and continued. "You see, Kevin Rain was once a client of mine."

"How interesting. Why did he hire you? If you don't mind my asking."

"It was a small but delicate issue." Bruno flicked his fingers. "I'm afraid the details are confidential."

"Of course." Jane decided not to press him. She had no doubt that she would wheedle the information out of him sooner or later. Besides, she already knew some of the story.

Bruno pressed his heavy chin into his chest. "Are you interested in signing up for the Bruno Caliostro

School of Detection?"

"Absolutely. If it's not too late and you have room for me."

"As a matter of fact, we've had a cancellation due to unforeseen circumstances."

Bruno jumped from his chair, afraid of losing a customer. In making a sale, it was all about getting that impulse buyer. He grabbed a pair of binders from the towering shelf next to the door. "These are the books you'll need for class."

She took the binders from him. "Thanks." They were heavy. She set them on the floor.

Bruno pulled some papers from his desk. "These are the contracts." He eyed Jane Bright, well-dressed and well-made up, and appraised her credit- and student-worthiness. "I'm afraid tuition isn't cheap."

"I don't mind. I have some money saved up. I'm sure it's worth every penny."

"Guaranteed." Bruno was liking her more and more. He showed her where to sign. The last paper was a confidentiality agreement spelling out that nothing from the class could be shared with other unauthorized persons. "What the School of Detection offers is exclusive," he explained.

Jane ignored the numbers and signed her life away. Somehow she'd find a way to pay for it later. Unless it turned out that Bruno Caliostro was guilty of murder, then she'd be home free.

"You were telling me about Kevin Rain." Jane was aware of the detective's eyes on her legs.

"The man suspected of murdering him was a student of mine." Bruno retreated behind his desk.

"No," she gasped.

"Yes, but not to worry. I suspended him. A young man by the name of Stewart, James Stewart. The Bruno Caliostro School of Detection is nothing without its stellar reputation."

"Do you think he's guilty?"

"I haven't been following the case that closely. I have no skin in the game, as they say. Plus," he shuffled some papers around on his desk, "I have paying cases of my own to deal with. But if you ask me…"

"Yes?"

"There is something very suspicious about this James Stewart. This time, the police might have got it right. He had argued with the victim. His prints were all over the murder weapon."

"Sounds bad. For him, I mean." Jane smiled inwardly. She couldn't wait to tell James what Bruno's opinion of him was. James Stewart was a total pain in the butt.

But he was no killer. She was convinced of that.

The question was why did Bruno Caliostro want her and everybody else to think he was?

46

James returned home tired and frustrated on all fronts. A good night's sleep was what he needed. And some fresh ideas. Maybe his dreams would provide some. His conscious mind was drawing a blank.

Unfortunately, a persistent knock on the door, shattered his dream of a quiet evening alone. He peeked out the curtains. Claudia Suarez and some strange girl.

"Now what?" He groaned. Were the others really expecting to meet at his place tonight? He hiked up his blue jeans and opened the door.

"Hey, Claudia. I wasn't expecting company."

"Why not? We had plans to meet tonight." She wore dark slacks and a long dark shirt. A silver cross dangled around her neck.

"I didn't think you were serious."

Claudia said something in Spanish to the young girl standing quietly nearby. The girl smiled.

"Who's this?" James looked uneasily at the girl. Standing about four feet tall, she had two tightly wound braids of black hair. Her dark brown eyes looked at him unapologetically as if he was an exotic specimen in a pet shop.

"My daughter, Zenia. I couldn't get a babysitter." Claudia Suarez pulled her daughter closer. "Say hello to Mr. James."

"*Olá*, Mr. James."

"Good. Now give me your jacket and go play while the grownups talk, *cariño*."

"What did you bring your daughter for?"

"Like I said, I couldn't get a babysitter." Claudia shoved off her backpack. "You got a problem with that?" She dropped her purse and Zenia's jacket on the table next to a chair.

"No. No." James threw up his hands. "I just didn't know you were married and had a kid." Hadn't she said something in class about a boyfriend?

"I'm not married. I *was* married," she replied savagely. "Her father, Enrique, works on cars in a garage in Little Havana. You think I can get him to babysit anytime I want to? It's not that easy."

"No, I'm sure it's not. Let's get down to business." The sooner they did, the sooner he'd get them out of his house and could go to bed. "So, where's everybody else?"

"You haven't heard from Ollie and Artie?"

"No, should I have?"

Claudia avoided eye contact. "I told them to call you the minute they made contact."

"Contact?" James didn't like the sound of this.

"With Phil Adler."

"You sent Ollie and Artie, the Abbott and Costello of the detective world, to make contact with Phil Adler? The man who is suing Smiley's for ten million bucks and may very well be responsible for murdering Kevin Rain?"

"I didn't send them. It was their idea. And who are Abbott and Costello?"

"You know. Who's on first?"

"What?" She was giving him that *I'm talking to an*

idiot look.

"Never mind. Artie and Ollie listen to you." James wasn't so sure the two men had an original idea between them.

"I wish a man would listen to me for a change." She hurled the words at James.

The sliding glass door glided quickly open at that moment and Jane Bright stepped inside. "Hi."

"What are you doing?" asked James.

"We have a meeting scheduled for tonight. Hi, Claudia." She waved. "Isn't anybody else here yet?" She popped open the fridge and helped herself to a can of root beer.

"No." James pushed the refrigerator door shut. "I mean, what are you doing coming in through the back door?"

Jane shrugged and popped open her soda and drank. "What's the big deal?"

"The big deal," James replied, locking the sliding door to prevent further intruders, "is that you don't live here. How about knocking next time?"

Jane tilted her head at him. "What if you don't hear me?"

"Oh, you can count on that." James snatched the can from her hands and guzzled the remainder. He slammed the empty can down on the kitchen counter.

"Wow." Jane winked at Claudia. "Cranky, isn't he? Has he eaten? Maybe that's the problem."

"You could be right." Claudia returned to the fridge and pointedly took a root beer for herself and handed another to Jane. "My Pedro gets cranky when he has low blood sugar."

"I thought you said your ex's name was Enrique?"

"It is." Claudia sat at the table. Jane joined her. "Pedro is our beagle."

Jane giggled. "Ollie and Artie aren't here yet?"

Claudia shook her head no. "I was telling James that I have not heard from them all day. They were going to try to have a word with Phil Adler."

The sound of somebody banging on a guitar with all the dexterity and skill of a tuna fish sandwich exploded from the bedroom.

James winced. Claudia's kid had found his remaining acoustic guitar, a vintage 1978 blonde maple Guild G37. He loved that guitar.

"What's that racket?" Jane wanted to know.

"That is my daughter, Zenia."

"Oh," squealed Jane, sounding almost as annoying as Zenia's thrashing, "I didn't know you had kids! How many?"

"Just the one."

"I can't wait to meet her. I always wanted kids," Jane added wistfully.

As if on cue, Zenia burst into the hallway leading to James' bedroom, clutching his guitar by the neck. "Look, Mama. A *guitarra*." She tilted it, whacked at the strings, and sang something in lilting Spanish.

James had no idea what the girl was singing about but Claudia smiled her approval. He had had enough.

"Here." He approached the girl and she backed up warily. "It's okay. I just want to show you how to play a couple of chords. You like SpongeBob?"

"Yes!"

James, against his better judgment, launched into the SpongeBob SquarePants theme song.

Zenia adored it. Suddenly, she adored James too.

Even Jane and Claudia clapped vigorously.

James handed Zenia back the guitar and showed her how to make simple G, C and Em chords. She fumbled a bit but was focused and seemed to get it. "Now, how about trying that on your own? In the bedroom. Quietly."

Zenia eagerly bobbed her head and retreated. James closed the bedroom door. "Can we get down to business now? Please?"

He vowed to vomit in the toilet bowl later. No offense to sponge-people everywhere, but performing that SpongeBob song was like eating a year-old, botulism-infected, dirty dishwater-soaked kitchen sponge.

"Let me try Ollie and Art once again." Claudia dialed their cell phones one after the other. No one was answering.

"What do we do?" Jane asked.

"Nothing," was James' answer.

"Nothing?"

"Are you not worried? What if Adler has killed them?" She banged her fist on the table.

James rolled his eyes. "And what if they've gone bowling? They could be gorging themselves on pepperoni pizzas and cheap beer even as we speak."

"We should telephone the police."

"We have nothing to tell them. Ollie and Artie are two grown men."

Jane and Claudia weren't satisfied and said so.

"Look," James said. "I'll go check out Adler's place tomorrow. Maybe he'll talk to me. He might know something."

And maybe the moon is made of green cheese and he'd climb a ladder up there tonight and make himself a green cheese sandwich.

47

The bedroom door opened and Zenia slunk towards them, dragging James' guitar across the floor.

"Mama, the string broke." She leaned the Guild against the kitchen chair. The busted G string flopped against the face of the guitar.

James held his tongue.

"Don't worry. I'm sure that happens all the time. Right, James?"

"Right." He pinned a smile on his face for Zenia's sake.

"Do you have anything to eat, Mr. James?" She swung her arm in his direction, bumping the guitar.

James dove for it but was too slow. The neck of the guitar bounced off the floor. James caught it on the second bounce.

"We'd better get going. Zenia has school in the morning." Claudia tousled her daughter's hair. "And Mommy has class tomorrow night."

"What class are you taking now?" James was curious. How did Claudia find time to be a mother, work security at a shopping mall and go to night school?

All the while, he was eying the neck of his guitar for cracks. Luckily, there appeared to be none.

On the subject of guitars, if he could just get paid by Kourtney and Dale or make a commission selling one of those overpriced luxury car on his brother's lot, he might be able to get his precious Martin and Vox out of hock before the ninety days were up and the pawn shop owner sold them both.

When he did get the Martin back, he'd keep it out of reach of little monsters like Zenia Suarez.

Claudia and Jane exchanged a look.

"What?" James was used to women exchanging looks. He was also very used to not understanding what those cryptic signals meant. That applied in this case.

When the two women remained silent, he said, "Does somebody want to tell me what's going on?"

"Mr. Caliostro has started Class 42 up once again."

James took a step back. Class 42 was the designation given to their class. "What? Are you sure?" He had been so busy trying to save his neck and keep his head above water, he hadn't even thought about cracking the books.

"His daughter texted us." Claudia helped her daughter into a blinged-out denim jacket with sequins and a pink pony on the backside.

"I didn't get any text." James scrolled through his text messages. "Nothing. Besides, he told us he wouldn't resume classes until I was exonerated."

"Or he found another pupil," added Claudia. She bustled Zenia to the door.

James tagged after her. "Wait. Are you saying he found somebody? Who?"

Claudia glanced nervously over her shoulder. "See you tomorrow!" She wriggled her fingers and fled into the night.

Jane waved back but lowered her hand to her side as if compelled to by the weight of James' glare.

"What do you think happened to Ollie and Artie?" She started cleaning up. "I hope they are all right."

"You." James loomed beside her.

"Me?" Jane gulped.

"*You* are the new student."

"Well, I—"

"You signed up for Caliostro's School of Detection?"

Jane slid around to the opposite side of the kitchen table. "Wow. You guessed right away. When I spoke with Mr. Caliostro, I got the impression that he didn't think much of your potential as a PI."

James lunged for her. He missed and went sprawling across the kitchen table while she went about her business. Which meant rinsing out his dishes and taking out his trash.

"I can't believe you did this to me," he said from his prone position on the hard tabletop.

"I didn't do anything to you. It seems to me that, so far, you, James Stewart, have done everything to yourself."

James rolled off the table, smacking his right elbow against the kitchen floor. But that wasn't why he cursed. He cursed because she was probably right.

48

James carried his first morning cup of coffee outside and stood barefoot on the cool deck. The sun was a smear of yellow on the horizon, fighting to pull itself out of the clouds.

He couldn't go back to class until the Kevin Rain murder case was resolved and he was exonerated. On the other hand, maybe he should forget about going back to class. Maybe he wasn't cut out for this detective business.

So far, even with his own life at stake, he'd bumbled and stumbled and come up empty-handed.

On the other other hand, he hated dressing like a preppie and selling high-end automobiles to overcompensated and/or born-to-the-manor snobs.

On the other other other hand...zilch zip nada. He had run out of ideas and options. Now, he was running out of hands.

James sighed as he took a sip of heavily sugared coffee. The tall weeds growing along the edges of the canal were a metaphor for the rangy weeds he found himself in.

Roberta Higgins sang inside her kitchen. What did she have to be so happy about?

A paddle boarder wearing baggy yellow board shorts and a navy- and white-striped tank top moved silently along the canal on a green and blue eleven-foot board. James wanted to warn the rider about the alligators he'd seen in that canal but, then again, alligators had to eat too.

Seeing no clear alternative, he resigned himself to going to the dealership.

The minute he got to Stewart Classic Motors, his brother put him to work on the phone in the office going down the list of contacts he wanted him to pitch to.

The dealership had taken in a low mileage Lamborghini Countach, white over red with a mere two thousand miles on it—who spends all that money to *not drive* a car? Apparently, lots of people, because several of Roger's customers said they were eager to come by for a look and a spin.

After which, they'd spend big bucks for it. The lucky owner would promptly park it in his or her climate-controlled garage where they could admire it at their leisure.

They'd sell it again when they got tired of looking at it and lovingly wiping the dust off its hood on a daily basis. By which time, the odometer would have nudged up barely a dozen or two miles due to the Lambo's owner having taken the car out for an Alaskan king crab and caviar Sunday brunch at The Breakers up in Palm Beach.

The Lambo was a steal at a mere three hundred grand.

James heard a commotion outside the office. Roger was yelling. That didn't happen often.

James put down the phone and went to have a look.

"Not here," Roger was waving his arms. "I didn't

order a food truck."

A big, boxy food truck blocked the entrance to the car lot. James ran outside. "It's okay, Roger." He laid a hand on his brother's shoulder. "I got this."

"You know these clowns?"

"Yes." Those clowns were Ollie and Artie. Ollie hunched behind the wheel. Artie was riding shotgun. The bright orange food truck read 'Ollie's Delights' in towering neon green letters. The menu was painted on the side beneath the ordering and serving dropdown panel. The smells of spicy cooking leaked out. A pair of construction workers waiting at the bus stop ambled over, hungrily sniffing the air as they approached.

The food truck shuddered then went silent as Ollie killed the motor.

"Claudia was looking for you guys last night. What happened?" James demanded as Artie and Ollie joined him and Roger at the edge of the lot.

"She was looking for us?" Ollie scratched his head. He was dressed in his chef whites. Artie wore baggy jeans and an orange and green Ollie's Delights T-shirt that was three sizes too large for him.

"Sorry, not open yet!" Ollie called to the workers whose faces fell. They shuffled back to the bus stop bench.

"We went to Miami," Artie explained.

"What's in Miami?"

"I got a call from a buddy of mine. He had a space at an art show down in North Miami Beach."

"But he had to cancel," put in Artie.

"He offered me the space. Artie and I worked all day. Since it was late, we camped out in her." He lovingly patted the side of his truck.

"Man, we were busy," exclaimed Artie. "I had no idea there was so much money in the food truck biz."

"What about Phil Adler?"

Roger pressed closer, sticking his nose through the open window. "What about moving this eyesore so my customers can get on the lot?"

Proving his point, a man in a blue Corvette convertible sat behind the truck, flapping his arms and leaning on his horn. Roger hastened to calm him.

"Quick, tell me about Phil. Then you'd better get this thing out of here," said James.

"There's nothing to tell," Ollie said. "We drove out to his house. He refused to talk to us."

"You actually saw him?"

"Yeah. Through a crack in the door."

"Sitting in a wheelchair," added Artie.

"I gave him a couple of sandwiches."

"We thought it might make him more friendly," said Artie.

"Did it?"

"Well, not a whole lot," admitted the kid. "But he did say he would count to ten slowly before siccing his dogs on us."

James wondered again what Phil Adler was hiding. He needed to find some pretext to talk to the guy.

Roger returned and ordered Ollie to move his truck. Ollie climbed aboard.

"See you in class tonight, James?" asked Artie, climbing into the truck.

Ollie scolded Artie and cranked up the food truck.

"Oh, right." Artie blushed. "I forgot you were *persona non grata.*" Artie stuck his head out the window. "You won't squeal on us to Claudia, will you, James?"

"Nah." James was as afraid of her as they were. He made them promise to stay away from Phil Adler. The last thing he needed was to have to bail those two out of a jam.

Artie had it right. James was *persona non grata* at the School of Detection. However, he was beginning to think that wasn't so much because Bruno Caliostro was worried about his reputation.

No, he was getting the idea that Bruno might be afraid that he might be on to him. Bruno was afraid James was going to unmask Bruno Caliostro, PI to the Stars, as a murderer.

49

"Thank you again for agreeing to meet with me, Mr. McRaney." The warm breeze tickled its way through Jane Bright's hair. She had nervously telephoned the actor and requested an interview on the pretense of writing a profile on him for her paper.

Parker McRaney agreed to meet her for lunch at Bourbon & Bifteck, an upscale chophouse near the Turnberry Marina in the small city of Aventura, situated south of Ft. Lauderdale and north of Miami.

Jane had a friend who worked in advertising sales for the tiny Aventura Biweekly News so she was familiar with the area and had arrived first.

Now, seeing the actor across the tiny table in the outdoor seating area overlooking the inlet with its exorbitantly priced yachts and sailboats bobbing in the water and gulls circling lazily over the water made her feel way out of her element.

She was more than a little star struck. Here she was having lunch with Parker McRaney!

Although he had to be in his early sixties, he looked every bit as handsome now as he had in his youth. His eyes were sharp and blue with fine eyelashes. His skin had a healthy tan and no wrinkles, only the merest of lines at the corners of his eyes and around his lips.

Sure, his sexy blond hair was a little thinner than it had been when he was starring as TV's Rocky Rhodes, but that was to be expected. He remained a very handsome man.

And charming.

She'd been giggling since he'd pulled up the chair across from her and introduced himself. As if he had needed any introduction.

The actor had an easy, athletic way about himself. He wore a lilac polo shirt and cream-colored trousers with tan boat shoes. As the breeze wafted over her, she caught a hint of lime aftershave.

"I'm flattered that you asked me," Parker was saying. "I'm no longer the hot commodity that I once was, as they say in Hollywood. California, that is." Florida has its own Hollywood and it wasn't far from where they sat.

The Florida town had been the dream of a businessman by the name of Joseph Young. The two cities had little in common beyond the shared name.

Parker McRaney waved for the server and ordered a bottle of sparkling white wine. "Then again, I am enjoying my retirement."

Over a small but tasty lunch, Jane peppered the actor with questions and plied him with wine. Both of which he attacked with alacrity. After dessert and the remains of a second bottle of wine, she had learned that he had retired to South Florida to "relax and enjoy life to its fullest."

Parker McRaney signalled for the check. "I hope you don't mind if we cut this short. I have a golf match in an hour." The expensive gold watch on his left wrist told him he was going to be late if he didn't get moving.

"I'd like to hit a few balls at the driving range first. Limber up."

"Of course." Jane ran a silky soft napkin over her lips and reapplied her lip gloss. "You've been more than generous with your time. And, like I said earlier, I don't expect you to pay for lunch. I invited you."

"It's my treat." He signed his name with a flourish to the bill, slipped it under his plate, and pushed back his chair. Smiling, he added, "And it has been my pleasure."

"There was one other thing I wanted to ask you about," Jane said, feeling warm and blushing pink. Was it the wine or the compliment? Or that sexy man sitting across the table from her?

Jane forced herself to focus. She had something to ask and had been having trouble working it into the conversation. Parker had been happy to regale her with stories of his colorful past as a star. Maybe she could charm Lou into running a celebrity profile on him in the paper.

That would be a feather in her cap.

The actor tilted his head at her and said with a smile. "Of course. Ask away. I never turn down a question from a lovely lady."

Jane's blush deepened and she cleared her throat. "It's about that book you wrote."

"My autobiography?"

"No. The other one. The Beginner's Guide to Detection."

A smile pushed out the actor's cheeks and his chest swelled with pride. "My book went to number three on the New York Times Bestseller List." He held up three fingers.

"I'm not surprised. It was brilliant."

"You've read it?"

"Of course."

The head waiter approached. "Excuse me, Mr. McRaney."

"Yes?"

"Your car is here."

Parker held up his hand. "Ask the driver to wait."

"I have a copy," Jane explained as the head waiter nodded and left. The actor had insisted that she call him by his first name. It still felt weird, surreal really. She was on a first name basis with a famous Hollywood actor!

She couldn't wait to tell her parents. They had never understood her work on the Broward County Times. Her maternal grandfather had been a world-famous concert violinist. Her father had taught classical music at the prestigious Stewart Institute in Philadelphia. He was also a noted symphonic composer. Dad was semi-retired now. Her paternal grandmother had been, in her day, a leading soprano. Her mother was a noted music journalist and historian.

Jane couldn't carry a tune and played the piano and violin—her poor parents had spent money on years' worth of lessons in both—as well as any blind warthog could be expected to—her brother's words, not theirs. Brothers can be so mean.

Said brother, Justin, was an in-demand session player in Nashville. He had also toured with several major country music acts. Jane's mom and dad weren't huge country music aficionados, but they had gotten a kick out of meeting Toby Keith. Although they never said a word to her, Jane could see in their eyes that Justin's success was a step, a giant step above her own.

"I've read it cover to cover," Jane answered in reply to his question about reading his book on detection. She had read it cover to cover, just not quite exactly every page in-between.

She would though, the first chance she got.

"That was some years ago. It has gone out of print, I believe. Did you bring it with you?" He extended his hand over the table. "I'll be happy to sign it."

"I'm afraid I didn't but I would love to have you sign it sometime, if that would be okay?"

"Of course, it would be my pleasure. It will give us an excuse to meet again," he said with a wink that made her shiver. "Do you have an interest in the PI business, Jane?"

"As a reporter, I like to discover as much as I can about a subject."

"That makes sense." Parker steepled his fingers. "Reporters and private detectives are often after quite the same information."

"Exactly." Jane wiped some breadcrumbs from the white linen tablecloth into the palm of her hand. She dropped the crumbs on her empty plate as the waiter came to take it. "In fact, there is a local murder case right now. Perhaps you read about it."

"There are a lot of murders in Florida. Which one are you referring to?"

"This one happened several days ago in Ft. Lauderdale. Kevin Rain, the owner of Smiley's Towing Service, was found dead inside the premises."

Parker pursed his lips. "I'm afraid I missed that one." He snapped his fingers and ordered a third bottle of wine.

"What about your golf game?" she reminded him.

He shrugged lazily, grinning boyishly. "What is hitting a little white ball compared to spending a sunny afternoon outdoors with a beautiful young woman?"

Heat climbed Jane's chest and neck.

"Tell me about this murder and why it fascinates you."

50

James felt the unforgiving metal light pole pressing into his back. Even dressed in shorts, sandals and a T-shirt, the unofficial South Florida uniform, it had been far too hot and muggy in the confines of the Ferrari.

The only relief would have been to turn on the AC but that would have meant burning fuel. In addition, any environmental concerns he might have had aside, that meant spending money—and that concerned him a lot.

His eyes drifted from the dimly lit stairway leading to Bruno Caliostro's School of Detection to the busy saloon across the street. The pulsating rhythms of pop music leaked out each time the door opened.

James had arrived twenty minutes before the end of class. A little after nine, students began trickling out. He stepped into the shadows of a shuttered store and watched as they drifted downward. He recognized them all, including Jane Bright. Ollie and Artie climbed into an old Toyota together and left first.

Bruno came down the stairs at Jane's side. His daughter, Sophie, followed behind. The three of them approached Bruno's van. He unlocked the door.

What was that silly reporter playing at? Was she going somewhere with them? Didn't she realize they could be a pair of murderers?

But then Jane waved goodbye and sheared off. James watched from his vantage point as she moved down the street to her VW and drove off.

He dodged across the street to the Ferrari. Luck had gone his way for once. Despite the nighttime crowd, he'd been able to tuck the sports car next to a dumpster in the alley across the way.

The van started up and James went after it, sticking as close as he dared without tipping off Caliostro.

Several minutes later, Bruno dropped his daughter off at a barrel tile-roofed condo building near the Fort Lauderdale War Memorial Auditorium and then kept going. Bruno took Sunrise Boulevard to I-95 northbound.

James tucked in behind a big rig and followed. Would Bruno notice he was being pursued? The man was a trained professional with many years' experience. He had to be careful.

Then again, Bruno had no reason to suspect he was being followed. Or did he?

Twenty long minutes later, sweating profusely, James cursed as he inched the Ferrari to the curb. He scratched his head. Bruno Caliostro had pulled into the dark driveway of Felicity Rain's house.

If he had known Bruno's destination, he could have saved himself the stress of trying to tail a car at highway speeds. Especially on South Florida's stretch of I-95, a virtual no-holds-barred obstacle course where one's main goal was to get on at point A and get off at point B without having been killed by some crazy Speed Racer type—and that could include anyone driving anything from the tiniest subcompact to the biggest big rig.

James cut the engine, pulled the handbrake, and climbed out. He had parked three doors down. Recycling bins lined the quiet street. Up ahead, a dark silhouette of a man or woman—he couldn't tell which—walked a dog. They were moving away from him.

A fine warm rain was falling.

Bruno let himself into Felicity's house. That in itself was interesting.

Wiping the rain from his face, he went slowly up the sidewalk—just another neighbor out for a stroll. Floridians didn't let a little rain stop them.

And when it rained hard and the streets flooded, which they always did—South Florida being a paved-over swamp—some of the state's more mischief-minded residents enjoyed surging through the deep and dirty puddles in their vehicles and casting a little love in the form of cold and wet rooster-tail spray on their pedestrian counterparts—figuring it served them right when they should be driving instead of walking.

Felicity's porch lights were off. Steam rose from the front of Caliostro's van as James crept between houses. Pushing damp hair from his eyes, he inched up to the nearest side window. Soft light from two table lamps revealed a large living area with twenty-foot ceilings. Strategically placed Chippendale-style furniture, a gourmet kitchen with professional stainless steel appliances, including a towering refrigerator that was wider than his bedroom closet, and an assortment of vases filled the open living space.

The room was unoccupied.

James tiptoed through the slick St. Augustine grass, past the screened-in patio covering a kidney-shaped swimming pool. His sandals thwacked against the bottoms of his feet. He walked stiff-legged for fear of Felicity or one of her neighbors poking their noses out, curious about the odd noise coming from her yard.

Diffuse light spilled from the room at the opposite corner of the house. James paused and considered his choices. Clouds obscured the night sky. A couple of doors down, he heard a man and woman laughing together.

James quietly approached the shoulder-high window and peeked inside. Felicity's bedroom. Two dimly lit figures writhed atop a king-size bed with an upholstered headboard.

Not what he was expecting to see.

Not what he wanted to see.

Seemingly out of nowhere, a curly-haired white poodle with a sparkly dog collar leapt in the air from a gray ottoman located beneath the window and angrily yipped at him.

The alarm had been sounded.

James fled back the way he had come, aware of lights flicking on inside the house as if chasing him. More lights came on at the house next door.

James raced to the Dino, grabbing for the car keys buried in his front pocket with wet fingers as he ran. His left sandal sailed backward through the air and hit the ground.

He left it for dead and fumbled the keyring. It fell to the curb, skidded and came to a stop over a drainage grate.

James heard the sound of a garage door rumbling to life. He imagined an armed and dangerous Bruno Caliostro gunning for him.

James swore under his breath and bent down. Despite his trembling fingers, he managed to get his fingers around the car keys. Clutching them in a death grip, he ran to the Ferrari and threw himself inside.

Glancing through the windshield, he saw a dark hulk standing in the road outside Felicity's house. Another joined it and then a tiny, four-legged third.

Careful to leave off the headlights, James backed up quickly in the nearest driveway and stepped on the gas. The fat, balding tires spun then caught a grip. He lurched down the narrow street, taking out four recycling bins along the way.

James stopped a mile away to catch his breath. He wasn't being followed and he wasn't hearing sirens.

All good signs. Bruno was right about one thing: a PI driving a red Ferrari is just asking for trouble.

Bruno.

He winced. That image burned in his brain.

How could he ever hope to erase the image of Bruno Caliostro, PI to the Stars, lying buck-naked atop Felicity Rain?

And what did it mean?

Well, he knew what it meant but what the hell did it mean?

51

James sat on the sofa in the Stewart Classic Motors office listening to Roger rattle on about sales projections and profit margins. Mercifully, the phone in his pocket vibrated. The thrumming against his butt reminded him of the moving image of Bruno Caliostro's hairy heinie the night before.

Nightmarish dreams had filled his sleep. Those dreams had culminated with a naked Bruno running through the streets of downtown Ft. Lauderdale, chasing James with a tire iron.

"Sorry," James interrupted. "I've got to take this call." He held up his phone apologetically.

Roger grunted and stepped out to check the inventory on the lot. The detailers were supposed to have every car spotless first thing in the morning. They always did, never fail, but Roger checked every day to be sure.

"We've got a situation."

"We?" James recognized Jane Bright's voice at the other end of the line. "What sort of a situation?"

"He hasn't come out yet. I'm beginning to worry that they may have kidnapped him."

"How about starting at the beginning, Jane?" James squeezed his eyes between his fingers. "Who hasn't come out yet? From where? And, most importantly, why should I care?"

"Parker McRaney."

"Okay. Parker McRaney. You talked to him, good."

"Not so good. You see—"

"Slow down. Where did you talk to McRaney?"

"At his house and, before that, a restaurant. But that's not where he is now."

"Okay, so where is he now?" James was aware of Roger's eyes burning into him from the parking lot. He turned his face to the wall.

"That's what I am trying to tell you, James. He went undercover but I'm afraid they figured out who he was and that they're holding him prisoner."

"Prisoner?" he repeated, skeptically.

Jane gasped for breath. "Maybe even killed him. Ohmygosh. It's all my fault. It will be all over the newspapers, cable, the Internet that I was responsible for Parker McRaney being murdered!"

James heard a sob. "Pull yourself together. Who is this *they* you keep talking about?"

"Ronnie Tench and her goons."

"McRaney's at Tow The Line? What's he doing there?"

"I told you, James. Why don't you ever listen to me? Parker went undercover at Tow The Line thinking he might find some clues, you know, to who killed Kevin Rain."

"Parker McRaney went undercover? Are you kidding me? Didn't he realize the chances of his being recognized?"

McRaney may have been out of the spotlight for decades, but for the occasional TV appearance, yet the actor's face still appeared in reruns somewhere in the world on a regular basis.

"He wore a disguise, James. He's not an idiot. He's very smart."

"Yeah, smart enough to have been taken prisoner by a towing company operator."

"I'm sure it wasn't his fault. Somehow they figured out who he was. The question remaining is whether he's okay and what we do about setting him free."

"Call the police."

"Are you sure that's a good idea?" Jane wasn't sure the publicity that it was bound to spark was a good thing and said so. "Besides, what if all the things we've been doing should come out? Some of it hasn't been quite legal."

James tried to ignore the growing headache. "Where is McRaney now? Tow The Line? I can drop in and see if I spot him."

"No, he's at Ronnie Tench's house. Why do men never listen?" she screeched.

"We listen. Women never talk straight!"

An ugly silence followed.

After a moment, the reporter said through gritted teeth, "Parker went to Tench's house yesterday afternoon with her and some guy who works for her. I staked them out. The guy left a couple hours later but Parker never reappeared."

"Are you sure?"

"I stayed out there all night, James. I'm sure." Jane was cold and tired and hungry.

"Don't you think it's possible that you might have drifted off?"

"No, James I did not drift off. Parker is still there. Get that through your thick skull, will you?"

James did some thinking. He wasn't convinced but there was no point riling her up any more than she already was. "Okay. Tell me where Tench lives."

Jane gave him the address. It was etched in her memory after what seemed like a lifetime of hanging around outside the house. "It's right on the Intracoastal, you can't miss it."

She'd had to dodge private security men who passed through the neighborhood every couple of hours.

"I'll meet you there in about an hour."

"An hour? What if something happens before then?"

"Handle it."

"Handle it? How am I supposed to—"

"Women." James cut the connection. Roger was going to kill him for missing work but this was more important. He ran out to the Ferrari and started it up.

"Hey!" Roger ran after him. "Where are you going? I made an appointment for you with a new customer. He'll be here any minute."

"Tell you about it later!" James waved his hand out the window.

"What happened to the Dino's front end?"

James ignored the question. He didn't have time and the answer was that he had smashed through a large number of recycle bins. His brother wasn't going to like hearing that answer, so why tell him?

Jane could wait. He wanted verification before wasting his time running around on her say so.

Stopping around the corner from Stewart Classic Motors, James looked up the old actor on his smartphone. Surprisingly, he found a listing for Parker

McRaney's home address. James pulled up a map with all the details he needed.

Parker McRaney resided out at the end of the Pelican Isle section of Fort Lauderdale in a too-big house with a turquoise tile roof. Golden gates at the end of the driveway bore the initials RR. An homage to the character and the show that had made it possible for the actor to afford this opulent estate?

The big gates hung open. James rumbled past a Mexican gardener standing on the back of a mower in a floppy hat, a red kerchief tied over his mouth and nose.

The gardener barely acknowledged James' presence. Which was fine with him. James parked at the end of the drive closest to the four-car garage beside a classic black on black Bentley.

Checking himself out in the Ferrari's tiny rearview mirror, James combed his fingers through his hair. All in all, he looked presentable. This was the sort of house, with its hand-carved, ten-foot oiled mahogany doors, manicured lawn and towering fountain where you wanted to look like you belonged at the front door rather than the service entrance.

A wizened woman with waves of gray hair and remarkably clear blue eyes for her age tilted her chin up at him. "Yes? Can I help you, young man?"

"Hi, I'm James. Parker asked me to drop by." It was a bluff, of course, but it didn't matter if Parker McRaney came to the door or not. James only wanted to discover if he was home.

If he was, Jane Bright had been very much mistaken. In which case, James planned to call her up and tell her so. Maybe he would gloat a little too.

Actually, yeah. Definitely he would gloat.

A lot.

"I'm sorry but Parker isn't here." The elderly woman wore a long light cotton frock covered with hummingbirds and red vines. Slippers covered her feet.

There was something vaguely familiar about her too.

James tilted his head. "Do I know you? Have we met?"

A smile transformed her face. Suddenly, she looked twenty years younger.

"You're Rocky Rhodes' mother." James snapped his fingers. "You're—"

"Mary Wilson." She held out her hand. James felt her bony fingers and papery skin as she squeezed his hand gently in hers. "You are a friend of Parker's?"

"Sort of." James stuck his hands in the pockets of his blazer. Wow, what was the actress who played Parker's TV mom on Rocky Rhodes, PI doing living in his house?

"Would you like to come in?" She held open the door. A cool breeze wafted through a huge entryway lined with old photos and modern paintings.

"No, I'd better not. Did I just miss him? Will he be back soon? I could come back." Jeez, what must this lady think of him?

She smiled benignly. "I don't believe Parker has been home since yesterday. He left in the afternoon. With a woman." She toyed with a ruby ring on the ring finger of her left hand. "I don't believe they've returned."

"You aren't worried?"

"No. Parker does that from time to time. He's like an old tomcat. You just have to let them do their thing."

"You said he left with a woman? Can you describe her?"

Suspicion finally flickered in Mary Wilson's eyes. "Who are you again?"

"James Stewart."

She scolded him with her eyes. "I have met James Stewart, young man. You are not James Stewart."

"No." James dug desperately into his back pocket for his wallet. This was also the kind of neighborhood where they called the cops on you if your dog so much as took a poop on their lawn. He didn't need the police showing up and wondering what he was up to.

"Not that James Stewart. This one." He handed the woman a business card.

"A car salesman?" She held the card up to the end of her nose. "This says *Roger* Stewart."

"Roger is my brother. I haven't had time to get new ones made yet." Sweat streamed from his forehead.

She flapped the card against her nose. "Parker does like his cars. Always has."

"Yeah. That's Parker, all right. When he gets back, please ask him to get in touch with me. I've got that Lambo he's been looking for."

James didn't wait for any assurance from Mary Wilson. He was in the Ferrari and down the drive before she'd even shut the front door.

52

Okay, so Parker McRaney wasn't home. Hadn't come home all night. Maybe Jane Bright, cub garden reporter, was right.

Following Jane's directions to Tench's house, James inched to the curb a solid half a block away. Away from prying eyes. He peeled off his SCM blazer and started walking.

Rounding the corner, a hand shot out from a six-foot crepe myrtle bordering the sidewalk and grabbed him roughly by the arm. "It's about time," Jane whispered harshly.

James took a step back. "What happened to you? You look like you got in a fight with a bear and lost."

Jane frowned, plucking leaves from her hair. "I've been on stakeout all night, that's what happened to me."

"Stakeout?" James waved his hand in front of his nose. "You smell."

"So don't breathe." She glared at him. "You got any other complaints?"

It had been a long night, a too long night. And this day wasn't over yet. In fact, it appeared to be far from over. And she had a column due at 5 p.m.

He combed his eyes up and down the length of her. "Your shoes are..."

"Are what?" Jane lifted her right leg and aimed a

shot at his shin. Her shoes were caked with dried mud and streaked with grass stains.

"Quite lovely," James said quickly. "Where can I get a pair?" He inched out of her reach and peeked through the branches. "Which house is it?"

"The pink one with the Mercedes in the driveway."

James nodded. "I recognize the car." He felt a sharp pain in the ankle and looked down. Red ants gnawed mercilessly on his flesh. He yelped and began swatting at them. "Help me!"

It was bad enough that the bottom of his left foot was scraped raw from last night's shoeless run, now a swarm of man-eating ants was making a meal of him.

"Keep it down. We don't want to draw attention to ourselves."

James ignored her. "My foot's on fire!" Racing to the nearest house, he grabbed a water hose tucked up close to the wall flanked by a loamy flowerbed. He hosed his leg down.

Throwing the hose on the ground, he looked down. The ants were now gone but the burning itch and accompanying pustules were going to last for days, weeks maybe. He cursed and shut off the water valve.

"Are you about done goofing around?" Jane shook her head at him.

"You aren't exactly Florence Nightingale, are you? Hell, you aren't even a Florence Henderson. Mrs. Brady would have offered sympathy—and salve."

"Get over yourself already. Any idea how we get inside?" Jane wanted to know, as she peeked through the bushes.

"You're sure Parker McRaney is in there?"

"Positive." Jane hesitated.

"What?"

"Unless they dumped his body in the canal or took off with him in the boat."

"What boat?"

"Tench's house sits on a canal off the Intracoastal. She's got a motorboat. Cabin cruiser I guess you'd call it."

"And you think she's holding him there?"

"No," the reporter said with little patience. "I'm suggesting that if he is not in the house then he might be one of those two places."

"On the boat or at the bottom of the canal." James frantically shook his damp leg. He knew his brother. If these expensive slacks were ruined, the price of a new pair was going to come out of his pocket.

"Exactly."

"All right." James resisted the urge to dig his nails in and attack the itch. It would only make it all the worse. As if that was possible.

It was midday, ninety-plus degrees outside and ninety-plus percent humidity. Maybe he should be back at Stewart Classic Motors sitting inside his brother's air-conditioned office sipping a lunchtime martini, shooting the breeze with a well-heeled client.

Why should he worry about some washed-up old Hollywood actor who might be in trouble?

"Well?"

James studied the sprawling one-story house. "Look at all those shrubs. There's plenty of cover around the sides between the houses. We ought to be able to get close enough for a look in the windows."

Had he really just said that? After what had happened last night?

"What if somebody sees us? There are laws against

peeping."

"Got a better idea?"

"How about if I knock on her door?"

"And say what, 'Excuse me but are you holding former TV heartthrob Parker McRaney hostage?'"

"Very funny. She knows I'm with the Broward County Times." Jane explained how she had tried interviewing Tench under the pretext of a gardening article.

"If she turned you down flat before, what makes you think you'll worm your way into her good graces this time?"

Jane considered. "I'll tell her that I spoke with Lou and—"

James threw up a hand. "Time out. Who is Lou?"

"Lou Edelstein. My editor."

"Right. Continue."

"I'll tell her that I talked to Lou and he suggested that I do a business profile on her."

Damn. That was good. Aloud, he said, "Not bad. I suppose it might work."

Then he had a thought. "You claim she kidnapped McRaney. What's to stop her from kidnapping you next?"

"What for? And in broad daylight? I don't think so. Why would she?" She gave him a patented do-you-know-what-an idiot-you-are look.

"Besides, I'll let slip that my editor knows that I was heading here." That was clever if she did say so herself. "Tench won't dare try anything."

Damn again, thought James. She wasn't as dumb as she sometimes acted.

Jane smiled because she knew she'd won. "Okay, then. I'll keep her busy while you check for sign of Parker. Do you need a description?"

"I saw the picture on that book jacket. I think I'm good to go." Besides, if there was a dead body lying around in Ronnie Tench's house or even a hog-tied one, whose else would it be but Parker McRaney's?

"All right. When you find Parker, get him out of there as fast as you can. I'll meet the two of you around the corner."

"What's around the corner?"

"My car."

James waited for a minivan slowly cruising past then hurried across the street.

"Don't run," yelled Jane. "It makes you look suspicious!"

53

James slowed to a walk, casually working his way between houses. The yards were big with plenty of space between homes. The house on the left seemed quiet. No barking dogs. No bored housewives or house-husbands, for that matter, or pesky kids with nothing better to do than snoop on the neighbors.

Hopefully, no jumping poodle would magically appear to alert anyone to his presence.

James got himself into position at the corner of the house and waited for Jane to ring the front doorbell. He couldn't hear what was being said but he recognized Ronnie Tench on the front stoop. After a brief discussion, Jane followed Ronnie inside.

Hopefully, not to end up at the bottom of the canal.

The first window revealed an empty office although the computer screen on the desktop displayed an open spreadsheet with row after row of meaningless numbers.

At the next window, he discovered a room filled with cardboard boxes spilling over with clothing and shoes, some books, odds and ends of furniture, a brass floor lamp and some fishing gear. All the useless things that Ronnie Tench couldn't bear to throw away or donate to her favorite charity apparently.

James' shirt ruffled in the breeze created by the spinning blades of a whirring AC unit sitting on a slab between two windows as he tiptoed past and approached the third window.

He took a careful peek.

Bingo!

The master bedroom suite. A king-sized bed with a red velvet-upholstered headboard floated on a sea of plush white carpet. A silver and crystal chandelier hung from the apex of the vaulted ceiling.

James caught a glimpse of a marble bathroom to the right. From the little bit visible, he estimated the bath could have held an entire Roman senate in full session.

A tousle-haired man in a fluffy baby-blue bathrobe sprawled in the middle of the bed. A pair of thin tan legs stuck out. Pillows were piled up around him. He was watching television with a teak tray balanced on his lap. The tray held food and drink.

Despite the obviously fake brown moustache drooping from the man's upper lip, he was sure who he was looking at.

Parker McRaney.

James watched for a minute, his sweaty fingers gripping the chalky edge of the window. There was no sign of shackles or handcuffs. Was Parker being watched? Was there someone in the room with him keeping an eye on him so he didn't escape? Did they have a gun?

Taking a risk, James pressed his nose to the window, trying to see more of the room. It was useless. Between the angle of the walls and the curtains bunched up at the sides of the window, he couldn't see any more than he was already seeing.

James ducked under the window and tiptoed to a row of windows on the opposite side. Inside, Parker took a lazy drag from a cigarette and coughed. The former TV star washed the cough away with a yellow liquid in a crystal glass and took another puff.

A sports fishing show playing on the television. There was no sign of anyone else in the room. James wondered how much longer Jane could keep Ronnie Tench busy before she burst into the bedroom.

Probably not long. Jane Bright could bore anybody to death in five minutes or less.

James bent his finger and rapped tentatively against the glass with his knuckle. The actor's eyes remained glued to the TV screen where some dude dressed up to look like Ernest Hemingway was trying to reel in a sailfish as big as he was.

When Parker failed to react, James knocked once again, harder.

Parker dropped the cigarette into his glass and stirred. His eyes swept over James and a look of surprise came over his face. Smiling, Parker waved a lazy hand in greeting.

James motioned for him to come to the window.

Parker pinched his brows together and spread his palms in a manner that let James know that he didn't understand.

"Come on," mouthed James, motioning wildly with his hands. "Let's go."

Parker maintained his puzzled expression.

James banged louder, rattling the glass pane.

Parker yawned and threw his feet off the side of the bed. His robe fell open. He ignored it.

The actor hobbled to the window and unlatched it. James pushed up the glass and said through the screen, "I'm James. A friend of Jane's. We came to rescue you."

Parker coughed.

James smelled alcohol and he smelled grass. But it wasn't the stuff under his feet.

"Rescue me? Jane?" Parker giggled. "You Tarzan, me Jane?"

James struggled with the flimsy window screen, yanking it out and tossing it on the lawn. "Come on." He held out a hand. "You'll have to come through the window."

Parker seemed amused and shrugged. "Why not?" He hitched up his robe, revealing pale blue boxer shorts covered in sailboats. He threw himself energetically at the window and hung his belly over the edge. "Hmm."

James heard voices. Somebody was coming but he couldn't make out who or from where. "Hurry. Come on. I'll help you." He grabbed Parker's flailing arms and pulled.

Parker grunted in anguish as his stomach scraped over the windowsill. James swore as Parker suddenly popped free of the window and landed atop him on the lawn. An in-ground sprinkler head punctured his flesh.

Parker giggled.

"Quiet." James worked himself to his knees.

"Parker!" James heard a woman call loudly. "Where are you, baby?"

"I'm—"

"Shh." James clamped his hand over Parker's mouth. The actor looked at him goggle-eyed.

James held his breath.

Ronnie Tench stuck her head out the open window and locked her red, angry eyes on James. "What are you doing there? What are you doing to Parker? What's going on?"

"Run!" James shouted. Grabbing Parker by the hand, he sprinted flat out.

54

"That is the last time I am ever looking in anybody's window," James swore. "Even my own." He keeled over, panting, in the side yard of the house down the street from Tench's place.

"Parker?" Jane looked at the disheveled actor standing complacently in his underwear. He swayed gently side to side as if caught in a soft summer's breeze. "What's wrong with him? Did Tench and her goons hurt him? Did she drug him?"

"He's drunk."

"Drunk!"

"And stoned."

Jane squished her cheeks between her palms and peered at the actor. "No way."

"Yes way."

"What happened to his clothes?" She pulled his robe closed and knotted the belt.

"Jane." Parker wiggled his fingers at her. Ronnie Tench's front door opened with a bang. Jane snatched Parker's hand. "Let's go."

Dragging Parker McRaney between them like an overgrown toddler, they managed to bundle him into the backseat of her Volkswagen.

Jane looked over her shoulder from the driver's seat. "What do we do with him?"

"Take him home, I guess." James closed the passenger side door. "He's obviously wasted."

"Parker, can you hear me?"

Parker's eyes popped open. "Jane."

"What happened last night? What did that woman do to you?" She ripped off the phony moustache hanging under his nose.

The actor leered at her. "Everything."

Jane blushed.

"I think he means—" James began.

"I know what he means." Jane angrily twisted the key in the ignition and started the Beetle.

Five minutes later, Parker was snoring in the cramped rear seat. Ten minutes after that, they were downtown. Jane and James each grabbed an arm and hauled the actor down the hall to Sheryl's office.

The city attorney was at her desk and she didn't look happy to see them. "What's this?" She looked at the motley trio over the top of her computer screen.

"You need to get a warrant. Raid Veronica Tench's house. Maybe even her business if you want. That's Tow the Line," blurted James.

Jane maneuvered Parker into a guest chair. "But her house, that's the important part."

Sheryl extended her palms. "Slow down, James. What are you two talking about?"

"He's talking about murder and conspiracy." Jane's eyes glistened with excitement. She'd managed to settle Parker down. However, his arms and legs were like rubber and he had a stupid grin plastered on his face.

James nodded. "We think Ronnie Tench and Bruno Caliostro are behind it."

"Probably Felicity Rain, too," added Jane.

"Are you sure about this?" Sheryl asked, tapping her pen against her knee.

"Rocky Rhodes, I mean, Parker McRaney was there. He can corroborate everything we're saying," insisted Jane.

"The actor?" Sheryl seared them with her eyes. "What's he got to do with this?"

"You know him?" James asked in amazement.

"Sure, Roger's got the complete series on DVD. He watches it sometimes when he works out on the treadmill in the morning."

"Wow. Did you hear that, Parker?" Jane asked.

"That's Parker McRaney?" Sheryl furrowed her brows and leaned in for a closer look at the robed spectacle.

"Jane," Parker said with a dopey grin, wriggling his fingers.

"What's wrong with him?" Sheryl wanted to know.

Jane blushed. "I'm sure he'd be flattered, if he wasn't so—"

"Drunk?" interjected Sheryl.

"Traumatized," Jane said, thinking fast. "And it's all Ronnie Tench's and Bruno Caliostro's doing."

"Would somebody in this room please start making sense," snarled Sheryl, quickly losing what was left of her patience.

"Jane," Parker said. "How's my Jane?"

James blocked Parker from Sheryl's view. "It's simple."

Sheryl rolled her eyes. "Nothing with you is ever simple, James."

Jane giggled as Parker grabbed her butt.

James glared at her. "It's simple," he insisted. "Parker McRaney infiltrated Veronica Tench's operations."

"This guy? *He* infiltrated her operations?"

"He went undercover."

Okay, it was more like under her bedcovers. There was no need to tell his sister-in-law that. It would only diminish things in her eyes.

"Parker was able to get a look at her computer. Where," James said firmly, "he discovered some things that would implicate Ms. Tench in the murder of Kevin Rain."

That much and little more they had gotten out of him on the ride over.

James held his breath awaiting Sheryl's reply. For once, just for once, she was going to take him seriously, see that he had done good.

Sheryl sucked in a breath, placed her hands flat on the desk.

Here it comes, thought James. My big moment.

Sheryl shot up from her seat. "What kind of an idiot are you? And what kind of an idiot do you take *me* for?"

James stumbled backwards under the force of her words. "Excuse me?"

"You heard me, James!" She shot around her desk and paced like a lioness in her cage. "I can't believe you. You go breaking into somebody's office? You're not a cop? And you've had one lousy intro class on how to be a detective. Are you nuts?"

"Actually, it was her house."

"Her house! Oh, that's good. That is so much better. You broke into Veronica Tench's house."

"No. No one broke into Tench's house. You aren't

listening to me, Sheryl. No one broke in anywhere."

"James' telling the truth," Jane said. "Ronnie invited Parker to her house."

"What is it you see in this guy?" Sheryl was talking to Jane whilst pointing her finger at James. "You're buying all this crap he's selling?"

Sheryl grabbed Jane by the shoulders. "Trust me, Jane. Just because he's your boyfriend does not mean you have to buy everything he sells."

"He's not my boyfriend!"

"She's not my girlfriend!"

Sheryl stared daggers at the two of them. She took a breath and methodically straightened some papers on her desk. Grabbing her purse by the strap, she waved it in their faces like a medieval mace. "You two had better be right."

She stomped to the door. "Because if you are wrong, the two of you will be spending the night together, whether you're dating or not."

Sheryl threw the door open with a bang. "In jail!"

Heels clicking officiously, Sheryl strutted down the hall. "Well," they heard her call, "what are you waiting for?"

Leaving Parker behind, James and Jane scurried after her.

Sheryl stopped outside Judge Renfro's office. "Wait here." She knocked and went in.

Twenty minutes later, she reappeared.

"Took you long enough." James groaned as he picked himself up off the floor. "Did you get the search warrant?"

Sheryl ignored the question. "Where's Jane?"

"She went to check on Parker." The guy had come

searching for the pair, complaining that he had the munchies. Parker and Jane had gone in search of a vending machine.

Sheryl ordered James to accompany her to Lt. Byrd's desk.

The lieutenant seemed even less happy to see him than his sister-in-law had been.

"Come to turn yourself in?" asked Lt. Byrd.

"Very funny. If I was a killer, I'd be in Belize by now."

"Good to know." She leaned back in her seat. "What's up, Sheryl?"

"This." Sheryl showed Lt. Byrd the warrant.

The two women ignored James and began talking strategy.

"You wait here," demanded Sheryl.

"Shall I lock him up to make sure he listens?"

Sheryl seemed to consider the idea, and then jerked a finger at James. "Wait in my office. You, Jane and Parker. Do not move until I get back."

55

James zonked out in Sheryl's Italian leather desk chair, his face mashed against her desktop. Parker McRaney was signing autographs for passers-by from a benchseat in the hallway.

Jane was the first to see Sheryl and the lieutenant return.

"Well?"

"Inside. Now," commanded Sheryl.

Jane meekly followed Sheryl into her office after getting Parker's promise to behave himself. Sheryl yanked her chair and sent James spinning from it and into a bookcase.

"What's going on? Did you get the goods on Tench?" James asked, picking up a handful of fallen books.

"We got nothing," Sheryl said icily.

"You wasted the department's time and money," added Lt. Byrd. "You got this, Sheryl?"

"Yes," hissed Sheryl.

Lt. Byrd sighed. "I gotta go write this up. Wait till my boss hears about this."

"You've embarrassed me, James. Me, the police department, the entire city."

"You didn't find anything?" Jane asked. "I don't understand."

"Neither do I." Sheryl threw herself into her chair.

"But Parker McRaney was so sure..." Jane's voice trailed off. She didn't know what to say.

The actor toddled through the open door. "Somebody call my name?" He waved hello to Sheryl. "You must be James' lovely sister. I've heard so much about you."

"That's sister-in-law," Sheryl corrected. "And I'm thinking, seriously thinking, about getting that *in-law* part changed."

Parker hiccoughed. "Is there a problem?"

"You've wasted my time and you're drunk. That's the problem."

"Actually, I'm not drunk, I'm—"

Sheryl threw up her hand. "I DON'T WANT TO KNOW!" The former TV star reeked of pot. "And, please, close your robe."

Parker shrugged and fiddled with the belt. It wasn't cooperating. "Didn't you find the evidence?"

"If you mean the nonsense that these two told me you found on Tench's computer, then no. We did not. As a matter of fact, we didn't find any evidence of any criminal activity whatsoever at her house." She threw herself into her chair. "Plenty signs of debauchery though."

"I'd hardly characterize my activities as debauchery," Parker replied, scratching his chest. "I was working under cover. Everything I did was for the greater good, I assure you." He aimed that last line at Jane and, to James' surprise, she appeared to be sucking it up.

"Right. The greater good." She'd seen empty champagne bottles, used condoms—a whip, for chrissakes—and enough Victoria's Secret lingerie to fill a catalog.

"Perhaps I was confused," Parker said. "That

woman…did things to me."

"I know," cooed Jane, patting his arm. "I'm so sorry. It's all my fault."

"I forgive you." He pecked her on the cheek.

Sheryl, wishing for something stronger, poured a glass of green tea from her travel bottle to her mug and guzzled it down. She'd read somewhere that it was good for one's nerves. "We'll be lucky if Tench doesn't sue the city. I'll be lucky if I keep my job."

"Sorry," James muttered.

"You sure are." The phone on Sheryl's desk rang. She glanced nervously at the number. "Great. It's the mayor. What am I going to tell her?"

Parker grinned. "Mayor Deborah Iyall?"

"That's right." Sheryl cocked her head at the actor. "You know her?"

"Deb and I go way back. She came to a fundraiser at my home some years ago. We've remained, shall we say, close. Maybe I can smooth things over." He wriggled his fingers.

Sheryl cautiously handed Parker the telephone. "Guess who. That's right. How's my foxy lady?" he asked smoothly. "Guess where I am?"

Sheryl gasped, sure the ax was about to fall. On her neck.

But it didn't. Parker sweet-talked the mayor for a minute or two and explained that Sheryl was assisting him in a personal matter. "Be right there, love." He handed Sheryl the receiver. "Deb's expecting us."

A change had come over the room and Sheryl. She ran her fingers through her hair. "What did she say?"

"She expressed her concern. And she asked me for a favor."

"What sort of favor?"

"She'd like a photo op. For social media. I told her it would be my pleasure."

"And me?" Sheryl's hand landed like a sparrow on her chest.

"You, too." Parker extended his hand. "Shall we?" He tugged at the lapel of Tench's bathrobe. "And might I borrow some clothes?"

"I'm sure we can find you something, Parker." Sheryl quickly smothered her hair some more then joined hands with the actor, giggling like a schoolgirl.

"I don't believe it." James watched Parker escort Sheryl down the hall towards the mayor's office. "I've never seen Sheryl act like that before."

"Parker can be quite persuasive."

"Let's get out of here before they come back." Parker might have a certain charm but when that charm wore off—and it would—Sheryl was bound to resume her attack.

56

James followed Jane to her VW. "Drop me off at my car, would you?" In their flight, they'd left the Dino behind in Ronnie Tench's neighborhood.

"I don't think so," replied Jane. "Ronnie could be out there watching us. Maybe even following us. We can't take a chance of her spotting you near her house. She's probably boiling mad."

"I suppose." James did not like the idea of leaving the Dino behind on the street but, in a neighborhood like hers, what were the odds of it being stolen?

The last thing he needed now was a confrontation with Ronnie Tench.

"Drop me off at Stewart Classic Motors then."

"Are you really selling cars now?" Jane asked as they pulled up to the dealership.

"It's temporary."

"Right."

Roger was talking up a customer drooling over a dark blue Mercedes-AMG Roadster. Good, that meant James got a temporary reprieve and would not have to listen to his brother complain. Not yet, anyway.

He stomped into the office and grabbed a cold Pepsi. "What the—"

"Like it?" Roger appeared in the open doorway, leaving his customer to take the Mercedes out for a test drive.

"Is that—" James' mouth hung open. He squeezed his fingers. Soda dribbled down the sides of the can and over his hand.

"Your Martin? Yep." Roger slapped his brother across the back. "The amp's in the storeroom."

James spun on him. "How did you get my stuff?"

Roger sank into his leather chair. "How do you think? I cruised down to the pawn shop and bought them."

"But they weren't supposed to sell anything for ninety days. We had a deal."

"What can I say? I made them an offer they couldn't refuse."

"Highly illegal, but thanks. I owe you." James set his Pepsi on his brother's desk and went to grab the guitar off the wall. Roger had screwed a guitar hook into the wall directly behind his desk. The Martin hung there like a trophy.

And James wanted it.

Roger wheeled his chair around, blocking James. "No, you don't. The Martin stays right where it is."

"It's mine. I want it back."

"And you'll get it back. You'll get everything back." He stroked the face of the Martin. "Just as soon as you pay me back."

Roger grinned the grin of victory as he ticked items off on his fingers. "For the guitar—I paid a thousand bucks for it, by the way. Plus, there's the amp. Another six hundred.

"And you'll have to repay me for the Dino. For the rent on the duplex." Roger's brows pulled together. "Where is the Dino, anyway?"

"At the duplex," James lied. "A friend dropped me off. Saves fuel."

"Good. Glad to see you're beginning to show some pride of ownership. Mind you, those Ferraris are hellishly expensive to repair. You'll see."

"Trust me, I see." James scratched his ankle. Those ant bites were killing him. "What happened to you? You used to be so easy-going. Sheryl has turned your heart to stone, bro."

"Me? You think I'm giving you a hard time?" Roger said. "I haven't asked why you ran off then came slinking back without a word of explanation. I'm not asking you about your clothes either. Your pants are wrecked. Your shirt's stained and one of the pockets on your blazer is coming unstitched."

"You haven't talked to Sheryl?"

"Nah." He glanced at his phone. "She left me a couple of texts but I've been tied up."

"Let me explain. You see, I was—"

Roger threw up his hands like a roadblock. "I do not want to know."

They stared at each other a moment, tension crackling between them. "Look, I'm doing you a favor, James. You never could have afforded to get your gear out of hock. You know that and I know that. This way, your stuff's safe. It's in the family. Better me than being in the home of some stranger, right?"

"I'm not so sure about that."

"Cheer up, James. Could be worse."

"How?"

"Sheryl wanted me to keep it at the house. Said she was thinking of taking guitar lessons."

"Sheryl? Lessons on my Martin?" James pictured

her fumbling fingers and long talons scratching the lovingly polished finish.

"See?" Roger spread his hands. "I'm doing you a favor."

There was a rap on the door. The customer for the Mercedes peeked inside.

"How was the ride?"

"Terrific," said the gentleman. "Can't beat that acceleration."

James rolled his eyes. Who needed to get from zero to sixty in three and a half seconds? And how many chances would one get to try it on the congested roads around here?

"Great. Let's talk numbers." Roger waved James off as he went into business mode, offering his customer a cold drink and a cheap pastry as he attempted to snatch a big wad of money from the man's bank account.

"James," Roger said. "There is one more thing."

James stopped at the door. "What's that?" His nerves bristled.

"Speaking of Sheryl, she texted she'd like a word with you. In her office."

James' shoulders sagged. "Forget it. I just left her office."

"What should I tell her if she asks for you again?"

And they both knew she would.

"Tell her I'm on my way," James lied.

57

A silver-haired, shirtless jogger with a deep bronze tan and knobby knees, dressed in floppy navy blue nylon shorts, waved at their car as he hobbled along on the shady side of the street. A monarch butterfly skipped from flower to flower in a neat little swath of blossoms—an island of life in an otherwise barren sea of lawn.

"Thanks for the lift, Hal," said James. "You can let me out here."

Rather than face Sheryl again so soon—he hadn't yet recovered from his last visit—James had bummed a ride to the Ferrari from Hal Linder, one of Roger's mechanics, as he was leaving work for the day.

"Where's your car?" asked Hal, peering out the window and scanning each side of the palm tree- and sea grape-lined residential street where James had asked to be let out.

"Up ahead a little." James pointed vaguely to an imaginary point in the distance. He didn't want the mechanic to know that the Ferrari seemed to be missing. Hal was bound to tell Roger. More trouble with his brother he did not need. "I feel like stretching my legs."

"Whatever you say."

James climbed out and the mechanic drove off. James walked over to where he was certain he had parked the Ferrari.

It was definitely gone.

A woman in a straw hat stood watering a patch of orange and yellow flowers in a bed alongside her house. James walked over. "Excuse me. Have you seen a red Ferrari? I'm sure I parked it right here."

James pointed to an oil patch where his car had once been. Had the Ferrari sprung a leak? That would be a pricey fix.

The woman twisted the nozzle of her hose to off. Small droplets fell on her toes. "Was that your car?"

James nodded.

"I'm sorry but I saw a tow truck take it away. Did you have a breakdown?"

"No." But he was about to. "Who towed it? Smiley's?"

If it was, it had to be Adam Mitchell's doing. James vowed to get even with him. Then again, it might have been Felicity, assuming she had any pull at the towing service, which he didn't doubt for a minute. Especially with Kevin dead.

Had she recognized him as the pervert peeking in her window the other night?

"No." She moved a few steps over and turned the spray on a patch of clematis. "It was that other one. I see their truck quite often. At that house down the street." She pointed the hose in the direction of Ronnie Tench's home.

"Tow the Line?"

"Yes, that's right."

James swore. The woman blushed. "Sorry," he said and walked away.

It turned out the odds of the Ferrari Dino being

stolen were pretty good when you left it unattended near the house belonging to the hard-nosed owner of a towing company, especially when she had a grudge against you.

James' duplex was miles away. He'd be lucky to make it by dark. Needing a ride, he fished out his phone and dialed Cindi's number. Hopefully, she was ready to forgive him now.

She was.

He waited for her to arrive under the shade of a live oak around the corner from Tench's house. Twenty minutes later she appeared.

"Thanks." James stepped out from the shade of a live oak and climbed into the Jeep.

Cindi smiled. "I can't stay mad at you, James." She shifted into gear and pulled away from the curb. "What are you doing out in this neighborhood?"

"We were investigating Veronica Tench."

"We?" She glanced at him.

"Me and Jane Bright."

"Are you and she..." Her voice trailed off.

"We're working together, that's all. Trust me," James said. "And I'm reluctant to even do that."

"Did you get Ollie's camera?"

"Alyssa gave it to me. I called my friend David. He promised to refurbish it."

"Thanks."

"I'll take it to him tomorrow. We have a sunrise shoot in South Beach."

"Sunrise?"

"David likes to shoot early. He says the light is perfect. Less people on the beaches too. I'm modeling the new Brees-Way bikini line."

"Congratulations."

"Thanks."

"Is the public invited?" Visions of a bikini-clad Cindi frolicking on the beach swam through his head.

"Sorry. I'd invite you to watch but David is sensitive. Doesn't like spectators."

"Too bad." In spite of the crazy hour, it would have been worth getting out of bed at the crack of dawn for.

"Alyssa is coming though. She's going to act as my assistant. Hair and makeup and stuff. David's cool with it. She didn't want to but I convinced her that it would do her good to get out."

"Good idea."

The sun was settling towards the west. Cindi removed her oversized dark sunglasses and rested them between the seats. A skintight pink dress clung to her skin. A white baseball cap shaded her forehead.

"Do you think Veronica Tench is the one? The killer, I mean?"

"I think she's involved. I'm not sure exactly how, but somehow. More and more, I'm thinking Kevin's ex-wife might be mixed up in this too."

"That's what Alyssa thinks."

"I know. How's she holding up?"

"Okay. I'm sure she'll feel better once Kevin's killer is caught."

"Me, too."

They talked about dinner and Cindi suggested her place. "I need to water my plants, pick up my mail, and check on things in the apartment."

James wasn't going to argue. Cheaper to eat in than out.

Cindi dropped him off at Tow The Line.

"I'll meet you at your place as soon as I've finished here."

The battered Dino was impossible to miss, sitting directly outside the entrance. James cupped his hands and peered through the car window. No sign of his keys. He'd been an idiot to leave them in the ignition in his haste to see what Jane was up to.

Now he'd have to go inside.

Skinny Tie greeted him at the door. "We've been expecting you. The boss is waiting for you upstairs."

"Terrific." James wasted no time. He took the steps two at a time and barged into her office unannounced.

Ronnie Tench sat behind her desk, unfazed. She waved for him to sit. "I talked to your partner yesterday." She studied her dark blue fingernails as if they held all the secrets of the Egyptian pyramids.

"Partner? I don't have a partner?" James settled in a squeaky red leather chair.

Through the glass, he could see Skinny Tie below, leaning idly against a filing cabinet, looking up at them. No doubt waiting to burst in and crack James' skull at the first sign of trouble.

"Jane Bright, that reporter. She said the two of you also run a detective agency."

"Ms. Bright has an overactive imagination." He leaned forward, pressing his elbows into his knees. "I want my car back."

"Car?"

"Let's not play games. It's parked right out front."

"You see, I'm not playing games," she said with a smile. "Nor am I hiding anything." She slid open the middle drawer of her desk and dropped his car keys at the far side of the desk. "Here. Bad habit leaving things where they don't belong. And with the keys in the ignition, no less."

James snatched the keys off the desk before she changed her mind. Roger would absolutely kill him if he lost the Ferrari. "What about you and Felicity Rain?"

"I'm trying to do the woman a favor. We businesswomen need to stick together. I offered to buy her out. Pay her enough to wipe out her debts and give her a little nest egg to start over with. But does she thank me? No. She gives me trouble. Nothing but trouble. Same as you." She leveled her eyes on James.

"Does Phil Adler work for you?"

"I'm not familiar with the name."

"What was one of your trucks doing at his house the other day?"

"I have no idea, Mr. Stewart. Perhaps one of my drivers is friends with him."

"Which one?"

"How should I know? I'm not their mommy." She rose and beckoned to Skinny Tie.

He bounded up the stairs, popped open the door and stuck his head in. "Yes, Ms. Tench?"

"Please see that Mr. Stewart finds his way out without getting lost on the way."

Skinny Tie guy grinned an evil grin and gestured for James to lead the way.

"One more thing, Mr. Stewart," said Ronnie Tench.

James stopped in the doorway. "Yeah?"

"It was rude of Parker to leave without saying goodbye. Tell him no hard feelings and to give me a call sometime."

58

James drove to Cindi's apartment and rapped on her door.

"It's open!"

Entering, he found Cindi sprinkling her houseplants with a small brass watering can.

"Hi, James. Help yourself to a beer while I finish up."

James grabbed a can from the fridge and carried it outside. He leaned over the balcony sipping and thinking through his problems.

No answers immediately came to mind. Maybe he should borrow The Beginner's Guide to Detection from Artie and try reading it himself. Speaking of which, he couldn't wait to hear Parker McRaney's full explanation of what he had been doing at Veronica Tench's house all night—once he sobered up enough to make sense.

Cindi called his name from the kitchen and thoughts of murder dissipated. Dinner had arrived.

A light breeze blew and jagged lines of lightning pulsed soundlessly to the east. Somewhere out above the Atlantic Ocean, a storm raged and boats large and small rocked in the roiling waves.

James and Cindi settled out on her patio—safe, warm and alone. That was the best part, he thought, alone. No intruding drunken sisters, no annoying brothers, no class clowns and no interfering reporters.

Life was good. Under the circumstances.

Over a meal of takeout Italian food, of which Cindi managed to eat a salad with no dressing and one artichoke ravioli pillow stating, "I don't want to look fat tomorrow," the conversation turned once again to her brother-in-law's murder.

"You mentioned earlier that *we* are investigating." Cindi tilted her wine glass this way and that, then took a sip. "There's Jane. Who else? Those people at your place?"

"Yeah." The corner of James' mouth turned down. "I seem to have picked up a few partners. The way a roadkill armadillo picks up maggots and flies. In particular, the one you just mentioned, Jane Bright, has been hounding me like a tick on a dog."

"She seemed nice when I met her."

"That's one opinion."

Cindi giggled.

"Plus, my classmates, ex-classmates. The ones you met from the School of Detection. Ollie and Artie have been doing some digging. Claudia's been digging too."

"Did they learn anything?" She toyed with a cold ravioli but it never made it to her mouth.

"Nothing much."

"Too bad." Cindi licked her fork clean. "Did I understand you right? You quit school?"

"Suspended. Bruno's afraid having a murder suspect in his class might tarnish his image. Such as it is." Flashbacks of Felicity and Bruno floundering atop her king-sized bed came to mind. "Remind me to tell you more about Bruno later."

She nodded and he continued. "Jane got this crazy

idea that Ronnie Tench was holding Parker McRaney captive at her house. She lives around the corner from where I had you pick me up."

"And was she?"

James smiled. "If he was a captive, he was a willing one." He described how and where he had found the actor. "Then we called the cops."

"And?"

"They got a search warrant for Tench's home based on our word. Parker's word, really."

"And?"

"And came up empty."

Cindi giggled. "Sorry." She cupped her hand over her mouth. "Maybe you should leave this to the police."

"I think you're probably right."

"When I met the others at your house and they talked about trying to find Kevin's killer, I didn't take them seriously. It's sweet of them but why would they care?"

"Because they're lunatics."

She laughed some more. "You're funny." She stroked his thigh under the table. "What does this Parker McRaney have to do with Kevin? Who is he? Do you think he had something to do with Kevin's murder?"

James swallowed, his breath catching in his throat. The sudden and too brief touch of her hand on his leg had temporarily disengaged his brain. It took him a second to comprehend the question. "You don't know?"

Cindi shook her head. She removed her sandals and placed a bare foot against the railing, revealing a length of sculpted leg. She rubbed her foot seductively. A silver ring graced her second toe.

"No, I guess you wouldn't. You're too young. Parker McRaney is, was, a TV star. I think he's pretty much retired now."

Cindi's eyes grew wide with interest. "You mean he was famous? How famous?"

James explained about the hit TV show. "I'm not sure what else he's done." He pictured a string of Love Boat appearances followed by Hollywood Squares, and a long fade into oblivion.

"Wow." She nodded yes when James offered her more wine. "I'll IMDb him."

It was James' turn to look confused.

"It's the Internet Movie Database. It lists everything an actor's done." She leaned across the table. "Do you think you could introduce me?"

"Well..."

"I'll bet he still knows lots of people in Hollywood. Does Mr. McRaney live here permanently or is he visiting?"

"I don't know if he lives in Fort Lauderdale year-round but he has a house not far from here."

"I'd do anything to meet him," Cindi said dreamily.

"I'll see what I can do." A girl saying she will do anything is a strong motivation to act for any male.

"Thanks." She stretched across the table and planted a kiss on his lips. "I'll be right back with the panna cotta."

James watched her go. Cindi had insisted on ordering a panna cotta with raspberry sauce of which she proceeded to eat a single spoonful, leaving him to enjoy the rest.

While James polished off the creamy dessert, he explained what he and his other classmates had come up with thus far.

Admittedly, it wasn't much.

"Tell me more about Kevin."

"How do you mean?"

James licked his spoon clean. "I know next to nothing about him. Only that he loved Alyssa and trains. What else can you tell me about Kevin Rain, the man?"

"Do you think it will help?"

"The more I learn about the victim, the more I might learn about the killer and his or her motives."

"That's smart."

"Thanks." No point bursting her bubble mentioning that he remembered a feature film detective, Charlie Chan maybe, saying something to that effect.

Cindi stretched her neck and thought. "There's not much to tell. You said it yourself, he loved my sister and he loved his trains. And the business. He practically never took vacations."

"Was he worried about Tench moving into the county?"

"Sure. But he said he could handle her." She stood and began clearing the table. "If you ask me, it looks like Ronnie Tench wanted Kevin's business at any price."

James stood and helped carry the empty food containers to the trash. Cindi kept her garbage can under the kitchen sink where it belonged. He'd point that little fact out to Jane the first chance he got.

"I spoke to a former tow operator named Larry Dobb up in Palm Beach. He had nothing good to say about Tench or her tactics. He liked Kevin though."

"That's nice. I remember seeing the name. He's invited to the memorial service. I helped Alyssa send out the announcements."

"When is it?"

"The day after tomorrow. All of Kevin's friends and family and his buddies from the Broward County Model Train Hobbyist Society are invited. Would you like to attend?"

"I don't think that would be a good idea. There might be news coverage." And wouldn't the news hounds like to get a shot of the number one suspect attending Kevin Rain's funeral. "Did Kevin ever mention Caliostro to you?"

"Sure. When I mentioned to Kevin that I was handing out flyers for the School of Detection, he said..." She closed her eyes a moment. "Those that can, do. Those that can't, teach. Then he laughed."

"Interesting. In the meantime, I've got Dale and Kourtney paying me to find out who murdered their dearly departed father."

"Like those two care."

"It's weird, isn't it?"

"Hey, I have an idea."

"Oh?"

"Uh-huh." Her blue eyes glittered with excitement. "Let's hold a séance."

59

"A séance?" James asked skeptically. "What for?"

"You said you wanted to learn more about the victim. Let me channel Kevin."

James cocked his head to one side. "You can do that?"

"Sure. I mean, I think so."

"Don't we need more people?" Images of a half-dozen or more people holding hands around a table came to mind. He'd seen that in countless films.

"Why? There's no minimum requirement," countered Cindi. "That's only in the movies, silly."

"I don't know…"

"Come on, James. This will be fun. Think what we can learn." She flipped the lights off and tossed a couple of sofa cushions to the middle of the living room floor. "I don't know why I didn't think of this before. We'll ask Kevin who killed him."

Cindi squatted and patted the cushion beside her. "Join me. Sit here."

"Do you really believe in this stuff?"

"Sure. There must be a spirit world. I mean, the dead have to go somewhere, don't they?"

James figured it was hard to argue with a statement like that so he didn't bother trying. He went another route. "Are you sure about this? Don't we need the collective energy of a bunch of people for a séance?"

Was he really having a serious discussion about the requirements for holding a successful séance? Was this what his life had come to?

"Nah. Like, I said, that's only in the movies. We've got enough psychic energy between the two of us." She crossed her legs and wriggled her butt. "Come on. Sit."

Copying Cindi, James experienced sharp pains in his knees as he lowered himself onto the cushion, crossing his legs as best he could.

"Oops. I almost forgot." Cindi jumped to her feet. Crossing to the credenza, she pulled out a candle, an incense burner shaped like a fat little Buddha, and a stick of incense. She placed the three things on the coffee table. She lit the candle then used the flame of the candle to ignite the sandalwood incense stick. A slow, hypnotic smoke began wafting toward the ceiling.

Cindi rejoined James. "Now, hold my hands."

James gripped her warm hands in his. She looked beautiful in the glow of the candlelight. He was tempted to reach over and steal a kiss.

"Now, close your eyes." She stroked her fingers gently across his eyelids and he complied. "Kevin, Kevin Rain. Can you hear me?" She drew in a long, slow breath and let it out again. "It's me, Cindi."

"With an i," muttered James. "Ouch!" He threw his eyes open.

Cindi had pinched him in the forearm. "Be serious." She pushed his eyes shut once more. "Kevin. We want to help you. Tell us, who murdered you?"

Despite himself, James found himself waiting for an answer from the Other World.

"Toe."

James snuck a peek out of the corner of his left eye. The deep sound had come from Cindi. The flame of the candle danced.

"Yes?" Cindi said. "Tell us more."

James felt a chill breeze against his back. Had they left the door to the balcony open?

"Toe," the husky voice emanating from Cindi repeated.

James shivered. He had only dealt with Kevin the one time, but she did sound eerily like him. Cindi tightened her grip on his hands.

"Fill."

"Maybe we can start narrowing the list of suspects down." James was running out of patience. "Ask your brother-in-law if his killer is a man or a woman. Then ask him if—"

The candle suddenly went out.

They both opened their eyes.

"Sorry." Cindi waved her hand through the smoke. "I think he's gone."

James rested on the palms of his hands. "Toe and fill. What's that supposed to mean? His skull was smashed, not his toe."

Cindi slowly smiled. "Maybe…maybe Kevin mean's t-o-w."

"Yeah, as in Tow the Line." He snapped his fingers. "And not fill with an f but p-h-i-l. Phil."

"The man who used to work for Smiley's," Cindi said.

"Okay. Maybe we've got something." Not that he believed in spirits or in the channeling thereof, but still. "Maybe your brother-in-law is trying to tell us that Phil Adler is responsible for his murder."

"I think you're right." Despite her earlier optimism, Cindi appeared almost as surprised by their improbable success as he was.

"And he's the one person I haven't been able to talk to yet. Well, that's going to change." James checked the time. "It's getting late. I should go. You've got an early shoot in the morning."

"You're leaving already?" Cindi laced her fingers through his. "Wouldn't you care for some dessert?"

"We had dessert."

"Not that kind of dessert, silly." Cindi led him down the hall to her bedroom.

60

Downstairs in the parking lot of the High Tide Apartments complex, Jane waited as patiently as she could. She was a reporter. She was used to waiting. Sometimes getting a story took time. Lots of time. Time and patience. And perseverance.

But there was a limit to how much one woman could take, wasn't there?

The VW was cramped and hot. The windows kept steaming up, her neck was stiff and she had to pee. Desperately.

What was keeping James?

When the lights went out in Cindi Keach's apartment and James didn't appear soon after, Jane decided she had had enough.

She went up and banged on the door.

Cindi answered. Her lipstick was smeared and her lips were swollen. The buttons on her shirt were undone down to her navel, exposing a lacy bubble-gum-pink bra. "Hello. You're the reporter."

"Jane Bright." She noticed a trail of light coming from the hallway. The scent of sandalwood filled the air. There was no sign of James.

"What's up?" asked Cindi, toying with a button.

In contrast, Jane's had pulled her hair back in a stiff ponytail, held in place with a rubber band. Her loose dark cotton shorts were wrinkled beyond hope and her peplum top was frilly but it was also damp with I've-been-cooped-up-in-a-car-too-long perspiration. "I was looking for James. I have some urgent information about the case."

Jane peeked past Cindi. "Is he here?" Could he have managed to leave when she wasn't looking?

"Come on in," Cindi said instead, moving inside and flicking on a lamp in the living room.

Jane trailed behind. She noticed two sofa cushions on the floor next to a candle and a still smoldering stick of incense.

"Would you like something to drink?" asked Cindi.

"No, thanks. I would like to use your bathroom."

Cindi pointed. "Straight down the hall."

"Thanks." Jane couldn't help feeling awkward and not just a little insignificant in comparison to Cindi.

All those photographs on the living room wall and more in the hallway. The camera loved her. How come she, Jane, always managed to be yawning, scratching her nose or looking like she'd smelled something funny in all of her pictures?

Even her official photo for her column in the Broward County Time made her face look too fat and her nose too big.

Jane started down the hall then stopped to say, "You never said, is he here?"

"Yes, he is." James stormed up the hallway, hair tousled, carrying his shoes. He'd barely had time to pull the bedroom curtains shut when he'd heard the banging on the door. He expected to find maybe Alyssa here. Instead here he was looking at Jane. "Why are you here?"

"I wanted to talk to you about the case." Jane

clutched her purse defensively against her chest. "I thought you would want to hear what Parker had to say."

"How did you find me?"

"Does it matter?"

"Yes, it matters.' James was frustrated and he was angry. She was spying on him and tailing him. Without him even being aware of it. Again.

Worse yet, she'd interrupted his Cindi time. He needed his Cindi time.

"Artie told me. I had him follow you."

"You what? Artie?" Artie had outsmarted him? How was that even possible?

Jane didn't see any reason to repeat herself. He'd heard her well enough. So she didn't bother.

"Okay, answer me this. *Why* did you ask Artie to follow me?"

"I wanted to make sure you weren't in any danger." Jane also wanted to keep track of him. Make sure he didn't shut her out of the investigation. She was going to get a newsworthy story out of the Kevin Rain murder whether James liked it or not.

"I was perfectly fine until you showed up." He stuffed in his shirttails.

"So I see."

"Anybody like a glass of wine?" Cindi asked. Both declined. She slid between them and poured herself a glass from the box in the refrigerator. Leaning a shoulder against the wall, she sipped quietly as James and Jane argued back and forth.

"Do you want me to fill you in or not?"

James scoffed. "Don't tell me, did can't-keep-his-pants-on Parker fill your head with more fairy tales?"

Cindi set her wine glass on the coffee table. "You met Parker McRaney?"

Jane nodded. "We're friends."

"You just met him!" James blurted.

Jane blushed and stuttered. "We've become very close."

James snorted and threw his hands in the air. "You're bonkers."

Cindi didn't seem to mind one way or the other. "Imagine, friends with a TV star. That is so cool." Moving to the living room, she picked up the sofa cushions and set them back in place. "I want to know what he said. Tell me everything. Please?"

"In a minute." Jane ran to the restroom. Finishing up, she splashed cool water on her face and fixed her makeup in the medicine chest mirror. Not great but presentable. She brushed her hair and took a deep breath before rejoining Cindi and James.

James stretched out on the sofa with his legs across Cindi's lap. Taking the chair, Jane crossed her legs, opened her purse, and pulled out her notebook. "Are you ready for a debriefing?"

The only debriefing James had been looking forward to having would have been at the hands of Cindi.

Another lost opportunity to add to his life list.

61

"Sure." James laced his fingers behind his head. "Debrief me."

Flipping her notebook open, Jane began. "Parker searched Ronnie's computer."

"He snuck in her office?" Cindi's eyes grew wide. "How did he manage that?"

"Trust me, he didn't," James told her.

"At her house." Jane explained how the actor had gone undercover and somehow been lured out to Ronnie Tench's house.

"Enticed by the offer of sex," James interjected.

"We don't know that." Jane's eyes sizzled at him. Though Parker had mumbled something about the woman's appetite and he hadn't been talking about food.

James shrugged and Jane continued.

"As I was trying to explain," Jane cleared her throat, "Parker believes that Ms. Tench could be the one funding Adler's lawsuit against Smiley's."

"Wow." Cindi looked at James. "You might have found Kevin's killer." She kissed him on the cheek.

Jane bristled. James hadn't done anything except manage to get himself bitten by a few lousy ants. And why didn't the slut button her shirt?

"Not so fast," James said. "The police checked

Tench's place out, including her home computer, and came up empty."

"So?" Jane replied. "Maybe she erased the evidence off the hard drive before they got there."

"The police have ways of finding things. Erased or not."

"How can you be so sure? And would you just be quiet and let me continue?"

"Okay, okay." James threw up his hands. The woman was nuts. The sooner he got rid of her, the sooner he could focus on Cindi. "Continue."

"The question remains," Jane said, "if Parker's correct, and Tench is helping Adler put the squeeze on Smiley's, why kill him now?"

"Good question," admitted James. "It sounds like Tench had Kevin on the ropes. Sooner or later, he would've sold out or been forced out of business."

"Poor Kevin." Cindi sank into the sofa.

"What else did Parker find out?" James asked.

Jane flipped through her notes. "Not much. Parker looked at her books. From what it looked like to him, Tow The Line is losing money, going broke fast. She's spending far more cash than she's taking in."

"So much for the great business woman," said James. "Maybe that's why she murdered Kevin. She knew she couldn't keep going the way she was much longer. The cash was running out. And fast."

Jane nodded. "Parker did say that Ms. Tench was looking for a partner. She asked him if he was interested in investing in her company."

"What did he tell her?" Cindi wanted to know.

"He told her he'd think about it."

"I thought you said he was working undercover?

Tench knew it was him?"

Jane blushed. "Yes. She recognized him right away. It seems she had a crush on him when his show was on the air."

"Great. Just great." James groaned. "How did Parker explain why he'd gone to see her?"

"Parker told her that he was researching a role for a Netflix movie."

"Oh, brother." James shook his head.

"I think that makes perfect sense." Cindi curled her legs under her butt. "I wonder if he could find a part for me..."

James gaped at Cindi. Were all women as crazy as these two? Was he the only person in the room with a home address in the real world? "I need a drink."

James went to the kitchen and helped himself to a glass of wine, drinking quickly. "Where's Parker now? Home sleeping it off?"

Jane looked down her nose at him. "For your information, he and the others are conducting an operation." She looked at her watch. "As we speak."

"What do you mean *operation*?"

"A surveillance operation, like Parker describes in his book."

"What?" James threw his feet to the floor and stood. "Where?"

"If you must know, Parker suggested we conduct a late night reconnaissance of the Adler residence." Jane jumped to her feet.

"You've got to be joking."

"How exciting." Cindi squeezed James' hand.

"Exciting? Are you kidding?" James turned to Jane. "What exactly are they intending to do?"

Jane blushed. "Parker has a plan."

"Oh, goodie. Is it as brilliant as his last plan? The one where he ends up in bed with the suspect and then jumps out the window in his underwear?"

"You are such an idiot!" Jane stuck her nose in James' face.

"And you are a—"

Cindi put out her hands and separated them. "Yelling isn't going to solve anything, you two. Am I right?" She scorched each of them with a stern, motherly look.

"Right," James grudgingly agreed.

"Sorry," Jane said, looking at the floor.

Cindi beamed. "Now," she planted her hands on her hips, "I suggest you go see what Parker McRaney and your friends are up to."

"I don't think—"

Cindi placed her finger against James' lips. "Don't think. Do. Go see what Parker and the others are up to. You can keep an eye on them that way. Keep them out of trouble."

"What about, you know, us?"

"There's plenty of time for us. Go. Your friends need you."

"Cindi has a point, James." Not that Jane was in the mood to flatter the woman in any way, shape or form.

"I suppose." James kissed Cindi's finger.

Jane rolled her eyes heavenward.

"You want to come?" James asked Cindi.

"I can't." Cindi replied. "I have a photo shoot in the morning, remember?"

"Yeah." Bikinis and beaches. He should give up this stupid detective idea and take a photography class.

How hard could it be?

James rubbed the nape of his neck. “Let’s go, Bright.” He stopped at the door and planted a kiss on Cindi’s lips. “I’ll call you tomorrow and let you know how it went.”

“I’m counting on it. Goodnight, Jane. Nice seeing you again. Oh, wait!” Snatching her purse off the floor near the sofa, she slipped a business card into the reporter’s hand.

“What’s this for?” Jane looked at the card.

“My contact info. Could you give it to Parker when you get a chance? Please?”

“I suppose.”

As Jane and James headed to the elevator, she stuffed the business card deep inside her purse where she hoped it would disappear along with every lip gloss, pair of nail clippers and bit of loose change she’d ever misplaced.

62

"There they are." James pointed out the passenger window to the dark hulk that was Ollie's food truck.

"I can see that," Jane replied, holding the wheel of the VW steady and easing up on the gas. The road was narrow, dark and bumpy. The heavens were closing in.

"Of course, you can. The whole world can see it," complained James. "I mean, did they really think they wouldn't get noticed sitting in an open field inside a food truck the size of Manhattan? Orbiting Chinese satellites can see it."

"You're just mad because you didn't get to have… relations with Cindi. You've been in a bad mood since we left." Jane rumbled off the road, bringing her car to a stop mere steps from Ollie's Delights. Light leaked out of the seams of the van.

"Relations?" James snorted. "Who talks like that? Your grandmother? It's sex. You ever have sex, Jane Bright, reporter?"

Jane thought it was a good thing it was so dark—he couldn't see she'd turned cherry red. "You're twice her age. And do you always have to talk about sex?"

"You started it!"

"Fine. Let's focus, shall we?"

"Whatever." He stared at Adler's shadowy property.

"I don't see the others."

"They must be inside the food truck." James stepped out of Jane's car and banged on the back of the truck. "Open up. It's me, James."

"James?" The door opened with a squeak and Artie poked his head out. He gripped a half-eaten, catsup-dripping cheeseburger with onions in his left hand, a 7-Up in his right. "What are you doing here?"

"We came to check on you."

"We?"

"Who's there?" James heard Ollie call from the belly of the truck.

"Me and James." Jane pushed James out of her way and climbed inside. The interior smelled like a beach barbecue.

To James' surprise, Parker rushed to her. "Jane, darling. Lovely to see you again." He locked her in his embrace and didn't let go until he caught sight of James.

"Ah, my knight in shining armor. Did I tell you boys how James stormed the castle to come to my aid?"

Ollie and Artie shook their heads in the negative.

"A pleasure to see you once again, James." The actor gave James a warm hug.

"Right, you too." James freed himself. "Fill us in. What's going on?"

"We were about to initiate phase one of our attack."

"Attack?" Jane didn't like the sound of that. "Where's Claudia?" She had promised Jane that she would keep an eye on the guys. Make sure they didn't get into trouble.

"Claudia did some reconnoitering." Ollie sucked noisily on a strawberry malt. "She said Adler appeared to be home alone."

"And where is she now?" James asked. "Not inside with him, I hope."

"No, I sent her on an errand." Parker examined his watch. "She took my car. We expect her to return any moment."

"What sort of errand?" James demanded.

"Parker's got a pair of night vision binoculars at home." Artie wiped his greasy fingers on his chinos. "He sent Claudia to get them."

"What are you doing with night vision binoculars?"

"We used them on my TV show. I kept them. A small souvenir."

"Which episode was that?" Artie asked.

"It doesn't matter which episode, Artie," James said.

"I'm not sure. Actually, I believe we used them in several instances, Artie. In any event, I texted Mary and told her to have them ready for your associate," Parker explained.

Jane squeezed her way past the others to the front of the truck where she had a clear view of Adler's house. Did he know they were here? It would have been impossible not to see Ollie's food truck. Was he watching them now?

The house was dark except for perhaps a glow coming from a room toward the back. The tall fence surrounding the yard blocked their view. Still, maybe Parker's night vision binoculars would come in handy.

As if on cue, Claudia burst through the back door of the food truck, binoculars in her hand. "Idiots!"

"What's wrong?" whined Artie.

"Aren't you watching?"

"Sure." Ollie scratched the top of his head with a spatula. "We've been keeping an eye on the house."

"Really? Because as I was driving up—which by the way, none of you even noticed and I could have shot you all dead—I saw someone leaving."

"Impossible." Parker snatched the binoculars and joined Jane up front. He plopped himself down in the driver's seat and peered out.

"Did you see who it was?" asked James.

"No. I only saw a car's headlights going in the opposite direction."

James shrugged. "The car could have been coming from anywhere."

"It was coming from behind Adler's fence," insisted Claudia. "I'm not stupid."

Jane rolled down the window on the passenger side. "I hear dogs."

The others heard them now too.

Artie stuck his head past Jane for a listen. "Sounds like he's let them out in the yard."

"Get some meat. Drug it up." Parker lowered his binoculars. "Might you have any more meat in this food truck of yours, Ollie?"

"Are you kidding? I've got a refrigerator full of beef, steaks, pork, bacon and turkey," boasted Ollie. He pulled open the under-the-counter fridge. "More in the commercial kitchen I rent space in downtown."

"I suggest we borrow some." Parker stuck his nose in the open fridge and beamed. He pointed to a pound of ground beef wrapped in cellophane. "This one looks nice."

"Borrow?" said James. "I doubt we'll be getting any

lightly licked meat back from the Rottweilers to return to Ollie."

Claudia thumped him in the chest. "Do you always have to make the stupid jokes?"

Ollie pulled out the packaged beef, slapped it on the stainless steel counter and ripped open the plastic. "Now what?"

"Slip in some sleeping pills," Parker said.

James cut his eyes at the TV detective. "This isn't a TV show, Parker. You can't just whistle for the guy from the prop department. I mean, where are we going to get sleeping pills out here in the middle of nowhere?" Parker McRaney's show may have come to an end twenty years ago, but the actor was still living in La-La Land.

"I'm warning you," Claudia said. "Give Mr. Parker a chance."

"Now, now. Our James has raised an excellent question," Parker told them. "A good detective should ask questions. As a matter of fact, James, there should be a small quantity of sleeping pills in the Jag."

"Why do you have—"

Jane cut James off. "I'll get them. The car unlocked?"

"*Sí*," said Claudia. "I leave the keys in the ignition."

Jane opened the rear door of the food truck and spotted the racing green Jaguar sedan parked beside them.

"Should be in the glove box, dear Jane," Parker cooed in her ear.

"I'll be right back."

63

Jane jumped down from the food truck.

Bending low, she tiptoed to the Jag, wincing in fear as the dome light popped on. She climbed inside on the passenger side and quietly eased the door shut. The overhead light blinked out.

Jane rummaged through the glovebox. She discovered several pill bottles, a travel-size bottle of mouthwash, a strip of condoms and a plastic baggie filled with leaves of some sort—she didn't want to know what sort.

She grabbed up all the pill bottles and carried them back to the truck. Ollie had laid several meat patties on the prep counter.

"Thank you, Jane." Parker found the brown plastic bottle he was looking for and screwed off the cap. He dumped a handful of pills in Ollie's cupped hands.

"You think this will do it?" Ollie asked.

"Let's hope so," replied Parker, resealing the bottle and pushing it into a pocket of his brown herringbone jacket.

Parker watched as Ollie stuffed the burgers with pills. "I could be wrong about the dose." He tapped his fingers against his chin thoughtfully, dug out the bottle and poured a couple more blue and maroon pills in Ollie's hand. "Better safe than sorry."

Following Parker's directions, Ollie shoved a couple extra pills in each patty.

"Are you sure this won't kill them?" asked Ollie. "I'm kinda fond of dogs. I don't want to see them get hurt."

"Positive," replied Parker. "They'll just take a nice little nap."

"Oh, brother." James folded his arms as he watched the dubious operation. "What makes you think this is going to work?"

"Easy. We did this in episode thirteen, season three."

"I remember that episode," gushed Claudia. "You had to infiltrate a Mafia gang who were holding two bank employees hostage in an abandoned warehouse."

"Yes. I tranquilized the guard dogs with sirloin and the bad guys with burgers."

"How did you get them to eat the burgers?" asked Ollie, wiping the slime from his fingers.

"I faked a delivery from the burger joint down the street."

"And it worked?" asked Artie.

"Like a charm," Parker avowed.

"Smart." Ollie returned the unused meats to the fridge and offered everyone a soda.

"It was a TV show," reminded James.

"Yeah, but it worked," countered Artie.

James gritted his teeth. "It was in the script, Artie. Of course, it worked. It was supposed to work. That's what the writer—"

"Shush, James." Claudia thumped him in the shoulder blade with a bony knuckle.

"Ouch."

Artie rubbed his hands with glee. "I love this."

"You should open a detective school yourself, Parker," gushed Claudia.

Parker planted a kiss on Claudia's forehead. Her cheeks turned pink and she giggled like a school girl. The grade school kind, not the School of Detection kind.

James didn't want to risk Claudia hurting him again by pointing out that the pills used on Rocky Rhodes, PI were most likely sugar pills and that the dogs would have been trained to feign sleeping on cue.

"These pills are quite fast-acting," Parker explained. "We'll give them a few minutes."

"How few? I've seen those Rottweilers in action," James said. "I don't care to see a repeat performance."

Let alone up close and personal.

"Let's make it twenty then," Parker said. "To be absolutely certain."

"Right. Come on, Artie."

"Be careful," urged Jane.

The others watched anxiously from the front of the truck as James and Artie ran the doctored meat patties up to the house.

There was no sign of life from the house as they approached, which James took for a good sign.

James pressed his shoulder against the sagging fence. "Ready?" he whispered to Artie, breathing heavily next to him.

They sheltered under the carport between the fence and an old pickup truck. There was no reason to keep his voice down. The Rottweilers were barking up a storm on the opposite side of the fence. Through the slats, they saw the Rottweilers' angry, glittering eyes and flashing teeth daring them to enter.

"Ready." Artie cupped an oversized, raw burger patty in his hands.

"On three. One, two..."

"Oops." Artie's meat fell from his hands and smacked the ground. He scrambled to retrieve it. "Okay. Ready when you are."

James glared at him. "Three!" He tossed his raw meat patties over the fence. Artie did the same, except on his first try the patty splattered against this side of the fence and stuck. Artie peeled it off the pickets and hurled it over the top.

The barking stopped, soon to be replaced with the sounds of the ravenous wolfing of raw meat.

"Let's get out of here and go wait with the others."

Twenty long minutes later and then another five because James wanted to make dead certain the dogs were out for the count, they tumbled out the back of the food truck and headed for the house.

"This is weird," muttered James, trudging over the uneven ground alongside Jane.

"What's weird?"

"It's too quiet."

"The sleeping pills are working. That's all. That's a good thing."

"So why hasn't Adler stepped out to check on his dogs?"

"What makes you think he hasn't? Maybe he has and we didn't see him."

"Maybe. But don't you think it strange that he hasn't checked out here even once to see what Ollie's food truck, a VW and Parker's Jag are doing out in his yard in the middle of the night?"

"It is kind of odd that he didn't call the cops on us,"

Ollie added.

"Men like your Mr. Adler never call the police," Parker McRaney explained. "The law makes them skittish."

"I agree," said Jane.

"You would," quipped James. It seemed to him that Parker could do or say no wrong in the enamored reporter's eyes.

"Adler sounds and behaves like your classic criminal type to me. Quite possibly a murderer," said Parker. "If you've read chapter twenty-three of my book, you'll recognize he fits the profile."

"Fascinating," replied Jane.

"You do realize that if Parker's right, this guy might just try to slaughter us all?" James reminded the besotted reporter. "And we're a mile from the nearest neighbor."

"And bury our bones in his yard," Artie said with a tremor in his voice.

"Especially if he thinks we hurt his dogs," Ollie just had to add, making everyone even more skittish.

"You worry too much," Claudia said to Artie. She reached the front door first. "And *you* talk too much," she said to James. She slowly tried the handle. "Locked," she whispered.

"Let's try the back door." Jane tiptoed toward the carport. The rest followed.

Ollie hoisted Artie up on his shoulders. Artie looked over the fence. "I see 'em. It worked."

"Are you certain the dogs are sleeping?" James asked.

"Dead to the world," whispered Artie. "And I see a back gate. That car Claudia saw could've left that way."

"See!" Claudia said.

"I'm going over."

"Careful," urged Jane.

Artie slithered over the fence, tiptoed to the gate and raised the latch. Ollie, Claudia, Jane and James peered inside the yard. The Rottweilers lay on their sides, breathing gently.

Jane stepped carefully over the sleeping dogs and followed the others to the junk-littered, poured concrete patio butting up to the rear of the ranch-style house.

Ollie and Artie crept to a window and peered inside the house.

"See anything?" whispered Jane.

"See anybody?" asked James.

"Not a soul," Ollie answered.

"Perhaps no one's home. That could have been Adler you saw leaving earlier, Claudia," suggested Parker. "The man may be more cunning than we have given him credit for."

"What if he's gone for good?" asked Ollie. "We may never get to the bottom of this."

That wasn't good news for James.

"And left his dogs?" Claudia retorted. "No."

"What are we gonna do now?" Artie thrust his hands in his pockets.

"Let's break in," suggested Jane.

64

"Seriously? We're already trespassing. I'm not sure I want to add breaking and entering to my list of crimes," James said. Not that any of the pending crimes trumped the murder charge he was already facing.

"You are skin and buns. Can you squeeze through the dog door?" Claudia asked Artie.

"Huh? Oh, bones. Skin and bones." Artie looked over at the dog door. "I think I could make it."

"That won't be necessary." Parker McRaney pushed his way past the others to the door. "Simple enough. Look at this lock." He rubbed his finger over the dirty keyhole. "This is as cheap a model as you can get. I can pick it in no time."

"Are you sure?" Jane stood at the actor's side, clutching his shoulder.

"I've done this a hundred times." Parker patted his pockets.

"On Rocky Rhodes, PI," muttered James.

"Hush." Jane kicked him in the shin.

"I may need a tool of some sort." Parker McRaney examined the keyhole at eye level. "Anyone have a Swiss Army knife on their person?"

"Sorry," quipped James. "I left my lock picking tools in my other pants."

"I've got a switchblade in my purse," Claudia

offered.

"You would," replied James, rubbing his shin. All women were nuts.

Artie jiggled the handle. "Hey, I don't think it's locked."

"Are you sure?" Ollie asked.

The door fell open.

"He's sure." James moved toward the door but Parker McRaney beat him inside.

"Everybody, keep your voices down." Parker McRaney motioned with his palm. "Our quarry may be out or he may be asleep but he may also be hiding in wait for us."

"You're right." Jane clutched the actor's arm. "This could be a trap."

"He may be armed." Parker pushed Jane behind him. "Stay close, dear."

"I only hope those dogs don't wake up," whispered Artie with a quivering voice, glancing over at the sleeping razor-toothed demon.

Parker rolled his tongue over his lips. "Mr. Adler? Are you here? I'm Parker McRaney. Perhaps you remember me from Rocky Rhodes, PI?"

There was no reply.

"I guess he's not a fan," grumbled James.

"Nonsense," replied the actor, refusing to believe that was even remotely possible. "You remember me. I won two Emmy's and a People's Choice Award," he shouted into the darkness, hoping that might draw the man out.

"Let's go in," suggested Jane, giving Parker a tiny nudge forward.

He nodded.

Using their cellphones to light their path, they crept inside single-file.

Matted, dirty green carpet covered the floor, including the small galley kitchen they had entered first. "Phil Adler's a lousy interior decorator and an even lousier housekeeper," whispered James.

"Look who's talking," quipped Claudia.

"I don't know," said Jane. "This place makes James' look like a shot out of Martha Stewart Living."

"Very funny."

The kitchen was littered but otherwise empty. Two big plastic dog dishes sat in the middle of the floor. A plastic rectangular box meant to hold plants rested against the far wall, serving as their water dish.

The calendar on the fridge featuring a buxom, bikini-clad blonde astride a motorcycle was more than two years out of date and declared that it was now December.

"I guess Adler couldn't bear to turn the page," James whispered to Artie who had stopped to study the girl on the calendar. "Let's keep moving." He gave Artie a nudge.

They continued on down a dark, narrow hall. The ceiling was low and the house smelled of dogs and beer. Junk was strewn everywhere.

James noticed some of the windows had been crudely boarded up from the inside. The remaining windows held blackout curtains. Phil Adler definitely liked his privacy.

"I'm beginning to think you were right, Parker. Adler probably drove off." What would Adler think, or do, should he come home and find six strangers in his house?

"Let's keep looking." Parker McRaney marched forward. The first bedroom they came to held a cot and an assortment of wooden boxes, along with several rifles in an open case. Countless cartons of ammo lay stacked haphazardly on a dresser. Lovely. All the comforts of home.

"Mr. Adler?" Jane called. "Yoo-hoo."

"He's gone," Claudia said.

"Maybe," said James. "But we're not alone."

65

James shined his phone into the living room at the front of the house. The weak light revealed three dumpy chairs and a rumpled sofa. A big screen TV hung crudely on the panelled wall across from the front door.

"Adler!" gasped Jane, falling back into Parker's arms.

Phil Adler sat in his wheelchair, a red and blue dog leash wrapped tightly around his neck. His cheeks and eyes bulged. His jaw hung slack.

The others pressed behind James as he moved closer to Adler, keeping the diffuse light of his quickly draining smartphone trained on the man. "This is Phil Adler?"

It was the guy with Kevin's kids that he'd seen in the Banana Reef.

"Yes." Jane was shaking.

"Are you sure?"

"I saw his picture online." Jane bit down on her lower lip. "Is he dead?" She felt her blood slowing as if cooling and turning to ice beneath her skin.

"Yes, he's dead," James snapped nervously, after checking for a pulse. "Can't you tell?"

"No, I can't tell," said Jane, backing up. This was more than she had bargained for. A lot more. She wanted to solve a crime, get her own byline, not see dead bodies. Especially not up close and personal. "I work the gardening and lifestyle pages. The only dead things I see are snails and slugs."

Parker snaked his arm over her shoulder.

"Well, this slug's been strangled," James said.

Claudia made the sign of the cross. "This is bad. We must leave." She started for the door.

"Maybe it's a trick," suggested Artie.

Releasing Jane, Parker reached inside his windbreaker and, to everyone's surprise, pulled out a small black pistol.

James gaped at the actor. "What are you doing? Is that thing real?"

"This? It's a prop from season six."

Jane moved closer to the wheelchair.

Artie turned on the table lamp beside the body.

"No!" hissed Claudia.

But it was too late.

"What's the problem?"

"You've left your fingerprints," Parker said. "A rookie mistake, Artie." He patted Artie on the shoulder with the hand holding the gun. The muzzle poking his ear. "Don't take it too hard, Artie. You didn't know."

Artie's head fell. "I've only had the two classes."

"Can we all concentrate on what's important right now?" insisted James. "We have something of a situation here."

A situation similar, far too similar, to the one he had found himself in just a few short days ago. He gnawed his lower lip.

"We should go," insisted Claudia, hands balled into fists at her side. "This is *muy mal.*"

Fighting her growing revulsion, Jane lightly

placed the back of her hand against Adler's cheek. "He's still kinda warm. He can't have been dead long."

A glass ashtray close at hand was brimming with cigarette butts. James noticed a half-spent matchbook beside it bearing the name and logo of the Banana Reef Bar & Grill. That confirmed it. This was definitely the guy he'd seen with Kourtney and Dale.

The dog leash cut into Phil Adler's flesh leaving red circles of blood and bruising.

"The killer could be close by," whispered Jane, a chill rushing up her spine.

"What do we do now?" Ollie asked, arms rigid at his side. "I didn't know there were going to be dead people when I signed up for detective school." He looked even paler than the dead guy and was sweating profusely. "I mean, really, nobody told me there'd be dead people."

"It's okay, buddy." Artie patted his new bestie on the back.

Parker McRaney suddenly lunged at the front door, fumbled with the lock and chain, heedless of fingerprints. He threw it open. The night sky looked down on the scene. Then he bolted across the yard.

James watched as Parker McRaney ran straight to his Jaguar.

"What's Parker doing?" Claudia wondered.

"I believe he's answering your question about what we should do," James said evenly.

"You mean—"

"Run!" James followed the word with the action. The others followed suit.

66

"I can't believe Parker ran away like that." Jane shook her head for the thousandth time. She and James sat alone in his sister-in-law's city hall office, staring at the walls and waiting.

"I can." James planted his feet on Sheryl's desk.

"At least he's here now." Jane couldn't help but defend the actor. There was just something about him.

"Yeah, after the mayor called him."

"Whatever. Your sister-in-law's not much of a plant person, is she?" said Jane, anxious to shift the conversation in another direction.

"If you say so."

"These plants are nearly indestructible. I've never seen one look so poorly."

"Sheryl has that effect on lots of things," James said.

Sheryl's lone office plant, a sansevieria trifasciata, also known as snake plant or mother-in-law's tongue, sitting in a clay pot on the corner of her desk, was in desperate need of some love.

Jane ran her fingers along the vertical, sword blade-shaped leaves. The sharp tips were dry and crispy. The plant could have used a little more water and a little extra light would help too. "Did you know that another name for the snake plant is the bowstring hemp plant?"

"Wonderful. I'll keep that in mind the next time I need to restring my bow."

"You don't have to be snide. Did you notice the carpet?" Jane asked.

James looked at the floor.

"Not here. Phil Adler's house."

"What about it?"

"Very few wheelchair tracks."

"Huh. You're right." James pictured the floor in Phil Adler's house. "Except near the front door." Why hadn't he noticed before?

James decided not to blame himself for Jane first noticing something that he should have seen himself.

Ollie, Artie and Claudia had run fast and hard to the food truck along with James and Jane. Parker McRaney had jumped in his Jaguar and left them in a dark cloud of dust that rolled through the open rear door of the food truck with them cowering inside and arguing.

The others had wanted to mimic the actor and hightail it out of there. Jane had insisted on telephoning the police.

James had taken Jane's side in the matter. He knew that running would prove futile. They'd left their fingerprints, footprints, and maybe even DNA inside Phil Adler's house.

There was no running away from this.

Jane made the call. After hours of intense interrogating by the Davie police, they were dragged down to Ocean Park where a furious Sheryl Stewart, roused from sleep and mad as a wet cat, had pummeled them with more questions.

"I'll bet Phil Adler was faking his injuries." Jane

crumpled an empty can of orange soda in her hand. "I mean, until he ended up dead." Everything was spinning out of control. Instead of writing a story about a murder, she just might end up the subject of that story herself.

And see her face plastered on the cover of the Sun-Sentinel. Maybe even the Miami Herald.

Her future as a crime reporter might be over before it ever got off the ground.

Why did everything in her life always go so wrong?

Men, she blamed it on men. Like James. And Parker.

"I agree," replied James. "I bet Adler was faking. You know, I saw him with Kourtney and Dale at the Banana Reef. I just didn't realize who he was at the time. He was wearing some sort of brace but he was walking."

James wondered if Kevin's children knew Adler was a fraud. Come to think of it, it might not have been Tench at all. The pair may have been the ones bankrolling Adler in his lawsuit against their father. He certainly wouldn't put it past them.

Thinking of which, he probably should be sending them a bill. Better to get paid before they got indicted.

Jane let out a heavy sigh. "I keep saying we should communicate with one another better, James. That's what partners do. Maybe now you've learned your lesson."

James grunted noncommittally. He'd partner up with Jane when hell froze over. Then again, Don Henley kept claiming The Eagles were dead, yet the band had been resurrected about ten times now. "The police interviewed Adler, remember? Nothing."

"Nothing? Then why is he dead?"

"Maybe because he surprised a burglar."

"Who would want to burgle Phil Adler? His house was a disaster."

"There were all those guns and that stockpile of ammo," James reminded her.

"Which were still there."

James frowned and was silent a moment before saying, "There were rumors, nothing confirmed, mind you, that Adler was dealing drugs."

"Did the police find any?"

"The Davie PD mentioned that they found evidence that would indicate there had been coke and meth on the premises."

"And now Adler's dead, ending his lawsuit against Kevin Rain and Smiley's."

"Seems like it," agreed James.

"But Kevin is dead. He can't be responsible for Phil Adler's death," stated Jane.

"No, but Felicity can."

"Right. Or her kids." "Where is Parker, anyway?" Jane stared at the door. "Sheryl and Lt. Byrd went with him to the interrogation room hours ago."

"Probably binge watching seasons one and two of Rocky Rhodes, PI," said James over the sound of approaching footsteps.

"Very funny. We slipped Parker out the back way," explained Sheryl, barging into her office. "His lawyer insisted." She gave James' feet a rough push. "Feet off the desk. Butt out of my chair."

James complied.

His sister-in-law appeared exhausted. That did not make her look any less dangerous. Maybe even more so.

Like a tired and very hungry great white shark.

"There must be a dozen reporters outside trying to get his picture and an interview," complained Sheryl. "He's already been on the phone with his agent in LA talking TV movie. I've never seen anything like it." Sheryl fell into her desk chair, her gray denim slacks and black sweatshirt bearing the Stewart Classic Motors logo looked as rumpled as she did.

"You two can get out of here, too. But I want to know where to find you at all times." Sheryl glared at James. "I want to be kept apprised of every step you take. If you so much as go to the toilet, you call me."

"You going to come flush for me too?"

"Just don't go anywhere you don't belong, James. Believe it or not," her voice softened, "you are family and I do care about you. Stay out of trouble and you just may stay out of prison yet."

"I will."

67

James took Jane's hand and led her out to the street where her Volkswagen sat waiting for them. Claudia had dropped it off earlier after the police let her and the others go after giving their statements.

Barking reporters immediately encircled Jane and James. They kept their mouths shut and ignored their questions, shoving their way past them into the car.

Jane drove James to his car in the visitor lot of Cindi's building. He climbed out of the Volkswagen, craned his neck and looked up, counting the doors until he came to hers. The lights were out. Cindi was probably fast asleep.

"Care for a drink?" James asked, pulling his car keys from his pocket.

"At this hour?"

"How about some coffee then?"

"Okay." They agreed to meet back at James' duplex. He stopped and picked up some coffee and donuts from an all-night grocery.

Once settled in, they spread out on the sofa. James popped open the coffees. Jane fished a wad of napkins from the bag. James popped the lid on the box of donuts and slid it in her direction.

"Thanks." Jane grabbed a chocolate donut sprinkled on top with blue and red decorating sugar. Folding the donut in two, she stuffed it in her mouth and chewed.

James watched with amusement as her jaw worked back and forth, up and down. She washed the glazed donut down with a couple sips of coffee.

Jane cocked her head at him. "What are you looking at?"

"Nothing." James threw up his hands.

"It's been a long night. It's going to be a long day. I haven't eaten anything in like forever. And I just saw a dead human being. Strangled with a dog leash, no less." Jane snatched a second donut and chomped down. "So indulge me."

Her eyes dared James to mock.

James was no idiot. He took a jelly donut and bit it in two. Strawberry jam oozed out over his fingers.

Jane tossed him a napkin. He licked his fingers instead and set the napkin on his lap.

"Let's go over what we know," began Jane.

"Good idea." James yawned and rubbed his stubbled cheeks. "You start because, personally, I don't know a damn thing."

"I wish Parker hadn't disappeared like that. We could use his help."

"He must have one helluva good lawyer. I envy the guy."

"Interesting." Jane said with a flicker of amusement.

"What?"

"I get the feeling you're jealous of him."

"Me? Jealous of Parker McLoony? Not a chance."

Jane snorted derisively. "Let's skip that for the moment." She cleared her throat and licked icing from her upper lip with the tip of her pink tongue. "We know for a fact that Ronnie Tench was paying Phil Adler's bills. Parker saw the records on her computer."

"So he says."

"And I believe him."

"The police don't. Besides, that does not mean that Kourtney and Dale weren't helping him too."

"Maybe they were all in it together."

"All for one and one for all." James swung a donut round and round on his finger before biting into it. "Let's not forget the widow, Felicity Rain. We both saw her with Ronnie Tench."

"Hold on a sec." Jane was writing furiously in her notebook. "Okay." She flattened the notebook across her knee. "We also know that Bruno Caliostro was once hired by Kevin Rain to get the goods on Felicity."

"Get the goods on?" James rolled his neck side to side. "You sound like you've been watching one too many Rocky Rhodes episodes yourself."

"Shut up."

James glared at her. "Okay, so Kevin hired Bruno to tail Felicity to see if she was cheating on him. What's funny to me is that Bruno doesn't just follow her, he ends up in bed with her."

"Disgusting, if you ask me. Men are pigs." Before James could reply, Jane went on. "So Bruno and Felicity decide to murder her ex? Why?"

"I have no idea. But how great it would be if the killer turned out to be Bruno Caliostro. I might get my money back for that stupid detective class."

Jane scribbled some more. "Don't forget, we also know that Dale and Kourtney hold the mortgage on Smiley's."

"I got the idea from Alyssa that those two would have been happy, more than happy, if dear old dad had defaulted on his mortgage payments."

"Giving them Smiley's."

"You're right."

A skinny green lizard had gotten indoors. They were common as New Yorkers in January. The jumpy lizard raced back and forth along the track of the sliding glass door. James grabbed a copy of the Sun-Sentinel and shooed him outdoors.

"Don't you read the Broward County Times?"

"Nope."

Jane huffed. "Do you think your brother might be interested in advertising? I could have Lou call him."

James smirked. "You should do that. Here's his number." He opened his wallet and dropped a business card in Jane's hand. "Tell Lou not to take no for an answer."

Roger deserved it for holding his guitar and amp hostage.

"Great." Jane slipped the card away in the back sleeve of her notebook. "Let's get back to the case." She held her pen poised and ready. "How did Dale and Kourtney murder Phil Adler or their father for that matter?"

James rubbed his sugar-sticky fingers against his temple.

"They have alibis for both murders, remember?"

According to Lt. Byrd, both Dale and Kourtney were in the Bahamas. The local police had interviewed them at the resort they were staying at, having checked in that morning. There was no way they could have murdered Phil Adler.

Unless they had hired someone to do their dirty work for them.

"Right. And why kill Adler now?"

Jane slumped in her chair. "Maybe they thought he was a loose end. Dispensable."

"So they dispensed with him. Makes sense," James admitted. "Maybe Dale and Kourtney went off to the Bahamas to provide themselves with alibis while they got some hired goon to kill Phil Adler. Ditto their father."

"That's exactly what I'm thinking." Jane thumped out a rhythm on her pad with the tip of her pen.

"You and me thinking alike? That's a scary thought." James reached into the box for an éclair.

"Ha-ha. Kourtney, Dale, Felicity, Veronica Tench." Jane pressed her pen firmly into the paper as she wrote their names in bold letters. "One of them must be guilty."

"Let's not forget Adam Mitchell. He wanted Kevin to make him a partner. Kevin refused. The guy's got a temper. I've experienced that up close and personal." He swallowed half the éclair in a single bite. "And our wild-card, Bruno Caliostro."

Jane wrote quickly. "That's six people who each had a good reason for wanting Kevin dead."

"A man that Cindi insists was a sweetheart who only liked to play with his toy trains." James sighed. "And we're no closer to figuring out which of these people, or which combination of them, is guilty."

James stuffed the remainder of the éclair in his mouth and reached for the container of coffee. "Want some more?"

"No, thanks. I'm all coffee'd out. In fact," Jane laid her notepad on the end table. "I'll be right back." She trounced barefoot to James' bathroom.

James' eyelids drooped. What he needed was sleep and plenty of it. He stretched out on the sofa.

68

Jane studied her sad reflection in the mirror. Dark smudges hung under her eyes and her hair was a mess. She splashed her face with water, ran her wet fingers through her hair and dabbed herself dry with a relatively clean washcloth hanging off the plastic towel rod.

A tube of peppermint toothpaste sat on the corner of the sink. She twisted off the cap and ran a bead of toothpaste along her index finger. She rubbed her teeth vigorously, rinsed, then spat and rinsed once more.

She smiled into the mirror.

Ugh.

All she needed was a story. One big news story and she'd be set. If she could name Kevin Rain's killer and Phil Adler's—and there was a good chance the killer was one and the same—she might even be able to sell to one of the big papers, the South Florida Sun-Sentinel, Palm Beach Post or even the Miami Herald.

If she survived the day.

Jane yawned and shoved her fist in her mouth to smother another. The narrow bathroom's backdoor led out to the deck. Deciding it couldn't hurt to touch up her makeup, she slipped out the door to fetch her purse from her car.

69

James' eyes popped open. For a moment, he stared at the ceiling, disoriented. Then he realized he was home in his living room. He saw the remains of the donuts, the coffee and the paper cups and remembered Jane. Where was she? Had she gone home?

James stumbled to his feet and banged on the closed bathroom door. "Hey? Are you in there?"

No reply.

"Are you all right?" He tried the handle. The door was unlocked and he pushed it open slowly, eyes half-closed. If she was taking a shower or sitting on the toilet, he did not want to see. Well, maybe the shower, but definitely not the toilet. "Jane?"

The room was empty. The bathroom sink was damp.

As James walked back to the living room, Jane banged on the glass sliding door to get his attention. "What are you doing out there?" James stepped onto the deck, looking side to side. "Where did you come from?"

"I went out the bathroom door. I wanted my purse." She held it up to him by its straps. "I couldn't get back in. Door must have locked behind me. Be right back." Jane pushed past James and headed once more to the bathroom to fix her hair and makeup.

"Damn."

Jane glanced over her shoulder, one foot in the bathroom, the other in the hallway. "What is it?"

"I think I know who killed Phil Adler."

"You do? Are you sure?"

"Sure enough." James fell onto the couch and clamped his hands on his knees. "But there's no way to be one hundred percent certain or prove it to the police."

"Who?" Jane asked, all thoughts of hair and makeup abandoned as she began composing her news story in her head. All she needed now was a name. She hurried over to the sofa.

"I don't know if I should say until I'm certain."

Jane grabbed him by the collar. "Oh, no, you don't. Speak now or suffer the consequences."

"Okay, okay." He told her. The name and everything else.

"You don't mean it." Jane's grip loosened as she digested the name.

James pulled free. "Yeah, I do. It was you disappearing a minute ago that gave me the answer."

"So we solved it together."

"Stop smirking." James pounded his fist against the sofa. "How could I have been so stupid? So gullible?"

"You're a guy. It goes with the territory."

"Very funny. Focus. We need a plan." He went to the fridge in search of a drink. He pulled out a bottle of cheap moscato, twisted off the cap and drank. He ran the back of his hand across his lips. "Want some?"

"After you put your dirty lips on the bottle?"

"Suit yourself." He took another slug.

"I thought we were focusing on a plan?"

"We are." James planted the bottle on the kitchen table. "And I think I have one."

"What do you have in mind?" Jane plopped herself at the kitchen table and grabbed her third donut. Or was it her fourth?

James told her. "Well?"

"Not bad." Jane licked raspberry filling off her fingers.

"Can you think of something better?"

Jane had already tried and come up empty. "No. Are you sure it's going to work?"

"Don't worry about it. Your job is to get Artie, Ollie and Claudia there."

"Why me?"

"Because the *gang* will listen to you."

"Fine," Jane relented, wearily. The sugar and caffeine rush she had been waiting and hoping for was refusing to show its face.

"Do you own a bikini?"

Jane narrowed her eyes at him. "Why?"

"Because you might want to wear it. It will give you a chance to do some undercover work."

"In your dreams." Jane grabbed her purse and stomped to the door.

"Where are you going?"

"To get a little sleep. I'll pick you up at six. Don't keep me waiting." She threw open the door with a bang.

James hurried after her. "Why don't I drive?"

"Because *you* are not dependable. I am." With that parting shot, she threw the door closed with an even louder bang.

James swore at the door. The door didn't seem to mind.

70

"Are you sure this is the place?" Jane looked blearily out the windshield of the Ferrari toward the deserted beach. The sea was calm. The breeze coming in through the window was warm and light.

"Yeah. There's Cindi's Jeep. Good, we're not too late."

"And whose fault is that? We wouldn't be late if you hadn't thrown a tantrum and insisted we take your car."

"It's faster."

"Right, except when you get pulled over for missing a sideview mirror and we lose twenty minutes," Jane replied. "Plus, you get a ticket. How much was that fine again, by the way?"

"It'll be worth every penny when I catch a killer."

"When we catch a killer, James. We. We're in this together."

"I know, I know." He had his eyes trained on the beach.

"I'm starving. Hand me a croissant, would you?" She had found the time to take a cool shower and changed into loose tan shorts and a short-sleeved blouse and open-toed sandals.

The mouthwatering scent of croissants and coffee mingling in the confined space reminded Jane of her profound lack of sleep and stirring hunger.

Going home had been a waste of time. She hadn't slept a wink and by the time she'd made it home it had been time to turn around and get James.

"Sure, but I still think you should have worn the bikini."

Jane rolled her eyes. "Is that all you men think about, women in bikinis?"

"I sometimes think about women *out* of their bikinis," James replied, nudging up his eyebrows. He'd dressed in faded denim shorts and a plain white tee and looked like he hadn't shaved in days. Which he hadn't.

"Pig." Jane held out her hand. "Hand me a croissant."

"Fine." James dutifully opened the white sack and dropped a warm, flaky croissant in Jane's hand. He then helped himself to one and bit off the end.

She brought the croissant to her nose, took a whiff, then bit into it. "And for your information, I'm not wearing a bikini." The truth was, she had worn a bikini under her clothes, but that was only for emergencies. Like jumping into the ocean to rescue James if he was drowning.

James didn't need to know that.

"And if you never see me in a bikini, it will be too soon."

"Glad to see we're on the same page," replied James.

"And if you—"

"Shh. There they are." James pointed down the beach. Cindi and her photographer friend were walking slowly down by the shoreline. The photographer had a camera and some gear slung around his neck and a tripod over one shoulder.

Jane followed his finger. "I see them. I wish we had binoculars." She twisted around in her seat. "I still don't see why you wanted the others here."

Ollie's food truck sat at an angle to them several hundred yards back. Inside, Ollie, Artie and Claudia kept watch.

"We might need backup." What he'd told Artie was to film the entire thing as it went down on his phone camera.

As real backup, that gang in the food truck would prove about as useful as a month-old toy poodle guarding a can of dog food.

"Then shouldn't we have let the police know what we're up to?"

"And have them stop us? No way. A killer might get away." And that would leave him on the hook for murder.

"Stop worrying. We've got this."

Jane was worried. A lot. "I wish Parker was here." She gobbled the rest of her croissant.

"Why? The man is useless."

"That's not nice, James. He's been a big help to us."

"Yeah, when he isn't running away."

"You're mean."

"I'll send him a Hallmark card when this is over."

"You said Alyssa was going to be here," noted Jane. Except for a solitary man walking a basset hound further up the beach, only Cindi and the photographer were in sight.

"That's what Cindi told me."

Jane pulled a small digital camera from her purse and checked to see that its battery was fully charged.

"Planning to get a photo for your Pulitzer prize-winning story?" James took a slug of coffee.

Jane blushed. "As a matter of fact, yes." She snapped a picture of his smirking face. "I'll post that one on our website for our goofy photo of the day feature." There was no such thing but maybe she'd suggest one to Lou.

James pushed the camera out of his face. "Show-time." He stepped out of the car, shucked off his sandals, and started walking diagonally across the quiet beach toward Cindi and her photographer.

Jane clung to his side carrying the croissants and coffees.

The sun was well over the horizon and the temperature was rising.

"I thought you were going to stay in the car? That was our plan."

"Plans change. I want to be where the action is."

"Suit yourself." What choice did he have?

Cindi looked like a sea goddess, long hair swirling, spilling over her breasts. Breasts barely concealed by the itsy-bitsiest of bikini tops. The bikini was shocking pink with silver sequins. The brief bottom rode tight and low across her hips.

"James, what are you doing here?" Cindi's smile moved from the photographer to James and Jane. "Hello, Jane."

"Hey, Cindi. Sorry to barge in on you like this." He stuck out his hand to the photographer. "You must be David. Cindi said you prefer working alone."

"I do." David said icily, gripping a big camera in his left hand as if debating whether to shoot photographs or club them to death like a couple of annoying baby seals.

"Jane and I won't keep you long. In fact, Jane was thinking of doing an article on you and Cindi for her newspaper."

"Is that right?" That news brought a smile to the dour photographer's face. He had a dark complexion and curly black hair. Big dark sunglasses hid his eyes. He wore a loose white button-front shirt open to the navel and baggy sand-colored board shorts.

Miami chic.

"Huh? Yes, right. Jane Bright, Broward County Times." Jane thrust the coffee and croissants at James and rummaged in her purse for her notebook. This was so not part of the plan.

"Coffee and croissants. Fresh." He extended the bags. "Who wants some?"

"Maybe later," said David. "Thanks."

"Sure thing." James set the stuff on the sand. "So where's Alyssa?" James scanned the beach. "I thought you said she was joining you?"

Cindi reached into a large yellow-and-white striped beach bag, pulled out a hairbrush and smoothed her locks. "She went to change."

"Change?" asked Jane.

"David said he'd include her in a few shots."

"I thought it might lift her spirits," David said.

Cindi planted a kiss on his scruffy cheek. "You are such a dear."

David snaked an arm around Cindi's waist. "Anything for you, love. A buddy of mine owns the Dive Shack." He pointed at a small beachside structure. "We're using it as a dressing room and for some location shots. In exchange, I take a few photos for his advertisements. It's a win-win."

"Sounds like it," James said.

David turned to Jane. "How about you?" He lofted the camera. "Care to pose? You've got the body for it."

"No, thanks." Jane blushed. "I have to maintain my objectivity."

James snorted. "I think I'll use the restroom. In the Dive Shack?" He bobbed his head towards the shop.

"Yep," answered David. "Near the back."

"Got it."

"I'll come with you," Jane said.

"Don't be silly. Stay and get your story." James put a hand on Jane's shoulder and spun her toward the photographer. "Tell Jane here all about your background, David."

David threw his shoulders back and began babbling. Jane was forced to listen as James abandoned her and slogged towards the Dive Shack.

Gazing into the distance, Jane saw no sign of the gang. Hopefully, they had their eyes glued on them from inside the food truck. If anything went wrong, at the very least, they could call out the cavalry.

As for Cindi, Jane wished the slut would put some clothes on.

71

What Jane didn't know was that Bruno Caliostro had taken up a position at a small picnic table at the beachside park with a cup of coffee and a breakfast sandwich. His disguise was a panama hat, Hawaiian shirt and a bulbous rubber nose from the time he'd done surveillance work for the Ringling Bros. He knew James had been sneaking around, checking up on him, peeking in the window when he was boinking the ex-Mrs. Rains.

What he didn't know was why.

He was here to find out.

72

James marched up the wooden steps leading up to the porch of the Ocean Park Dive Shack. The place was something of a landmark. Hurricanes had come and gone and done their worst, yet the shack had withstood it all, staying steadfast in its same location since the mid-1960s. Not that it hadn't sustained serious water and wind damage, but its various owners had always persuaded the town to let them rebuild.

The ramshackle building now included outdoor storage sheds for beach chair and umbrella rentals, plus a small ice cream shop, now shuttered, with several weathered picnic tables scattered in front facing the water.

Laughing gulls had made themselves at home on the picnic tables waiting for another day filled with junk food scraps. The birds shifted their feet only slightly as James walked past them.

Twin palm trees swayed at the edge of the deck.

James took a deep breath, enjoying the salty smell of the ocean. He was about to unmask a killer. Maybe he should have asked Jane to come along and photograph his big moment. He'd like to see the look on Sheryl's face when she read in the paper how he had solved Kevin Rain's murder. The murder of Phil Adler, too, for that matter—he'd bank on it.

Because the killer had to be one and the same, Alyssa Rain.

And he, James Stewart, was about to rain on Alyssa's parade.

The door hung open. James stepped inside. "Hello? Anybody here?"

A long, cluttered sales counter stood to his right. Rows of shelving climbed to the low ceiling. Scuba, sailing and fishing gear hung from the ceiling and spilled from the shelves.

Must-have beach-going paraphernalia, everything from colorfully-striped folding chairs, to coolers, sunscreen, sun-tanning oil for those who still believed in getting their skin color up to a nice burnt toast as much as they disbelieved in skin cancer, beach balls, paddle boards, surfboards, skimmers and more occupied virtually every inch of the damp space. The Dive Shack had gorged itself on all things beach and was in danger of bursting at the seams.

Speaking of bursting at the seams, Alyssa Rain stepped out from behind a beaded curtain flaunting the merest of seafoam green bikinis with shimmering clear glass beads at the ends of the tie strings.

"Shouldn't you be wearing black?" he asked, struggling to catch his breath. She might have been a cold-blooded killer but she wasn't all bad.

"James!" Alyssa smiled and did a turn on tiptoes. "Like it?" Her body was tan and just the right amount of firm.

"Not bad for a tow company operator." James tried not to let all that exposed flesh sidetrack him.

"What are you doing here?" Alyssa moved closer, lifting her dark hair off her neck. "Do you mind?" She turned around and offered the loose ends of the bikini top to James.

He tied them with trembling fingers. She smelled of fresh coconut and mango.

"Thanks." She kissed the tip of his nose. "Come to watch my sister do her thing?"

"Actually, no." James cleared his throat and took a measured step backward, bumping into a carousel of polarized sunglasses. The carousel went spinning, several pairs fell to the sandy floor. He picked them up and set them on the nearest shelf atop a box of over-priced protein bars.

"Oh?" Alyssa admired her reflection in the mirror next to the cold drinks vending machine. "What are you doing here then?"

He couldn't help admiring it too.

"I came to see you."

"Lucky me. She smiled coquettishly, batting her eyelashes and taking his hands in hers. "You are cute. But what about Cindi?"

"She was only the accomplice. You're the murderer."

Alyssa stiffened a moment but quickly recovered. "What do you mean?"

"I mean you murdered your husband. I'm betting you murdered Phil Adler too."

Alyssa laughed, glancing out the window towards the beach. "I see you brought a friend. The reporter?"

"She likes the beach."

James had missed a pair of fallen Ray-Bans and scooped to pick them up. "Tell me," he began as he straightened, adding the dark-tinted glasses to the already precarious pile he had begun, "how did my sunglasses end up under Kevin's desk?"

Alyssa hesitated a moment as if thinking over her options. Finally, she said, "Easy. I picked them up at the Banana Reef. I was there at the bar drinking my troubles away. Waiting for Cindi to finish. We were going to get something to eat. I noticed you but you didn't notice me. I ran after you. Imagine, I was going to be a Good Samaritan and return them."

Alyssa helped herself to a bottle of sunscreen from a shelf, squirted some into her palm and carefully rubbed her arms. "Then I saw you talking to Cindi. I couldn't believe my luck. A complete coincidence. I took it as a sign. And an opportunity. Too good to pass up, really." Alyssa grinned. "I realized you could be so much more useful to me. You could be the cure for all my troubles."

"Kevin."

"I'd been wanting to dump Kevin forever. I finally saw my chance."

"It was a complete setup from start to finish. Cindi was using me."

"Family comes first, James. You know that." She applied sunscreen to her belly. "Can't be too careful. Wouldn't want to get a sunburn, or worse."

"The night of the murder, you showed up at Cindi's apartment pretending to be wasted. Cindi makes up an excuse to run an errand, leaving me alone in her place without witnesses to prove it and you sneak out the front bedroom window."

"Cindi isn't the only one in the family who can act," Alyssa said with a big grin. "I keep an extra car key at her place. We had everything set up for when you came."

"And I fell right into your trap." How could he have been so stupid? Vanity. Vanity and ego. He'd really believed that Cindi was into him.

Lesson learned. Not that it would do him any good now. "And getting my car towed?"

"That was easy. I called it in. I needed something to connect you to my husband."

"So you had my car towed and arranged for Cindi to *accidentally* run into me after class."

"We couldn't believe how perfect it all went. We weren't sure what you'd do. I really didn't expect you to go down to Smiley's until the next day. Instead, you surprised us both." She stopped and applied more sunscreen to her thighs and calves. "You played your part perfectly, James."

"Glad to be of service."

"Oh, you were. You were. Then while you were waiting for Cindi to return, I snuck out, drove to Smiley's and gave my dear hubby his final exit papers. Smashed the window to make it look like you broke in. Left your sunglasses in the office. Nice of you to help out by picking up that tire iron and plastering your fingerprints all over it."

Alyssa set the sunscreen bottle back on the shelf and wiped her hands across her ribcage. "Not to mention the fact that you actually went back there that night to try to get your car. We figured you'd have no alibi for the time of the murder, not that you'd be stupid enough to try to snatch your car from the lot after hours. I knew the first time I laid eyes on you that you'd be perfect."

"Yeah, the perfect patsy." And a fool. An A+ fool.

"Cindi knew to use her credit card everyplace she

went and to stay far away from Smiley's. That gave her an airtight alibi. I returned to the apartment with you none the wiser. Thanks for providing me with an airtight alibi too."

"My pleasure," James said sardonically. "But why kill Kevin? I thought the business was losing money? Why not simply divorce him?"

"It was. Kevin was an idiot. Too busy with his toy trains. Felicity and his kids were running him into the ground. Squeezing him on all sides. Then Tench came along and I knew he was going to crumble sooner or later. I would have been left with nothing. When I married Kevin, I thought I'd be set for life."

"So you decided he had to go."

"We all have to go sometime, James." Alyssa moved quickly to the next aisle. "And this way, at least I have the business."

James followed her and wished he hadn't. He rounded the bend to discover Alyssa in the center of the aisle facing him. Her feet planted firmly, she aimed a very ugly and deadly looking spear gun at his soft midsection.

He took a step backward and raised his hands. "Take it easy, Alyssa. Let's not do anything we're going to regret."

"I have no regrets, James. Well, Cindi does like you but what's that they say? There are plenty of fish in the sea? Sis will just have to hook another. I mean, it's not as if you've got any money or anything anyway. So it'll be no real loss to her."

Alyssa's eyes danced with deadly mischief. "For you, however..."

73

James fumed.

Alyssa and Cindi had set him up. He'd been hoping he'd been wrong. What a fool he had been. "I still don't understand. Smiley's was struggling to remain in business. Kevin had no life insurance. What good is a failing business? Is it really worth killing for? What am I missing?"

If he fought for time, maybe the owner or an employee of the Dive Shack would show up, thwarting Alyssa's plans to make a sport-fishing trophy out of his corpse.

She released the safety catch on the spear gun. "I inherited a business that's bleeding red ink. That actually made me less a suspect in the eyes of the police. But I'm not worried. I'll turn Smiley's around now that I'm in charge. People like Tench don't intimidate me."

"She's still out there, gunning for Smiley's."

"Then maybe I'll have to go gunning for her first."

"Another murder, Alyssa? Is that really what you want?"

"If that's what it takes."

Her face pinched into a mask of anger.

"You'll never get away with this." James had heard people in movies say it a thousand times. Those times he'd believed it. It was in the script. Parker McRaney had probably said it more than a few times himself.

This time, James found it rather likely that Alyssa would get away with yet another murder—his.

"I already have gotten away with it. You're dead. You just don't seem to know it yet."

Alyssa's ominous words sent an electrical surge through James' body. Should he dive for the door? Better to take a harpoon in the back? Or in the chest?

So many choices, yet so few good ones.

"What about Phil Adler? Why kill him?" James said in a rush.

"Because he refused to end his frivolous lawsuit against Smiley's. I tried to warn him. I tried to reason with him. I even slept with the jerk." Her fingers grew white as she tightened her grip on the spear gun. "He still refused to listen. Too afraid of Ronnie Tench. That was his biggest mistake. It was me he should have been most afraid of."

James could see the truth in that.

"Cindi told me you and your class clowns were determined to talk to him. I couldn't let you do that. I couldn't take a chance that Adler might say the wrong thing."

"So you killed him."

"I beat you out there and disposed of the problem. Like I'll have to dispose of you. You should have quit. Like Adler should have quit." Her head shook side to side. "People just don't listen."

Alyssa took a step closer, the barbed tip aimed at his heart. At this close distance, he wondered if the spear would go straight through him.

James braced himself. "Jane and David are going to wonder what's happened to me." Cold sweat dripped into his left eye but he didn't dare lift a finger to wipe it away. "They'll come looking. If they don't find me, they'll phone the police."

Alyssa shrugged a shoulder. "I'll think of something. I always do." Her finger twitched against the trigger.

James held his breath.

"Maybe I'll tell them we fought. I could tell them you confessed to murdering my dear, departed husband." She removed her left hand from the barrel of the spear gun and tugged at the tie string of her bikini top. "Maybe I'll tell them how you tried to rape me and I had to fight you off."

She ripped the string loose, revealing her breasts. The top fluttered to the ground. She kicked it towards him. "A girl has to defend herself. Pick it up."

"Alyssa—" James took another step back. He'd hit a wall, literally and figuratively. Shelves of tacky unisex tee shirts aimed at the tourist crowd covered the wall blocking his escape.

74

As David gave Cindi direction on her poses, Jane glanced in the direction of the Dive Shack. What was taking James so long? Had he forgotten that they were supposed to be solving a murder?

More annoyingly, had he forgotten that they were supposed to be a team?

He was probably investigating on his own. He might even be hitting on Alyssa. The widow was every bit as beautiful as her sister.

"Men do so little thinking with their actual brains, I don't see why they're included as standard equipment," Jane muttered. She excused herself and slogged through the sand toward the Dive Shack.

Cupping her hands over her eyes, she peered through a corner window of the store. A topless Alyssa Rain was aiming a loaded spear gun at James. The weapon had a mahogany barrel and held a sharp metal spear with a barbed tip.

James was about to be skewered by a topless Amazon.

Jane frantically scoured the area for a weapon of her own. A trashcan and a beachload of sand. Throw sand in her eyes and toss the barrel over her head?

What were the chances of that succeeding?

Jane wracked her brain.

There wasn't time to phone for help and, if she yelled, it would alert Alyssa who might then shoot James and make a run for it.

She needed something to stop Alyssa with or at least to distract her long enough to allow James to make his escape.

With her options limited, Jane grabbed a sharp-nosed wood paddleboard from the rack at the edge of the porch. It was over ten feet long and must have weighed thirty pounds.

She grappled with it, struggling to maintain her grip on the board and her balance. She'd never surfed or paddle boarded, nor so much as held one of the unwieldy things in her arms before.

A fuzzy plan formed in her brain, although she acted mostly on impulse. If she stopped to think things through, James could end up with a spear in his chest.

With the board at her side, Jane ran awkwardly through the soft sand, retreating about thirty feet from the shack. She struggled to lift the board and balanced it on her head.

Gritting her teeth, she took a deep breath. "One, two…" She ran as fast as she could, her hands struggling to keep the board in the air and pointed in the right direction as it slip-slided atop her head.

The hard tip of the paddleboard struck the window. The glass shattered instantly and shards fell like snowflakes. The board flew from her hands and sailed into the shack like a rocket—heading straight for Alyssa.

Jane's forward momentum carried her into the wall of the shack, forcing the breath from her lungs.

Her vision dimmed.

75

James watched in surprise as the blue paddleboard shattered the window and flew between himself and Alyssa.

Alyssa spun sideways to see what was happening. Her finger squeezed the trigger of the spear gun as the paddleboard hit her in the shoulder.

The spear shot from the gun and whizzed past him. It lodged in a poster advertising Billabong board shorts on the wall on the far side of the Dive Shack, quivering.

James was doing a little quivering too. The tan, bare-chested surfer in the poster now sported a spear in his crotch. Ouch. That could have been him.

The paddleboard clattered noisily to the floor. Alyssa hurled the now useless spear gun at James, turned and ran out the side door. "Cindi!"

Jane was waiting for her. She dove for Alyssa's legs and brought her to the ground hard.

James raced outside in time to see Jane and Alyssa locked in arm-to-arm, leg-to-leg and chest-to-bare chest combat. "Now, now," he said. "You two don't have to fight over me."

And was that flash of pink fabric a bikini top peeking from Jane's torn shirt?

Cindi sprinted towards them, kicking up sand.

"Now, now." James grabbed her arms and pinned them behind her back, ignoring her curses. "It's all over," he told her.

Cindi head-butted him. He dragged her to the water and threw her in. She came up sputtering, spitting up saltwater, and cursing some more. She clenched her fists.

David ran up and took her picture. Cindi screamed at him.

"Keep an eye on her!" ordered James, jogging back up the beach to Jane and Alyssa.

Alyssa was surprisingly strong and as wiry and slippery as an angry tomcat. Jane yelled at James, "Don't just stand there, give me a hand!" For emphasis, she slammed her foot into his shin.

"Ow!"

Alyssa snarled and sank her teeth into his opposite ankle.

"Hey!" James grabbed his ankle and howled like a wounded banshee. Bouncing up and down on one leg, he tumbled over Alyssa's thrashing legs and landed on her stomach, knocking the wind out of her.

Jane pinned Alyssa to the sand. "Thanks."

"For what, bitch?" hissed Alyssa, futilely twisting her arms to free herself.

"For finally getting me out of the Gardening and Southern Living section." Jane beamed. "Just wait till Lou and Eduardo hear about this!"

"I'm so happy for you," replied James, hoping she'd pick up on his sarcasm. "She bit me." He rolled off Alyssa and rubbed his ankle. "Look, tooth marks!"

"Don't be a wuss. Have you got your phone?"

"Right." James reached into his pocket. "We'd better call the police."

"Huh? Oh, sure." Jane straddled Alyssa, balancing her weight between her torso and arms. "But first, can you get a shot of me? I mean, me and Alyssa. From the neck up," she hastened to add, staring jealously at the woman's boobs. "I want to sell to the newspapers not Playboy."

Jane turned her head towards James' smart phone and tried to look fierce. "I can see the caption now: Local Reporter Solves Murder."

James climbed to his feet. Alyssa wasn't going anywhere. She had stopped struggling. Cindi was kneeling in the sand, head in her hands, sobbing. The photographer was standing a few yards away, camera whirring like mad as he took a bunch of photos of his own.

Half a dozen folks out for their morning strolls, gawked at the scene. Some had their phones out, too.

James limped off to call the police and then maybe see about getting an icepack and a rabies shot.

"Hey! Where are you going? What about my picture?"

76

"I cannot believe you two idiots." Sheryl slammed a handful of papers against her desk, fixing her frosty eyes on James and Jane.

James hung his head, for once not daring to look his sister-in-law in the eye. How did Roger manage it? "I admit it, in retrospect, I never should have confronted Alyssa alone."

"It's a basic rule of police work. Never confront a killer without backup." Sheryl threw herself into her chair and tried vainly to pull her hair out by the roots. "What have I done to deserve this?"

"You're lucky I was there," Jane said primly.

"But did you have to kick me?"

"I got carried away. Sorry. I thought you were Alyssa." A total lie. The jerk had had it coming.

"I tried to help."

"Please, you were too busy staring at her breasts."

"Not true! I didn't want to get in the way. I figured you could handle her. Nice bikini, by the way, girl who wasn't going to wear one. When do I get to see the rest of it?"

"The day after NEVER."

"Yeah, well, thanks for saving my life. I guess if you kicking me is the price I have to pay for you preventing me getting speared in the first place, I should be happy. I have a bruise the size of a grapefruit though, I'll have you know."

Sheryl groaned.

"Yes, you should be happy," Jane replied. "And I said I was sorry."

James didn't think she sounded sorry at all but there was no sense arguing about it. The whole thing was over and done with. They had found Kevin Rain's killer and accomplice.

And patsy, but that was best forgotten.

Both Alyssa and Cindi would be locked away for years to come.

Cindi with an i would now become Cindi with a criminal record.

Ollie and the others had proved useless. Tired of waiting, Ollie had opened up the food truck for breakfast business at the beach. Claudia and Artie assisted. Between the three of them, they had raked in nearly three hundred dollars while Jane and James were raking in a killer.

Bruno Caliostro, detective to the stars, had been one of their customers and had missed all the action too. It wasn't until the police cars came, sirens howling and guns ablazing that he realized anything untoward at all was going on in front of his nose. He claimed he had been following James around to test his detective skills.

Nobody had been able to prove otherwise.

James rubbed his ankle. "I'm going to need a rabies shot."

"Do you know how insulting that is?" Jane made a face.

"Do you know how much rabies shots cost?"

“Out!” Sheryl pointed to the door.

77

It couldn't have been too soon for James and Jane. The reporter took pity on James and gave him a lift home.

"What's this?" James stooped at the front door and picked up a package. It was from his mother. "Huh." He shook it. "I wasn't expecting anything from Mom till next week."

"It must be the fruit cake."

James threw open the front door and Jane followed him inside without waiting for an invite. He set the brown paper-wrapped package on the kitchen table. "Fruit cake?"

"Belizean black fruit cake, to be precise."

"Belizean black what?" James tore at the wrapper with his fingernails. "How do you know that?"

"I ordered it."

James paused mid-action and gaped at her. "You ordered it?"

"Uh-huh. I was talking to your mother and she said—"

"Stop!" James threw up a hand. "You were talking to *my* mother? When was this?"

"A couple days ago, I guess." Jane pushed him aside and finished tearing open the package. Sure enough, a foil-wrapped dark fruitcake lay inside. "Evelyn and I got to talking and she said she had this recipe for fruit cake."

James couldn't stop staring—at the crazy woman in his kitchen, not the dessert on his table. "So you ordered one? From my mom?"

"That's right." Jane yanked open the silverware drawer and pulled out a knife. Carefully unwrapping the cake, she sliced two substantial pieces and handed one to James.

"This is delicious," she gushed between mouthfuls. "You should try it."

The dense cake contained loads of raisins, currants, citron, cherries, pecans and dates, not to mention healthy doses of rum and stout.

"Thanks, I will." James carried his slab out to the backyard deck and chewed. The fruitcake was good but what was Jane doing having a telephone conversation with his mother? A mother who was a thousand miles away?

Not to mention, the two women had never met.

"What do you think?" he heard Jane say.

James turned in time to see her licking her fingers clean. "It's pretty good."

"I mean about being a detective. Pretty cool, right?"

"If you could call getting almost skewered cool, yeah, pretty cool."

"I gotta go. Tell your mom thanks for the cake."

"Where are you off to?" He tongued at a bit of pecan that had lodged in a tooth.

"I've got a story to write and I've got to hit the ground running if I want to beat the other papers. See you tonight."

"What's tonight? Another meeting of the gang at James' Clubhouse?"

"Class, dummy."

78

Jane wrote up her story at the Broward County Times news office. Lou assured her a front page byline and that the paper would go out first thing in the morning. He was afraid the bigger papers would beat them to the punch if he waited any longer—worse yet, lure Jane away with the offer of more money and a larger cubicle.

To celebrate her rising fortunes, Jane selected a new blue sundress to wear to class at the School of Detection that night. Life was good.

79

Back at the duplex, James reluctantly scooped up his books and drove to Fort Lauderdale for class. What choice did he have?

Though he had argued with Bruno's daughter for over an hour on the telephone, she had refused him a refund. It was either take the class or take a hike.

Her words, not his.

So he was taking the class.

His next-door neighbor was watering the plants in her front flowerbed with a long green hose as he warmed up the Ferrari.

"I hear you didn't kill anybody."

"Not yet," James replied through the car's open window. "But give me time."

Arriving downtown, James grudgingly fed coins into a parking meter up the street from the Edsel Building and hauled himself up the steps. He recognized Jane's car, so he wasn't surprised to see her already inside the classroom. There was no escaping the woman

Sophie arched a brow on James' appearance. That arch was filled with unspoken commentary. James ignored her and took a seat in the second row near the door and the breeze, such as it was.

Bruno stood in front of his classroom. He paused and waited for James to settle in.

"Sorry I'm late." James spread his books on the table and slapped a pen on top of the manual. Ready for business.

"Welcome back, Mr. Stewart."

"Thanks. It's good to be back." Sort of.

"I had faith in you," Bruno Caliostro told James. "I knew you'd succeed. We'll make a detective of you yet."

Artie gave James a friendly punch in the arm.

"You have had quite the education the past few days. It goes to show, class, experience teaches us things that mere books cannot." Bruno loomed over James and pinned a smile on his face. "By the way, I hear you are a good friend of Parker McRaney?"

"Oh, yeah," James said. "We're like this." He wound his fingers around each other.

"That's wonderful. Perhaps you could ask him if he would like to come speak with the class one evening? Would we like that, class?"

Enthusiastic voices, especially those of the ladies, assured Bruno Caliostro that they would indeed.

"I'll see what I can do," James replied. When hell freezes over. "Why didn't you tell us you were involved with Felicity Rain?"

"It wasn't relevant to the investigation. Her husband hired me to tail her. I did. And I gave him a full report. Later, she and I became friends."

"You should have come clean about your relationship with her."

"I didn't see how it could be relevant to Kevin Rain's murder. And it wasn't. Besides," he said, "a good investigator discovers these things for himself."

"Believe me, I've seen things I never expected. Some I wish I could un-see." The horrible image of

Bruno Caliostro riding Felicity naked in her bed jumped into his mind's eye.

Bruno Caliostro rubbed his hands together. "Now, where were we before we were interrupted? Oh, yes. We were meeting our newest student, Edna Flowers."

"That's me." An old lady who hadn't yet registered in James' consciousness wiggled a handful of thick, arthritic fingers. Her voice was deep and scratchy, like a wizened old three-pack-a-day troll speaking from the bottom of a deep river rock-lined well.

"So, Mrs. Flowers—" Bruno Caliostro stopped, cocked his head. He paced a moment back and forth then tried again. "So, Mrs. Flowers what made you decide at your, uh, um..."

"He means age," quipped Artie.

Claudia poked him between the ribs with her elbow. "Shut up, Artie."

Mrs. Flowers glared at the both of them before replying to Bruno. "My husband is dead. All my friends are dead. I needed something to do."

Edna winked at Bruno. "I always dreamed of being a detective. Like Joan Blondell in *There's Always Another Woman.*"

Bruno blinked numbly. "I-I see."

"He drove his car into a condo."

"Who did?" Artie leaned toward Mrs. Flowers.

"Abner, who do you think?"

"What happened to Joan?" Artie couldn't let go.

"Joan Blondell? She's dead, I guess. Who knows? Who cares?" Mrs. Flowers cackled like an old hen. "Maybe she drove into a condo too. In Palm Springs, I'll bet."

"Right." Artie slumped in his seat.

"Excuse me?" Bruno was regretting he'd taken the old woman's money—almost.

"Into a condo?" Ollie squinted in puzzlement.

"First floor unit. Nice one, too. Two bedrooms, one and a half bath right over at Century Point. That's the big retirement village where I live. I don't know why they call it a village. It's more like a giant concrete beehive. Know what I mean?" She fluffed her pink hair. "Not Palm Springs."

"I'm so sorry," Ollie replied. "It must have been awful losing your husband in a crash like that."

"Oh, it wasn't the crash that killed him. That Oldsmobile of Abner's was rock solid. You shoulda seen the bumper on that thing. Tough. Took out the whole living room wall."

"Of the condo?" Bruno leaned his butt on his desk. Even his daughter had given up surfing the web on her smartphone to watch and listen.

"Yep," replied Mrs. Flowers.

"But it didn't kill him?" Artie asked.

"Nope."

"What did?" Ollie continued.

"Well, after Abner ran the Oldsmobile through the Brickmans' living room wall, he decided to go for a swim."

"A swim?" Bruno mopped his forehead with a paper towel.

James said nothing. He was enjoying the show. It beat listening to Bruno Caliostro lecture about boring Florida statutes.

Jane, however, ever the reporter, was scribbling notes furiously in that omnipresent notebook of hers.

"Yep." Mrs. Flowers massaged her sagging neck.

"Abner figured since there was nobody home at the Brickmans and seeing how he'd brought his towel and his sunscreen—always use sunscreen, young man, keeps you from getting wrinkles." She was eyeing James now. "Anyway, he took his towel and went for a swim."

"Okay." Bruno drew the word out. He glanced at his daughter as if it were her fault Mrs. Flowers was in his class.

James wondered what the Oldsmobile meets condo story had to do with her husband's passing, if anything. "How did your husband die? I mean, if you don't mind telling us, Mrs. Flowers."

"Drowned. Abner walked down to the community pool, set his towel on one of those chaise lounges, waded in, had a heart attack and drowned." She eyeballed the class. "At least that's what the paramedics and the doc said. I wasn't there. I had a hair appointment with Lucy."

"While his car was—"

"Parked in the Brickmans' living room. Under a pile of concrete block, dry wall and chintz curtains. Ugliest curtains you ever saw."

There was a numbed silence.

Edna Flowers broke it. "Shouldn't we be getting started, Mr. Caliostro, sir?"

Bruno Caliostro's face turned red as a ripe tomato. "Of course." He grabbed his pool cue like he always did.

"Welcome to class, Edna," Jane extended her hand. "We're happy to have you."

"Thanks. You the two who nabbed that murdering bitch?" Her watery gray-blue eyes swept over Jane and James.

"That's right."

James introduced himself.

"Is that how you dress to come to class?" Edna Flowers snapped.

"Excuse me?"

"You ought to dress up. Show some respect."

"Yes, ma'am. Excuse me." James excused himself and found a seat nearer Jane and the others, figuring they were the lesser of two loonies.

Edna Flowers rose from her seat and followed, sitting down next to him. "My husband's gone."

"Yes, I heard. Sorry." James avoided eye contact. Maybe she would go away.

The odd woman had a long Modigliani face and fluffy pink hair. It was as if she had leaned over too far into the cotton candy machine at the county fair. She had gray eyes and looked old as Time itself. Why had she followed him?

"Abner—that's my husband—Abner he used to say, when the kids are grown, you and me, will make whoopee on the kitchen table. That's what he used to say."

James found himself blushing.

Jane sniggered and gripped her pencil tighter.

"You ever make whoopee on the kitchen table, sonny?"

James cleared his throat. "Me?"

"Well?"

"No, ma'am. I think we should be quiet now. Class is about to begin." Bruno was setting up his ancient slide projector on the edge of his squat desk.

"Sure, sure." She poked his calf with her pointy shoe. "What's your name, sonny?"

"James." Hadn't she heard him the first time?

"I know that. You already said so. I mean your full

name."

"James Stewart," he whispered out the side of his mouth.

She pinched her brows together. "Anybody ever tell you that you look like James Stewart the actor?"

"Actually, no." James wished the woman would stop prattling.

"That's good." Just when James thought she had shut up, she said, "Because you don't look nothing like him."

She reached out and took his chin in her hand, stabbing him with sharp, teal-painted fingernails. She moved his head side to side. "You have got Bea Arthur's cheekbones, though. Anybody ever tell you that you look like Bea Arthur? You know, Blanche, the Golden Girl?"

Color ran up his shoulders, neck and face. "No, ma'am. Really, I think we should be quiet."

Jane prodded James in the shoulder. Looking past James at the unusual woman, she said, "You know, now that you mention it, I can see a little Bea Arthur in James. Say, maybe the two of you are related, James."

James bit his lip. "Very funny. Ha-ha. Now, if you ladies wouldn't mind."

"Is everything okay, Mr. Stewart?" Bruno was looking at him severely.

"What?"

"You were practically shouting. I asked if you were all right."

"Sorry. Was I shouting?" James tugged at his collar. "It's nothing."

"I worked in a diner," said Edna, apropos of nothing. "Fenster's 24-hour over on State Road 84. You ever hear of it?"

James nodded yes.

"Abner sold meats wholesale. He's dead now."

"Yes, ma'am."

"Call me Edna."

"Right, Edna." James smiled at her and hoped she got the message that the smile signaled the end to their conversation.

"Can I call you Bea?" she asked James.

Jane guffawed.

James tightened every muscle in his body, clamping down on his jaw so hard he was pretty sure a molar cracked in two. Did Roger provide dental insurance?

"It's not so bad," Edna said out of the side of her mouth. "Abner may be gone but that Oldsmobile still runs great."

ACKNOWLEDGEMENT

Hi, thanks for reading Detective School 101. If you enjoyed this novel, please support me by sharing your positive review online and on your favorite social media platforms. Trust me, every little bit helps. And maybe check out some of my other books, too.

Thanks again!

J.R. Ripley is the bestselling author of the Todd Jones comic thrillers, A Bird Lover's Mystery series, the Maggie Miller mysteries, the TV Pet Chef mysteries (writing as Marie Celine), and other novels. He also writes as Glenn Eric Meganck, and is a critically-acclaimed singer-songwriter-musician. Feel free to search the interweb for the good, the bad, and the ugly. Some of what you read might even be true.

www.ingramcontent.com/pod-product-compliance
Lightning Source LLC
LaVergne TN
LVHW041059080826
845145LV00007B/1629

* 9 7 8 1 8 9 2 3 3 9 4 4 7 *